"I found the storyline quite fasci............ midst of all the trials the characters had to go through. Dudley has a great imagination, and he is indeed a very interesting storyteller. He draws you right into the story. It causes the reader to feel empathy for the characters."

Elmer Allen,

Edmonton, Alberta Province, Canada.

THE APPEARANCE

THE
APPEARANCE

WILL GOD'S BELIEVERS HAVE THE STRENGTH TO ENDURE THE PEACE COVENANT?

DUDLEY FAIRBAIRN

TATE PUBLISHING & Enterprises

Published by Tate Publishing & Enterprises, LLC
127 E. Trade Center Terrace | Mustang, Oklahoma 73064 USA
1.888.361.9473 | www.tatepublishing.com

Tate Publishing is committed to excellence in the publishing industry. The company reflects the philosophy established by the founders, based on Psalm 68:11,
"The Lord gave the word and great was the company of those who published it."

Book design copyright © 2008 by Tate Publishing, LLC. All rights reserved.
Cover design by Lynly D. Taylor
Interior design by Summer Floyd-Harvey

Published in the United States of America
ISBN: 978-1-60696-467-5
1. Fiction: Futuristic
2. Fiction: Religious: Apocalyptical
00.00.00

Dedication

This novel is lovingly dedicated to my late, beloved mother, Annie, and my late, beloved father, George Fairbairn, who went on to their reward in heaven. This novel is also dedicated to all the saints who were martyred for the cause of Christ Jesus, our Lord and Savior, since the birth of the Church. And many others who are still suffering for the name of Christ Jesus.

May the reading of *The Appearance* be instrumental in bringing many souls into the kingdom of the Lord God, through their faith in the Lord Jesus Christ by the power of the blessed Holy Spirit.

Acknowledgements

The Appearance was inspired by my interest in the end times. The inspired Word of the Lord God has been my main source, guide, and inspiration in writing of this novel.

Understanding how end times prophecy fits together is not always easy. I trust the pieces of this amazing puzzle of prophetic events will give the reader a better understanding of the prophetic teachings of Jesus and the apostles.

I want to acknowledge my wife, Verna, for her tireless assisting in the proofreading of this novel. Not forgetting my sister-in-law, Emma Melnyk, who always encouraged me when we discussed the novel.

I trust that the information in *The Appearance* will be a source of inspiration to those who read it and that it will strengthen their faith in the Lord Jesus Christ no matter what the prophetic outcome may be. Remain faithful to the Lord Jesus Christ is my words of encouragement to you!

Table of Foreign Words

Anabaino—Ascend
Axum—City in Northern Ethiopia
Diaspora—Dispersion of the Jews
Hatikva—The Hope
Imam—Muslim Priest
Intifada—Uprising, or rebellion
Isa—Muslim name for Jesus
Knesset—Israeli Parliament
Mitre—Pope's hat
NIsan—Corresponds with the Month of April
Shalom—Peace [Hebrew]
Salaam—Peace [Arabic]
Quorum—Minimum number of People Required

Introduction

The inspiration behind the writing of the novel, *The Appearance* is to give the reader a balanced perspective concerning the end-times. We have been mostly exposed to one side of the prophetic coin. I want to give the reader the opportunity to discover what is on the other side of the coin and for the reader to make up his/her own mind. The reader will never know until he/she takes the plunge of faith to pick up the coin to see what is hidden on the opposite side.

Some people want to know whether it is Biblical to believe in what is commonly known as the *rapture*. Their argument is based on the fact that the word *rapture does* not appear in the English Bible. They are absolutely correct! The word *rapture* does not appear in the English Bible.

However, the action is clearly described in the writings of the apostle Paul. He used the words *caught up* three times in his writings, and John used it once in the book of Revelation. Paul said:

> I know a man in Christ who fourteen years ago—whether in the body I do not know, or whether out of the body I do not know, God knows—such a one was caught up to the third heaven. And I know such a man—whether in the body or out of the body I do not know, God knows—how he was caught up into paradise and heard inexpressible words, which is not lawful for a man to utter.
>
> 2 *Corinthians* 12: 2–4

In the most famous *rapture* passage, Paul describes it in the following fashion.

For the Lord Himself will descend from heaven with a shout, with the voice of an archangel, and with the trumpet of God. And the dead in Christ will rise first. Then we who are alive *and* remain [survive] shall be caught up together with them in the clouds to meet the Lord in the air. And thus we shall always be with the Lord. Therefore comfort one another with these words.

1 Thessalonians 4: 16–18, emphasis added

John received this revelation via Jesus' angel.

And she [National Israel] brought forth a man child, who was to rule all nations with a rod of iron: and her child was caught up unto God, and to his throne.

Revelation 12:5 KJV

The author of the book of Acts wrote:

Now when they came up out of the water, the Spirit of the Lord caught [harpazo] Philip away, so that the eunuch saw him no more; and he went on his way rejoicing.

Acts 8: 39

The Greek word for 'caught up' according to the Strong's Concordance is called: *Harpazo.* It means to seize (in various applications)—catch (away up), pluck, pull, take (by force). The word *rapture* is derived from the Latin word *raptus,* which means to snatch up or caught up. It is found in the Latin Vulgate Bible. The Greek word for *harpazo (caught up)* must not be confused with *Anabaino* (ascended). Jesus was not caught up to heaven. He ascended to heaven. *Harpazo* describes a fast action whereas *Anabaino* describes a slow action.

The Appearance was written with the intent to broaden one's understanding of the end times. We believe that Jesus is coming in the very near future to *rapture* His redeemed. The majority of believers believe that Jesus will *rapture* them before Antichrist makes the seven-year Covenant of Peace.

However, there is just a small percentage of Bible students who believe that Jesus will *rapture* them before the start of three and a half years of The Great and Awesome Day of the Lord. That Awesome Day will culminate with the introduction of the Antichrist's mark. The above-mentioned Day starts soon after the *rapture* of the redeemed. It is good to be acquainted with both views. The most important thing is to be ready, both day and night.

It does not matter what happens on the religious or political world scene, nothing is going to stop Jesus from coming to evacuate His blood bought redeemed. The blessed Holy Spirit is preparing a people for God who will be ready at a moment's notice. The Spirit filled Church of the Lord Jesus Christ, is going to rise to the challenges of the end times.

one
CHAPTER

All over the world, the spirit of euphoria was reigning. "What was the reason for it?" Unknown until this time, The Man, as he was referred to, had brokered a truce between the Israelis and the Palestinians.

"Who is he, and where did he come from? Where has he been all this time?"

Here follows a little about his history. Both his great grandparents were Assyrian-born Jews who immigrated to Italy and who lived in the former Vatican states.

He was trained in military warfare by the shrewdest generals and in the art of politics by the most, shrewd politicians. He was taught Jewish and European history by learned historians and economics by the most influential economists. He received training in the mysteries of the occult and was one of the foremost linguists in the world. In his well-kept secret place, he was abiding his time, hidden away in a cloister somewhere in the mountains in Italy.

He had been schooled for twenty-four years in order for him to be prepared for the greatest calling of his life. As a brilliant student, he was eager for knowledge. His training started at the early age of six. He grew up amongst the Jesuits. The only woman that he was exposed to for the first five years, nine months, three weeks, and four days of his life was Mary Bianchi, his nanny.

Mary was a spinster whose desire was to become a nun, but her parents refused to send her to a nunnery. Mary did not see him again after his sixth birthday. Her position was abruptly terminated on that same day. She prepared him for bed as usual and reminded him to pray to the Virgin Mother.

He knelt next to her and prayed, "Beloved Virgin Mary, Queen of heaven, and mother of God, please bless the brothers here at the cloister and please bless Brother Marcus and Nanny Mary, with a double blessing. I thank you for her because she is taking such good care of me. You are my mother in heaven, but Nanny Mary is my mother here on earth, and I love you both very much."

Mary, who could no longer hold back her tears, started weeping softly. Just before she came to prepare him for bed, Brother Jonathan Mancini gave Mary severance pay and told her that her services were no longer required. She was shocked, but knowing Bother Jonathan, the way she did, she knew that it was no use arguing with him. She kissed the boy and gave him a hug. Then she tucked him in for the very last time, said goodnight, and switched off the light.

For days they both pined for one another. Mary was sworn to secrecy. Soon after leaving the cloister, she received an anonymous phone call from a man with a foreign accent. He threatened to kill both her and her parents should she tell anyone about the boy. The stress that she was under severely affected her health. Mary died of a broken heart, taking the secret to her grave.

• • • •

It was a cold and blustery winter's morning. It had snowed heavily the night before. Brother Marcus Giordano was on his way to the cloister. He was following a car when suddenly he saw it going out of control. It crashed through the guardrail and landed sixty yards down the embankment. It seemed to him that there were three adults in the car.

This is how Brother Marcus' related the story.

I stopped my car and I scrambled down the embankment as fast as I could. One look behind the steering wheel was enough to convince me that the driver was dead on impact. He had a deep gash on his forehead, and his brain was exposed. On the back seat, I saw a woman holding an infant who was wrapped in a thick blanket.

She was bleeding, and I could see that she was in great pain. There was no trace of the third adult passenger. It did not seem that anyone was thrown through the shatterproof windows. It was cracked but still intact. All the doors were still locked. I broke the passenger's window on the driver's side and opened the door.

With great effort, the woman tried to speak to me, but I told her not to speak but for her to conserve her strength and that I was going to get help. I could swear that I saw three adult passengers in the car. The passenger who was sitting next to the driver was dressed in a black-hooded coat. The driver had on a camel-colored coat, and the woman sitting in the back had on a deep red-colored coat. I was amazed to find only the two adults and a little baby in the car. The passenger with the black-hooded coat had d*Isa*ppeared into thin air.

The woman seemed very anxious, and with a faltering voice, she pleaded with me. She said, "Please do not go. I have a grave problem that is weighing very heavily on my heart."
Referring to the driver she said, "Philip and I had both dabbled in the occult, and he was a very heavy gambler and had a huge debt to repay. The Mafia threatened to kill him if he did not come up with the money within two days. Philip jokingly made a wager with Satan and said, "Satan, the stakes are very high. If you help me win at blackjack tonight, then I will give you my future son.

"He only told me afterward about it. I was terribly upset as I thought that he had completely broken with Satanism." She gave a sigh and said, "I fear for the life of my illegitimate and fatherless child." Somehow, she knew that the man behind the steering wheel was dead.

"Both our parents were Assyrian-born Jews, and so were their parents before them. Our great grandparents immigrated to what was then known as the Vatican States. They were some of the Jewish elite who lived there before Benito Mussolini, signed the concordat between the Italian Government, and the

Pope of Rome. Both Philip and I were born in Rome, making our son a Roman citizen."

She was gasping for breath but pressed on. "My grandparents had made a lot of money in stocks and bonds, and they were able to hobnob with the European aristocrats. Because of their riches, they were welcomed and fully accepted by the Roman aristocracy. Soon after, both my parents, for their own safety, and the safety of their children and future grandchildren, became members of the Church of Rome and they took on Christian names.

"My mothers name was changed from Miriam Jacobs to Mary Handel, and my father's name was changed from Jacob Jacobs to James Handel. Because of Philip's gambling addiction, my parents d*Isa*pproved of our relationship."

She paused for a few moments then with great effort continued speaking again. Because I knew that she was dying I did not want to stop her from telling her story. She said, "My parents warned me that if I did not break off my relationship with Philip that they were going to disinherit me and that they did not want to see me ever again. I loved my parents and Philip very much. When I told Philip that I was expecting his child, he said that he did not want the responsibility of fatherhood. He said that he wanted to be free to enjoy life and that he was *too* young to get married.

"In the meantime, he met someone else and told me that we should put our child up for adoption." She gasped again for breath but continued speaking, "Philip had no plans to marry an aristocrat who was going to become penniless. When we heard about the cloister, we decided to bring him to the Jesuits in order for them to raise him as a Jesuit Priest and that they may protect him from Satan.

"I was planning to return to be with my parents after we delivered our son to the Jesuits. Philip was going to go his own way. When we came to the bend in the road, a foul smell filled the car. "Satan materialized in the car and said, 'I have come to claim my son,'" She closed her eyes and then continued, "Philip got such a fright that he let go of the steering wheel. He shouted, 'Saint Frances, help me!'"

It was at that same moment that I saw the car going out of control and crashing through the guardrail. She was breathing with great difficulty now, and her eyes looked very tired but she continued with her story.

She said, "Satan! You cannot have our son! You will have to kill me first. He gave a sinister laugh and then he d*Is*appeared." With a very weak voice and with tears running down her cheeks she said, "Please take good care of my baby. I love him so much."

She was barely speaking above a whisper, and I had to put my ear very close to her mouth to hear what she was saying. I replied, "We, the Jesuits shall take good care of him." She said, "Thank you and God bless you." "I could see that death was close at hand and her time on earth was running out. I quickly asked her, "What is your baby's name? She whispered, "Messiah," then she died with her baby's name on her lips. I quickly checked to see if the baby had any injuries and found none.

Brother Marcus, who was a fully trained doctor, examined the baby and found that Messiah was unhurt. He was cooing away contentedly, unaware of the great tragedy that had befallen both his parents. The thick blankets served as a protective barrier. He first transferred Messiah to his car then he returned and opened the cases looking for one containing baby clothes, which he found.

He then inspected the contents of a bag that was on the seat next to Messiah's deceased mother. He was hoping to find some identification. His search paid off. It contained their passports and a smaller bag containing a letter addressed to "The order of the Jesuits." It also contained a check in the amount of two million dollars, which was to secure Messiah's future, and it was also for the needs of the Jesuits.

Messiah's mother's name was Anna Handel, and his father's name was Philip Largo. Brother Marcus made sure that he left the cases as he found them. He removed any evidence that could prove that there was ever a baby in the car at the time of the accident.

He then carefully wiped the car for fingerprints and lightly sprinkled snow on the car where it had been touched. He also used a branch to remove his footprints. It started snowing just as Brother Marcus was busy erasing his footprints.

He then drove to the cloister and handed baby Messiah over to Brother Jonathan, who was one of seven medical doctors at the cloister.

The medical staff at the cloister was responsible for taking care of the frail and sick Jesuits, and they also served the community. He quickly explained to Brother Jonathan what had transpired on his way to the cloister, and then he phoned the police station to report the accident without mentioning Messiah.

• • • •

Twenty-eight years, nine months, two weeks, and four days had passed since that blustery wintry morning. Nobody knew about Messiah's existence, except the Jesuits. Messiah had an intuition that he was born for something great. Sometimes he was champing impatiently at the bit to get going, and the Jesuits had to restrain him.

Since a very early age, Messiah had experiences with the supernatural. At the age of thirteen, while he was meditating, a spirit materialized in his room. Unafraid he conversed with the spirit.

He asked the spirit, "What is your name?"

The spirit replied, "You can call me Father. As from today onwards, I shall be your guiding spirit. You were born for a very special purpose, and you shall become very great and renowned in the world."

Through the years, the visits of Messiah's guiding spirit became more and more frequent.

During one of his guiding spirit's daily visits, Messiah became very impatient with his father.

Messiah asked him, "Father! When can I start the vocation for which I was born? I am twenty-nine years of age, and I am getting tired of being hidden away from the world as if I were a monster," said Messiah with a grim expression on his face.

His father replied, "Son! You are not as yet finished with your training."

"What more knowledge is there still for me to acquire?" said Messiah with an angry tone in his voice.

"Be patient, my son," his father said, trying to pacify him. "There is yet one more year of training left for you. I have already planned for you to go to a monastery in Tibet, which is situated in the Himalayan Mountains."

With a frown on his forehead and an angry look on his face, Messiah inquired, "What for?" he said with a sullen expression on his face.

To his question his father replied, "I want you to take an intensive course in the art of meditation and of occultism. One of my high priests will infiltrate the monastery. He shall teach you everything there is to know about me and my kingdom."

Messiah walked over to where his father was sitting and sat down next to him. He put his head against his father's chest, and his father embraced him and whispered soothingly in his ear.

"Now close your eyes, my son, and sleep. When you awake you will be in the Monastery in Tibet." Messiah dosed off into a very deep sleep.

It was the first time Messiah was going to experience physical astral travel. Satan summoned some of his strong demons, and they quickly and quietly whisked Messiah away. When he awoke the next morning, he found himself in strange surroundings. A stranger in a pure-white flowing-robe was bending over him to check whether he was awake. He had slept for twelve hours. Messiah sat up with a start, and enquired. "Who are you?"

two

CHAPTER

The stranger spoke to Messiah and said, "I am Prophet Elijah, and you are Messiah. Your father told me everything there is to know about you. From this day forward, I shall be your closest confidante. We shall be together until the end of time."

Monks, clad in saffron-colored robes, ministered to his every beck and call. Messiah's day started very early in the morning. He was served breakfast at six o'clock. Only vegetarian meals were on his menu. He could be found sitting in the lotus position, busy meditating for hours on end. It was during these times of intensive meditation that the spirits of the underworld manifested themselves to him.

His training started in earnest when the high priest from the satanic order, disguised as a monk, was flown in from Burma. His assignment was to train Messiah in the art of Satanism. He was always surrounded by hundreds of monks, young and old, meditating with him. He looked like a white flower planted in saffron colored soil because of his white robe. He was soon to discover that his spirit had mastery over his body.

One morning after many hours of meditation, he opened his eyes and saw all the monks levitating. He wondered why he was looking down at them, and why they were looking up at him. It was then that he discovered that he was on a higher spiritual elevation than they were. His spirit had reached mastery over his body, and he had gained mastery over them. Messiah's training was now complete.

On his thirtieth birthday, he was accompanied to the river, by Prophet Elijah to be christened. All the monks were present. Prophet Elijah and Messiah both entered the river where Prophet Elijah sprinkled water on Messiah's head.

While Prophet Elijah was sprinkling water on Messiah's head, he said, "Messiah, I christen you in the name of the Supreme Father and of the Supreme Son and of the Supreme Spirit."

Out of nowhere, an ugly looking crow appeared and hovered over Messiah, and an unearthly sounding voice said, "You are my son. Go! Dethrone Esau in the hearts and minds of the masses and my spirit be with you."

When the monks saw the crow and heard the voice, they fell down and worshipped Messiah, believing him to be a god. Back at the monastery, and again after an intense time of meditation, very early that evening, Messiah took a shower and went to bed.

During his last night at the monastery, he dreamt that he was leaning with his head against his father's shoulder.

In his dream, he heard his father distinctly say to him, *"Son! Go now! Now is the time! And my spirit, go with you."*

Messiah replied, *"Yes, Father, I am now ready."*

The very next moment, he was again physically transported by demons to Israel. It all happened in a twinkling of an eye. When he awoke the next morning, he found himself in a luxurious suite at the Intercontinental Hotel on the Mount of Olives.

According to Jewish tradition, he was now the correct age to start his mission as prophet and Messiah over Israel. Satan's goal was that Messiah be eventually crowned king over Israel and over the whole world.

• • • •

In the most crucial time of Israel's history, Messiah appeared on the horizon. The *Intifada* had been dragging on for a very long time now with hundreds dead on both sides. The Palestinian leader wanted the United Nations to send in an International Peace-keeping Force. Their job would have been to replace the

Israeli armed forces, which were presently in the so-called occupied areas.

The Peacekeeping Force would have been a force without teeth, as the terrorists had no fear of the International Peacekeeping Force. Israel was against it from the very start, and the United States of America vetoed it.

There was a groundswell of support from the nations of the world for an Independent Palestinian State, with Jerusalem as its capitol city. The United States of America was under severe pressure from within and without to give up Israel as a lost cause.

Then the satanic terrorist attack came, which destroyed the twin towers of the World Trade Centre. Demonized Muslim fundamentalist pilots crashed two aircrafts into the towers killing hundreds of innocent people. A few hundred more were killed when another aircraft crashed into the Pentagon, the nerve centre of the United States Defense Network.

Another aircraft crashed in Pennsylvania when the passengers fought the terrorists preventing the aircraft from crashing into heavily populated areas. These brave men and women knew that they were going to die, but they did not die in vain.

President Barabas of the United States of America was able to get the support of a number of nations who were willing to fight terrorism. A broad coalition of nations was formed, Great Britain being the strongest ally.

The bombardment of Afghanistan was to flush out and kill Osama Bin Laden who was the mastermind behind the attacks and also his demon-inspired, brainwashed Al-Qaida-terrorist network with him. The Taliban was in control of ninety percent of Afghanistan.

They were given enough time to surrender Osama Bin Laden, to the American authorities, but they stubbornly refused. The bombardment stirred up the fervor of the Moslems worldwide. They declared a holy war against America or any nation who would dare kill their Muslim brothers. Other nations were now also experiencing terrorist attacks of horrendous proportions.

A broad coalition was formed to oust Saddam Hussein, which eventually happened. They found him hiding in an underground hideout. The search for weapons of mass destruction did not deliver up any thing because months before the invasion of Iraq, planeloads of W.O.M.D. were flown out to Syria.

In Afghanistan their had been a resurgence of the Taliban. The coalition in Iraq is stuck in the quagmire and unable to extricate itself from Iraq without handing the country back to the religious fanatical terrorists.

Opposition was building up in Britain, America, and other European countries against the war. Satan was working overtime in both Afghanistan and Iraq to cause the military interventions to be a failure.

Pressure from the members of the coalition against terror was now mounting against the United States of America to abandon Israel. They were now voicing the opinion of the terrorists that America's biased foreign policy toward Israel was responsible for the worldwide terrorist attacks.

A high-ranking terrorist said, "The attacks will only come to an end when the Palestinians become an independent Nation with Jerusalem as its capitol and also when America leaves the holy soil of Saudi Arabia."

In one of the corridors of the United Nations Headquarters, a politician said to his colleague, "The Arabs, Israel's life-long enemies, are going to destroy her, and Jerusalem is the bone of contention."

His colleague replied, "The Israelis believe Jerusalem to be the capitol of Israel, and the Palestinians are claiming it to be the capitol under a unified Palestinian State."

"They are like two dogs fighting over the same bone. Neither one is going to give in. It is going to be a fight to the death." *I just know so*, he thought.

"There is only going to be one winner to gloat over the prize. And I can assure you that it is not going to be the Israelis but the Palestinians." his colleague replied.

"The whole world is rooting for the Palestinians."

Then the message that Mordecai Rabin, the Israeli prime minister and the Israelis had dreaded for a long time came. The

Minister of Defense, Moses Sharon, told the generals about the e-mail that he had received.

> You are now on your own. This is a war of your own making. We have bent over backward to accommodate you. I have personally visited you a number of times trying to bring you, the Israelis, and Palestinians together, but to no avail. We have exhausted all ways and means to make you comply. You have rejected the Oslo Accord, the Wye River Agreement, and the Tenet Plan. You are just too stubborn. We have permanently broken off diplomatic relations with the Nation of Israel. You are now on your own. Please do not contact us ever again.
>
> *Mr. Joseph H. Morgan*

• • • •

Messiah could not have come at a more opportune moment. The Arab League, Russia, and China were in a state of readiness for war to the death with Israel. Over the last few months, Russia and China had secretly flown in their most sophisticated warfare-machinery to a secret place in the Iranian desert, or so they thought.

To the Israeli Intelligence Department, it was no secret at all. It was no wonder that the Israeli military generals were talking so much about the Samson syndrome lately.

One general said, "We shall take them down with us. The world will just wake up and find over six-hundred and fifty million Arab corpses."

His friend replied, "Our intercontinental nuclear ballistic missiles shall kill hundreds of millions of Chinese and Russians inside their territories."

"The nuclear fallout, also called the invisible death, shall be airborne to the Western hemisphere, and a few hundred million more will die. That will teach the Americans and the Europeans a lesson for not coming to our aid."

With a voice filled with emotion his colleague said, "Who would have thought the United States of America, once one of our staunchest allies, would ignore our repeated pleas to come to our aid and fight on our side."

. . . .

The Israeli Prime Minister Mordecai Rabin, the generals and the Chief Rabbi of Jerusalem gathered in a huge bunker under the Negev Desert that houses the missile control-room. Prime Minister Rabin addressed the generals and said, "We are not going to warn the Israeli public that we are going to be engaged in a nuclear war. There is no need to start a panic. They have been living in bombproof shelters in fear for months now. The shelters shall become our tombs. There is no other alternative for us but to start a nuclear war."

He turned to Rabbi Rabinovitz and said, "Please offer up a prayer."

With a voice filled with emotion, he prayed. "Dear Lord, God, please forgive the sins of your people, Israel. We have been a very rebellious nation, and have served our own interests and the gods of our own making. Take to Yourself, the souls of Your people, Israel. Amen!"

After a few seconds of silence, the minister of defense said with a commanding voice, "We have been through this drill many times before. Let us synchronize our watches. The time is now exactly 2300 hours. Every man to his station! The countdown begins right now!

"Within one hours time the two ignition key-switches which are separated by a mile shall be turned on at exactly 2400 hours. As a safety precaution, I shall switch the key under my command to the on position, and the other officer in the other control room (a mile away in the other bunker) shall turn the other key-switch to the on position.

"We shall be in constant communication via close-circuit television and by other sophisticated means of communication. Should our enemies be willing to declare a unilateral declaration of peace, the delay will give us enough time to abort the operation. If they do not make contact before midnight, then we have no other alternative but to fire the missiles," he said with a sad tone in his voice.

Israel's enemies and the general public did not know that they had nuclear missiles in secret missile silos in the Golan Heights, in Gaza, and the former buffer zone in Lebanon. It was Israel's most well-kept secret. Not even America, her former closest ally, was aware of it.

The minister of defense continued, "None of us are to leave our stations. If our enemies do not declare a unilateral peace within exactly one-hour's time, that is, before midnight, then all hell is going to break loose. Should a miracle take place, then a worldwide catastrophe will have been averted. Only God can help us now, if He is interested. He has deserted us for over two-thousand years."

For over two-thousand years, the Jews have rejected Jesus who is Jehovah's salvation. Because of fear, the faces of those present went pale as the blood drained from their faces. Prime Minister Mordecai Rabin stared intently at the white phone.

He was praying in his heart, *Please God, let someone phone. Please speak to us and tell us that this is all a terrible mistake. Please reassure us that there is not going to be a nuclear war.*

God did not reassure them and neither did the phone ring at that time.

A number of officers with concentration etched out on their faces were monitoring numerous instrument panels, while others were manning a number of phones. An agonizing fifty-four minutes and fifty-nine seconds had lapsed when the white phone rang. The multi-headed nuclear missiles would have received the all-clear signal to strike its targets right in the heart of the enemies' territory.

Prime Minister Rabin quickly lifted the receiver, placed it to his ear, and said, "Israeli prime minister here."

The voice on the other end said, "I am Messiah, the Messiah of Israel, but at present, I am to be addressed as The Man. I am speaking on behalf of the Arab League and for the presidents of Russia and China. I have been in constant contact with them since your minister of defense gave the okay for the nuclear attack on their countries.

Mordecai Rabin asked, "How did you know?"

The Man replied, "That is not of importance now. That which is of real importance is Russia, China, and the Arab League are willing to sign a unilateral declaration of peace with Israel.

With a commanding voice he continued, "You must desist from activating the nuclear missiles, right now! Or you will blow us all to hell! We can talk about the finer details later on," he said, with an angry tone in his voice.

The minister of defense, who listened in on the conversation on the other phone, immediately relayed the message to the other high-ranking official, informing him that the mission had been aborted.

The Man addressed himself to Moses Sharon, the minister of defense, and asked, "Did you give command to abort the mission?"

The minister of defense replied, "Yes, I did." He remained silent for a few seconds, and the thought crossed his mind. *The Man had phoned just in the nick of time.*

Since he phoned, only one minute had remained in the most crucial time of Israel and the world's history. The Man picked up the conversation where he had left off. "The Russians and the Chinese and the Arab nations are willing to unilaterally withdraw their forces and make peace with you."

Sighs of relief were heard from those present. The minister of defense, the prime minister, and the others in the other bunker were as if mesmerized. The minister of defense knew, against his better judgment, not to trust anyone with something so serious. But he had a gut feeling that this man, who calls himself Messiah, was telling the truth.

The Man on the other side of the phone asked, "Are you still there?" came his impatient voice.

Moses Sharon replied, "Yes, I am still here, and God answered our prayers just at the right time."

There were a few seconds of silence on the other side. A thought crossed The Man's mind, *There is no God but me.* When

Messiah spoke again, he addressed himself to Prime Minister Mordecai Rabin. "I am going to broker a seven-year peace covenant on the first of *NIsan* (*NIsan* corresponds with April) that will guarantee Israel's security. Russia, China, and the Arab Confederation have all agreed to be signatories to it, and I told them that I shall make sure that they comply." His dominating spirit was shining through.

"The King David Hotel will be the venue. Go ahead with the preparations and security matters. My confidante, Prophet Elijah, shall contact you shortly. *Shalom!*" And he rang off.

"Did you hear that? Did you hear that?" the prime minister exclaimed, "Seven years of glorious peace. The prophets were correct all along when they prophesied that Messiah was going to come. He has come, just as they had prophesied. His arrival will bring us the promised peace and prosperity." He could hardly contain himself and was beside himself with joy.

Messiah appeared on Israel's horizon at just the right time. He appeared at a time when the United Nations were up in arms with Israel. They did not know what else to do with Israel to make her comply with their demands.

The Secretary General of the United Nations said to his colleague, "What threats do we still have to make to break Israel's stubborn spirit. What must we do to make her comply to give up ownership of the whole of Jerusalem and to concede ownership of all of the West Bank and even more?"

His colleague replied, "We have tried everything to bring peace to that region. Yet peace seems even more allusive. Is Israel ever going to reach an agreement with the Palestinians? The way Israel is stalling, it is never going to happen. I tell you, a full-scale war is inevitable. Even Russia and China are willing to fight on the side of the Arab Confederacy." *We should just throw them to the wolves.*

• • • •

Those who saw The Man said, "He has hypnotic eyes, and it seems as if he can read your very thoughts. His presence commands attention, respect, and complete obedience."

A preacher from a certain church said, "This charismatic man is made of the right stuff. He alone can bring the warring factions together." He sounded overly optimistic.

Even the Israeli's prime minister, who adamantly said in the past, "We shall never negotiate with terrorists," was now willing to sit around the negotiating table with them. The enemy was none other than Mohammed Pharaoh, the newly elected Palestinian leader.

The Presidents of Russia, China, the high-ranking members of the Arab Confederacy, and the Secretary General of the United Nations were also present. They were all pro-Palestinian. During the last session, the members of the United Nations had lambasted Israel because of her obstinacy.

• • • •

Through satellite communication, the nations of the world heard the breaking news as it was unfolding.

The newscaster from Central News Makers (C.N.M.) came on and said, "At the very last minute a nuclear war has been averted in the Middle East. It would have had devastating consequences for the whole world. The Arab countries, Russia and China, and the countries bordering them, would have been completely obliterated.

"The nuclear fallout would have killed hundreds of millions of Americans and Europeans. The person responsible for this great miracle is simply to be called The Man. He must be a genius from another planet to have been able to pull it off. I have a gut feeling, mind the expression, that we are going to hear a lot about The Man. The world needs someone like him to be its president."

• • • •

The newscaster was making a prediction and he was not even aware of it. Central news Makers then showed live coverage from all over the world. People were rejoicing and celebrating in the streets because of the averted nuclear war.

Prophet Elijah had mysteriously booked in at the Intercontinental Hotel. The very next day, he called in at the office of Prime Minister Mordecai Rabin to discuss the preparations for the conference. No one knew what the finer points of discussion were going to be, except The Man. The King David Hotel, in the heart of Jerusalem, was chosen for this auspicious occasion.

Five days before the start of the Jewish New Year, the delegates started arriving. Many of them, who had never been to Israel before, used the opportunity to do some sightseeing. With great fanfare, the day of the signing of the seven-year peace covenant arrived.

three

CHAPTER

The Man; Prophet Elijah; Mordecai Rabin, the Israeli prime minister; a high-ranking official; the Palestinian President, Mohammed Pharaoh; representatives of the Arab Confederacy; and the vice-president of the United States of America were present. The newly elected president of America had sent the following apology.

> I would have loved to be present at the signing of the peace covenant as Israel and America have had a very long history of friendship. But due to a pressing domestic situation that needs my personal attention, I am unable to attend the signing ceremony.

The newly elected presidents of Russia and China, the prime minister of Japan, the king of Saudi Arabia, the Pope, and two high-ranking cardinals were also present. They gathered in an auditorium that had been thoroughly swept for explosives and listening devices. The Israeli prime minister was smiling broadly at his once hated enemies.

There appeared to be more congeniality between the Israeli prime minister and his Arab counterpart, than between him and the American vice-president. There was a visible aloofness between them. What was the reason for it? The democratic government of America had put undue pressure on Israel to introduce the agreements they had agreed to implement.

Because of Israel's stalling tactics, the present democratic administration had withheld billions of dollars in aid that had been passed by a majority vote in the house of congress by the previous republican administration. They wanted Israel to reach an agreement with the Palestinians even at the cost of their security.

Pressure was put on Israel to unilaterally withdraw its military from all of the so-called occupied territories. They also demanded that the Israeli government give up claim to the Jerusalem, the Eternal City. Israel stiffened her neck and bluntly told America to go to hell.

The State of Israel recalled all her ambassadorial staff from across the whole of America. The American Jewry expressed their concern that with the latest outbreak of antagonism against America; the Israeli Government had gone *too* far. They chose to side with their host country. And now this breakthrough! It is like a dream come true.

One American Jew said, "There is a God in heaven who answers prayers."

After what seemed like hours, The Man and his very important entourage emerged from the conference room. Accredited journalists and reporters from all over the world were present. They were behind protective bulletproof barriers, not for their own safety but for the protection of The Man and the world leaders.

A chorus of voices filled the air. "What was the outcome of your secret meeting? Did Israel agree to withdraw from the West Bank? What is the status of Jerusalem?"

They were all talking at the same time, and what they said was lost in the noise of their own making. Prophet Elijah replied, "Ladies and gentlemen you will have to wait with the rest of the world to hear it out of the mouth of his Excellency, he who was sent by God."

Central News Makers, one of the world's most prestigious and richest television broadcasting companies, had the sole rights to beam the breaking news to the world. No outsider, as yet, knew whether the announcement was going to be positive or negative.

Camcorders were recording everything that could be seen and heard. Digital cameras and old fashion cameras were clicking, and flashlights blinded those who were nearby.

With tears in her eyes, a very emotional reporter whispered under her breath. "This time it must not be a failure. Too much is depending on it. The Israeli public has suffered *too* much, already." Her sympathies were clearly with the Israelis.

Someone near to her said, "It has been rumored that worldwide economic sanctions will be of immediate effect against Israel should she refuse to comply." A sombre spirit was hanging like an ominous cloud over the conference area.

Those nearby could hear anti-Israeli rhetoric all around them. "Should talks fail, all blame should be laid squarely on the Israeli government."

Another speaker said, "Israel should be completely annihilated."

His friend replied, "The Holocaust should be repeated again. But this time they must make sure that not one single Jew lives to tell the story." Others who heard him nodded their approval. The atmosphere was very foul. A Messianic sympathizer, who heard him, said to himself, *Jehovah, our God, shall never allow it to happen to His, chosen people.*

Those who had a close-up view of The Man, said, "His eyes look like the eyes of a god. It seemed as if a supernatural entity was manifesting through him."

Even the most detestable politician was feeling optimistic and sounding religious. President Mohammed Pharaoh looked very pleased with himself as he chatted away very amicably with The Man. They both had a smirk on their face, and every now and then they would sneak a glance at Israel's Prime Minister Mordecai Rabin, who was talking to Prophet Elijah.

The Man was dressed most impeccably. He could have been mistaken for the president of one of the richest countries in the world. On the other hand, his confidante, Prophet Elijah was dressed like an Old Testament prophet or someone from the epic movie *Lawrence of Arabia*. He was making a very good impression on the leaders of the Arab Confederacy with whom he had a very good report.

The people immediately stood to their feet when The Man and Prophet Elijah, walking side by side, entered the auditorium, followed by the various dignitaries. The main hall was packed to capacity. All conversation came to an abrupt end, and a hush came over the audience. After The Man had taken his seat, the prophet lifted up his hands in prayer.

• • • •

As he moved his hands from side to side, the Jewish follow-ers of Jesus, who had gate-crashed the conference, discerned that he was casting an evil spell on the audience. They had pled the blood of Jesus Christ over them for protection before entering the premises.

Prophet Elijah told the people to remain standing. He clapped his hands once, and as a hypnotic spirit emanated from him. He now had their full and complete attention. The people appeared to be in a trance, and their eyes took on a strange hypnotic look.

He began, "Ladies and gentlemen. It gives me great pleasure to introduce to you, the Honorable, his Holiness, The Man, who is going to influence the course of history and the lives of the inhabitants of the whole world."

Looking away from the people, he turned his attention to The Man. Prophet Elijah clasped his hands and bowed before him.

Still talking through his lapel microphone, he addressed the conference and said, "Behold, The Man!"

At the hearing of his words, the people went wild with frenzy. At the back of the auditorium, a commotion broke out. A young man, who was a follower of Jesus Christ, shouted loudly from the back.

"Do not believe Elijah. He is the false prophet, and The Man is none other than the Antichrist. The Bible calls him the man of sin and the son of perdition."

To drown out his words, those nearest to the young man started shouting and cursing him. It seemed as if an evil spirit had taken possession of them. They grabbed the spokesman of the followers of Jesus and those of his group and started manhandling them. Some of them were bleeding.

The spokesman of the group who spoke in English said, "Because Jesus had exposed the devil, religious people like you crucified Him. We are here to expose Satan and his advocates. We are willing to suffer shame and even death for His name."

A Gentile grabbed Andrew by the throat and started verbally abusing him.

With an aggressive voice, he shouted, "Shut up or I will kill you, you stupid Christian. How dare you talk to us about Jesus! We do no want to hear His name mentioned in this holy atmosphere. We do not need Him. What has He done to bring peace to this region or the world? It is because of Him that for the last two-thousand years we have had so many wars and problems in the world. We have The Man now! He will solve the world's problems."

They would have killed Brother Andrew (as he was called by one of his group) had the security guards not intervened. Within minutes, policemen were on the scene and apprehended them and took them to the police station where they were booked.

One of the bystanders said, "May they rot in prison. Christianity should be outlawed."

Someone else said, "They should be thrown to the lions like they did during Imperial Rome. I would *love* to see them torn to pieces."

Another agreed with him and said, "We should make this suggestion to Prophet Elijah."

Still another interjected, "How dare these illiterate Christians insult men of such stature."

An evil spirit from hell had been let loose when the prophet made his incantations. In the auditorium, people fell to the floor, as if in a trance, and started writhing like snakes. Some were foaming at the mouth. Their yellowish-colored eyes were rolling in their heads. They were very quickly removed by the medical staff, who were on call, and taken to another room.

Some calmed down, but others lost it completely and had to

be taken to a psychiatric hospital for observation. Prophet Elijah gestured with his hand for the people to sit. He walked backward to his seat. His head was slightly inclined, but still looking at The Man.

Order was immediately restored when The Man started speaking. A hush fell over the audience and you could hear a pin drop. The people were in awe at the sound of his voice.

He said, "Brothers and sisters! The world has entered a new dawn. I have signed a seven-year peace covenant that will guarantee Israel's security. All the signatories are in agreement. I am very elated to announce that Jerusalem is now the sole property of the Israelis, and they have my blessing and approval to rebuild their temple. The West Bank and Gaza are again to be incorporated into broader Israel." With a sinister look on his face he looked across the audience

"The Palestinians have agreed to concede all claim to the land and are willing to be governed by Israel. The West Bank is again to be called by its Biblical names, Judea and Samaria. The Palestinians are henceforth to be called Arabs. All terrorist groups are henceforth commanded to disband or they shall experience the full fury of the law, governing terrorism. From today onward, the death penalty shall again be in effect.

"Let's give Mr. Mohammed Pharaoh, the former president of the previously called Palestinians, a very warm applause."

Very reluctantly the people applauded. Mr. Pharaoh and the Israeli prime minister were seen warmly embracing one another. Those present were confused at The Man's announcement.

They were not sure whether they had understood him correctly. They were expecting Israel to get a lambasting from him for having dragged out the peace process for so long—also for having refused to withdraw its soldiers from the occupied territories. And for having refused to hand Jerusalem over to the Palestinians, who claimed it to be their Capitol City under a unified Palestine.

According to them, Israel was also guilty of applying segregation against the Palestinians. A resolution equating Zionism with the former South African segregation policies had been passed at the conference in Geneva Switzerland, against racism.

They blamed Zionism for the deaths of hundreds of Palestinians. They conveniently forgot about the thousands of Israeli Jews, who through the years had lost their lives at home and abroad at the hands of demon-possessed, religious fanatical Muslim terrorists.

They were waiting for an announcement to start killing the Jews and, therefore, were not prepared for what was announced. The murmurings of discontent could be heard all over the auditorium. Then another sound filled the air. Prophet Elijah again took his place behind the lectern and started enthusiastically applauding The Man. Within seconds of the prophet applauding The Man, the whole conference gave him a standing ovation.

Prophet Elijah had a very powerful influence over the people. He again bowed before The Man, and the crowd followed his cue, also bowing. A thunderous applause broke loose, which lasted for about ten minutes. They applauded as if they never had any qualms before with his announcement.

Their faces were now exuding approval. The Man quietly left the auditorium with his personal bodyguards, after which Prophet Elijah announced that the conference has been adjourned. Everyone was to receive a brief. He encouraged them to go and spread the good news. Prophet Elijah said, "Messiah's peace, be upon you."

Everywhere people were sharing The Peace, which they demonstrated by embracing one another. The proceedings in the auditorium were broadcasted live. All over the world, people were glued to their television sets, having waited long for this breaking news.

When the newscaster came on, the first words he said were, "The New World President has brokered a truce between Jew and Arab."

First, the picture of the Prophet Elijah came into view. His hands were outstretched as if he was reaching right into the homes, hearts and minds of billions of viewers. He was chanting something that was unintelligible to the listeners. They were now also under his spell.

The camera moved away from him, and The Man was now in full view. The people were beside themselves with excitement. Nearer to home, where history was in the making, the spirit of festivity and euphoria was reigning everywhere. The sounds of the Jewish and Muslim greetings of *Shalom* and *Salaam* were being exchanged.

The streets were crowded with people who were dancing and singing. Others again were seen talking excitedly. Tens of thousands of overseas visitors were mingling with the crowds of people. The peeling of church bells could be heard in the distance. Jews and Arabs were embracing one another and toasting strong coffee, while others again were toasting strong liqueur and beer.

• • • •

There was something that the ordinary Israelis and the citizens of the world did not know. The Man and Prophet Elijah had a secret meeting at Ras El-Tin in Egypt with Mohammed Pharaoh, the leaders of the Arab Confederacy, and the presidents of Russia and China.

Because of America's past sympathies and partiality toward Israel, the president of America was not invited. According to Prophet Elijah's evaluation of them, the Americans were not to be trusted. Those present were sworn to secrecy or face death should they divulge the points of the discussion.

Prophet Elijah, who was the spokesman for The Man, was chairing the meeting. He very carefully explained The Man's designed master plan. The Man did not participate in the discussions, but he was busy reading the minds and hypnotizing those who were present.

Prophet Elijah said, "You, the Palestinians, Arabs, Russians, Chinese, and his Holiness, The Man, all want the same thing. And that is the total annihilation of Israel as a Nation. If you, the Palestinians, agree to fully cooperate with his plans, he will give you the whole of Palestine. Palestine shall be only for the

Palestinians. Jerusalem shall be the capitol city of the reborn, Palestine.

"Israel as a nation and country, as we know it today, shall cease to exist. All he asks of you is to only give him three and a half years to reach his goal. He shall then give you Palestine on a platter. In order to obtain your desire over your archenemies, you, the Palestinians will have to give up your dream of an independent state for now.

"You must also concede all rights to East Jerusalem, and allow the mosque. The Dome of the Rock is to be relocated to Jordan. In this first vote, you may raise your hand if you are in favor of his Holiness' suggestions. Let me see your hands."

Everyone present voted in favor of the resolutions. A second round of voting was deemed unnecessary.

They also brought out a *yes* vote because all they could think of in their perverted minds was the annihilation of the Jews. Having The Man on their side would make it a sure possibility. Therefore, they were all willing to fall in line with his plan.

By their desire to kill the Jews, they also wanted to prove that Jehovah God, of both the despicable and misguided Jews and Christians, did not exist and that Allah was the only true god.

Only Jehovah, the true God is able to stop these anti-Semites from destroying the nation of Israel. They forgot the beating Jehovah gave them during the six-day war. But because the Jews were so desperate to live in lasting peace they were unaware that The Man's objectives were to deceive and destroy them in the end. The Man was just abiding his time. He remembered his father's words.

His Father said to him, "Son, do not rush things. After you have signed the peace covenant, you must wait a full three and a half years. Be patient until the Jews are completely on your side. Then and only then you must strike at them like a serpent."

Individuals from amongst the crowd were voicing the opinion that The Man was Israel's long-awaited Messiah. The more they mused about it, the more it sounded right. On television that very same evening the spokesman for the Rabbinical School made an announcement.

The Rabbi said, "Our Messiah has come at last and is amongst us. He is no longer to be addressed as The Man. He must be addressed as Messiah or the Anointed One. The new millennium has dawned for us who are the Lord's chosen people. *Never* again shall we experience another Holocaust. We, the nation of Israel, must give Messiah our full support. His peace, be upon us."

• • • •

Not far from where all the excitement was taking place, Brother Andrew and some of the believers from the local church in Jerusalem were busy praying. They were all huddled in a prison cell at the police headquarters. They were bruised, hungry, and thirsty and covered in blood.

After they were locked up, the officer in charge of the station said to his subordinates, "Today is not a day to be watching these ignorant Christian criminals. Let's go and enjoy the festivities. We have to celebrate the coming of our Messiah. We shall deal with these misguided Christians later on."

When the police officials left, Brother Andrew led the group in prayer. "Jesus, we read in the book of Acts that the Holy Spirit transported Philip, who was in Samaria, to Azotus. We are not afraid to die for your name, but there are so many young believers, who are dependant on our leadership.

"Dear Father, there are so many Jews, nominal Christians and Muslims, who must still be reached and won for you. Father, please transport us to our brothers who are praying for us in Bethlehem. We ask this in Jesus' name. Amen!"

He was praying by divine revelation, for at that same moment, the Holy Spirit revealed to Brother John, that Brother Andrew and his team were in prison. He told the believers about the revelation that he received. He prayed, "Jehovah God, You delivered the Apostle Peter and also Paul and Silas from prison. You are no respecter of persons. You can deliver our brothers and sisters right now, in Jesus' name! Amen."

When they said amen, there was a knock at the back door of the house. One of the brothers ran to open the door and saw Andrew and the team standing in front of the door. God's Spirit had transported and brought them straight to the house. They quickly entered the house and together they thanked God for His deliverance.

Pastor Andrew shared what had happened to them and how the Holy Spirit told them that Pastor John and the believers were praying for them.

"And here we are," Andrew said.

Their experience strengthened the faith of the believers to trust God for anything and everything. The mothers tended to their wounds and bruises and rejoiced in the greatness of Jehovah, their God.

Joseph, who had a weight problem, said, "Boy, am I ever hungry! I could eat a whole lamb!" The others in the group started laughing.

"He has been grumbling about food in prison already as we started fasting the day before yesterday," said Andrew.

Hannah, John's mother said, "Nothing to worry about. I baked twelve loaves of bread in the oven outside, and I have a huge pot of warm vegetable soup, ready and waiting."

Joseph responded with, "Hallelujah! That is just what a growing boy needs!" *If only they knew how hungry I really am!*

Mother Hannah laughed, "Jehovah is so good. He sure had a sense of humor when He made you."

"What a growing boy needs! If you keep on growing you won't be able to get into the van, and we will have to leave you behind," Andrew interjected.

Again, laughter filled the air. Joseph, being a real sport, did not take offence at his pastor's remark. Andrew introduced him to Jesus, and they were the best of friends. He would always be grateful to Lord Jesus, for sending Andrew to cross paths with him.

Andrew who continued speaking said, "Joseph! We are all very proud of you. Tell us how much weight you have lost since you accepted Jesus as your Savior?"

Joseph replied, "Before my conversion, I weighed 150 kilograms. I have lost 50 kilograms so far. My goal is to weigh 80 kilograms."

A chorus of hallelujahs filled the air.

Mother Hannah said, "The reason I baked twelve loaves of bread and made a huge pot of soup was because the blessed Holy Spirit gave me inside information. He told me that we were going to have unexpected guests and that they were going to be *very* hungry.

"I am glad that I listened to His voice," then she turned to Martha and Miriam and said, "Come on, girls, let's feed these hungry men and women."

The other women also followed Mother Hannah. Being a sensitive woman, she singled out Martha and Miriam was because they were somewhat shy. They only came to faith in Jesus a few weeks ago.

four
CHAPTER

Back at the police headquarters, another scenario was unfolding. When the officers returned, after some time celebrating, they were amazed and perplexed to find the prison cell empty but still locked as they had left it. No one stayed behind when they locked the doors of the cell. It was even a bigger mystery to them when one of the officers pointed out a Bible lying on the bunk bed.

One officer went to his desk and punched in the code on his computer keyboard and the door slid open. Joel, one of the officers entered and picked up the Bible. As he picked it up the Bible fell out of his hand and it opened up at Acts chapter five. A few verses were highlighted. He had a strange look on his face when he read the verses to himself.

He shouted excitedly, "Look here! This is what must have happened to them. It is nothing short of a miracle. The Lord's angel came to deliver them." Joel got all excited. The other officers looked at him as if he was not right in the head.

The chief officer said, "Come on! Be realistic! We are living in the space age, and you are talking about the existence of angels!" *Joel must be unstable in his mind.*

Ignoring him, Joel read the verses aloud anyway.

> Then the high priest rose up, and all those who *were* with him (which is the sect of the

Sadducees), and they were filled with indignation, and laid their hands on the apostles and put them in a common prison. But at night an angel of the Lord opened the prison doors and brought them out … But when the officers came and did not find them in prison, they returned and reported, saying, "Indeed we found the prison shut securely, and the guards standing outside before the doors; but when we opened them, we found no one inside!"

Acts 5:17–19, 22–23

With a strange look on his face the chief officer said, "That the Bible fell open just at that spot, was no coincidence. We must destroy *all* evidence that the Christians were booked in at our police station. Do not mention it to anyone, or we will be in big, big trouble! And I sure do not want trouble with God or His angels." He quickly changed his tune.

Joel had been under conviction for a long time that Jesus was the promised Messiah. He thought to himself, *What happened here tonight is a sure confirmation to me that the followers of Jesus are right about Him. I have to find out where they meet. I want to know more about Jesus. My life is so empty and meaningless. I just cannot get excited about The Man they claim to be Israel's Messiah.*

When Joel finished his shift that evening, he took the Bible with him, as none of the other policemen wanted it. While he was walking home, he saw a man standing under the light of the lamp post, about a half a block away. The man was waving to him, but Joel was on his guard and he had his hand on his holster. A thought crossed his mind, *With all the terrorist attacks of the past, one cannot be too careful.*

When he was a few feet away from the stranger, he saw that it was a young man about his age. He had an honest face. As a policeman, Joel was also a good judge of character. He was shocked when he recognized the young man as one of the Christians who was locked up in prison, but who had mysteriously d*Is*appeared.

The stranger spoke first. "I see that you have brought my Bible. Thank you for keeping it safe for me. Bibles are becoming very expensive and scarce nowadays. Lord Jesus told me to

wait for you here. He told me that your name is Joel Levenski."
Andrew stretched out his hand and greeted Joel then he introduced himself.

Joel was dumbfounded and exclaimed, "Wow! You mean that
Jesus knows my name?"

"Yes, He knows your name, and He also said that you were
going to become a great witness for him. Do you want to become
a follower of Jesus Christ?"

"I sure do, but I do not know how," came Joel's reply.

Andrew, asked Joel, "Are you a sinner?"

"Yes, I am. I am a drunkard, I swear, and I get angry very
quickly. I have disobeyed my mother many times and hurt her
very deeply," came his honest reply.

Andrew said, "Please, pray this prayer after me, 'Jehovah
God, I believe that Jesus is the Savior of the world. I confess that
He died and shed His blood on the cross for me. I believe that
He rose again after three days from amongst the dead. And I now
accept Jesus as my Savior. Amen!"

Sobbing with emotion and with tears running down his face,
Joel repeated the prayer of commitment. They stood to their feet
and embraced one another.

Joel responded, "I have peace in my heart at last. It feels as if
a heavy burden has been lifted from off my shoulders. The con-
demnation that I for so long had carried is gone. Praise, be unto
Jesus."

Brother Andrew responded with, "It is because Jesus has
made you a brand new person."

Before they parted, Andrew asked for Joel's contact number.
He said, "I will contact you and let you know where we are gathering tomorrow evening."

The Holy Spirit spoke to Andrew's spirit and said, *You can
trust him. You can tell him where the service is going to be.*

Andrew wrote down Brother John's and his address and told
him the place and the time of the meeting. Andrew then drove
back to John's home with the car he had borrowed from him.
Andrew shared with the believers what had transpired between

himself and Joel. Later that evening, John drove Andrew back to his home in Jerusalem.

. . . .

About a year before the signing of the false covenant of peace, a group of born again believers came together for a Bible study in the Christian enclave in Bethlehem. At that time, they were only thirty in number. They were mainly in their mid twenties and early thirties.

John Weisman was the pastor of the local church in Bethlehem, and Andrew Levinson was the pastor of the local church in Jerusalem. On one of their previous visits to Israel, they were baptized in the Jordan River in the name of Jesus Christ.

That was long before they studied at the University of Christ for all Nationalities, in the United States of America. They came to Israel for the sole purpose to plant home churches for the Messianic believers. They had to be very careful as it is against the law to convert Jews to Jesus.

Jehovah's anointing enabled both John and Andrew to plant a hundred home-churches, consisting each of no less than twenty believers, across Israel. They have experienced that once a Jew accepts Jesus as their Messiah, they make very faithful disciples for the rest of their lives, just like the early apostles and disciples.

Both their fathers had died in America, and they were both an only child. When they immigrated, they brought their mothers along with them. Some of their strongest support came from certain Orthodox Jews, who discovered that Jesus was indeed the Messiah of Israel.

He had revealed Himself to them through dreams and visions. They were a secret group within Orthodox Judaism, who decided that as soon as they formed a *Quorum (minimum number of people required)* they were going to declare that Jesus was both Lord and Christ.

As for now, they had to be satisfied to be secret disciples. They just marvel when John and Andrew showed them from both the Old and New Testament that Jesus was indeed the promised

Dudley Fairbairn

Christ (the true Messiah) who walked the dusty streets of Palestine over two thousand years ago.

Before John and Andrew's encounter with Jesus, they were members of a Reformed Jewish Congregation in New York. Being Jews made it easy for them to immigrate to Israel. They never told their Rabbi that they had accepted Jesus as their Christ. That information would have caused problems with the Israeli authorities and their application for immigration would have been rejected. They were not ashamed of being followers of Jesus, but they had to use wisdom, as they did not want to jeopardize their chances of a new life in Israel.

John, once said, "Atheistic and Communistic Jews have no problem being accepted as immigrants. They are welcomed with open arms. But the applications of law-abiding Jews, who believe that Jesus is Israel's true Messiah, are rejected."

• • • •

The day after the signing of the false covenant of peace, a group of about thirty believers gathered at Andrew's home in Jerusalem where he was the leader of the house churches. They warmly greeted one another. Rachel, a young Jewess, was asked to open in prayer. Peter, an Italian Jew, led the worship.

The songs were written and put to music by some of the most talented singers and musicians in the group. The songs were in Hebrew and in English. They knew that assimilation was very important if they wanted to win souls for Jesus. The songs were exalting Jehovah and expressing their love for Jesus.

The worship lasted for an hour. The group was now waiting with great anticipation for Brother Andrew, who was the overseer of the greater Jerusalem, to share the word of God. He believed that all members should be trained to function in the local churches.

Tonight, however, it was his turn to share the word. He had sought Jehovah God for divine revelation, and it was burning in his heart like a fire. The happenings of the day before had impressed upon his heart how close they were to the coming of Jesus, to transport His Church to heaven.

He greeted the believers, who had their notebooks and pens in readiness. "*Shalom,* brothers and sisters. I have something important to share with you."

He read from the Book of Daniel. "'Then he shall confirm a covenant with many for one week; But in the middle of the week He shall bring an end to sacrifice and offering. And on the wing of abominations shall be one who makes desolate, Even until the consummation, which is determined, Is poured out on the desolate' (Daniel 9:27)."

Andrew bowed his head and prayed, "Heavenly Father, we come to you in Jesus' name. We love you with all of our hearts. Let Your Holy Spirit be the teacher of Your word. Amen!" And they all chorused, "Amen!"

Andrew addressed the fellowship. "You are all aware of what had happened at the conference yesterday. A seven-year covenant of peace was signed. Where does that leave us, and where does it all fit in Jehovah's eternal plan? Daniel said that the Antichrist will make a seven year covenant, but in the midst of the week, or three and a half years into the seven years, he is going to break the covenant. The apostle Paul had warned us in the Epistle to the Corinthians. 'For when they say, "Peace and safety!" then sudden destruction comes upon them, as labor pains upon a pregnant woman. And they shall not escape. But you, brethren, are not in darkness, so that this Day should overtake you as a thief' (1 Thessalonians 5:3)."

Andrew paused for a few seconds then, continued, "Peace is the subject on everyone's lips. But I can assure you that the peace covenant that was signed yesterday was not from God, but from the devil. It is a covenant with death according to *Isa*iah 28:15 and 18."

The believers quickly turned to the scripture.

"I will paraphrase the following scriptures. *Isa*iah recorded in *Isa*iah 28:15–18. He said that our nation had made a covenant with death and that they were in agreement with Sheol. He warned that when the overflowing scourge passes through that our people believe that it would not come near them because they had made lays their refuge, and under falsehood, they have hidden themselves.

"*Isa*iah warned us that the agreement with Antichrist had made would not stand. When the overflowing scourge passes through our land, those who accepted the agreement shall be trampled down by it. Thanks be unto our God that we as believers in Christ Jesus had rejected it. He shall safeguard us against it.

"Here it plainly states that their covenant with Sheol shall be made invalid. It will happen three and a half years into the seven years of false peace and security, according to Daniel 9: 27." Andrew waited for his words to sink in before continuing. "Paul tells us what is going to take place in, the middle of Daniel's seventieth week.

Andrew addressed the believers. He said, "During the visible and physical coming of Jesus Christ, our gathering together unto Him would take place. The gathering together is the same as the *rapture*. Paul warned us not to be shaken in our faith. We should not allow anyone deceive us by any means. He said that before the gathering together unto Jesus could not take place two things must happen first. Firstly, the falling away or rebellion against God must take place, and secondly that the Antichrist would take up his seat in the rebuilt temple and declare that he is God, before our gathering together unto Christ can take place.

"Paul said that the rebellion precedes the *rapture* of the redeemed. The sacrilege or abomination when Antichrist declares himself God will take place when the allotted three and a half years of tribulation comes to an end. It shall take place on the twelve hundred and sixth day after the signing of the false covenant of peace.

"This is the abomination that Jesus referred to is recorded in the book of Matthew. Jesus said, 'Therefore when you see the "abomination of desolation," spoken of by Daniel the prophet, standing in the holy place' (whoever reads, let him understand) (Matthew. 24: 15a).

"Yesterday, when Antichrist made the covenant, he did not declare himself God. Had he done so, the wrath of all Jewry would have been against him. He is abiding his time. Paul connects the coming of Jesus, our Lord, and our gathering together unto him when Antichrist declares that he is God in the rebuilt temple. He will be crowned king over all the earth on that very same day.

"The gathering of the believers unto Christ will take place at that same time. It will culminate with Antichrist's coronation as God. A worldwide darkness shall then cover the earth and a war shall break out in the atmospheric heavens. "John the revelator gave us a clear insight concerning the war in Revelation 12:7–9.

"John said that war would break out in the atmospheric heavens. Michael and his angels would fight against Satan and his angels. Satan and his angels will suffer defeat and that they will be cast down to the earth."

"Listen to what Jesus alluded to in Matthew 24:29. 'Immediately after the tribulation of those days the sun will be darkened, and the moon will not give its light; the stars will fall from heaven, and the powers of the heavens will be shaken.'

"When Satan and his angels are cast down to the earth the way will be cleared for Jesus to descend to the purified heavens. Daniel connects the deliverance of the Jews with the emergence of Michael the archangel according to Daniel 12:1–2.

"The *rapture* of the redeemed of all ages, whether they be, Jew or Gentile, shall take place here. Bear in mind that there is only one rapture of both the Old and New Testament saints. There is only one evacuation for the Bride of Jesus Christ.

"Some Bible scholars are of the opinion that Jesus never did say when He was going to return. However, Jesus taught that He was going to come for us after the tribulation and the total eclipse of the sun and the moon. It depends upon whether they believe what Jesus said.

"Jesus said in Matthew 24: 29–31, that immediately after the tribulation, there will be a total eclipse of the sun, and the moon will not give its light; and the stars will fall from heaven, and the powers of the heavens would be shaken. It is during this time of total darkness that Jesus will return to banish the darkness and *rapture* His redeemed."

Dudley Fairbairn

Because of Andrew's inspired teaching, the interjections of amen and hallelujah could be heard. Andrew continued, "Jesus warned us: 'Now when these things begin to happen, look up and lift up your heads, because your redemption draws near' (Luke 21: 28).

"This redemption does not refer to the redemption of our souls. Our souls were redeemed when we accepted Jesus as our Savior. This redemption refers to the redemption of our bodies. To what signs was Jesus referring? He was referring to the signs in Luke 21: 25–26. Those signs would be the indication that His coming mentioned in verse 27, is at the door.

"Jesus said that there would be signs in the sun, moon and in the stars; and there would be distress amongst the nations, with perplexity. Nature shall experience convulsions. People hearts' will be overcome with fear because of the occurring calamities. The powers of the heavens will be shaken. It is during this time of natural d*Isa*sters that we will see Jesus coming in a cloud with power and great glory to *rapture* His redeemed.

"Beloved it is going to be a very spectacular sight to behold," said Andrew.

"Beloved this is all for now. We will continue with this study during our next Bible study, God willing! But before we leave, I have one announcement to make. We will fax and e-mail the notes of tonight's Bible study to the leaders of all the other house-churches. From now on, we must be very cautious.

"Our places of fellowship must be kept top secret. It shall be safer if we do not walk in large groups to the places of fellowship. We should not have the meetings at the same houses all the time. We must confuse our enemies. Do not tell strangers where our gathering places are unless you are very sure where they stand concerning Jesus Christ.

"Things are going to change drastically for us in the next few years. I will share it with you tomorrow evening at Brother John's house in Bethlehem. Jesus forewarned us, 'You will be betrayed even by parents and brothers, relatives and friends; and they will put *some* of you to death' (Luke 21: 16). *It sounds awful but true.*

"Your own family may turn against you. When witnessing to

your parents or family members or friends, it will be wise to ask questions to find out what they believe concerning the teachings in the Old Testament concerning Christ. Start a discussion and subtly steer the conversation in the direction of Jesus. Use wisdom. The Holy Spirit will help you choose the right words."

Dudley Fairbairn

five

CHAPTER

Hannah, a twenty-year-old girl raised her hand and asked if she could share a testimony. She said, "Last week Mother was very sick with a fever. I prayed for her in Jesus' name and He healed her. When I told her that it was Jesus who healed her, she got very angry with me and said, 'Do not mention that name ever again in my house or I will disown you.'

The believers were eager to hear more so Hannah continued, "Since then I have been praying that, the Holy Spirit would reveal to Mother that Jesus was indeed Israel's true Messiah. Yesterday morning about ten o'clock she again became violently sick. I tended to her needs with all the love and care of Jesus in my heart.

"She was getting sicker by the hour. My heart was aching for her, but I was not going to pray for her unless she asked me to. I could see that she was not able to bare the pain any longer." She shouted, 'Hannah! Pray to your Jesus to heal me or I am going to die.'

"In my heart, I said, *Thank you, Lord. You heard my prayer!* I laid my hand on her fevered brow and said, 'You spirit of infirmity! Come out in the name of Jesus, the Son of Jehovah.' My mother immediately sat up in bed, and all her pain was gone. She was miraculously healed!

"She asked me how to become a follower of Jesus. I showed her from the Bible, and I prayed the sinner's prayer with her, and she was gloriously saved."

Those present clapped their hands and praised the Lord.

"You are sure an impatient bunch," said Hannah and with that, she burst out laughing.

"I am not finished yet. There is still more to come," then she continued, "I love Mother very much. But she sure loves bossing us around, but I believe that Jesus is going to change her." Some in the group started laughing again.

"Last night when my dad came home from work, she met him at the door and marched him to a chair."

Those in the room could just imagine the expression on his face.

"'Sit down,' she said, 'and listen very carefully.'" The blood drained from Dad's face.

Someone said, "Go on, Hannah! We want to hear more. You are sure a good story teller," said Martha.

Then she continued, "His face was white with fear. He knew what that tone in Mother's voice, meant. He thought that Mother was going to beat him up again. But instead of a beating, she knelt in front of him, embraced him, and started crying."

Some of the believers in the room started sniffing.

"At first, he thought that someone in the family had died. But then she started asking him to forgive her for having been such a terrible wife and for the beatings she had given him in the past. He started crying, I started crying, and my young brother, Amos, who had been listening in on the conversation in the kitchen also started crying.

"To make a long story short, both my dad and my brother accepted Jesus as their Savior when they saw the change in my mother. Or should I say? She commanded them to accept Him, and they did."

This time everyone in the room roared with laughter—even Pastor Andrew, could not contain himself. Even the young children started laughing.

"They asked if they could attend our Sabbath, and Sunday services, and I said I would let them know tonight when I got home."

The blessed Holy Spirit bore witness to Andrew and John and Moses, the guitarist, that it would be safe for them to come.

"They are welcome," said Brother Moses, and Brother John nodded his approval.

It was as if the floodgates of heaven opened up above them and a spirit of laughter and joy descended upon the fellowship. It was *so* refreshing to them to listen to Hannah's testimony, and they were all looking forward to meeting her family.

Enoch, who is quite shy by nature, said, "We are going to hear more testimonies about power evangelism." The believers were pleasantly surprised to hear him interact.

"What do you mean by power evangelism?" asked Mary, who seldom said anything in the services.

Enoch replied, "It means that Jehovah is going to lead us to pray for key people in our communities to win them for Him, with the result that their colleagues and families will also come to know Jesus as Savior."

Moses exclaimed, "Wow! I never thought about it in that way."

Enoch picked up the conversation again and said, "We must trust Jehovah for signs, wonders and miracles. When someone is sick, we must see it as an opportunity to pray for them in Jesus' name. We must not force our convictions on them. We must pray for them and let the precious Holy Spirit do the work.

"Always be kind, considerate, and friendly to them. No matter what! After we have prayed for them, we must leave them in the capable hands of the Holy Spirit and allow Him to continue the work. Make sure that you leave a contact number with them so that they can inform you of the healing, the miracle, or God's intervention in their lives. Or maybe they just want you to visit them again. What we need is a volunteer to man the phone; someone who is home most of the time."

Miriam, who was stricken with polio at the age of eight and who was confined to a wheelchair, said, "It will bring me great joy to man the phone. It will give me something useful to do for Jesus."

Hannah said, "But Miriam! You *are* useful to Jesus and us.

You pray more than all of us." Miriam, being a very shy girl, looked down at her hands.

Enoch spoke again, "Miriam! You are not going to be confined to that old wheelchair for long." Miriam looked up at Enoch. Her eyes were brimming with tears, "In my spirit, I see you walking, running, and jumping for joy." The sounds of amen and hallelujah, filled the air. It was settled that Miriam was going to man the phone until Jesus healed her.

Andrew said, "Let's bow our heads for the benediction. May now, the grace of Jehovah, the love of Jesus our Lord, and the fellowship of the Holy Spirit, the blessed trinity, remain with us. Amen!"

• • • •

There was a beehive of activity on Solomon's Mount. Construction crews were busy sawing the brickwork of the Dome of the Rock into exact pieces. Each piece was properly marked. It was to be reassembled and reconstructed in Jordan just across the border between what used to be called the West Bank and Jordan. The West Bank was again called by its Biblical names, Judea and Samaria.

The king of Jordan had given his blessing for the relocation of the mosque, as it would be a big boost to their tourist industry. They hoped that the relocation of the mosque would lure tens thousands of Muslim tourists to their country. Because Jordan had sided with Sadam Hussein during the Kuwaiti war, the financial supporters from the West had cut off their financial support.

The relocation of the mosque was another coup that Messiah had pulled off. The Dome of the Rock had to make way for the rebuilding of Solomon's Temple. No cost was going to be spared for its reconstruction. The temple had to be painstakingly replicated, even in its minutest detail. Only the most intelligent Jewish architects, art*Isa*ns, and technicians were brought in.

Messiah had made the Jews proud again of their Jewish heritage. Jews, who had taken on Christian names and surnames to escape the pogroms of the Nazis and escape imprisonment and even the gas chambers, had their names changed back to their birth surnames. Donations were flooding in from all over the world. Russia, Australia, the United States of America, and the Republic of South Africa pledged millions of ounces in pure gold.

The roof and the inside walls were to be overlaid with gold. With all the modern equipment and technology, it would take about three to four months to rebuild the temple. Three shifts of men were working non-stop around the clock until a few hours before the start of the Sabbath. For decades, the world's Jewry had been anticipating the rebuilding of King Solomon's Temple, and they were not going to stop until it was finished.

All during that time, they had been preparing certain specific utensils, clothing for the priests, and musical instruments that would be needed in order for temple worship to be implemented. For a very long time, the Orthodox Jews have been making preparations for the rebuilding of the temple, because they knew that the rebuilding of the temple was inevitable. They were busy cutting huge golden sandstone blocks by the tens of thousands in the quarries.

Because the sound of chisels and hammers was not to be heard at the temple site, the huge blocks had to be cut to precision at the quarries. The joints were to fit so perfectly that not even the blade of a knife would be able to be shoved in between the grooves. The logs, likewise, and all the wooden parts were pre-made by hand at the factories. The best Jewish art*Isa*ns from Jakarta, Indonesia were flown in to assist in this task. They were Jews from the Netherlands who had settled there.

· · · ·

Messiah took a keen interest in the progress of the rebuilding of the temple. Smiling contentedly, he watched the progress at the temple sight.

He said to himself, *Only the best is good enough for me. I am going to replace Esau. The temple is going to be my headquarters. Build on you fools, as you built Pharaoh's pyramids and his holy cities. Only*

Father, Prophet Elijah and I, know about my plans to declare myself God of the universe, three and a half years into the seven years.

Antichrist could not have been more mistaken. He did not keep reckoning with the Christian sect, as they were called by the unbelievers. They were working overtime, praying, fasting, preaching, and winning souls. They were warning people about Satan's evil plans for their lives, and exposing Antichrist for who he really was.

They were preaching to people who were willing to listen to them about the coming catastrophic storm that would make the coming catastrophe look like a Sunday school picnic!

Huge excavation and earth-moving equipment was brought in to remove the foundations of the Dome of the Rock, and other buildings associated with the worship of Allah. Professionals were brought in to lay out the plans for the digging of the temple's foundations. The huge golden sandstone blocks that were being used in the building of the temple were being lifted by huge cranes.

For the first time in two-thousand years, the Jews saw Levitical priests dressed as if they had just walked out of the pages of the Old Testament. They were busy praying and sanctifying the ground of any pollution that may have been caused by corpses, the shedding of blood, immorality, false gods, and devil worship.

The architects and the art*Isa*ns were busy day and night on the Temple Mount. Bright floodlights were used during the night. It actually seemed to turn the night into day at the temple sight. A few hours before the start of the Sabbath, the workmen would start cleaning their tools to have it all ready for their working day on Sunday.

The Rabbis were present to make sure that the laws governing the Sabbath were not being transgressed. Every working day started and ended with prayer. Because of the sacredness of the area, only Jews were allowed on the sight. Unauthorized people were not allowed on the grounds surrounding the temple area.

The reporters and journalists got their briefs from the Rabbi Hershel. With great anticipation, the people of Israel and the world's Jewry waiting for the dedication of the temple. The Levites were also receiving last minute training and instructions through refresher courses.

Although Israel was preparing for many years for the rebuilding of the temple, they had to make certain that everything was going to run smoothly for the dedication. All across Israel stock farmers were busy raising oxen and sheep for the temple sacrifices. Twenty-two thousand oxen and twenty thousand unblemished sheep were needed for the holy occasion.

The celebrations were to go on for days. Only the best was good enough for the Lord their God. Friendly countries also donated sacrificial animals. With all due respect to other religions, a new law was passed in the *Knesset* that forbade the farming of pigs within the borders of Israel. The government compensated the farmers. Some of them changed over to farming livestock and fishing.

Since the epic announcement by Messiah, the day for which the world's Orthodox and Reformed Jews were praying, talking, and dreaming about for years was now close at hand. But the Levites were burdened with a very serious problem. They could not commence ministering to the Lord without the ark of the covenant. The archaeologists were unsuccessful in finding the ark of the covenant in the digs around Jerusalem and beyond.

Time was now of the essence. According to, Jeremiah 3:16, the Jews were not allowed to replicate the ark. It had to be the original one. The only alternative was to check the rumor that the ark was in *Axum,* in Ethiopia. Every lead had to be fully investigated. That the ark was in Ethiopia had been part of the Ethiopian tradition for many years.

According to oral and written tradition, Solomon had fathered a son by the Queen of Sheba of Ethiopia. When his son visited King Solomon, he ordered that a replica of the ark be made as a gift for his son. But his son took the original one instead, without the king's knowledge.

The military was approached, and "Operation Ark" was born. They knew the exact town and church where it was rumored the ark was being kept; under the faithful and watchful eyes of the dedicated Coptic Priests. Only the Keeper of the ark was allowed to be in its immediate presence. In the dead of night, a group of brave soldiers was flown to Ethiopia. Their helicopters landed about a half a kilometer away from the church.

Four soldiers, who were decorated for their bravery and whose linage could be traced back to the tribe of Levi, accompanied them. They had to be the bearers of the Ark. They did not want the soldiers to die should they accidentally touch the ark. When they arrived at the church, it was in total darkness.

Two soldiers used bolt-cutters to cut the strong locks that secured the gates. Eight other soldiers released sleeping gas through some of the broken window panes. They waited a few minutes for the gas to take effect. The soldiers all wearing gas masks, forced open the church doors and systematically searched the respective rooms.

They found the priests fast asleep. The sleeping gas had done its work. Because the gas was harmless, the priests would sleep it off and eventually would wake up with a terrible headache and a nauseating feeling in their stomach. "Operation Ark" would be history by that time. The ark would then be, safely back on Israeli soil, in The Most Holy Place where it belonged, not in an Ethiopian Coptic Church.

The soldiers knew that the ark would not be in the main sanctuary, but somewhere in an anteroom hidden away from prying eyes. Within minutes upon entering the church, one of the soldiers shouted very excitedly.

"I found it! I found the ark of the covenant!"

The four Levites ran to where the shout came from and the rest of the soldiers converged onto the room with great excitement. The soldier, who found the ark, had stuck his hand through the steel bars of the security door and drew the curtain aside. It was then that he saw the ark.

Again, they used the bolt-cutters and the door swung open on its hinges. The Levites took one look at the ark, and they knew from the many years of research that the ark was indeed the original one.

Excitedly, the Levites exclaimed, "This is it! This is the original ark of the covenant!"

The ark stood in front of them in all of its glory. The gold was glistening in the beams of their flashlights.

One of the Levites said, "There is no time to waste. We must get out of here as quickly as possible."

The other three Levites got hold of the end of the poles, started lifting it, and, at the same time, made for the door and kept on walking through the gate as fast as their legs would carry them. The soldiers were afraid to touch the ark because they were afraid that they would be struck dead. They were unaware that the Shekinah glory of Jehovah God, which was the source of the ark's power, had departed long ago.

Once the soldiers were in the helicopters and airborne they breathed sighs of relief. The captain immediately called Messiah, Prophet Elijah, and the High Priest. And lastly he called Prime Minister Mordecai Rabin to inform them of the success of "Operation Ark."

six

CHAPTER

To crown it all, after years of experimentation, an Israeli farmer bred a pure red heifer. The ashes of the red heifer, was crucial to the implementation for the temple ceremonies. The television station and the main newspapers were immediately informed.

Early the next morning, the newspaper vendors shouted out the news, "Read all about it! The ark of the covenant has been found! The ark of the covenant has been found."

When the newscaster announced it during the early morning television news broadcast that the ark of the covenant had been found, it caused great joy amongst the Orthodox Jews. On the front page of the morning newspaper was a picture of the ark. It showed Messiah and the High Priest standing on either side of the ark. The whole story of the retrieval was told in detail. For the security of the soldiers their names were withheld.

• • • •

A journalist said to Pastor Andrew, "This is one of the greatest achievements in the history of the Jewish people since Moses brought our forefathers out of the Land of Egypt."

Andrew replied, "I agree with you in part. But I beg to differ with you. The greatest achievement was when Jesus died as our Passover Lamb

The Appearance

69

on the cross for the sins of the whole world, was buried, and arose again from the dead after three days."

The journalist responded, "You must be a member of that stupid Christian sect who believes that Esau is the Son of God, the Messiah of Israel."

Andrew had learned from past experience that it was no use to argue about who Jesus is, as He is able to defend Himself. By inspiration, Andrew said to the journalist, "Three years ago you were ambushed by two members of the *Intifada,* and you lost two fingers on your right hand. Jesus the Son of the living God is able to save your soul and give new life to your paralyzed arm. And, not only that, but He is able to create two new fingers for you."

The journalist was amazed that the stranger knew about the ambush, as it was never, made known. Andrew took him by the hand and said, "Be made whole in Jesus' name. Jehovah God's power went through his body and he fell to the ground shaking."

His friends, who were with him at the time, were busy talking to other people. When they heard the commotion, they turned around and were shocked to see the journalist shaking and laying on the ground.

"What did you do to him?" The journalist's friend asked Andrew.

"It is not what I did to him, but what Jesus Christ is busy doing for him," came Andrew's response.

A friend who was bending over the journalist exclaimed, "Look! Look! His fingers are growing out, and he is lifting up his paralyzed arm."

His other friend said, "It is indeed a miracle."

By this time, the journalist sat up. When he saw the two new fingers he exclaimed, "Esau be praised! Eh! I mean, Jesus be praised! He even created the wedding ring that I had lost during the ambush."

Soon a very big crowd gathered, and Andrew asked the very well-known journalist to tell the people what had happened to him. The people were amazed and also wanted Andrew to pray for them. Andrew preached about the seriousness of breaking God's law and that the punishment was eternal death.

He elaborated on the nature of sin, and he told them that only Jesus was able to deliver them and remove Satan's curse from their lives. He then gave an altar call and many accepted Jesus as their Messiah and personal Savior.

A group of believers from the local church in Jerusalem joined Andrew. They walked amongst the crowds of people and prayed for the sick. They also prayed for those who wanted to put their faith in Jesus and those who had other problems. Through the ministry of the believers, Jesus revealed Himself to them as Savior and Healer.

Andrew said to John who had joined him, "I firmly believe that signs, wonders, and miracles are still the key to prove to the unregenerate that Jesus is indeed the Christ. And it proves beyond a shadow of a doubt that He was indeed whom He claimed to be when He walked the dusty streets of Palestine two-thousand years ago."

In many Jewish homes, a lot of questions were still being raised around the supper tables. For some of them it was still hard to believe that peace had come to Israel and if Messiah was *indeed* the promised One.

• • • •

The dedication of the temple that everyone had been talking and dreaming about had come at last. The day before the dedication of the temple, the high priest and four of the Levites placed the ark of the covenant behind the heavy curtain in the most holy place. The streets of Jerusalem and surrounding areas were beautified, and even the smaller towns and villages had undergone a face-lift. Beautiful flowers were in full bloom in huge clay pots.

Hundreds of dignitaries from all over the world were amongst the tens of thousands of tourists who had arrived for the auspicious event. The hotels, motels, and guesthouses, were packed with visitors. The day before the dedication of the temple, the minister of tourism made an appeal to the Israeli public via the evening national television broadcast.

As his image filled the screen, he said, "People of Israel! I know that we as a country can depend on you. Israel has been host to tens of millions of tourists throughout the years. Our hotels and lodgings are filled to capacity. I want to make an appeal to the citizens of Jerusalem, and the surrounding villages, to open up your doors of hospitality to the visitors. At the same time, you can earn some money with your Eastern hospitality. And may I add, please do not overcharge the visitors."

• • • •

The temple was very impressive and breathtaking and could be seen from a great distance away. People living in the east, west, north, and south had a very clear view of the temple. The people who arrived very early that morning were amazed at the magnitude and magnificence of the building.

The temple was 125 feet long and forty-one feet and eight inches wide. The walls were sixty-two and a half feet high. The porch in front of the temple was forty-one feet and eight inches long and twenty feet and ten inches wide. The gold-plated roof glistened in the sun. It would have made King Solomon proud had he been present for the inauguration of the temple. The honor to dedicate the temple had befallen Messiah.

Not to defile the temple area and offend the Jews, the outer court that was generally reserved for the Gentiles during Old Testament times was chosen for this great and auspicious event. A brand-new marquee was erected to give shelter from the sun to the many dignitaries. Thousands of chairs had been placed in neat rows facing the marquee. Lovely palm trees, displayed in huge clay pots adorned the area.

People arrived as early as seven o'clock that morning to secure a seat. Nearly everyone was carrying an umbrella or a parasol to shield them from the sun. In case of any eventualities, a huge makeshift tent-hospital was also erected. By nine o'clock, all the seats were taken up and hundreds had to stand, which they gladly did. Nobody wanted to miss this once in a lifetime experience.

Jewish musicians from all over the world were flown in to thrill the people with their best Jewish compositions. They played with

Dudley Fairbairn

deep emotion for their God, their Messiah and Fatherland. The audience immediately stood up when they played the national anthem. At that same time, Messiah followed by Prophet Elijah walked up the steps onto the podium.

The people went wild with frenzy and started chanting, "Long live Messiah! Long live Messiah!" while applauding enthusiastically at the same time.

Prophet Elijah lifted his hands, and the applause died down. The high priest was followed by the Pope and a high-ranking cardinal, Prime Minister Mordecai Rabin, and the Dalai Lama also joined them. Then they were followed by kings, queens, princes, princesses, presidents and prime ministers, and other unknown notables.

The people were applauding as the dignitaries were being ushered to their designated seats. Something that was very noticeable was the absence of Mr. Mohammed Pharaoh from the platform. The reason for him being dropped from the V.I.P. list was because, he was no longer the president of the Palestinians.

• • • •

Prophet Elijah took his place behind the lectern and signaled the people to be, seated. His robe was as white as snow. Again, he started chanting in the ancient Babylonian language that only Messiah knew. He was moving his right hand from side to side. His incantations had an effect on the people, and again some fell to the pavement and started writhing like snakes as they did on the day of the signing of the covenant.

Unknown to the ignorant people his incantations were releasing demonic spirits. The spirits took control of their minds, and it made it easier for them to be manipulated and controlled by Messiah, making them totally dedicated to do his will.

The medical volunteers who were monitoring the area via close-circuit television were on the scene within minutes, to remove them to the tent-hospital that was erected in front of the Western Wall, formerly called the Wailing Wall. Even some of the dignitaries on the podium felt cold shivers going down their spines.

The Appearance   73

Prophet Elijah firstly greeted all the very important guests on the podium, and then he greeted the larger audience. "Citizens of The New World Order. I greet you in the name of Messiah. Two-thousand years ago a man called Esau, claimed to be the Son of God. Esau was hailed by his followers to be the Messiah of the Jews and the Savior of the world! Did He bring peace? No! He did not! The world has not known peace for the last two-thousand years since He set foot on planet earth. He was an imposter."

The people started cheering and the majority on the podium, and those in the crowd stood to their feet. Prophet Elijah smiled broadly. As usual, his spell had worked. He continued his speech, "Since the coming of the true Messiah, peace has swept the world from sea to sea, and from coast to coast." Those on the podium nodded their heads in approval. "It gives me great honor in presenting to you, 'His Holiness Messiah. The one who was born to be the Messiah and the deliverer of the world."

As one, the crowd stood up, and a deafening applause broke loose. The people were in ecstatic mood. Messiah took his place behind the lectern, and in a commanding voice, he addressed the conference. "I bring you greetings from another planet. I am he of whom it was prophesied thousands of years ago. If you obey my commands, for my commands are not grievous, you shall live long and happy lives." With great pride, he looked across his audience.

"However, there are certain rebellious Christians who are out to disrupt the peace that I have brought. They are guilty of blasphemy. They called me the Antichrist, the son of perdition," he said with a very angry tone in his voice. "Judge me by my works. Through my own power, I have prevented a Goliath of about 650 million Arabs from killing Israel who represents little David, a nation who only numbers about five million souls.

"Single-handedly, I have averted a third world war." Messiah pushed out his chest with pride. "These illiterate Christians should be eradicated like vermin. Like cancer, they must be cut out of the fabric of society or they will destroy our, New Age

Society. No disobedience shall be tolerated! The heads of state and their governments are answerable only to me."

Again there was a thunderous applause with the people taking up the chant, "Who is like unto Messiah? Who can make war with him? Long live the king! Long live the king!"

Prophet Elijah looked with great admiration and approval at Messiah, who continued his speech. "All of you are my servants, my little children whom I love dearly." Men and woman were seen wiping away tears. "In the Holy Book it is written of me, 'He shall judge between nations, And rebuke many people; They shall beat their swords into plowshares, And their spears into pruning hooks; Nation shall not lift up sword against nation, Neither shall they learn war anymore' (*Isa*iah 2:4)."

• • • •

All across Israel, the followers of Jesus boycotted the dedication of the temple. They preferred to stay indoors and listen to live television or radio broadcasts. The secular world was enthralled at what Messiah had accomplished. But the Pentecostals, Evangelicals, Charismatic, and Baptists were appalled at the course the events in Israel had taken.

The followers of Jesus in Israel and abroad were very concerned for the Israeli Jews. They had read the books of Daniel, Matthew, and Revelation, and they knew that it was not the right time for the Israelis and the Jews of the *Diaspora* to express elation.

• • • •

At a house meeting, where the leaders of the local churches were gathering, the spirit of prophecy came upon Brother John, and he started speaking under the unction of the Holy Spirit.

" ... continue in the faith. We must through many tribulations enter the kingdom of God. But he who endures to the end shall be saved. Do not fear, little flock, for it is the Father's good pleasure to give you the kingdom ... being confident of this very thing that He who has begun a good work in you will complete *it* until the day of Jesus Christ

The believers started praising Jehovah, and there was not one dry eye in the room. One believer wrote down the prophesy and immediately faxed and e-mailed it to the other ninety-nine house churches all over Israel, where they were also in earnest prayer at that very moment.

Dudley Fairbairn

seven

CHAPTER

Back at the dedication of the temple, the Gentile guests were kindly asked not to cross the demarcated area that was marked with a red line. The temple guards were out in full force. The guests on the podium were also asked to take their seats on the first few empty rows of seats facing the podium.

With military precision, the marquee and podium were removed giving those present a most glorious view of the temple. For the first time the people could see it clearly from the front without the obstruction of the huge marquee. The people were in awe at the splendor of the temple.

Messiah was accompanied by Prophet Elijah, the high priest, a selected few of the many Levites, and the prime minister of Israel. They were followed by some Jewish notables up a few flights of steps leading up to the porch of the temple with its magnificent golden doors.

Messiah took his place behind the lectern and he motioned the people to stand. He lifted up his hands and said, "The Lord said that He would dwell in the dark cloud. I have surely built you an exalted house, And a place for you to dwell in forever." Then Messiah turned around and blessed the whole assembly of Israel.

Messiah said, "Blessed *be* the Lord God of Israel, [*but in his head he replaced the last four words with—my father the devil*], who has fulfilled with His hands *what* He spoke with His mouth to my father, David, 'Yet I have chosen Jerusalem, that

My name may be there, I have chosen [Messiah] to be over My people Israel' (2 Chronicles 6:1–4, 6)."

After the prayer session, Brother John looked at the believers who were listening to the broadcast and said, "Antichrist is deceiving the people, and he is plagiarizing himself by applying King Solomon's words to himself."

• • • •

When Messiah had finished praying, they moved to where the offerings were to be sacrificed. The prophet lifted up his hand fire came down from heaven and consumed the burnt offering and the sacrifices, and the glory of Satan filled the house.

> When all the children of Israel [and the Gentiles] saw how the fire came down, and the glory of the LORD on the temple [they thought that it was Jehovah God's glory, but it was Satan's glory], they bowed their faces to the ground on the pavement, and worshiped, and praised the LORD, saying: For He is good for His mercy endures forever.
>
> *2 Chronicles 7:3*

Prophet Elijah took his place behind the lectern again and said, "What more proof do you need; you saw the fire. God has put His seal of approval on Messiah. The temple is now officially dedicated to the Lord because he has accepted the sacrifice. The sacrificing of animals shall again, from today on, become an integral part of the worship of the Nation of Israel."

• • • •

For days on end, animals were sacrificed. The festivities lasted until the early hours of the morning. The people were given an official holiday for seven days. The Levites were very busy. However, to them it was heaven on earth because Messiah had come. Since there were so many Levites, they were divided into different shifts, which made the workload so much lighter.

• • • •

The regular early morning news bulletin was interrupted. The newscaster came on but was very fidgety. He was not his normal self, and he looked very nervous. Without greeting the viewers, they showed the breaking news as it was unfolding at the Jordan River. The cameraman zoomed in and two strange-looking characters appeared in focus.

The Jordan River could be seen in the background. With their preaching of doom and destruction, they had scared the living daylights out of the people who were having a picnic on the river banks. They were dressed like Old Testament prophets. Prophet Moses said, "Jehovah is going to pour out His judgments on those from amongst the nation of Israel, because they had accepted a false Messiah."

Prophet Elijah said, "The Messiah you have accepted is none other than the Antichrist. Repent! Or you shall all perish. Accept Jesus, the crucified Savior and you shall receive eternal life. He alone is Israel's Messiah."

Some people looked very upset. Others again had furious expressions on their faces. A burly man took offense at what the stranger had said. He said to one of the prophets, "I will give you a beating you will never forget. We do not like the looks of you or your companion. If you do not leave in the next few minutes, you'll be sorry that you were ever born."

The crowd encouraged him, saying, "Give it to him."

Someone else said, "Knock his teeth out. That will shut his mouth for him."

Just at that moment there was a commercial, and the people watching the news were very dIsappointed.

• • • •

A group of Messianic Jewish believers, who had just finished baptizing new converts, stood nearer to listen to the prophet's warning. Brother John, the leader, and his group were from Bethlehem. They were busy with personal evangelism. He said to the man, "This is fulfillment of Bible prophecy. These men are the two prophets of Revelation."

As the believers stood nearer, they heard the burly man's

threatening words. Some of the people who always enjoy a good fight also stood nearer. Brother Andrew addressed the angry man and said, "Do not lay a hand on the prophet, you will regret it. He is Jehovah's anointed servant."

The man replied, "If he is, what does that make me, the dog's breakfast? I will fight ten like him at the same time." His face was oozing with hatred.

As he approached the prophet, fire came from the prophet's mouth.

Brother John said to the man, "I warned you."

The man stopped dead in his tracks. Had he taken one more step he would have been burnt to a crisp! Because of the fervent heat, the rocks that were touched by the fire melted like wax. Like a scared rabbit, he turned in his tracks and ran to where his wife and children were sitting on a blanket. He grabbed his children by the arms and told his wife that they should immediately leave the beach.

They were not the only ones who left the picnic-area in a panic. Several people scampered to their cars, leaving blankets and picnic baskets behind. The man who nearly lost his life contacted the chief police officer.

The minister of defense was also informed. He immediately dispatched two-hundred heavily armed soldiers of the Israeli army who arrived within the hour.

The officer in charge of the battalion commanded the people, "Vacate the area immediately," he said with a commanding tone in his voice. "Should you refuse to leave then we cannot be held responsible if anyone should get hurt or killed."

The people who were still in the vicinity left in a great hurry, except the followers of Jesus, and the television and radio crews.

The believers chose to remain with the prophets. The soldiers took position and aimed. They had received direct orders from the minister of defense, who in turn had received his orders from Messiah. Prophet Elijah had informed Messiah that their two rivals were causing trouble. Prophet Elijah's orders were, "Shoot those imposters on sight. Shoot to kill, and anyone who dares to choose to take sides with them."

John, the leader of the group, said, "Let's pray and do not be afraid. If Jesus Christ chooses not to spare us from the bullets then we shall meet Him in the next few minutes."

They knelt on the ground and closed their eyes. Those who were filled with the Holy Spirit started praying in the Spirit, while the others prayed in their Hebrew tongue. They were expecting a hail of bullets to rain on them when they heard a great commotion.

When they opened their eyes, they could not believe what they were seeing. Some of the soldiers were rolling on the ground others were scratching themselves like rabid dogs. While the believers' eyes were shut, some of the zealots ran to the river and jumped in.

While the believers' eyes were shut, one of the prophets pointed his finger at the soldiers and a plague from Jehovah fell on them. They were now incapacitated to do the assignment they were sent to do and that was to kill the prophets.

Prophet Moses walked up to John and his group. "As a scholar of the Bible you must be aware that the tribulation started with the signing of the false Covenant of Peace. You, the followers of Jesus Christ must continue to remain faithful to Him during this time of tribulation.

"His grace is sufficient for you. The retaliation of the Antichrist is going to be very fierce against you. But you shall overcome them by your faith in Jesus and by the power of His name."

Prophet Elijah said, "We have been sent by Jehovah God, to you who are Christ's brethren. We are to fight on behalf of all the true followers of Jesus in the world. Be on the alert because you are living in a wicked world. Jesus said, 'Go your way; behold, I send you out as lambs among wolves' (Luke 10: 3)."

Jehovah God is depending on all of you to preach Jesus' Gospel of the kingdom. He shall confirm your ministry with signs, wonders, and miracles. You are going to experience divine intervention in your lives as you have never seen before."

The prophet who spoke first said, "Be not afraid! You will see and hear much about us during the duration of the three and a half years of tribulation." They greeted the believers with the customary greeting of, "*Shalom*," and vanished into thin air and the believers left soon afterward.

The soldiers were still in great straits because of the plague. However, they managed to get to their vehicles and drive off to the military hospital, where they were treated for their discomfort. Nothing happened to the television and radio crew who followed the soldiers.

· · · ·

Benjamin, the chief cameraman said to his colleagues, "I have never been so scared in my whole life. I was afraid that fire would rain down on us as well."

His colleague said, "The thought that crossed my mind was ... should I die, what would happen to my wife and children?

Benjamin picked up the conversation again, "I do not know about you, but I am going to make drastic changes in my life. I now know that the Jehovah God truly exists, and I now believe that Jesus is truly Israel's Messiah."

All four in the vehicle decided to accept Jesus as their Savior. They stopped at a secluded spot and bowed their heads in prayer.

Benjamin prayed, "Lord, I do not even know how to pray; please forgive my sins and the sins of my friends. We accept Jesus, Your Son, as our Messiah and Savior." His three friends prayed along with him.

As the believers were driving home, Andrew said, "The soldiers can be thankful to The Lord that the prophets did not call fire from heaven or they would all be in hell right now. We must stand firm as witnesses for Jesus even if our lives are in danger. It is written, 'What then shall we say to these things? If God *is* for us, who *can be* against us?' (Romans 8: 31)."

Joel, the converted policeman, who was also baptized, said to Andrew, "Jehovah must help me never to exchange the hard times we are about to face in the tribulation for the security that would be mine if I joined the apostate church. Jesus said, 'He who finds his life will lose it, and he who loses his life for My sake will find it.' (Matthew 10: 39) The security that the world offers is only temporary."

Since the day of his conversion, Joel showed tremendous growth and maturity in his Christian life. The other policemen had already questioned him about the drastic changes that they now witnessed taking place in his life.

He used to be short tempered, and he got angry very quickly, and cursed like a sailor. On his days off, he would sit in the bar for hours and get very drunk. As a rule, his friends had to take him home so he could sleep it off.

His mother would say to him, "Joel! You must stop this nonsense of yours or find another place to live. I cannot stand your behavior anymore. You are driving me to an early grave."

Joel loved his mother very much, but he just could not help himself. After his conversion, she commented, "Joel! What has come over you? You are a changed man. You do not come home, drunk anymore. Still you are out nearly every night when you are not working night shift. You are not sick, are you?"

His replied, "No Mother! I am not sick."

Joel had enough time to ponder over his mother's questions. His mother was waiting for him when he arrived home from the Jordan River. She gave him a warm plate of food to eat and then waited for him to finish his supper before she broached the subject again.

She asked him, "Joel what has come over you. You are so different?"

He thought to himself, *Should I tell her of the new love in my life? I know that Mother loves me very much. I know she did not mean it when she said that I should find other lodgings.* Joel was all she had. His father had died when he was five years old, and he was an only child. How is she going to react when he tells her that he has rejected The Man whom Israel believes to be their Messiah, and that he has accepted Jesus as his Messiah. "Mother! Do you really want to know what brought on the change in my life?

With great sincerity in her voice, she said, "Yes, I want to hear the whole story."

He looked into his mother's eyes and said, "Promise me that you will not get upset. Only then will I tell you."

She replied, "I promise."

He knew since a very young age that he could always take his mother at her word. He prayed a silent prayer in his heart, and his heavenly Father gave him the courage.

"Mother, something happened to me the day of the signing of the Covenant of Peace. We arrested a group of Christians because they caused a commotion at the conference. Their leader said that The Man was the Antichrist." Joel paused for a few moments.

His mother nudged him on, "Go on, Joel."

"We locked them up, and all of us at the police headquarters left the premises to join in on the celebration. When we returned, we found the cell empty but still locked as we left it." He took a sip of lemon juice and waited a few moments.

There was a puzzled look on his mother's face. "Go on, son. You are keeping me in suspense," she encouraged him again. Her curiosity was getting the better of her.

A smile crept across Joel's face. "We found a Bible that was left in the cell. As I picked it up it fell out of my hand, and it opened up at Acts Chapter 5. A few verses were highlighted. It was about the apostles of Jesus who were delivered from prison by the Angel of the Lord.

"I told the other officers that the Lord's Angel had delivered them. At first, they were skeptical, but when I started reading the scriptures the others agreed that this was nothing short of a miracle. While I was on my way home, a young man was waiting for me a half a block away from the police station. He was standing in the light of the street lamp post.

"He said that Jesus Christ had told him that my name was Joel Lewenski. He introduced himself to me as Andrew. I was amazed that Jesus knew my name. He said when Jesus delivered them, his Bible was left in the cell. He thanked me for taking care of it.

"He asked me if I wanted to accept Jesus as my Savior. I knew that it was the right thing to do. Mother, I got baptized today in

Jesus Christ's name, and I am now a brand new creature in Him." A tear rolled down his cheek and fell onto the table.

He was expecting a negative reaction from his mother. But to his surprise she put her hand on his. "Son! I also want to accept Jesus as my Messiah, and I also want to be baptized."

"Mother, are you serious?" Joel asked.

"I have never been more serious in my whole life," she replied.

With an enquiring look on his face Joel asked, "What brought on this sudden change?"

"I was watching the afternoon news, and I saw you and your friends on television. The soldiers could have killed you, and I also witnessed when the plague fell on the soldiers. It sure was so very funny when some of them started rolling on the ground." His mother giggled.

"It was such fun to watch the soldiers scratching themselves like rabid dogs because of the terrible itch. And when the others soldiers jumped into the river for relief, I could not help laughing through my tears. I was already under deep conviction then that Jesus was our Messiah."

Joel and his mother knelt on the carpet, and she prayed the prayer of consecration prayer after him. His mother's face was beaming with real joy. "Mother! Welcome to Jehovah God's family." Joel hugged and kissed his mother on both her cheeks.

eight

CHAPTER

At the Military Hospital, the nurses smeared the two-hundred soldiers with a special ointment to relieve them from the itch. Their bodies were covered with red blotches and welts. The doctors had never seen such a condition before.

One of the doctors, a Doctor Abraham, asked them, "Did you come into contact with poisonous plants or hazardous chemicals?" The answers were in the negative.

The dermatologist said, "If it was not poisonous plants or chemicals, what was it then?"

"The finger of the prophet caused it."

"The what caused it?" the dermatologist exclaimed. The commander had to explain the whole episode from the time they arrived on the scene, until the prophet pointed his finger at them, and the rest is history!

"We never ever want to be confronted by them again. Had they called fire from heaven, we would all be dead. I believe that not even an atomic bomb would be any match for them," said the commander, as he looked the dermatologist straight in the face.

Doctor Abraham just scratched his head while the other doctors had a look of amazement on theirs faces. He knew that the commander was telling the truth, as he was not one to be intimidated. He was man enough to acknowledge that he and his soldiers had met their match

. . . .

The false prophet, as he was called by the Messianic believers, had posted a reward of ten million dollars to any man or woman who would bring the prophets in, dead or alive! The newspapers carrying the story sold like hot cakes. People, who never bothered buying newspapers were buying them now.

The headlines of the two newspapers read like this, "Two Men from Outer-space Conquered Two-hundred Heavily Armed Soldiers" and "Soldiers Were No Match Against the Itch."

The people were making fun of the soldiers in their homes and at their places of work. Someone said, "I never had such a good laugh in a long time."

• • • •

Since the appearance of Messiah and Prophet Elijah, a spirit of gloom, despondency, and lawlessness descended on planet earth. Since the signing of the Peace Covenant, peace appeared to have been removed from the earth. The utopia of heaven on earth the world had been looking forward seemed abruptly to have come to an end.

Ethnic and religious wars were breaking out all over the world. The United Nations had its hands full with rebellious nations. Soldiers were sent to various countries to keep the peace; trouble flared up the moment the soldiers left. India and Pakistan threatened one another with nuclear missiles over Cashmere.

In Russia, Chechen rebels blew up a number of buildings in the City of Moscow, killing hundreds of people. In East Timor, thousands of rebels joined up as suicide fighters to fight against the United Nations Peace-force. Killer earthquakes in Greece, Indonesia, Turkey, Iran, and Taiwan had killed hundreds of thousands of people.

Tsunamis decimated coastal populations in many countries, killing hundreds of thousands and causing trillions of dollars in damage. Killer tornadoes killed thousands in the United States of America, causing billions of dollars in damage to property and the end was not yet in sight.

• • • •

The arrival of the two prophets brought a revival amongst the Orthodox and reformed Jews. An interest in Old Testament prophecies, concerning Messiah, had been rekindled. They were now researching their tribal affiliation because they had read Revelation 7:1–8.

John and Andrew, the overseers of the home fellowships in Israel, were now very busy since inquiries were coming in on a daily basis from all over the world concerning Jesus.

Since the outpouring of the Holy Spirit, a holy boldness now took possession of them. The Messianic believers were no longer afraid to come out in the open. Since the visitation of the Holy Spirit, the number of the local churches have increased. Some of the local churches now numbered over a thousand members or more, and the number, kept increasing daily.

From all over the world, wonderful testimonies were pouring in. At one of the meetings, Hannah shared her testimony. "I heard the sound of a mighty rushing wind. I saw tongues like as of fire falling on us. Then I heard myself and the rest of the believers speaking in a heavenly language. We were all witnesses to it." She looked across the congregation and they said amen in response.

"Brother Joel came over to me and said, 'Rise up and walk in the name of Jesus.' I did not rise up, but I literally jumped out of the wheelchair and started running. Miracles were happening all over the large hall."

Joel picked up the story and said, "I was standing about ten yards away from Hannah when Jesus said to me, 'Command Hannah to rise up and walk in My name.' I walked over to her and said, "In the name of Jesus, rise up and walk.""

"As I saw you coming toward me, I knew my miracle was on the way," said Hannah.

Joel responded, "I have never been so brave in my whole life. I remembered Jesus' promise. 'But you shall receive power when the Holy Spirit has come upon you; and you shall be witnesses to Me in Jerusalem, and in all Judea and Samaria, and unto the end of the earth' (Acts 1: 8)." The believers were all ears to hear what

Joel had to share. "I witnessed it with my own eyes tonight. God's Word is the truth."

Thousands of people had gathered outside the hall. The Holy Spirit drew them, and they were intrigued by the supernatural fire that was now hovering over the hall.

"We thought that the place was on fire. When we got nearer we realized that it was a supernatural fire because the building was not being consumed," commented some of the bystanders.

In the meantime, someone had called the fire brigade, who rushed to the scene of the fire. The fire brigade wanted to rescue and evacuate the people they thought were trapped inside the burning building. They were shocked to find no evidence of fire in the hall, and not even a whiff of smoke was to be detected in the air.

The bewildered firemen just shook their heads in disbelief. They had never experienced anything like this before. The fire could still be seen on the building. The believers left the hall mingled with the crowds of people. They were now busy witnessing about Jesus' saving grace. Others were laying hands on the sick and seeing undeniable healings and miracles.

. . . .

From all over the world reports were coming in of an unprecedented revival that was sweeping the nations of the world. The prophecy of the Prophet Joel was literally being fulfilled before their very eyes.

The Gospel was being confirmed by signs, wonders, and miracles. Literally multiplied millions from amongst the nations, tribes, peoples, and tongues and of various religious persuasions accepted Jesus, as their Savior. They were breaking with their sinful lifestyles and rejecting their false gods.

. . . .

In Jerusalem, Messiah and Prophet Elijah were busy earnestly discussing the two prophets. Messiah's concern was growing by the day. "We must stop the prophets before they do anymore harm to our cause," he said with great concern in his voice.

Prophet Elijah, who was in a pensive mood for a few seconds, said to Messiah, "I can get a number of zealots who would be willing to give their lives for you. They believe that you are God's anointed one and, as such, they would do *anything* for you. They hate the two prophets with a passion."

"Do that which is in your heart. And do it immediately." *What I say is law,* crossed Messiah's mind.

Prophet Elijah left Messiah's presence and walked to his private office. Messiah knew that the prophets could not be killed, just yet. He knew that only he had the power to kill them by Satan's authority three and a half days before the middle of the seven years.

• • • •

Seated at his bureau, Prophet Elijah immediately picked up the receiver and dialed a number from memory. The person on the other end picked up the receiver, and with a gruff, he said, "Judas here."

The prophet responded, "Prophet Elijah here."

Judas was the ringleader of a large group of about five thousand zealots. They were well-trained, ex-military men. They were dishonorably discharged from their military duties.

They were kicked out of the Israeli Military Force because they had no respect for authority, and they were very brutal. The only way someone was considered for conscription into their order was if they had killed someone.

Prophet Elijah said to Judas, "Messiah has an assignment for you." It went, very quiet on the other side of the line. "Are you still there?" Elijah enquired.

Judas was in shock when he heard that Messiah had need of his services.

"Yes, I am still here. *Whatever,* Messiah requires of me, I will do," came, Judas' immediate response.

"He wants you and a group of zealots to kill the two prophets. Your snitches will tell you where to find them."

"Do you want to have them killed?" Judas inquired. *Have I heard him correctly?* he thought to himself.

"Not later than the end of the week," came, Prophet Elijah's reply, "and do a neat job. I do not want the evidence to lead to Messiah as it would tarnish his image."

He has no image to tarnish. If he only knew what people are saying behind Messiah's back, thought Judas.

Exuding great confidence, Judas assured him, "Have no fear. We are willing to lay down our lives for Messiah." Judas had not felt this good in a very long time. *Wait until I tell my comrades,* he thought to himself. *This will prove to them that they did not make a mistake when they chose me to be their leader.*

Prophet Elijah ended the conversation. "This is all for now."

Judas still wanted to say something more, but the connection was broken. He wanted to ask about payment. *That will have to wait for now until the prophet calls me again.*

Judas had heard that Messiah was very rich. He had heard rumors that the gold in the temple's storehouse was at his disposal to do with it as he pleased. As soon as Judas got off the phone, he started calling some of his snitches. Prophet Elijah could not have called at a better time. Tonight was their regular night for their meeting.

Because their organization was outlawed by the Israeli government, they held their meetings in secret, though that didn't matter much anymore. Since the coming of Messiah, the Israeli government was a government only in name. Messiah had become the real ruler. The government was there only to do his dictates. Messiah was king, and he was the sitting on the throne of David, so the people was made to believe.

nine

CHAPTER

In Prime Minister Mordecai Rabin's office, Prophet Elijah was chatting away very amicably with him over a glass of wine. They had become very good friends since the signing of the Peace Covenant.

Mordecai, who discerned that the prophet wanted a favor from him, inquired, "Is there something I can help you with Elijah?" Only when they were alone would he address the prophet on a first name basis.

"Yes, there is. I am glad you asked," he replied.

"What can I do for you?"

"I want your government to promulgate a law that makes it a criminal offence for Christians to belong to any unauthorized religious organizations. By that I mean that all house fellowships must be banned as soon as it becomes law and is published in the government gazette."

The prime minister was shocked at Elijah's request and said very apologetically, "It was a most unfortunate misunderstanding at what had happened on the day of the signing of the Peace Covenant."

Elijah nearly choked on his sip of wine. "You call it an unfortunate misunderstanding. It was no misunderstanding!" he shouted. "One of those demented Christians called me the false prophet and he called Messiah the Antichrist. And you call it a misunderstanding?" His voice had reached a very high pitch and his face was as red as a strawberry.

The prime minister who has a very high regard for the followers of Esau was shocked at the prophet's request because they never harm anyone and they always help the poor. He also heard, via the grapevine, that they regularly pray for him, his family, the government, and the nation of Israel. They are not guilty of breaking any laws like the zealots who are the enemies of the state.

Are the followers of Esau right about Elijah and Messiah? he thought to himself. Elijah made him feel very uncomfortable. Mordecai replied, "I will see what I can do."

"That is not good enough for me. I want a commitment from you now!" Elijah shouted again.

"*Now?*" exclaimed Mordecai.

"Yes, *now!*" Elijah shouted again, while banging his fist on the bureau, "And do not forget you are running for office again in six months time, and I can make it very difficult for you and your party."

The prophet was showing his true colors. The prime minister was amazed that he did not discover the true character of Elijah earlier.

"Okay! I will do it," Prime Minister Mordecai said with a very heavy heart.

"I knew that you would come around," Elijah replied, smiling. "Why don't these so-called Christians join the Church of Rome? If I were not a Jew, I would have no problem in becoming a full-fledged member of the Church of Rome.

"Oh! I forgot to tell you that I am hosting a Church Unity Conference in Jerusalem next week," he said quickly, changing the subject. "The World Council of Churches and the Ecumenical Movement have also been invited. Something very good is going to come from it. We are planning to form a One World Church. The permanent seat of Parliament of the One World Church is going to be here in Israel.

"I foresee that in the future Judaism, Christianity, Hinduism, Buddhism, Islam, and other religions will one day all become one. We shall, then have fewer problems in the world. Messiah shall be the head over them all."

As if nothing unpleasant had transpired between them, Elijah was his friendly self again. The prime minister thought to himself, *The prophet must have a split personality.*

Elijah had another drink then left with his chauffeur-driven limousine.

The prime minister, thought to himself, as he left his office. *I have to work fast. I have to warn the followers of Esau about Elijah's plan for them. I have to find out where the leader of Jerusalem can be contacted. How could I have been so wrong about Elijah?*

· · · ·

In Bethlehem, the believers gathered in a hall seating about five hundred. Since the Holy Spirit's visitation, Jehovah had added daily unto the Church those who were being saved. In many villages and towns, they had to get bigger accommodation as the houses were *far* too small.

They had now prayed for two hours. As they sang the last song, the gift of revelation operated through Brother Mark who had come from Gaza to report what the Lord was doing there. He said under the inspiration of the Holy Spirit, "The false prophet is formulating a plan to have all the house fellowships banned, and he is recruiting the help of the government. We must pray and fast as never before."

After the prayer meeting, Mark went home with John, as he was going to stay overnight at his house. He was scheduled to preach during the Sunday morning service. He planned on leaving immediately after lunch. When they arrived home, a delicious meal was awaiting them, prepared by Hanna, John's mother.

Mark immediately felt drawn to her and called her mother. His mother had gone on to be with the Lord, a year ago. His late mother was a staunch believer in Jesus Christ. After mother Hanna had bade them goodnight, the men went to the lounge where they would be more comfortable.

Mark told John, "Jehovah's Spirit told me that Prime Minister Mordecai Rabin wants to contact you. The false prophet paid him a visit today, and he wants to warn us. You must go and see him on Monday if it be God's will."

John responded, "That is more reason why you should stay until Monday, and you may leave after we have seen the prime minister. I would appreciate it if you would accompany me when I visit the prime minister.

"It would be very beneficial *for* God's people to have a friend in the *Knesset*. One of the Rabbis who is a member of the Religious Party is also a very good friend of mine. He also believes Jesus to be the Messiah of Israel. What do you say, Mark? Will you stay?

Mark, who was silent for a few seconds, replied, "In my heart I have the conviction that I should stay. Yes, I will go with you," and the matter was settled.

John immediately contacted the prime minister's office by e-mail, informing him that he would be at his office on Monday morning at ten o'clock.

· · · ·

Two days later Judas' snitch contacted him about 7:00 a.m. "Brother! Have I got good news for you! The two old fogies are here at Tiberius and are scaring the living daylights out of the people," the snitch said, with excitement in his voice.

"Judas said, "Keep them busy until we get there."

"Do you think I am crazy? I heard what happened to the two-hundred soldiers at the Jordan River. I'd rather handle a nest of rattlesnakes than mess with those two old fogies. And don't forget! You owe me big time, pal!" the snitch reminded Judas.

"I will score with you when Prophet Elijah pays me," and he ended the conversation.

· · · ·

It was a warm sunny day, and many people were having fun at the beach. The majority of the people chose to ignore the prophets, who were warning the people of the coming judgment of Jehovah God. Some believers from the local churches in the area were on the beach busy witnessing and distributing tracts.

The front page of the tract depicted a beautiful picture in color of a shepherd carrying a lamb across his shoulders. It was a favorite with the children and their parents.

From what the brethren from Jerusalem and Bethlehem had told them and from what they had seen on television, the believers immediately knew that these men were Jehovah's prophets. Without fear, Brother David the leader and the group walked over to them and greeted them.

"*Shalom!* Prophets of God."

The prophets returned the greeting. "*Shalom,* children of the Most High God."

When some the people saw the group of believers talking to the prophets, they also took courage and stood nearer. Prophet Moses quoted from the word of the Lord. His words were like a two-edged sword.

> Behold, the day is coming,
> Burning like an oven,
> And all the proud, yes, all who do wickedly will be stubble.
> And the day which is coming shall burn them up," Says the
> LORD of Hosts,
> That will leave them neither root nor branch.
> But to you who fear My name
> The Sun of Righteousness shall arise
> With healing in His wings.
>
> *Malachi 4:1–2a*

Prophet Elijah picked up where the other had left off. "You have transgressed Jehovah's commands. Repent of and forsake your sins, and Jehovah shall forgive you. Accept His Son, Jesus who died for your sins on Calvary and you shall be saved and healed!

"Jesus is the Son of Righteousness, He is the Savior of the world, and Israel's Messiah. The present Messiah in Israel is an imposter. He is none other than the Antichrist! Come and kneel here, and these believers shall pray for you and show you the way of salvation."

About one hundred and fifty in number, both men and

women, young adults and children stepped forward and knelt on the ground. Some were weeping softly. Some of the bystanders started making fun of them. Prophet Elijah walked over to them and just looked at them causing them to look down in shame.

Others walked away, but a few more joined those who were kneeling. The majority were enjoying themselves, sunbathing, while others again were enjoying a swim. Little children were frolicking in the water under the watchful eyes of their parents.

Every convert was prayed for received instruction from the Bible. Edifying spiritual reading matter and also a schedule of the regular services was given to them. They left the believers with the promise that they were going to attend one of the many local churches in the area.

Because of their encounter with Jesus, their lives would never be the same again. The two prophets also made a very deep impression on them. For some of them, it was their first encounter with the followers of Jesus.

To many of them, religiosity was synonymous with being a Christian. These believers were different. They did not talk about religious personages or revere relics. They spoke with deep conviction about Jesus, whom they believed to be the Jewish Messiah.

They also believed that He died on the cross for the sins of the whole world and that He arose from the dead after three days and that He is alive this very moment. The prophets themselves had confirmed it.

The group of believers who were involved in the evangelistic outreach lingered near the prophets. All of a sudden, a deafening noise filled the air. Two-hundred motorbikes, each having a passenger stopped at the parking area. They were all bearded, and they were slovenly looking. They were revving the engines to impress the people on the beach.

It caused a terrible racket, and they were very rowdy, and vulgar. The believers knew from past experiences that big trouble was on the way. Some of the bikers decided to ride right onto the beach area sending people scattering in all directions.

The people quickly grabbed their belongings, gathered their

children, and drove off. The beach was nearly deserted. Some stayed and watched from a safe distance. They were more interested to see how the prophets were going to react.

Some of the people saw the prophets on television and what had happened to the two-hundred soldiers at the Jordan River. On the backs of the bikers' leather-jackets were printed in big red letters, "Messiah's Angels." Some of them wore knuckle-dusters, and some were armed with chains, batons, and knives; while others were in possession of guns.

The prophets motioned the believers to leave. They knew that it was not their fight. This was between the prophets and these mobsters. Those who drove onto the beach went to park their motorbikes in the parking-area. They now also joined those who were walking in the direction of the prophets.

The bikers encircled the prophets, while at the same time taunting and cursing them. They were about fifty yards away and were still coming closer. Judas was leading the group of zealots. When they were about forty yards away, he shouted two words, "Charge! Kill!" *This is your last day on earth,* he thought.

The believers and the other onlookers were standing about three hundred yards away.

Suddenly, a number of the onlookers started shouting, "Look! Fire is falling from the sky."

Brother David said, "This looks like Sodom and Gomorrah being re-enacted again."

Someone else shouted, "The fire is consuming them."

All around the prophets the earth was scorched. The fire consumed every gang member, except Judas. To the naked eye, there was not a trace of human flesh left or the weapons they had on them.

Like a pathetic bundle of human flesh, Judas was found lying in a fetal position. He was shaking and crying like a child. He could not believe his eyes, as he saw his friends being vaporized before his very eyes. Soon he realized he was the only one alive. As Prophet Moses approached Judas, he shrunk away in horror. He stopped two yards away from him and pointed his finger at him.

Judas started screaming like a deranged man, "Please don't kill me. I beg of you. Don't kill me. I am not going to serve the devil anymore."

His eyes were as big as saucers. The followers of Jesus and the others had now also approached the prophets but were still a safe distance away. Smoke was still ascending up from the scorched ground. If the situation had not been so serious, the believers would have burst out laughing because Judas' reactions were very funny.

Brother David said to the brother standing next to him, "I am going to talk to the man who gave the command to the zealots to charge. He is just another human being who is in need of Jesus' forgiveness and love."

Prophet Moses spoke to Judas and told him, "You go tell those two demon-inspired men, the Antichrist and the false prophet, that the bottomless pit is waiting for them."

While those present were concentrating on Judas, the two prophets mysteriously vanished. Judas slouched off to his motorbike, a broken man. He wondered what he going to tell the families of his dead comrades.

Brother David walked over to Judas, who was about to mount his motorbike. He started conversing with the stranger. David said, "Excuse me, mister. My name is David. I witnessed what happened to your friends. You sure need a friend right now."

He looked sheepishly at David and said, "My name is Judas. Who wants to be my, friend?"

David replied, "The Lord Jesus wants to be your friend, and I speak for all my friends. They feel the same way I do."

Judas was amazed. His eyes brimmed with tears, and with an emotion-filled voice, he said, "You really mean what you have just said, my friend?"

David nodded. "I meant every word I said. You must be exhausted."

"I feel faint. I have not eaten since last night," came Judas' response.

David's heart was filled with compassion toward this stranger. "Come home and have supper with us, then you will feel much better." David had something better in mind to offer him. He was going to offer him, Jesus, the bread and the water of life.

Someone had phoned the local police about what had transpired at the beach. Soon the deserted beach was swarming with policemen and forensic scientists. The sergeant started questioning Judas.

"Tell the truth. The truth shall set you free and start right at the beginning." David admonished Judas.

Because of the number of policemen taking statements, the believers and a few of the community who did not leave after the fire fell, were free to leave within the hour. David left his phone number where Judas could be contacted as one of the officers had been requested Judas to be at the police station at ten o'clock the following morning.

A few army trucks arrived and the soldiers loaded the motorbikes onto the trucks and took them to the army barracks. It was part of the evidence of something that was very bizarre! The forensic team was testing the ground to see if they could find any trace of human remains. A few strong men were digging trenches. They were sifting the dirt for clues. They were amazed to find that the soil was scorched to more than a yard deep.

• • • •

One of the brothers drove Judas' motorbike to David's home. Susannah, his wife, had cooked a simple but delicious meal. After they had washed their hands, the seven men and Susannah found a place at the extended table. Susannah thanked Jehovah God for His manifold blessings. After a delicious meal, they went to the lounge where it was more comfortable.

David looked over to where Judas was sitting and said, "Welcome, friend. You are free to stay here this evening. We have a guestroom. That will save you time from having to drive back to Jerusalem tonight and returning early tomorrow morning."

Judas took a few seconds before he replied, "I do not want to impose on you anymore than I have to. You have already done so much for me. I do not want to cause you any inconvenience." He seemed broken and humbled man by his experience of just a few hours before.

"You are not an inconvenience to us. You are as welcome as any other person for whom Jesus died," came, David's reply.

"Thank you. I will stay. I do not have the energy to drive back to Jerusalem tonight," Judas' replied, and it was settled.

When they arrived at John's home, one of the brothers prepared Judas a hot bath. David fetched Judas a change of clothing, as they were the same size and height. He also supplied him with a towel, face cloth, a new tooth brush, comb, and razor. He then showed him where the bathroom and the guestroom were located.

"See you tomorrow morning God willing. Breakfast is at eight fifteen. We have to be at the police station at ten o'clock. Have a good night's sleep and do not worry. The Lord is in control. We shall be praying for you."

Judas was up early the next morning and heard the believers praying. Just as he was walking into the living room, he heard David praying for him.

"Dear Jesus, Judas is in serious trouble." Judas came and knelt next to David. "You have the power to deliver him from his sin and transgressions. Still the storm that is raging in his heart and restore peace and order in his life."

Judas started praying the best way he knew how. "God! I am a bad person. I wanted to kill your prophets. I am a thief, a liar, an adulterer, and I have disgraced my parents. Please forgive me. Amen!"

He was crying his heart out, and David put his arm around him. When David opened his eyes to look at Judas, he did not recognize him.

He was cleanly shaven and he had also cut his shoulder-length hair with a pair of scissors that he had found in the bathroom, and he did a good job of it. He was neatly dressed with the change of clothing David had given him the night before.

David asked him, "Do you want to dedicate your life to the Lord Jesus Christ?"

"Yes!" came his reply. "With, my whole heart." He prayed the prayer of dedication after David and invited Jesus to take possession of his life. A smile crept over Judas' face.

Those in the room congratulated him on his spiritual birthday. "Welcome to Jehovah's God's family!"

David took him by the hand and said to him, "We are not going to call you Judas anymore. From today onward, we shall call you Judah, which means to celebrate. We have reason to celebrate because you have passed from death unto life."

The believers gathered around him and welcomed him into the fellowship of believers.

ten

CHAPTER

At the police station, Sergeant Rubenstein was livid with anger. "I have just received a call from Prophet Elijah. How dare that what-cha-ma-call-it, that hypocrite of a prophet, tell me how to do my job! He had the audacity to tell me that if I did not obey his orders, he'll personally see that I lose my job. Why doesn't he keep himself busy with religious matters?"

The other officers were shocked at his out-burst. They had never seen him so angry, as he seemed always to be in control of his emotions. One officer said, "Please! Calm down. You may suffer a stroke or a heart attack." *Wow! This is another side if him we had never seen before,* he thought to himself.

The sergeant held his hand to his chest. An officer pulled up a chair for him and said, "Sergeant, please take a seat," while still another officer handed him a glass of water and an aspirin.

With a tired note in his voice, Sergeant Rubenstein said, "I was to take a complete state-ment from Judas about how his friends, three-hundred and ninety-nine to be exact, were vaporized before his very eyes. Now it won't be necessary. All charges against Judas have been dropped,." and he gave a deep sigh.

"Wouldn't it be fantastic if we had God's prophets on the force? We could win the battle against crime in no time." The officers nodded in agreement. "When Judas shows up, tell him the charges against him have been dropped. He is free to go home."

He addressed officer Levinson and said, "Please destroy the charge sheet and all the notes of yesterday. The prophet was in contact with the minister of security. He gave the clearance to drop all charges against Judas."

As David and Judah were driving to the police station, they were preparing themselves for staying a very long time. The police have the habit of asking the same questions over and over again. These matters could take hours. They met Sergeant Rubenstein at the door as he was about to leave. He was on his way home as he decided to take the rest of the day off.

"*Shalom,*" both David and Judah greeted the sergeant.

"This is Judah."

"You mean Judas. You must be kidding me!" Amazement was written all over the sergeant's face.

"He has come to give a full statement of yesterdays happenings," said David. The sergeant had a frown on his forehead. He did not recognize Judah.

"*Shalom!*" He returned their greeting. "But this is not the same man I met yesterday."

David replied, "You are right sergeant. This is *not* the same man you met yesterday. Yesterday you met a murderer, a mobster, a rogue, and a thief. But today, standing before you is a brand new man. He has been reborn of Jehovah's Holy Spirit. His name is no longer, Judas. His new name is Judah, which means to celebrate. He has become a follower of the Lord Jesus Christ."

The sergeant said, "It is amazing! Wow! It is mind boggling. I can actually see the change in him. It is not just his outward appearance that's different. It is the change in his eyes. Yesterday, he had the eyes of a murderer, but today he has the eyes of a compassionate human being. Jesus must be who He claimed to be."

Now it was Judah's turn to exclaim, "Wow! No police officer has ever said such nice things about me." A tear was glistening in the corner of each eye. Having been faced with death the day before had left an indelible impression on him. All Judah could think about during the night was, *I could have been in hell, right now.*

The sergeant was also moved by what he saw and heard. "Judah! I have very good news for you. All charges against you have been dropped. You are free to go."

Judah's jaw just fell open. "It is amazing!" he exclaimed. "Thank you, Sergeant. I promise you that with Jesus' help, you will never have problems with me ever again. I have also made a promise to the two prophets that I will no longer serve the devil."

Before leaving, the sergeant said, "Keep your promise and may the Lord's blessing abide on you." Then turning to David, he said, "Here is my business card, if in any way possible, please pay me a visit at my home tonight. Come at six and join me and my family for supper."

David thanked him and accepted the invitation. As the sergeant was leaving, he discovered that he was feeling much better. David and Judah returned home rejoicing and shared the good news with the believers who were praying for them. They gave Judah the contact numbers of the leaders of the house-churches in Jerusalem and Bethlehem. He stayed for lunch, and after prayer, Judah left for Jerusalem a new and a very happy man.

All David could say was, "God is so good! God is so good!" He immediately phoned both Andrew and John and told them about Judah's conversion. "Being a follower of Jesus is sure an exciting and full life. We gave him your contact number, and he is sure to give you a call tomorrow morning. Jesus did great things for him. Judah could have been dead, had it not been for the grace of Jehovah God."

• • • •

In Prophet Elijah's private suite, all hell broke loose. He was pacing the floor like a deranged man. He was cursing his personal attendants and servants, and throwing things around. He shouted, "Those lunatics who pose as prophets may have the Lord on their side, but I have Satan on my side!"

His servants were just staring and listening to his tirade.

They had heard what had happened to the zealots. They had no sympathy for the zealots because they themselves had suffered at the hands of that murderous mob. Elijah raved, on and on! "Do you know what those two lunatics did to my men? They zapped three-hundred and ninety-nine of them with fire. They were vaporized! Vaporized! I tell you. And now Judas has also betrayed me, like Judas betrayed Esau. If Judas has enough sense then he will hang himself like Judas of the New Testament did."

• • • •

In Jerusalem, John and Mark were on there way to the prime minister's office. They had sent him an e-mail and had also phoned his secretary to make an appointment. He was very pleased of their decision to pay him a visit, as he urgently needed to meet with them.

Prime Minister Rabin told Ruth, his personal secretary, "Cancel all further appointments. Should Prophet Elijah or Messiah call, tell them I have gone to see my personal physician, and I will be absent for the whole day. Please phone my wife of my plans in case Elijah phones my home."

"Okay, Mr. Rabin. I will do just that," came Ruth's reply.

He continued, "I am expecting two young men named John and Mark. Send them in and I do not want to be disturbed."

Being very witty, Ruth replied, "How can you be disturbed if you are not at the office?"

Mr. Rabin just smiled. He has great confidence in Ruth's efficiency.

"I will order lunch for three," said Ruth.

The prime minister nodded his approval.

• • • •

John and Mark had just entered the main entrance of the government building. A guard stopped them and asked for their identification. They told him that they had an appointment with Prime Minister Mordecai Rabin.

The guard accompanied them to the receptionist desk. They showed the receptionist their personal identification, and she checked their names against the file and told the guard that everything was in order. She gave them directions to the prime minister's office. "It is down the hall, door number seventy-seven, to your right."

The door was open, and they stepped into the very spacious office area. Ruth was sitting behind her desk. She looked up and smiled at them.

Mark thought, *Here is another precious soul we must win for Jesus, but we will start with her boss, first.*

"You must be John and Mark?"

John answered, "Yes, we are. I am John." Pointing to Mark, he said, "This is Mark."

"I am Ruth. Mr. Rabin is expecting you." She thought, *What clean cut young men they are.*

She informed Mr. Rabin of their arrival and asked them to follow her. Mr. Rabin pressed the unlock button on his desk, and the heavy security door slid open; Ruth ushered them into the prime minister's spacious office. She turned around and went back to her desk.

The door silently slid shut behind her. Once seated behind her desk, Ruth phoned one of the restaurants to deliver barbeque fillet steak and all the trimmings for three adults for lunch.

The prime minister stood up, stretched out his hand and said, "I am *Mordecai* Rabin."

John pointed to Mark and said, "This is Mark, and I am John."

Mr. Mordecai Rabin said, "Take a seat and make yourselves comfortable." He then continued, "How did you know that I urgently wanted to see you?"

Mark said, "Jehovah our God revealed it to me by His Spirit, and I told Brother John to follow it up, and here we are. You wanted to see John, didn't you, Mr. Rabin?"

"Yes, I did," the Prime Minister Rabin replied.

"I am not going to waste your time, so here it is. Prophet Elijah wants the government to promulgate a law that would make it a criminal offense for house-churches to operate in Israel. It is to become law in two months time.

"We have been receiving a lot of complaints at the office of the Ministry of Religion that a great number of Jews have accepted Esau as their Messiah. Some of the secular Jews have promised their full support to the prophet. I want you to know that I am your friend. You must warn the leaders of the local churches to be very careful in the future.

"I fear for their safety. Prophet Elijah will stop at nothing. An enemy of Messiah is also his enemy. One of your house leaders called him the false prophet, and he also called Messiah the Antichrist. To him that was unforgivable." John had to hide a smile. He knew it was Brother Andrew who exposed the terrible two-some.

When the prime minister was more relaxed, Mark said, "Mr. Rabin, I discern that you are deaf in your right ear. When you were six-years old, you had a terrible ear infection. It completely destroyed your eardrum. Even wearing a hearing aid is of no use to you. Your mother blames herself even to this day for your loss of hearing."

Amazement was written all over Mr. Rabin's countenance. He exclaimed, "How did you know about it?"

"There is nothing that the Lord Jesus Christ does not know about us. Every time you visit your mother she would say, "Mordecai, Mama is so sorry.""

"It is amazing!"

John joined in on the conversation. "At school you were the brunt of cruel jokes. They teased you and said that you were as deaf as a stone."

Mr. Rabin just shook his head in amazement.

"Would you mind if John and I ask Jesus to heal you?"

Mr. Rabin replied, "I have never experienced the supernatural,"

John responded, "There is always a first time."

"I am open to whatever the Lord has for me," came his response.

John pulled his chair four feet away from the bureau and motioned Mr. Rabin to take a seat. John who was standing at the back of him gently placed a hand on each shoulder.

Mark stood in front of Mr. Rabin and placed his fingers gently on each ear. He prayed softly, "Blessed Holy Spirit, please create the eardrum which was destroyed by the fever many years ago. This I ask in Jesus' name. Amen!"

It was a simple but powerful prayer. Mr. Rabin was under the impression that Mark was going to pray very loud. He had heard strange rumors accredited to the followers of Esau. But he had no evidence that it was true. About a minute after prayer, with no one saying anything, the phone rang. Mr. Rabin picked up the receiver and placed it against the ear that was deaf without realizing it.

After Mr. Rabin finished his call and had placed the phone on the receiver, John said, "Mr. Prime Minister! You can hear quite well out of the ear that was deaf, can't you, Mr. Rabin?"

He was truly amazed and said, "The Lord, be praised. Blessed be His name. I can hear! I can hear from the ear that had been deaf for forty-four years. It is indeed a miracle!"

Ruth pressed a button on her desk informing Mr. Rabin that she was on her way with the trolley of food. Mr. Rabin saw Ruth on the monitor and pressed the unlock button, and the door slid open.

He said to Ruth, "Come in, Ruth. Something wonderful has hap ... " Just at that time, the phone rang.

He was not able to finish the sentence. It was his wife, reminding him not to forget to buy a chocolate for David, their four-year-old son.

Ruth, exclaimed, "Mr. Rabin! You were listening with your deaf ear."

He laughed, "That's what I was about to tell you when the call interrupted our conversation. These two men, or should I say brothers, prayed for me in Jesus' name, and I can hear perfectly well now."

"Impossible!" said Ruth.

"I will close my good ear, and I want you to look toward the door and whisper anything."

Ruth whispered very softly, "It is a miracle." *Why was I ever so against Jesus?* she thought.

Mr. Rabin repeated, "It is a miracle." Ruth just shook her head in amazement.

As she was leaving, she said, "I want to hear more about what happened here today."

John and Mark responded at the same time. "You surely will."

After a hearty meal and a lengthy conversation about Bible prophecy, Mr. Rabin summoned Ruth over the intercom. She thought that she had to clear the dishes. When she entered the room, the prime minister said, "I want these young men to pray for us."

They bowed their heads, and John prayed, "Father we come to you in Jesus' name. Thank you for our prime minister and Ruth. I pray that they both would come to know Your Son, as their Savior. Thank you, Jesus for healing Mr. Rabin. Bless his family, the government, and the Nation of Israel. Bless all the staff and especially Ruth who took care of our natural man. Bless her and her family. We give you all the glory. Amen!"

As Ruth was leaving to go back to her station, she greeted Mark and John with tears in her eyes. Mr. Rabin said to them, "I do not know when I last had such a refreshing time. All my tiredness is gone. But before you go, I want to accept Jesus as my Savior."

Both John and Mark shouted a loud, "Hallelujah!" It was the first time any one had ever shouted hallelujah in Mr. Rabin's office.

They knelt on the thick carpet, and Mr. Rabin asked Jehovah to forgive his sins, and he accepted Jesus as his Savior and Messiah. Mark and John congratulated him and welcomed him into the family of God.

Mr. Rabin said, "For now, I will have to be a secret follower of Jesus or I will be kicked out of my office as prime minister."

John responded, "You are worth more to us as prime minister than someone who is against Jehovah God's children."

Mr. Rabin said, "I know that it won't be long before my wife and all my children will also come to faith in Jesus Christ."

They greeted him with an embrace and left his office. They

walked over to Ruth. Her eyes were all red and puffy, as she had been crying. Mark enquired, "What's wrong Ruth?"

She replied, "I have a problem that is weighing heavily on my heart. My husband was killed in an ambush in Lebanon a few years ago. I was pregnant at the time. When my son Jonathan was born, the doctors discovered that he had a problem with his spine. He is six years old and is unable to walk. Will you please come and pray for him tonight."

Mr. Rabin heard the conversation because the intercom was still on. He got up and went to Ruth's office. "Ruth, why don't you take the rest of the day off? Your work is finished for the day." Then looking at both John and Mark he said, "You will be more than willing to pray for her son, won't you?"

John replied, "It will give us great joy to pray for her son. I do not have to be at a service tonight. The day of miracles has not ended with today. It shall continue until Jesus comes to take us to heaven.

"Brother Mark is only leaving for Gaza tomorrow morning God willing. I will quickly give Mother a call and let her know that we will be late and also to find out if there are any messages for me."

• • • •

At Ruth's home, her mother responded to her knock and opened the door. She was pleasantly surprised to see two handsome and clean-cut young men with Ruth. Ruth embraced her mother. "*Shalom*, Mama."

Looking at the two men her mother responded with a *Shalom* which also included them. They returned the greeting, "*Shalom*, Mother."

"Mama, John and Mark have come to pray for Jonathan."

Won't it cause problems for us? There are so many rumors floating around since Prophet Elijah and Messiah appeared on the scene. I do not trust them.

Ruth saw the worried look on her mother's face and reassured her. "Do not worry, Mama. The Lord will take care of us." Her mother was surprised that Ruth would even mention the Lord, as she has never been a religious person. "Mama, will you please fetch Jonathan for me." Then turning to Mark and John she said, "I have been very moved in my spirit today. I always thought that the stories about Jesus healing the sick, was just fabricated by people with weak minds. Today, I saw it with my own eyes. What you believe about Jesus to be true."

Mother Sarah came in carrying a boy with black curly hair and dark brown eyes. He looked very pale and frail.

When he saw Ruth, he said, "Hello, Mommy."

Ruth stretched out her hands to take him and said, "Mommy's sweet child. Please greet these uncles."

With a weak voice Jonathan said, "*Shalom*, Uncles."

With compassion in their voices, they responded, "*Shalom*, Jonathan."

Ruth said, "Jonathan! Uncle John and Uncle Mark are going to pray for you and you are going to be healed."

Jonathan responded, "But, Mommy! You always told me that Esau won't heal me because I am Jewish and that he only heals Gentiles."

Ruth felt embarrassed at Jonathan's revelation and that he called Jesus by the derogatory name that she had taught him. "I have had a change of heart," came her reply. "I now know that Jesus will also heal little Jewish boys."

Jonathan was overcome with excitement when he heard that Esau also heals little Jewish boys. "Mommy I believe that Esau is going to heal me and then I will also be able to take part in sport, just like all the other boys and girls!"

"Yes, my son, you will." By the sound of her voice, you could hear that she was close to tears. Both John and Mark were touched in their hearts.

"Mommy, what are we going to give Esau as a gift of appreciation? Oh, Mommy! I know what I am going to give Esau. You always tell me that if I have nothing to give you, all you want is my heart, because you say that my heart is so full of love.

"I am going to give my heart to Esau. Mommy, one heart is not enough for the miracle Esau is going to perform. You and grandma must also give Him your heart. Won't you, Mommy!? Won't you, Grandma?"

Both Ruth and her mother were weeping softly.

John intervened on their behalf by saying, "Jonathan, Uncle Mark and I are first going to pray for you, and Jesus is going to heal you. Then afterward your mommy and grandma are going to give their hearts to Jesus as a thank you present."

John had experienced so many miracles since he had accepted Jesus as his Savior that he just knew that Jonathan was going to be healed! He took him from Ruth and both he and Mark laid hands on him. Mark started praying while John agreed in prayer.

Mark prayed, "Lord Jesus, You are the same yesterday, today, and forever. Your power has not diminished. You healed the sick two-thousand years ago, and You are able to heal Jonathan today! There is not a sickness you cannot heal." Then he addressed the spirit and said, "You spirit of infirmity, I command you to leave Jonathan's body in Jesus' name," and they both said, "Amen!"

Mark said to Ruth and her mother, "I know that the miracle has taken place. I felt the anointing go through me."

"I also felt the power," came John's response.

He placed Jonathan on the carpet and held onto his hand and said, "Jesus has healed you, Jonathan. Now start walking."

With feeble steps, he started out, and as his legs became stronger, he started taking bigger steps. He looked up into his mother's face and said, "Look, Mommy! Jesus has healed a little Jewish boy." Without being corrected, he started saying Jesus.

John let go of Jonathan's hand, and he started walking without effort holding onto the furniture. Then he let go of the chair and started walking on his own. Both Ruth and her mother were crying unashamedly now.

Jonathan was laughing and running around the living room as if he had never been paralyzed. He ran to his mother. "Mommy! It is now time to give our hearts to Jesus."

Without anyone having to tell him, he knelt on the carpet and both Ruth and her mother knelt down beside with him, followed by John and Mark.

Jonathan started praying a simple childlike prayer, "Dear Jesus. Mommy, Grandma and I are giving our hearts to You because it is the most precious gift anyone can ever give. My mommy told me so. Thank You, Jesus for healing a little Jewish boy."

John also prayed for them and led them in a prayer of commitment and dedication to Jesus. Soon after John and Mark left, Ruth phoned the prime minister and shared the good news of the miracle with him.

He was so excited that he shouted, "Hallelujah! The Lord's name be praised!"

• • • •

Tired, but satisfied John and Mark arrived back in Bethlehem. After bathing, they felt refreshed and sat down for a home-cooked meal, John's mother, Hanna, had cooked for them. Although no service was scheduled for the evening, a few believers came over to visit with John and Mark. They had a wonderful time of fellowship, sharing the great things that the Lord God had done during that day.

It was already early in the morning and both John and Mark were still pondering on their beds about the way Lord Jesus was leading the local churches. They did not rule out the fact that some of them might die as martyrs for Jesus' sake.

Dudley Fairbairn

eleven

CHAPTER

The great conference that was arranged by Prophet Elijah to discuss Church unity was to start in earnest on Friday morning. It was to get worldwide coverage, as journalists from all over the world were present in Jerusalem.

The journalists from Central News Makers, who covered the signing of the covenant of peace and the dedication of the temple, were back in full force. They felt honored to be covering this once in a lifetime event.

Jerusalem was crowded with religious leaders from all over the so-called Christian world. At home, people were glued watching to the proceedings. The Pope and cardinals from all over the world booked in at the King David Hotel. Ernest Johnson, the Archbishop of Great Britain, arrived with the Dalai Lama in tow. Security personnel were seen everywhere.

The Bishops of Ethiopia boycotted the conference to demonstrate their abhorrence to what Israel had done when they stole the ark of the covenant. Only their cardinal represented Ethiopia. Representatives of both the World Council of Churches and the Ecumenical Movement were present. Jews, Buddhists, Hindus, Muslims, and the Shinto religion also sent representatives. However, they only had observatory status.

The auditorium was packed to capacity, with only standing room at the back. Some people felt let down because Messiah was not present. They had especially come to get a glimpse of the greatest man on earth. Prophet Elijah greeted all the dignitaries, the representatives, and the visitors.

He then called on Ernest Johnson, the Archbishop of Canterbury, to open the conference with prayer. As he prayed, he lifted up his hands and said, "God of all creation. We are all your children. You are our Savior no matter whether we are, black, white, or brown. Thank you for sending Messiah to us. Lord, Your church is *so* divided. Please make us all one through Your servant Messiah. Thank you for Your servant, Prophet Elijah, who is our mediator between Messiah and us. Only through Messiah can we come to know who You really are. Amen!"

While listening to the prayer, Prophet Elijah thought to himself, *Through Messiah, you shall soon discover that Satan is your father and not the Lord God.*

After the opening prayer, the Mayor of Jerusalem stepped forward to welcome the guests. "It gives me great pleasure to welcome all our guests to Jerusalem, on behalf of Messiah and Prime Minister Mordecai Rabin. Jerusalem is not only the greatest city on the face of the earth; it is the city of the great King. It is for this reason that this very important conference has been arranged." After his welcoming words, he took his seat again.

Prophet Elijah took his place behind the lectern. "I declare this conference officially open in the name of Messiah." The people stood to their feet and a deafening applause broke loose. He motioned to the people and the applause died down. He continued, "We are not here to waste time. Time is of the essence. We have wasted enough time already. To be exact, we have wasted over two thousand years. We are not here to draft new resolutions that are not going to be implemented.

"Today, I want a commitment on paper from His Holiness the Pope, the Archbishop Ernest Johnson of Canterbury, pastors, moderators, or leaders from every church organization. It does not matter whether you have a billion or seventy million, tens of thousands, ten thousand, a thousand, five hundred, or a hundred or less members.

"Before you leave Jerusalem, the Cradle of Christendom, I

want a commitment from all of you. You must all join the One World Church. No one is going to be exempted!"

Some leaders were shocked to hear that they had no say in the matter. They knew that the prophet was ruthless, but this crowned it all. Many representatives of the mega organizations decided then and there to take the first flight home the following morning. As the conference proceeded, they were in for even a greater shock.

Prophet Elijah continued, "For nearly two thousand years, you, the religious leaders, allowed the Church to be torn by schisms. Some of the worst culprits are dead now. Many of you are party to the more recent schisms. Enough is enough!" He shouted hysterically, "Messiah and I are not going to stand for it any longer!" His voice was filled with anger.

Prophet Elijah sounded like someone who was suffering a nervous breakdown! He was banging the lectern with his fist. His face was as red as a beet and the veins were standing out on his forehead. He took a sip of water and waited a minute, glaring at those sitting at the back and front of him. Then he continued with his address. After venting his anger, he looked much calmer. The representatives were shocked at his outburst and childish behavior.

"The reason Messiah is not present here today is because he is heartbroken. He is heartbroken because the Church is *so* divided. For his sake and his sake alone, we desperately need a Super Church. We need a Church which speaks with one voice."

The reason he gave for Messiah not being present had the desired effect on the conference though the real reason for Messiah's absence was because he got stupefied drunk the night before and woke up with a terrible hangover. Prophet Elijah had to come up with some excuse. He turned around and beckoned the aged Pope, who had his designated seat next to him, to come and stand by his side. I have the greatest respect for His Holiness the Pope. Now here is a man who is the head of the true Church. His church is not like these disorganized, happy-clappy churches we have here in Israel, which they call house churches.

John and Andrew who attended the conference as observers,

looked at one another. "The reason the false prophet singled us out for criticism is because we are the real threat to Antichrist and to him and the apostate church."

Andrew replied, "With Jesus on *our* side we can never go wrong because we are on the right track and we are on the winning side."

The Pope took his seat again, and Prophet Elijah continued, "If I were not Jewish, I would gladly become a member of the Church of Rome. Things are changing so fast in the world that I foresee no problem in the very near future that a person can have duel loyalties.

"We can be both a practicing Jew and a professing Christian at the same time. After all, the first Church was Jewish in origin. Together we are going to make the Church strong again. We want Messiah to be proud of both Judaism and Christianity."

Someone murmured, "I believe he wants all of us to become members of the Church of Rome. That will be the day! I am going to pack my bags, and I am going to leave on the first flight out tomorrow morning." He was not the only one in the crowd who was voicing discontent.

The prophet continued, "The Church of Rome was the first church. All the churches, which broke away from her, must return to the Mother Church. No church organization is going to be allowed to function if they do not subscribe to the unified doctrine and principals that have already been drawn up by the Church of Rome." A large contingent of representatives stood up and were about to leave the proceedings.

When Prophet Elijah saw their intention, he shouted, "Sit down! No one is to leave the auditorium. I repeat! No one leaves the premises! Guards! Lock the exit doors of the auditorium!" *That will teach them a lesson for rebelling against me.*

Those who stood up immediately sat down again. Then he continued as if nothing, untoward had happened. Many were red-faced and fumed with indignation as they took their seats again.

"Let me continue and listen very carefully. I do not want any further disturbance to the proceedings of the conference. Do I make myself clear? The Pentecostals, Charismatic, Baptists,

Evangelicals, the Plymouth Brethren, The Seventh-Day Adventists, Jehovah's Witnesses, Mormons, and the host of other small *insignificant* small Christian groups must also join."

The presence of religious demons were everywhere. To many, the suggestion of the prophet was palpable because they saw the need for a Super Church. For others, the concept was *too* horrible to contemplate.

Prophet Elijah said, "Seeing that we had such a long session, our next session will start Saturday morning at ten o'clock. Do not even think of leaving the country before the end of the conference. We have already been in contact with the ministry of immigration. All flights from the country have been canceled." You are dismissed!" The prophet looked at his watch and was amazed that they were busy for straight eight hours.

The following Saturday morning, the conference started in earnest again at ten o'clock. Without wasting time Prophet Elijah said, "We are not going to have a secret vote. This matter is far too serious to have a secret vote. How many of you are not in favor of becoming part of a Super Church, please stand to your feet."

To the prophet's amazement, about twenty percent of those present voted against the formation of a Super Church.

"You may sit down now," he said with a voice sounding like ice. "We are only having two sessions today. Some of you may still be entertaining the thought of leaving the country. I repeat do not even think of leaving the country before the end of the conference."

Many people were murmuring. Someone said, "He is keeping us hostage." *Who does he think, he is?*

A preacher said, "The Evangelicals and Pentecostals said that Prophet Elijah is the false prophet of Revelation 16:13, and Messiah is none other than the Antichrist. What they said about them must be true."

His friend next to him whispered harshly to him. "Do not talk so loud. You may end up in a dungeon."

Prophet Elijah stuck to his schedule and announced that the dining lounge at the auditorium was open for service. Many of the representatives had lost their appetite and did not go to the dining lounge. Others returned to their hotels and preferred to stay in their rooms to contemplate and pray. Everywhere groups were in deep discussion about the remarks the prophet had made. Some were in favor and others were against it. The camp was split. By seven forty-five that evening, most of the people had already taken up their seats in the auditorium.

The prophet took his place behind the lectern and said, "I have very good news for you. Messiah is going to be here on Sunday morning for the last session."

Again, the people applauded enthusiastically but not as enthusiastically as when he first mentioned Messiah. The mood of the conference had changed dramatically.

Prophet Elijah went on to say, "I want to make myself very clear. We are going to have church unity no matter what the cost. And to show you just how serious I am, I have arranged for you to see a DVD, which shows how the Spanish inquisitors punished heretics and dissidents."

The lights in the auditorium were dimmed, and the picture was projected onto a very large screen on the wall behind the lectern. The dignitaries on the platform found seating in the first few empty rows which was reserved for them. It showed a woman who was found guilty of heresy because she had accepted Jesus as her Savior. She was tied down to a table. Her mouth was pried open by an evil-looking man. He was pouring a mixture of water and course sand down her throat. She was in great distress and was unable to breath. Some of the mixture ended up in her nostrils, and she choked to death.

It also showed a family, consisting of a husband and wife and a son and daughter. Each one of them was tied to a stake that was planted in the ground.

A church official was shouting, "Recant! Recant! You heretics and we shall spare you."

The man responded, "We cannot recant. Jesus is our Savior. We are willing to die for Jesus."

The official cursed him and said, "May you burn in hell," and lit the dry tinder which ignited the dry wood.

Both the man and his wife started praying, "Lord Jesus, into your hands we commit our family."

The children started crying out, "Mommy! Daddy! Please help us."

The fire started burning very fiercely at this time. The family was overcome by smoke inhalation and fell into unconsciousness by the time the flames started licking at their flesh. Some of the people in the auditorium were holding their hands over their eyes and others were crying. They could not believe that people could be so wicked.

Someone commented, "The prophet must be crazy if he thinks that the organization that I represent is going to become part of such a gang of murderers. We'll never become part of the church he envisions." He was not the only one who was expressing that sentiment. The film also showed two other martyrs. The one was a pregnant woman and the other a young man about twenty years of age. The woman's legs and arms were tied to the rings screwed onto the sides of the table she was laying on.

Her dress was ripped to pieces. A mean-looking man had a sharp knife in his left hand. In one corner of the room, two ferocious-looking dogs were tied to a ring in the wall. They were very hungry, as they had not been fed for more than three days.

The woman was struggling and screaming, "Please do not hurt my unborn baby. Please do not hurt my baby!" The man said, "I will spare you and your unborn child if you reject Jesus."

Her eyes filled up with tears. "How can I reject Jesus? He is my Savior; He is all I have." She started praying, "Please, Lord Jesus, receive my baby and me into your eternal kingdom. You are our only hope of eternal salvation."

The man became violently angry and hit her over the head with a blunt object, and she fell into unconsciousness. The man started cursing her for having fallen into unconsciousness and robbing him of the pleasure of seeing her suffer. Because of the stress the woman was under, she prematurely gave birth to a baby boy who died soon after. The man's superior called him on another assignment, and he left the scene of the crime, and he never returned.

Some of the people present were so nauseated at what they saw that they ran to the washrooms where they vomited. They just could not take it anymore.

There was still one more incident the prophet wanted them to witness. It showed two men dragging a young man. They tied him to a stake in the ground. He *too* was given the opportunity to deny the Lord Jesus.

He shouted, "I won't! I won't! You killed my parents and my sister. Jesus is all I have and need. You can do with me as you please." Two angry-looking men approached him. One had a red-hot poker in his hand and the other had a very sharp knife. The young man cried out, "Lord Jesus, soon I will be in heaven with Mama, Papa, and my sister Joan. Into Your hands I now commit my spirit."

The spectators shouted, "Shut your mouth, you heretic. You deserve to die."

Someone else said, "Because you rejected Messiah, you must die!"

The man with the red-hot poker was approaching the young man. He laughed as someone possessed and he had evil intentions in his heart. The young man cried out, "Jesus, help me." The people cowered at the mention of the Lord's name. In the distance, the bellowing of bulls could be heard. They were stampeding in the direction where the young man was tied to the stake. In the confusion that ensued, the people, including the men who wanted to do the young man harm, ran away from the approaching danger. A believer saw his opportunity and cut the young man loose and helped him to escape certain death. The Lord answered the young man's prayer.

The lights in the auditorium went on. Prophet Elijah who was standing behind the lectern had an evil look in his eyes. "What you just witnessed does not need any explanation. You now know what will happen to you, should you refuse to join the One World Church. The Spanish had given birth to the inquisition and had perfected the art of dealing with heretics. We shall avail ourselves of their expertise. Spain's archives are full of manuals that can be helpful to train a new generation of inquisitors how to deal with rebel Christians."

Many of the conference attendees were looking with shocked expressions at one another. They were not sure whether they heard Prophet Elijah correctly.

"You heard me correctly," he said. Unbeknown to them the prophet was reading their minds. He continued, "On either side of the auditorium are two rows of tables. I want each one of you to register, row by row, and I will be watching you like a hawk. The ushers will tell you at what table you can form a line. The information we want from you is, your full name, your date of birth and address, province or state, and country of domicile. We also want the name of your denomination."

The tables were manned by eager men and women, whose sole ambition was to please Messiah, and Prophet Elijah. Prophet Elijah continued, "The Church of Rome shall undergo a complete transformation. The new Church shall be the only Church that shall be acknowledged by both Messiah and me."

Fear was written on many faces. Some decided to register but would refuse to comply when they returned to their country of origin. Others again thought that it was the greatest thing that could have befallen Christianity.

One preacher said, "Maybe this is God's way in bringing the prayer of Jesus in the Gospel of John to fulfillment." He flipped through the Bible and started reading softly to those around him.

> I do not pray for these alone, but also for those who will believe in Me through their word; that they all may be one, as You, Father, *are* in Me, and I in You; that they also may be one in Us, that the world may believe that You sent Me.
>
> *John* 17: 20–21

John and Andrew, who had been quietly taking notes and also taping the sessions, heard the man's explanation. They were sitting just behind him.

John who was listening to him, said, "This is not from God.

This is of the devil. That man is the false prophet who is working hand in hand with the Antichrist. I would rather choose death than join this worldly religious system. Take heed to Jesus' warning. Jesus said, 'Then they will deliver you up to tribulation and kill you, and you will be hated by all nations for My name's sake' (Matthew 24:9). Jesus said, 'And do not fear those who kill the body but cannot kill the soul. But rather fear Him who is able to destroy both soul and body in hell' (Matt. 10: 28)."

"Read Hebrews chapter 11 and Matthew chapter 24 in your hotel-rooms tonight," said Andrew. "Jesus will give you the answer to your questions. Confess your sins to Jesus and accept Him as your Savior. We have to leave now. May God protect you under Jesus' precious blood! *Shalom,* be upon you all."

"*Shalom,*" they said in return.

The man who read from the Bible said, "I believe I was wrong after all. I do not know about you, but I am going to give my life to Jesus right now."

As it was not yet time for them to register, they sat down with him. They bowed their heads in prayer. The man started confessing his sins and the others joined him. It was a very humbling experience for them to acknowledge that they were guilty before God.

He prayed, "Father God, we thought that we were Christians. We were under that impression because we were christened as babies and because we were members of a church organization that this was all that was required of us to be a Christian. We know now that we were dead wrong. Please forgive our sins. We now accept Jesus as our Savior. This we ask in Jesus' name, Amen!"

twelve
CHAPTER

Just before the representatives went to register, great excitement broke loose in the auditorium. The people were ecstatic. Even Prophet Elijah was greatly surprised when he saw Messiah walking into the auditorium flanked by his personal bodyguards.

When the people saw him, they took up the chant, "Long live the king! Long live the king!"

For many representatives who were seeing Messiah in the flesh for the first time, it was the highlight of the conference. The prophet lifted up his hand and a silence descended over the audience. Prophet Elijah warmly welcomed Messiah and beckoned him to take his place at the lectern.

Messiah started his speech. "My dear children. I have something very important to share with you. I just could not stay away although my personal physician advised me to stay in bed." He was lying through his teeth. "I just had to come."

"You left your families to be in Jerusalem with Prophet Elijah and me. Upon entering the auditorium, I heard Prophet Elijah say that all churches who broke away from the Church of Rome must return to the Church of Rome. That will not be necessary anymore,"

Prophet Elijah had an inquiring look on his face. He could not believe that Messiah would correct him in front of the Pope and all the representatives from the various religious bodies from all over the world.

The Appearance   127

Then Messiah continued his speech and said, "Just as I entered the auditorium, my father told me that the time was ripe for a new Church to be established. He also gave me the name of the church. He told me to name it the Mystery Babylonian Universal Church."

When it dawned on Prophet Elijah what Messiah had just said, a broad smile lit up his countenance! As one man, those present stood to their feet, with the exception of a few thousand who refused to sell their souls to the devil. The approval of those who stood up exploded like an electric storm over the conference. It lasted nearly twenty minutes. Prophet Elijah wanted to call them to order, after ten minutes but Messiah beckoned him and whispered in his ear to let them continue.

"I have summoned the powers of darkness to bewitch them. They will now be willing to give me their souls."

Those who refused to compromise their convictions were protected under the blood of Jesus. When the twenty minutes came to an end, a deathly silence descended on the conference, and as one man, they sat down. The silence was broken by Messiah's charismatic voice.

"What I am going to share with you this moment, my best friend and confidant, Prophet Elijah, does not even know about. He looked at Elijah and said, "Come here, my friend," And he put his arm around his shoulders and gave him a warm embrace. "Today, the Mystery Babylonian Universal Church, has been birthed and a new Church needs a new head."

The aged Pope, hearing that he had outlived his welcome, fainted and was declared dead by his private physician and by one of the cardinals who was also a medical doctor. The shock was too much for his frail heart. He suffered a massive heart attack.

All over the vast auditorium, the Roman Catholics started weeping followed by members of other churches. Their beloved Papa, who had relentlessly worked for church unity, died on the eve of his lifelong dream becoming a reality. None of the cardinals seemed to be overly upset. They wiped away a few tears and that was all.

The dear Pope's body was immediately taken to Mount Sinai

Hospital. In the auditorium, many people were wondering what had brought on this sudden heart attack.

Central News Makers again beamed this breaking news to their worldwide audiences, as it was unfolding in the auditorium in Jerusalem. Prophet Elijah was very upset over the uncontrollable show of emotion, and he wanted to call them to order.

With a twinkling in his eye Messiah whispered in his ear and said, "Let them weep; they truly loved him. The Papacy has been a very great help to our cause. The late Pope has brought 1.2 billion members to the table. They are going to be our staunchest allies. They are very faithful to their religious beliefs and convictions, and they believe in the supernatural."

A half an hour had gone by and the crying had now all but died down. A few people were still sniffing.

Messiah took his place at the lectern, pretending to be very moved by the Pope's sudden death. With an emotion-filled voice, he said, "I want to express my sincerest condolence to the Catholic family worldwide and also other church denominations and religions which held our Holy Father in very high esteem. His untimely death is a great shock and a great loss to us all. He shall be sorely missed by everyone." Messiah called on the Archbishop of Rome and the cardinals who were all sitting behind him to stand up. Then he motioned everyone to stand. "We are not going to waste time with the tedious process of electing the next Pope." All the cardinals nodded in agreement.

"I have just the right candidate for the second highest position in the world." Messiah beckoned Elijah, and he walked toward him. With a voice as smooth as velvet he said, "Please kneel on the cushion my friend."

· · · ·

The cushion was covered with genuine, gold-embroidered fabric. One of the cardinals handed Messiah a purple covered, velvet box. He opened the box and took out a golden, fish-head *Mitre* hat that was specially crafted for this auspicious occasion. Satan had everything planned in the minutest detail.

Messiah placed the *Mitre* on Elijah's head and said, "May the powers of the Prince of the air be with you. May your rule be long and prosperous!" Then addressing the audience he said, "I present to you, your Sovereign Pontiff, Prophet Elijah."

A thunderous applause broke loose. Some shouted, others whistled. Some stomped their feet and shouted all at the same time. Others again were crying as if their lives depended upon it. Messiah started clapping and everyone followed suit. He took Elijah by the wrist and lifted up his left hand into the air, thereby signifying, *I am still number one.*

He continued talking, "I want every one of you to register at the tables and cast your vote in favor of a One World Church. The One World Church will be a precursor to the One World religion. And when that time arrives, I shall be the head of the One World Religion. Cast your ballot in the boxes standing on the tables. The voting starts now! "

The people were very eager to vote for the formation of the Mystery Babylonian Universal Church. Prophet Elijah was blown away at what had just happened to him. He felt like someone who was dreaming. About eighty percent of the representatives voted in favor of The One World Church, and twenty percent of the representatives voted against it.

Those who voted against it decided to boycott the remainder of the conference and went on sightseeing tours. Many visited the holy sites after the afternoon session.

Those who had finished voting were chatting up a storm. It sounded like hundreds of finches. When the last vote was cast, Elijah, the newly elected Sovereign Pontiff, called the conference to order. "We shall only have one confession of faith. There is no salvation outside the Mystery Babylonian Universal Church. The Virgin Mary shall no longer be worshipped as the Mother of God. We shall revert back to the worship of the original Queen of Heaven, Mother Semiramus. Prayers are only to be directed to her.

"The Babylonian Priesthood shall be revived. Sins must be confessed only to the priests and not to Esau the false Christ. Messiah is the Lord's anointed one. Prayers and requests to the saints must continue.

"Infant baptism in the name of the Supreme Father and of the Supreme Son and of the Supreme Spirit shall from today on be the only formula that is to be used. It shall be administered by way of sprinkling. The name of the Lord Jesus Christ must never *ever* be used when baptizing infants or adults.

"That name is too powerful. We do not want the name of Him, who claimed to be the Messiah, to make an impression on their pure minds of the infants," He refused to mention the name of the Lord Jesus Christ, again. "Baptism by immersion in the name of the Father and of the Son and of the Holy Spirit, or in the name of the Esau shall from today forward be a criminal offense."

• • • •

The few representatives of the Pentecostal, Baptist, and Evangelicals, who were present, knew that they were right in the devil's camp. They knew that the sooner they could get out of there the better. They were not prepared to sell their souls for the sake of, Church Unity, a unity that was not based on divine truth. They were not the only ones who believed that a sinister plot was being spawned against them by the devil.

The last session ended at ten o'clock, that Saturday evening. Prophet Elijah made the announcement that the Sunday morning session was canceled. Many were d*Isa*ppointed but others again were very elated.

He said to the conference, "I want you to discover the beauty of Israel. Go on sightseeing tours tomorrow and buy a lot of souvenirs to take home to your families."

People were seen shaking hands and embracing one another. Some got the opportunity to personally greet Messiah and Elijah, their new Sovereign Pontiff.

Very late that evening Prophet Elijah said to Messiah, "I am greatly relieved that the conference has come to an end."

Messiah replied, "I was surprised when you announced that the Sunday conference sessions had been canceled."

"We had such a good response in this evening just before you arrived."

"What do you mean by, 'just before you arrived,' said Messiah with a smile.

"I did not mean it in that way." Messiah's remark made Elijah feel somewhat uncomfortable. "I showed them something they will never forget for the rest of their lives. I'll clue you in over a late supper. Eighty percent voted in favor of joining the One World Church."

"That is fantastic!"

"They were very d*Is*appointed when I told them that you were indisposed and not able to attend the conference. Your presence was the crown jewel of the conference."

Later that evening at Messiah's private lounge, his valet served them thinly sliced barbecued fillets and vegetables smothered in white sauce. Messiah's curiosity was getting the better of him. He inquired, "What are you going to do with the twenty percent who voted against the formation of the One World Church?"

Now it was Elijah's time to smile though it was more like a grimace than a smile. "I showed them a DVD about the inquisition and how they killed the heretics. It sure shook them up. I told them bluntly that if they resisted that they were going to suffer the same fate."

Messiah put his hand across the table, laid it on Elijah's hand, and said, "That was a brilliant maneuver. I could not have done better." And they both laughed to their hearts' content. Let's have a drink and celebrate our victory, your royal Sovereign Pontiff," and again they laughed hilariously.

"Everyday we are getting nearer to our goal. With the Israeli Jews and the apostate Christians on our side as well, our victory is assured. We shall soon have to make a move against the followers of Esau, and we shall start right here in Israel," said Messiah.

"One of my snitches gave me information as to where these misguided Christians are meeting in Haifa. Tomorrow morning, right after breakfast, I am driving to Haifa. I want to catch them red-handed," said Elijah with great bravado.

Messiah inquired, "Has it been written in the law that it is a crime to attend a house church yet?"

"Does it matter whether they are killed before or after it

becomes law? If we want to be successful, certain rules or regulations do not apply to us," said Elijah.

"When I declare myself God three and a half years into the seven years, we will not need anyone's permission." *I thought that he would know better,* crossed Messiah's mind.

"If you do not want them to be killed tomorrow or any other day then it is good enough with me." *I hope he wants them killed!*

Messiah looked at his closest confidante and thought, *Prophet Elijah knows everything about me. He knows that we are both in league with the devil. He is fully aware about my plans to take control of the whole world.*

As Messiah removed his hand from Elijah's hand, he said, "Do as you have decided, but do a good job. Make sure that it is not traced back to us."

They both lit up a cigarette, and then enjoyed their late, supper and a few more drinks. Prophet Elijah bade Messiah good night and left for his private suite.

The news that a *One World Church* had been birthed and that Elijah was crowned the Sovereign Pontiff, after the death of the Pope was confirmed, was beamed to the whole world. A seven-day mourning period was declared across the whole so-called Christian world to mourn the death of the beloved Pope. Everywhere on government buildings, churches homes, schools, and hospitals flags were flying half-mast.

thirteen

CHAPTER

In Haifa, the Sunday morning service was well attended. The church had grown to over two-hundred believers. They were praising Jehovah God for His greatness and rejoicing in the salvation of Jesus Christ their Savior. Brother Peter the leader of the local fellowship in Haifa read the fax that John had sent him.

In it, John informed them of the false prophet's decision to ban all house churches and that all the followers of Jesus and all the nominal Christians *must* join the Mystery Babylonian Universal Church. The believers entered into intensive prayer for about a half an hour after which Pastor Peter encouraged the flock with the following scriptures.

> Stand fast therefore in the liberty by which Christ has made us free, and do not be entangled again with the yoke of bondage.
>
> *Galatians* 5:1

Pastor Peter said, "We have entered a time called, The Tribulation. Our faith is going to be severely tried. But no matter what happens to us, we must not forsake the Lord Jesus Christ. His grace is sufficient for us. According to the God's word, Tribulation is not foreign to those who serve Him."

The believers were in an expectant spirit to hear what he had to share with them. They listened very attentively to Pastor Peter as he quoted the scriptures.

> Beloved, think it not strange concerning the fiery trial which is to try you, as though some strange thing happened to you; but rejoice to the extent that you partake of Christ's sufferings, that when His glory is revealed, you may also be glad with exceeding joy.
>
> 1 *Peter* 4:12

Pastor Peter continued, "In the Western world believers have become so obsessed with prosperity that when they hear you mention the word, *tribulation,* they think you are a false prophet. Partaking of Christ's sufferings was not foreign to the New Testament believers. Jesus said, 'These things have I spoken to you, that in Me you may have peace. In the world you will have tribulation; but be of good cheer, I have overcome the world' (John 16: 33). Through Jesus, we can have peace in the midst of tribulation.

"Did Jesus make a mistake when He told His disciples that in the world they'll suffer tribulation? No my brothers and sisters, Jesus did not make a mistake. Our faith is going to be tested by fire according to the following verses.

"Peter declared, ' ... you have been grieved by various trials, that the genuineness of your faith, *being* much more precious than gold that perishes, though it is tested by fire, may be found to praise, honor, and glory at the revelation of Jesus Christ, whom having not seen you love. Though now you do not see *Him,* yet believing, you rejoice with joy inexpressible and full of glory, receiving the end of your faith—even the salvation of *your* souls' (1 Peter 1:7–9).

"Beloved, in the eyes of God, the trial of our faith is more precious than gold that perishes. I am appealing to all of you to rededicate your lives to Jesus because in the midst of life we are in death."

The believers knelt on the floor and collectively they rededicated their lives to Jesus. Jehovah God's sweet Spirit filled the place, and the believers broke out in spontaneous praise and worship. As the believers were caught up in the Spirit, the sound of angels' voices mingled with theirs, they who were part of the redeemed.

Prophet Elijah was standing just outside the building in the shadows across the street. The sound of praise and worship sent shivers down his spine. He had on a black-hooded cassock. In his hand, he held a broken cross.

Ten masked zealots, armed with machine guns, stood in front of the door of the hall. Prophet Elijah signaled to them to go ahead with their deadly mission. They opened the door, which was unlocked. Someone had forgotten to remove the key after unlocking the door. The zealots quietly snuck into the hall.

The believers were oblivious to the presence of the bearers of death. One of the zealots silently closed the door behind him. Their leader gave the signal and a hail of bullets rained on the unsuspecting believers who were praising and worshipping Jesus. The sound of gunfire was ear splitting.

When the noise broke loose, the brothers jumped up to defend their wives and children. Some were mowed down as they tried to put up a resistance.

Chaos was reigning as mothers cried out, "Please do not kill my children. Blessed Jesus, help us!"

Others were calling out, "Jesus receive the souls of your children."

Another hail of bullets brought their prayers, to an abrupt end. Bodies were sprawled all over the building. A dying mother was still clutching her dead baby.

One brother, who was dying, said, "I see heaven opening up, and I hear angels singing. I see Jesus beckoning me to come," *then* he died.

Brother Peter shouted to the masked men and said, "Let them go! It is *me* that you are after! Kill me, but please let the rest go." Pastor Peter was under the impression that some believers were still alive.

A zealot approached him and shot him point blank. With the last bit of breath, he said, "I love you, Jesus," and he died. One zealot still had time to spray-paint a slogan on the wall, "Death to the pigs, death to the heretics!"

Before leaving the scene of the massacre, the zealots made sure that no one was alive. They quickly left the building, locking the door behind them and leaving the key in the lock. It took them four minutes to do their evil work. When the first shots rang out, Prophet Elijah jumped into his chauffeur driven limousine, which took off with great speed in the direction of Jerusalem.

Three stolen getaway cars were waiting for the zealots, and they too sped off in different directions. Ten miles away from the ghastly scene, they dumped the cars and transferred to other vehicles that were arranged to pick them up. In a dingy motel, they changed their clothes and threw their blood-splattered clothes in the motel's incinerator. They then drove off to a deserted well.

A sign over the well written in Hebrew, Arabic, and English warned the people not to drink the water because it was contaminated and that it could cause certain death. They moved the heavy cement slab, discarded the machine guns into the murky waters of the well, and covered it up again.

One zealot commented, "No one will ever suspect what is lying at the bottom of this well," He handed each zealot a wad of hundred dollar bills. "Let's go home," he said nonchalantly, "Our work is finished."

Within minutes of their departure, a woman walked past the building where the massacre took place. She thought it strange when she saw the key in the lock. Her curiosity got the better of her and she unlocked the door.

She pushed the door open and let out a soul-wrenching scream. Her eyes quickly scanned the building. She saw bodies sprawled all over the hall. Some were lying slumped over the chairs. Others again were lying on top of one another on the floor.

A number of bodies were lying a few meters away from the door. The walls were splattered with blood. Most of the victims were shot in the back of the head and others in the chest area. She quickly withdrew and pulled the door shut, and locked the door and held onto the key. She was literally shaking from shock. She ran to the nearest public phone booth and contacted the Police Headquarters. She immediately got through.

One of the officers manning the emergency phones responded. "Officer Ruben Cohen here!"

The woman was still in great shock at what she had just witnessed. Her heart was pounding against her chest as she began to speak. She stammered, "I ... I ... ammm ... Miriam Feinstein. There has been a massacre. It is ... It ... is terrible! They are all dead. Please come immediately."

"Please take your time, ma'am. What is the address?"

She thought for a few seconds before she replied, "The address is number 777 Mediterranean Street, opposite the huge, wild fig tree."

"You have been very helpful, Mrs. Feinstein."

"Miss Feinstein," she corrected him.

"Please wait at the building, Miss Feinstein, until we get there."

Within minutes of her call, the place was swarming with police officers, detectives, and forensic specialists.

Miriam looked like a scared child. The horror she had witnessed was seared in her subconscious mind. The officer, who was informed that she would be waiting for them, approached her. He could see that she was badly shaken up. He took her to the caravan that was set up for an office. He gave her a drink of water and summoned the doctor, and he gave her a sedative, which had the desired effect. The officer then took her statement. She told him everything she had witnessed in the thirty seconds upon entering the hall.

The officer said to her, "Miss Feinstein, I will arrange for you to be taken home."

She replied, "Thank you, officer." *I don't have the strength. How will I ever get over this!*

"Will you be available again should we have need of you?"

"Yes," came her prompt reply.

She gave him her residential address and that of her employment. She was relieved to get away from that somber place

Inside the hall, the forensic scientists were fine combing the building for clues. "These guys are professionals. They did not leave any fingerprints," said a detective to one of his colleagues.

A few strands of black hair were found in the area of the doorway and outside. They took hair samples of all the deceased. The policemen went from door to door inquiring whether any unsavory characters were seen in the vicinity of the hall.

The journalist for the newspaper, *The Jewish Voice,* was on the scene within minutes after being tipped off by an unknown caller. The journalists; were followed by the Israeli TV broadcasting crew. The regular programs were interrupted by the breaking news of the massacre, within minutes on their arrival at the scene.

A somber-looking TV announcer came on and said, "We have just received word that over two-hundred followers of Esau have been brutally murdered while they were having a church service."

The building was now in focus. The cameraman zoomed in and door number 777 was now in focus.

The police officer who stood in front of the door said, "We are making an appeal to the citizens to stay away at this time, as we do not want you to interfere with police operations. Should anyone have information that would help the detectives with their investigation, please feel free to phone our emergency number. Your calls will remain anonymous. Our emergency number is 777–4677."

All the newspapers were carrying the story of the massacre the following Sunday morning. Some of the headlines read:

"A Christian Tragedy is Awaiting the World"
"The Last Days Are Upon Us"
"Is This Leading Up to the Rapture of the Church?"

The followers of Jesus were in shock, but their faith was not shaken. Everywhere in Israel, where the Messianic believers gathered, their places of worship were jam-packed to capacity. The leaders of the local churches were encouraging the flock to remain strong in their faith. They were told that their brothers and sisters were in heaven with Jesus.

Pastor Andrew e-mailed these encouraging scriptures to the various pastors in Israel.

> But we have this treasure in earthen vessels, that the excellence of the power may be of God and not of us. *We are* hard-pressed on every side, yet not crushed; *we are* perplexed, but not in despair; persecuted, but not forsaken; struck down, but not destroyed—always carrying about in the body the dying of the Lord Jesus Christ, that the life of Jesus also may be manifested in our body. For we who live are always delivered to death for Jesus' sake, that the life of Jesus also may be manifested in our mortal flesh.
>
> 2 *Corinthians* 4:7–11

The Monday morning following the massacre, most of the believers stayed home from work. They were in no condition to work. The news of the massacre was beamed worldwide. The so-called Christian world was also in shock at what had happened so soon after the Church Unity Conference in Jerusalem.

Their religious leaders still had to tell their congregations of the decisions that was decreed by his Sovereign Pontiff, Prophet Elijah. Their spiritual leaders, who attended the conference, knew who was responsible for these barbarous killings. But, they were afraid to voice their opinion. All over Jerusalem, the members of the local fellowships came together to pray for the bereaved families. They also gave liberally to assist with the funeral arrangements.

Many Jews, who were sympathetic to their cause, also contributed. The leadership of the fellowships decided to have the funeral two days after the massacre. John, the pastor of the greater Bethlehem area, was called upon to officiate at the funeral.

He asked Pastor Andrew to assist him. Their eyes were red and swollen from crying.

They did not ask, "Why did they have to die Lord Jesus? They prayed, "Please give us the strength and the courage that when our time comes to die as martyrs that we will be willing to lay down our lives for You."

. . . .

A sea of faces from all over Israel attended the funeral; many were from Orthodox, Reformed, and Jewish backgrounds. Hundreds of Muslims also attended the funeral.

John, Andrew, and all the Messianic male believers had skull-caps on and prayer shawls covered their heads. The married Messianic woman wore headscarves. The followers of Jesus dressed in the distinct Jews garb. They did not want to offend the Orthodox Jews, because they wanted to win them for God's kingdom.

A combined choir sang the "Hallelujah Chorus," followed by "What a friend we have in Jesus" sung by four brothers.

The melody of "What a Friend We Have in Jesus" wafted on the gentle breeze.

The Holy Spirit's anointing rested upon their singing. The Jews and even their Rabbis, who had never heard such anointed singing, could be seen wiping away tears.

Prime Minister Mordecai Rabin sat between John and Andrew. The Chief Rabbi of Jerusalem was on the program to open the service in prayer. As he took his place behind the lectern, he lifted up his hands in prayer. His white beard and side curls were hanging out from under his skullcap were blowing in the light breeze.

He prayed, "God, creator of heaven and earth. We come before You with humility of heart. Our hearts are broken and our prayers are with the bereaved families who have lost their loved ones. I pray for the Messianic believers who have lost brothers and sisters in the faith. We beseech You, Lord, comfort them and heal their brokenness of heart and spirit.

"These martyrs have died with faith in Jesus whom they believe to be the Messiah of Israel. Who are we to condemn them? We cannot condone what has happened to them Lord, we leave the judgment in Your hands. Amen!"

The mass choir sang one last hymn entitled, "When I Survey the Wondrous Cross."

A wonderful anointing rested on the message that was conveyed by the mass choir who sang the hymn. The message of the song made such an impression on those present that women were seen wiping away tears with their handkerchiefs and men were blowing their noses as to not give the impression that they were crying. The blessed Holy Spirit was hanging like a cloud over the cemetery.

It was during this time that Brother John took his place at the lectern. He lifted up his hands and prayed, "Lord! Let the balm of Gilead cover us. Heal us and we shall be healed of all our sins, in Jesus Christ's name. Anoint, the preaching of Your word to our hearts. Amen!"

Some of the Jewish fundamentalists took great offence when Brother John made the assumption in his prayer that Jesus was the Messiah.

John continued by saying, "I extend greetings to David Cohen, the Chief Rabbi of Jerusalem, our Prime Minister Mordecai Rabin, our councilors, the bereaved families and friends, and all the visitors from far and near, in the name of Jesus the Messiah.

"I want to share a brief message with you as recorded in the Book of John. Jesus said to Martha, 'I am the resurrection and the life. He who believes in Me, though he may die, he shall live. And whoever lives and believes in Me shall never die. Do you believe this?' (John 11:25–26).

"Martha and Mary were heartbroken because all their hope was gone. Their beloved brother Lazarus had died four days ago, and his body was decaying in the tomb because of the hot summer weather. Martha, bore witness to it. For she said, 'he stinks.'

"Then Jesus appeared on the scene and brought them new hope. Death is not the end for those who believe in the Lord's salvation, Jesus the Messiah.

"Some people's hope comes to an end at the open grave. But for those who put their trust in Jesus, a beautiful journey begins, when the spirit leaves the body. Jesus the great Jewish Rabbi said that He was the resurrection and the life. No man before or after Him, has ever uttered these words. Rabbi Paul said, 'For to me, to live *is* Christ, and to die *is* gain' (Philippians 1:21).

"The Jewish Apostle named John penned these words uttered by Jesus. 'For God so loved the world that He gave His only begotten Son, that whoever believes in Him should not perish but have everlasting life' (John 3:16)."

The believers were praying in their hearts that Jehovah's Spirit would move on the hearts of those who were present.

"Everyone here has transgressed God's law. We have transgressed His commands and the penalty is eternal punishment and separation from Him. The Lord has spoken. What are you going to do with this message? You can do either of the two. You can accept it or reject it." With great compassion in his heart, he looked across the crowd of people.

Brother Andrew stood up and came to stand next to John who gave him the microphone. He addressed the crowd. "All of you can have the assurance of the forgiveness of sins. If you forsake your sins and accept Jesus, you shall have eternal life. If you reject Him, you shall be eternally separated from Him.

"I am going to give you a personal opportunity to make up your own mind. We know for a certainty where these loved ones have gone. They are in the presence of our heavenly Father, because they died with faith in the Lord Jesus Christ. If you want to accept Him, raise your hand."

Literally thousands of Jews and Moslems responded to the call of salvation with the exception of a few. The sweet presence of Jesus was present. Then, something out of the ordinary happened. The blessed Holy Spirit descended upon the choir, and they started singing in a heavenly language other tongues for about five minutes. In their many tongues, they sang in harmony.

The Chief Rabbi exclaimed, "Amazing! It sounds like a heavenly choir." He again said, "Amazing! In all of my fifty years as a Rabbi, I have never heard anything like it," and for the third time he said, "Amazing!"

John requested them to repeat the prayer of consecration after him, "Heavenly Father I come to You in the name of Jesus Christ. I acknowledge that I am a sinner, and I confess that Jesus is Your Son. I believe that He died on the cross and shed His blood for the remission of my sins. I confess that He was buried and that

He arose again after three days. I renounce the devil and all his works and I now accept Jesus as my Savior. Amen!"

The police orchestra played the Israeli Anthem titled the "*Hatikva.*"

David Cohen, the Chief Rabbi prayed, "Lord, giver of life. We commit the bodies of our brothers and sisters to the earth from which you made them. Together with them, we wait for the day of the resurrection, of all the just dead. Amen!"

The families were now stationed at the open graves of their loved ones. Loudly and clearly the voice of the Rabbi Cohen came over the P.A. system, "Dust to dust," as the caskets were being lowered into the graves. The people quietly left the cemetery to allow the bereaved families to bid their last farewell to their loved ones.

Many people came to John and Andrew afterward and made very positive comments.

One man said, "My spiritual eyes were opened today. It seems like scales have fallen off from my eyes. Some of my relatives and friends want to know where we may contact you. We would appreciate it if you would come and teach us more about Jesus the Messiah. We learned things today we had never known before. We never knew that Jesus was the resurrection and the life."

"You may contact us through Rabbi David Cohen and you are most welcome to attend our services."

John and Andrew had a few words with the prime minister before they left for their car. He said to them, "The enemy thinks that he is going to scare us with his intimidation, but today it backfired in his face. He killed two hundred and seventy of our brothers and sisters and over five thousand or more took their place. Andrew, you once told me that the blood of the martyrs is the seed of the Church of Jesus Christ. We must get together again soon. Call Ruth, my secretary, and make an appointment. I understand that Ruth and her mother want to be baptized, and so do I."

Andrew said, "We shall do it soon," and they parted.

John said to Andrew, "A day of sadness was turned into a day of great joy. There is joy and excitement in the presence of the angels of God, even if it is only one sinner who repents, and today over five-thousand accepted Jesus." And then he shouted a loud, "Hallelujah!"

fourteen

CHAPTER

From all over the world, news of the tribulation was filtering in that followers of Jesus were being killed for their faith. Brother Peter Scott, from England, visited a large secret gathering arranged by Andrew. Peter reported what was happening in countries around the world.

He said, "There is not a country where the followers of Jesus Christ have not paid the ultimate price.

A brother, visiting from North Korea, said, "To force the parents to denounce Jesus, children have been slaughtered in the presence of their parents, which they refused to do. Inquisitions are operational in many countries already. The believers chose death, rather than to betray their faith in Jesus, the Son of God."

An Italian believer shared this testimony. "A priest from the Mystery Babylonian Universal Church asked an Italian believer in Christ, 'What causes you choose death over life?' The believer replied, 'The empty tomb in Jerusalem. Jesus has risen from the dead. And we too shall live again after we die.' Eyewitnesses said, 'He just shook his head and walked away leaving the believer to his fate.'"

Not all the news was negative. There was not one country that had not been touched by the fires of revival. Brother Matthew, who worked amongst the headhunters in Borneo, paid Andrew a surprise visit. "I can only stay a few hours," he said. "I just flew in from South Africa. I want to share with you what the Lord is doing in our ministry amongst the headhunters in Borneo.

"The headhunters would kill any white man who would dare set foot on their territory. Three missionaries had already been martyred there. One evening after wrestling for four hours with the Lord in prayer for the salvation of the headhunters, I fell into a very deep sleep. Jesus appeared unto me in my dream and said, 'Set out tomorrow and visit the tribe of headhunters.'

"I said, 'Lord. You know that they have killed everyone of your servants whom You have sent to them.'

"Jesus replied, 'You do not need to be afraid because I have already begun a work in their lives.'

"The team that works with me was headhunters before accepting Jesus as Savior. To get to the plateau where their village was, we had to walk for seven days through forests infested with swarms of mosquitoes, poisonous snakes, and wild animals. It rained most of the time."

Andrew's mother, Anna, brought them sandwiches and coffee. "Thank you, Mother. I am hungry and thirsty. Be free to join us. You will enjoy this testimony," said Matthew, then he continued, "I would be telling a lie if I said that we were not afraid. It crossed our minds many times to turn back. Then the headhunters spotted us. They made soul-piercing sounds and started running toward us.

"They were naked except for the string around their waist. Their bodies were covered in various colors of clay, and they had a bone through the lobes of their noses. They had feathered head dresses on. They were armed with spears, and we thought that at any moment they were going to spear us. We expected to die the martyr's death. But to our amazement, when they got to where we were they stopped dead in their tracks.

"Instead of killing us, they fell on their knees, lifted up their hands, and started talking in a language that my team did not understand, or so I presumed. One of the team members, who after his conversion was named Thomas, said to me, 'They are praying to the God who created the heaven and the earth. The

Great One who sent Jesus His Son to die on the cross for their sins.'

"I could not believe what I was hearing. Afterward, Peter told me that his mother used to be a member of that tribe. His father had kidnapped her over fifty years ago. She used to speak her language to him, and he grew up learning both the languages of his parents. Thomas interviewed the chief and here follows his story."

"He said, 'We were about to sacrifice a young girl who we had kidnapped from one of the tribes who was our enemy. We tied her hands and feet with rope to the rings in the sacrificial rock. I was just about to cut out her heart when two men descended from the sky. My people fell to the ground in fear. I was *so* petrified that I stood like a wooden idol holding the knife. One of the men walked over to me and took the knife from my hand and then I fell to the ground.'" Peter was astounded at what he was hearing. "'The men were covered in pure white sheets.'

"It was his way of explaining that they had white robes on. 'The one man spoke our language and the other one spoke the girl's language. While cutting her loose, he spoke comforting words to her. The one man who took the knife from me told us a beautiful story about the God who so loved us that He sent His Son, Jesus to die for us. All my people now believe in the God who created the heavens and the earth. We also believe in Jesus, His Son, who died for the sins of the whole world and who came back from the dead.

"'The man who descended from the sky told us that Chief Jesus was going to send His servant, Matthew, and some of His children to us. We have to confess our sins to Jesus and that God's servants will baptize us on the confession of our faith in the Lord Jesus Christ. When we opened our eyes, the men were gone. We immediately fell on our knees and confessed all of our sins. We sent the girl back to her parents with a few of our warriors. Because of what we did, the two tribes have now become family. They also want to hear about the God who made the heavens and the earth and about His Son, Jesus who died for our sins and came back from the dead."

Andrew and his mother Anna had tears in their eyes. Andrew prayed God's blessing upon him and gave him an undisclosed amount of money to him for his family and for the ministry. It was with heavy hearts that they took leave from one another.

• • • •

Andrew and John also had another unexpected visit from Mohammed Sulayman, an Indonesian evangelist. After Andrew's mother Anna had served them lunch, Mohammed shared what God did on one of his visits to a heathen tribe.

"I led an evangelistic team to a heathen tribe who lived in the jungle to share the Good News of Jesus with them. When we arrived there, everyone was in mourning. We made inquiries and heard that their chief had died. I said to one of the tribal elders that the Lord Jesus whom we serve is able to bring your chief back to life." The elder replied, 'If your God does not bring the chief back to life then we are going to sacrifice your whole group to our gods.'

"I asked him to take us to his chief which he did. The chief's hut was crowded with the chief's many wives, children, grand-children. A great number of the tribal elders were also present. The elder allowed only my brother, Ishmael, and I to enter the hut. Before I followed him, I told the believers to pray as they had never prayed before in their lives. I told them what we were up against and if the Lord chose not to bring the chief back to life that they were going to kill us all. We could hear the believers praying above the wailing inside and outside the hut. The elder, who took us into the hut, shoved us toward the corpse. When our eyes became accustomed to the dim light in the hut, we saw two witch doctors.

"They were not happy at all to see us. The stench of the decaying corpse was unbearable. The chief must have been dead for a few days. The witch doctors had used up all their spells but without any success. The anointing of the Holy Spirit descended upon us, and we started praying in the Spirit. We prayed with our eyes, open. As one man, we stretched out our hands toward the corpse and I said, 'In the *name* of Jesus. Satan! We bind you; you who have the power of death. You, spirit of death. Release this man and come out of him right now, in the name Jesus!

"The chief took one big breath and sat up. Those who were present started screaming in horror. They trampled one another to get to the door. The door was *too* small for them to make a hasty exit. They had to literally force their way through the bamboo walls, which were covered with clay.

"In their haste to get out, they trampled on the little children. Only the first and the last wife, of the chief stayed behind. Even the witch doctors and the elders ran away. Because of the great miracle the whole tribe accepted Jesus as their Savior."

Andrew exclaimed, "Wow, what a tremendous testimony to the power of Jesus."

"I agree with you my brother," said John, with an emotion-filled voice.

Wiping away her tears with her apron Andrew's mother said, "I never cease to be amazed at our Savior's love."

fifteen
CHAPTER

Brother John stood before the open grave of Judah, whose name was Judas.

When the false prophet heard that Judas had turned traitor, he ordered an assassin to eliminate him. One evening, while he was on his way to the prayer meeting, an assassin slit his throat. Over one-hundred thousand believers came to show their last respects to a brother who became a martyr because for his faith in Jesus.

John read, "'Great *is* my boldness of speech toward you, great *is* my boasting on your behalf. I am filled with comfort. I am exceedingly joyful in all our tribulation' (2 Corinthians 7:4).' John bowed his head and prayed from the scriptures, "'Now, Lord, look on their threats, and grant to your servants that with all boldness they may speak Your word, by stretching out Your hand to heal, and that signs and wonders may be done through the name of Your holy Servant Jesus' (Acts 4:29–30)."

The believers and the nonbelievers, were moved by his prayer. It was God's word in the prayer that was so powerful.

John went on to say, "Beloved! Since the start of the tribulation, Jehovah God has sent an unprecedented revival in the history of the Church. It is resulting in literally millions upon millions, being swept into His kingdom.

"The tribulation is backfiring in the face of Satan, Antichrist, the false prophet, and the adherents of the Mystery Babylonian Universal

Church. I believe that for every soul being martyred for Jesus, a thousand souls are being saved.

"The blood of the martyrs is truly the seed of the Church of Jesus. We are not going to slack off or back off. We are not going to run away either. Neither Satan, Antichrist, the false prophet, nor their followers are going to stop us from preaching the Gospel of the Kingdom. We shall overcome them—time and time again—by the word of God in our testimony and by the blood of Jesus, the Lamb of God.

"The death of our Brother Judah should be an encouragement to everyone who is born again, to be faithful. The word faithful means to be full of faith, fearless, and loyal to Jesus even in the midst of death. May Jehovah our God keep us close by His side and full of the Holy Spirit in these last days.

"Just listen to what Jesus said in the following verse, 'And do not fear those who kill the body but cannot kill the soul. But rather fear Him who is able to destroy both soul and body in hell' (Matthew 10:28). Jesus told us not be afraid. Why? 'For God has not given us the spirit of fear, but of power and love and of a sound mind' (2 Timothy 1:7).

"If the enemy can succeed in making us afraid, it is then that we become cowards. It will stop us from witnessing to the unsaved, and we will stop winning souls for Jesus and we will neglect praying for the sick and the needy.

"It is then that signs, wonders, and miracles stop happening. The result is that we will not see people saved, healed, and we will not see the dead being raised anymore. That is when we stop experiencing the miraculous. The greatest revival that the Church of Jesus has ever experienced is upon us. We receive reports on a daily basis of the supernatural workings of the blessed Holy Spirit from around the world.

"It is happening in the midst of the greatest tribulation the people of Jehovah God, has ever faced. It is written, 'For the eyes of LORD run to and fro throughout the whole earth, to show Himself strong on behalf of those whose heart is loyal to Him' (2 Chronicles 16:9).

"Our heavenly Father knows and sees what we are faced with,

and He will show Himself strong on our behalf. All He expects of us is to remain loyal to Him. This very moment tens of thousands of our brothers and sisters are paying with their lives.

"Two-thousand years ago, soon after the birth of the Church on Pentecost, a fierce tribulation broke loose. The disciples were scattered and fled to Asia taking the gospel of Jesus with them. Everywhere they went, local churches were established. The tribulation then, and even today, has a positive effect on the Church.

"Jesus' Church is going to be caught up to meet Him in the air when this present tribulation draws to a close. He said, 'These things have I spoken to you, that in Me you may have peace. In the world you will have tribulation; but be of good cheer, I have overcome the world' (John 16:33).

"Jesus said that that He was going to return after the tribulation and the total eclipse of the sun, moon, and stars (Matthew 24:29–31). If we cannot take Him at His word, whom are we going to believe? I want to conclude with 1 John 4:4. John said, 'You are of God, little children, and have overcome them, because He who is in you is greater than he who is in the world.' Amen!

"Those of you who have not experienced Jehovah's Salvation must break with your sinful lifestyles. You must confess and forsake your sins and accept Jesus as your personal Savior."

John gave an altar call and thousands of Jews and Muslims accepted Jesus for the very first time. As the coffin was lowered into the grave, the mass choir of a thousand voices sang a new composition of "We shall overcome." Melodious voices filled the air as the choir sang with great enthusiasm.

Pastor Andrew closed with the benediction.

• • • •

Israel's Aruts Sheva's television newscaster read a statement prepared by Prophet Elijah.

I, Prophet Elijah, your Sovereign Pontiff of the Mystery Babylonian Universal Church, declare that from today onward, the Mystery Babylonian Universal Church will be the only officially recognized church in Israel and in the rest of the world.

Most of the indigenous churches have already joined Mystery Babylonian Universal Church. But we have a problem, however, with a minority in Israel who go by the name of Messianic believers. In the rest of the world, they are called born again believers.

They are refusing to accept the hand of friendship that we have extended to them. Although they are but a small minority, they are causing great harm to the unity of our great Church. Churches or individuals who do not comply shall experience the full force of the law governing the inquisition.

From today onward, it shall be a criminal offence for anyone to attend the services of these dissenters and heretics. Anyone contravening the law shall be arrested and jailed indefinitely, without trial. They shall be released only on these conditions: They must denounce their faith in Esau whom the English speaking world call Jesus. They believe Him to be the Savior of the world and they believe Him to be God. We prefer to call him Esau, and He isn't God." *How can he be God when Antichrist is going to be crowned God?*

A Babylonian priest must re-administer the Babylonian mode of baptism by way of sprinkling in the name of the Supreme Father and the Supreme Son and the Supreme Spirit, to all who have strayed. They must break all communication, either by contact or conversation, with the followers of Esau. The Jordan River and the Sea of Galilee, or any body of water for that matter, is off limits to the so-called Messianic believers, for the purpose of baptizing by immersion. Baptism by way of immersion is dangerous and irresponsible. Sprinkling with water is by far a safer mode of baptism. I also want to bring it to your attention that the members of our great church are no longer to be called Christians but Babylonians. The name Christian is associated with the man called Christ, whom his Jewish followers believe to be the true Messiah.

I have already brought it to your attention that he was a false Christ and an imposter. The true Messiah is with us in the flesh this very moment in Jerusalem. He is the personification of the Babylonian Messiah. Do not allow the Christian sects, who call themselves Messianic believers, to fool you.

Be at the Western wall tomorrow morning at ten o'clock and you shall see the power of the true Messiah. Also, take note that the entire Babylonian world is daily updated with the changes taking place at the *Palace of Religion,* here in Jerusalem. Ignorance is no excuse for breaking the laws of our great Church.

. . . .

The following morning, thousands of people made their way to the square in front of the Wailing Wall, now called the Western wall. The square was crowded with followers of Israel's Messiah. Many of them had never seen him in the flesh, before.

The followers of Jesus took recognizance of the law prohibiting them from gathering together for any religious purpose. They refused to become part of the false church. Because of its devilish nature, they decided to ignore the law.

. . . .

Only Andrew, the leader of the local churches in Jerusalem, and John, the leader of the local churches in Bethlehem, were present at the Western Wall. They stood about thirty yards away from the wall. Together with the rest of the people, they were standing behind an iron barrier.

The barrier was put into place for the protection of Prophet Elijah, to prevent him from being trampled by Messiah's followers. Thousands had gathered just to get a glimpse of their Messiah, whom they believed to be the true anointed one. A small marquee was pitched against the Western Wall. The front of the marquee was covered with a crimson curtain.

The thing that puzzled John and Andrew the most was the crucifix that was planted about eight yards away from the marquee. They were soon to discover the reason for it.

Prophet Elijah, commanded one of the temple guards to pull the curtain cord, and as it slid open, it revealed a person inside the marquee. When the people saw Messiah sitting on the throne they believed to have belonged to King David, they exploded with excitement and applauded with great enthusiasm. Some fainted, and others again cried unashamedly.

Messiah stood up, stepped onto the crimson carpet, and joined Prophet Elijah behind the lectern. The prophet said, "Welcome, Your Holiness, King of kings, and Lord of lords." It was the first time that Elijah ascribed these titles to Messiah. Again, a thunderous applause broke loose which went on for about ten minutes.

Prophet Elijah continued, "In yesterday's newspapers and on national television, I promised you that today Messiah shall prove once and for all that he is indeed the Messiah of Israel. Many of you may have wondered why the crucifix, which is an abomination to the *sensitivities* of some people in Israel, is planted here so near to the temple. You shall see the reason for it in a few minutes." Elijah lifted his hands to heaven and started with his incantations.

Andrew looked to John and said, "The false prophet is calling on demon forces to come to Messiah's aid." He opened his Bible and read two verses to John, "Jesus said, 'For false Christs and false prophets will rise and shall show great signs and wonders to deceive, if possible, even the elect. See, I have told you beforehand' (Matthew 24:24–25).

"He performs great signs, so that he even makes fire come down from heaven on the earth in the sight of men. And he deceives those who dwell on the earth by those signs which he was granted to do in the sight of the beast' (Revelation 13:13–14)."

. . . .

Antichrist and Prophet Elijah nodded in agreement to one another. The countenance of Prophet Elijah changed as he laid his right hand on Messiah's right shoulder. What seemed to be a bolt of lightning went through Antichrist's body. He was levitating about two yards above the ground.

Messiah then pointed his finger at the crucifix and fire fell from the sky. The crucifix exploded and disintegrated into billions of dust particles, which rained on the spectators. In spite of Messiah's demonstration of power, John and Andrew remained unfazed in their faith in Jesus.

Some people went hysterical, others fainted, and others again went into deep shock and had to be hospitalized! Prophet Elijah took up the chant, "Long live Messiah! Long live Messiah! The people took his cue and also took up the chant, and it continued for nearly half an hour.

Messiah's bodyguards escorted him away, while the people were caught up in the shock and excitement of the moment. With a broad smile on his face, Prophet Elijah, said, "I hope that this settles it once and for all that Messiah is indeed the promised 'One' of Israel and not Esau. You saw the demonstration of his power."

The people responded with, "He is our Messiah! He is our Messiah! Away with Esau! Away with Esau!"

John and Andrew were still standing at the very same place behind the barrier. The prophet spoke again and said, "You must think it very sacrilegious that Messiah called down fire from heaven to destroy the crucifix. There is a great reason for it, which I will explain to you right now. I have already told you that Esau, who was born two-thousand years ago, was a false Messiah.

"He and His followers planned everything so that it would seem to the ignorant people that he fulfilled Bible prophesy. Starting from today all crucifixes and crosses in Israel and in the whole world are to be destroyed! The doctrine of the crucifixion rests on a false premise."

"Esau never died on the cross. He was only in a coma and was resuscitated in the tomb by his disciples. They afterward smuggled him out of Palestine by boat to India where He married and had children and lived a long and healthy life and died a normal death."

Because the people believed his lies, they shouted, "Amen! Amen!"

Andrew looked at John in amazement at the utter nonsense the prophet was talking. And again, he quoted a portion of Scripture.

From that time Jesus began to show His disciples that He must go to Jerusalem, and suffer many things from the elders and chief priests and scribes, and be killed, and be raised the third day.

Matthew 16:21

"The false prophet wants to rob the people of the knowledge of Jesus' atoning death. If He did not die on the cross, it eliminates the need for a resurrection. If there was no resurrection then in the end analysis there remains no salvation for the human race.

"He is robbing the people of their only hope of salvation and of ever having their sins forgiven. Outside Jesus Christ's atoning death on the cross and his subsequent resurrection, there is no salvation," came John's affirmation.

"I wholeheartedly agree with you," Andrew said to John. "The New Reformers around the world and the Moslems have found an ally in the false prophet and Antichrist. They do not believe that Jesus is Jehovah God's Son, and that He died on the cross.

"Let's shake the dust off our feet!"

They both stomped their shoes on the pavement, and Andrew said, "Let's go home and get something good to eat; I am starving. I believe Mother has prepared, as always, a delicious meal for us."

They pressed their way through the crowd, walked to John's car, and drove home. The evening news carried the story.

"Fire from heaven confirmed that Messiah, and not Esau, is the real Messiah of Israel."

The cameraman zoomed in and showed Messiah calling fire from heaven and how the crucifix exploded into billions of dust particles. It was also front-page news in Israel and all over the world.

• • • •

The newscaster of Central News Makers said, "The New Testament must be rewritten. All reference to Jesus being the Messiah, Son of God, and the Savior of the world and His phony miracles must be excised from the Bible. What we need is a New Age Bible, which teaches about a multifaceted and a multi-face God. We need a God who can be called by various names such as, Jehovah, Buddha, and Allah. We are all his children and he loves every one of us, no matter how we live. Therefore, it is unthinkable that he has created a place called hell.

"I prefer the teaching of the Mystery Babylonian Universal Church concerning purgatory. It at least gives us a second chance to get to heaven after we have messed up here.

sixteen

CHAPTER

Later that week, Andrew went to visit John, in Bethlehem. While they were enjoying a glass of cold pomegranate juice, John said, "Have you been aware that Antichrist has not been seen of late? He has not appeared in public here in Israel or on television for sometime now."

While they were conversing, the phone rang. John picked the receiver. The person on the other end of the line said, "Jose from Timor here."

John placed his hand over the mouth of the phone and whispered to Andrew, "Brother Jose from Timor is on the line. Take the phone in the kitchen."

Andrew hurried to the kitchen, picked up the receiver, and made himself known to Jose, as they were acquainted with one another.

Jose, said, "Revelation 6:2 is being fulfilled here in Timor. Antichrist has been seen in Timor, riding a white horse and wearing a crown. His only weapon was a bow. The moment he appeared, an evil spirit exploded over this region. He has inspired Muslims rebels to kill people who voted in favor of an independent East Timor.

They are burning down buildings in the residential and business areas and are killing men, women, and children. Tens of thousands have been uprooted from their homes and have fled into the jungle.

They are living as our ancestors did centuries ago. They are *not* going to survive the harsh winter months. Only the coming of Jesus will be

The Appearance

161

able to bring an end to their suffering. Stand firm in your faith, my brothers. Please convey my greetings to your mothers and the saints." After they have said their good-byes, Brother Jose rang off.

• • • •

In Jerusalem, a group of religious fanatics attacked a group of the followers of Jesus who were witnessing on the streets and handing out tracts. They were all bundled into two vans without windows and driven to a secluded spot. Someone reported the kidnappings just minutes after it happened. By then the kidnappers were far away, zigzagging through the residential areas and backtracking to throw the police or anyone who was following them off their tracks.

In a secluded spot, they violated the young women, while the brothers were forced to look on. In the midst of their terrible ordeal, they were praying for their enemies.

One of the kidnappers took his revolver and hit one woman over the head, knocking her unconscious. One of the young men prayed, "Jesus, into your hands we commit our spirit."

The kidnapper pulled off his mask, revealing a terrible scar across the right side of his face. He shouted at the young man, "Shut up! If you mention that name again, you will regret it for the rest of your life."

The young man thought in his heart, *They are going to kill me anyway. I'd rather die, calling on the name of Jesus because I am going to be with Him for the rest of my life, anyway." He shouted as loud as possible, "Jesus! Here I come.* The young man was shot in the head, and he died instantly and was ushered into the presence of Jesus.

The other young men were struggling to free themselves in the hope of helping the young women. One of the kidnappers shouted, "Shoot them!" Without hesitation, six shots rang out, and seven young men in the prime of their lives were dead. The girls were screaming and kicking their attackers. One attacker said, "Slit their throats and let's get away from here." At that same moment, they heard police sirens and their kidnappers fled the scene. In their now blood-splattered clothes, they sped off in different directions.

When the police officers eventually arrived on the scene, they made the gruesome discovery of the murder of the seven young men. Their torn Bibles were lying scattered amongst the deceased. They took the young woman to the hospital for treatment and counseling. The news was released nationally and internationally. The news sent shock waves through the communities of the Messianic believers and their sympathizers from amongst the Orthodox Jews.

The born again believers from all over the world were praying for their Israeli brothers and sisters, and for the Nation of Israel. It was heartbreaking for the families who had just recently come to faith in Jesus to stand in front of an open grave of one of their loved ones. However, it made them even more determined not to forsake Jesus their, Savior.

In great numbers, the believers from all over Israel attended the mass funeral. They were unafraid of the Prophet Elijah's threats. Andrew preached about the awfulness of sin and that Jesus paid the penalty for mankind's sin and that only He was able to take away God's, eternal judgment.

Andrew asked those who wanted to accept Jesus to confess their sins to the Lord, right where they were standing. Everywhere people were unashamedly confessing their sins to Jehovah God, and experienced His favor and forgiveness. Andrew waited for ten minutes to pass before he extended an invitation for salvation, and again hundreds responded to the call of Jesus upon their lives.

A time of great sadness turned into a day of rejoicing before God's throne in heaven for the followers of Jesus. The believers encouraged one another to stand firm even in the face of opposition, torture, and even death.

• • • •

A great number of Jesus' followers dIsappeared without a trace. The zealots were responsible for the kidnappings. The pastors of the house churches and their families were left in the dark as to their whereabouts. The believers were called to a time of fasting and prayer when Hannah received a word of knowledge as to their whereabouts.

She approached Pastor John and told him, "The Holy Spirit just revealed to me where our brothers and sisters are being kept in seclusion. They are held prisoners in a cave in Jericho. The zealots are responsible for their d*Isa*ppearance. They are fed thin soup once a day, and some of them are very emaciated and sick."

John made the revelation known to the fellowship. "Beloved we cannot sit still and do nothing about our brothers and sisters. In our own strength, we are not able to win the battle against these reckless men, who do not even blink an eye when they kill men, women, and children. We do not war as they do, with knives, hand grenades, and machine guns.

"The Apostle Paul declared, 'For though we walk in the flesh, we do not war according to the flesh. For the weapons of our warfare *are* not carnal but mighty in God for pulling down strongholds, casting down arguments and every high thing that exalts itself against the knowledge of God, bringing every thought into captivity to the obedience of Christ, and being ready to punish all disobedience when your obedience is fulfilled' (2 Corinthians 10:3–6)."

He drank some juice and paused for a few moments before he continued, "Beloved, our obedience has been fulfilled. We have fasted and prayed for weeks now, seeking God for the whereabouts of our brethren. Our God has deemed it fit to reveal that information to Hannah. He will also protect us by sending His angels to help us according to His word.

"Our brothers and sisters need us. Those who are responsible for preparing meals, please prepare enough soup and sandwiches. The medical doctors and nurses amongst us must take whatever is needed in case of any emergency. The strong and able-bodied men will have to help carry the sick and wounded.

"'Operation Angel' will be under way tomorrow morning at four thirty, God willing. We shall acquire twelve buses. Each bus has a seating capacity of sixty passengers. We are going to take two busloads of believers with us. That includes the doctors and nurses. We are to take no weapons with us. Jehovah is going to fight on our behalf."

They then bowed their heads, and together they called on the name of Jehovah to send His angels ahead of them. Some of the believers did not sleep that night, as they got everything prepared. Early the next morning, the buses were loaded with containers of hot soup and fresh homemade bread sandwiches.

The doctors had everything they needed as they packed boxes containing medicines, salves, and bandages. Under the cover of darkness, the convoy of buses left for Jericho. With the description of the whereabouts, which the Holy Spirit had revealed to Hannah, the place was easy to find.

Although it was a hilly and rugged terrain, they were able to drive close to the entrance of the cave. They were not afraid for one moment that they would be greeted by sniper fire. It was all in the hands of their Heavenly Father. They alighted from the buses and stood in rows of seven.

The sisters were right in front with their tambourines, and the doctors and the nurses followed. They were followed by those who carried the stretchers; then the rest of the group followed. John and Andrew, who were walking in front, gave the signal, and they started marching and singing an old favorite chorus.

"'Not by might, not by power, but by My Spirit says the Lord of Hosts. Not by might, nor by power, but by My Spirit says, the Lord.' (Zechariah 4:6)."

Their singing echoed through the hills, causing rockslides. The zealots, who were in the cave, thought that an earthquake had struck the area. They left the prisoners unattended and ran to the exit of the cave toward the narrow steel doors. The doors were locked, and they had to wait for their leader to unlock the door.

Simon, their leader, pushed his way through about eighty men to get to the door to unlock it. Everyone was trying to get out first and had no regard for rank. With a scowl on his face, Simon glared at them.

After the believers had sung the song for about seven times, they broke out in spontaneous praise. The glorious anointing and power of the Lord descended upon them and that same moment the steel doors opened. Simon frowned at the men and women who were praising Jesus, with their hands lifted toward the sky.

He shouted, "What the … is this?!" His men started laughing at what seemed so stupid to them. He barked at his men, "Shoot these crazies!"

Then consternation broke loose amongst them. Exactly at that very moment, the angels of Jehovah God descended upon the zealots who were now standing in the open area in front of the cave. They were unable to see the angels. The believers who were praising Jesus, could see them, all around them. The angels smote the zealots, causing welts to break out all over their bodies. Their clothes were bloody and torn. They, who showed no mercy to the followers of Jesus Christ, whom they held captive, were now crying out for mercy.

They were all bundled together by the unseen force and were unable to make an escape. The doctors and the nurses immediately entered the cave and the others followed them. There they discovered over four-hundred and twenty believers. All of the men and a few of the women were chained to the walls.

They were emaciated and filthy. Many of them were covered with bruises, and others had running sores. The children started crying when they saw what seemed to them to be strangers.

One of the sisters found a few sets of keys, and soon two of them started unshackling the captives. When the captives realized who their deliverers were, they started praising and thanking their heavenly Father. Those who came to rescue them joined them in thanking Father God. Water was brought, and they washed their hands and gave thanks for the food they were about to eat.

Nurse Esther encouraged the captives, "Make sure that you and your children get something to eat. Many of you are still very weak. You don't want to get sick, do you? There is enough for everyone." After they had eaten, the doctors examined the captives. They then disinfected and bandaged their wounds. Two hours later, the very sick were carried out on stretchers while the others who could walk were assisted to the buses.

The little children were carried by their fathers or mothers, who came on the buses. They took them to the homes of the doctors for further examination. A few doctors stayed behind to tend to the wounds and gashes the zealots received at the hands of the angels.

They were still at the same place where the angels had driven them. Some were standing, some were sitting, and others again were just lying on the ground. It seemed that the angels had punished them according to what they deserved. Although the angels were no longer with them, not one of the zealots tried to run away.

John asked them, "Why did you kidnap the followers of Jesus? *Who* put you up to it? John spoke to them with compassion in his voice.

One of the zealots said, "My body is burning all over. It feels as if someone had rubbed sulfur into my wounds."

Everywhere hardened criminals were groaning. John's heart went out to them.

Simon, the leader of the zealots, said, "Our Sovereign Pontiff told us to kidnap the followers of Esau."

John said, "Friend! His name is not Esau. His name is Jesus."

"Please forgive me," the zealot quickly apologized, "I should have said Jesus." John turned to the believers who had remained behind and requested. "Please fetch some water that we may clean and dress the zealots' wounds. Jesus taught us to bless our enemies." The zealots could not believe what they had just heard.

Hannah came forward and informed John, "There's lots of soup and sandwiches left over. May we give the food to the zealots?"

"You certainly may," replied John. "Proverbs 25:21–22 encourages us feed the hungry and to give water to the thirty even if they are our enemies. Jesus died for us, as well as for the sins of these men. These men need Jesus."

Some of the nurses started disinfecting the zealots' wounds, and the doctors helped dress the wounds. Those who were already helped were seen eating the most delicious meal they had ever eaten in months.

After the zealots had finished eating, John stood in front of them and said, "Do you know that it is a capital crime to kidnap a person? We forgive you as God in Christ has forgiven us. We shall not hand you over to the authorities—but to a loving and compassionate Father God.

"Some of you have done despicable things. You have broken God's laws. Antichrist, your false Messiah, and your false prophet are responsible for what happened to our brothers and sisters. You were just pieces on their chessboard. They are in league with Satan, and you were manipulated by them. Jesus Christ died on the cross of Calvary for our sins. We should have been crucified, but Jehovah God, in His great mercy laid our sins on Jesus.

"He rose again after three days, and He is alive and is here right now. If you are willing to break with your sinful lifestyles, confess your sins to the Lord, for He is merciful. It is a personal choice whether you want to accept Jesus as your personal Savior. I cannot force you to accept Him. Please excuse me now; we have to get organized for our journey back to Jerusalem."

After fifteen minutes, Simon approached John and said, "I, and some of my men, have come to a decision to accept Jesus as our Savior."

John shouted a loud, hallelujah, causing the believers also to give a shout of victory. The zealots started confessing their transgressions and crying out for forgiveness and they willingly accepted Jesus as their savior.

Some of the zealots were crying unashamedly. Some fell on their knees, and were praying from their hearts, seeking God's forgiveness for their hideous crimes. It was a very happy group of people who drove home that afternoon. Heaven came down, and the joy of Jehovah filled the hearts of the zealots.

One of the brothers said, "Truly Jehovah is no respecter of persons."

While they were singing, the Holy Spirit fell on them in the buses, and many of the zealots were filled with the Holy Spirit. After some time, John stopped the buses near Jerusalem, and they all disembarked and gave thanks to God for having undertaken in delivering their brethren and also for having saved the zealots.

Dudley Fairbairn

John addressed the zealots saying, "After the morning Sabbath Bible study, we are going to the Jordan River for a baptismal service. All of you are going to be buried with Christ Jesus in baptism. Then at the Sunday (*resurrection*) morning service you are going to receive your first communion and you are also going to receive your very own Hebrew Bible containing both the Old and New Testaments."

seventeen
CHAPTER

It has been reported that millions of people worldwide had seen the red horse as recorded in Revelation 6:4, flying through the sky. The psychiatrists said that the people were deluded and were suffering from mass hysteria, resulting in a severe psychosis. Many of the people were being treated for severe depression. Others again had to be institutionalized because they had totally lost control of their faculties.

On the other hand, the followers of Jesus were thrilled as they witnessed Bible prophesies being fulfilled before their very eyes. They were encouraged by the appearance of the red horse. They continued to disobey the authorities in complying with their demands that they become part of the Mystery Babylonian Universal Church.

The fellowships made use of the warm summer evenings to have open-air services in spite of the possibility that they might be attacked by radical elements in society. The soldiers and the zealots were afraid to attack the believers, as the fear of Jehovah had fallen upon them.

They heard and saw on television what God's prophets had done to the zealots and what had happened to some of the soldiers. They knew that they were only able to hurt or kill the followers of Jesus—if He even allowed it—because their lives were in His hands.

The believers from Jerusalem and Bethlehem were out in full force early that evening. They were having a combined open-air meeting at the

The Appearance   171 square in Bethlehem. It was during that time that the fiery red horse flew across the clear blue sky.

It was very huge, and there was no possibility that the red horse could have been mistaken for a cloud, as there were no clouds in the sky. The meteorologists could vouch for that. And it was no weather balloon either! The forecast for the evening was clear skies over the whole of Israel and the neighboring countries.

John was preaching at the time of the appearance of the red horse. He said, "The rider of the red horse is going to take, peace from the earth. Jesus, forewarned us. He said in Matthew 24:6–7, that there will be wars and rumors of wars. He encouraged us not to be troubled because all these things must come to pass. Nations and kingdoms shall be embroiled in wars. And there will be famines, pestilences, and earthquakes in various places.

"Jehovah God is calling the world to repentance. Things are not going to get better on earth. But for the children of the Lord, a very bright future is coming. The news on television and in the newspapers is very depressing and disturbing to those who do not have faith in Jesus."

The anointing was resting on both Andrew and John. They both had their own microphone, and Andrew took over from John as they had done many times before.

"The only good news that we have for you is that Jesus is coming to *rapture* those who have accepted Him as their personal Savior. He shall return when the three and a half years of tribulation we are now in come to an end. A worldwide eclipse of the sun will herald the end of the tribulation. It shall be the sign to all born again believers that the coming of Jesus to *rapture* His children is at hand.

"Jesus said in Luke 21:25–26, that there will be signs in the sun, moon, and stars. Nations shall be in distress, perplexed, and be in turmoil. Mankind will lose heart at the calamities they will be experiencing. It is going to be of such severity that the powers of the heavens will be shaken.

John took over again and connected Luke 21:25 with Matthew 24:29.

Immediately after the tribulation of those days the sun will be darkened, and the moon will not give its light; the stars will fall from heaven, and the powers of the heavens will be shaken.

"Jesus encouraged us in Luke 21:28, to look up and to lift up our heads during the time of total darkness. Some people may argue and say that it is total stupidity to look up when you are not even able to see your hand in front of your face. We do not care about man's opinion. We care about Jesus' opinion. He said, 'Now when these things begin to happen, look up and lift up your heads, because your redemption draws near' (Luke 21:28)." *I will look up, even if I have to look up alone. But, I am assured that multiplied millions will look up together with me to see our blessed Savior.*

To drive home the point for those who gathered, Andrew asked John, "Why must we look up and lift up our heads?"

"The answer is in Luke 21:27. 'Then they will see the Son of man coming in a cloud with power and great glory,'" replied John.

The people who gathered around John and Andrew had eager and inquiring expressions on their faces. They wanted to hear more on the subject about the end times.

Andrew asked John another question. "Is there any physical deliverance from the tribulation for Jehovah's children without Jesus' personal intervention?"

Again, John supplied the answer. "No! There is no personal deliverance or escape after three and a half years of tribulation without Jesus' intervention. He alone has the power to *rapture* us to be with Him in heaven.

"Jesus is going to rescue us before the start of the three and a half years of 'The Great and Awesome Day Of The Lord.' The *rapture* happens immediately after the three and a half years of tribulation comes to an end! The *rapture* of the redeemed will take place at that juncture in time."

Andrew then asked another question, "Does the Bible tell us when Jesus Christ is going to deliver us?"

John replied, "In Matthew 24:29, Jesus gave us the signs leading up to His coming. He placed His coming after the tribulation and after the total eclipse of the sun. Jesus said, 'Immediately after the tribulation [which lasts for three and a half years] of those days the sun will be darkened, and the moon will not give its light; the stars will fall from heaven, and the powers of the heavens will be shaken' (Matthew 24:29).

"It is during this time of total darkness that Jesus is going to appear in the sky to dispel the great darkness."

"Do we have any assurance from God's word, that it is so?"

"Yes there is. Jesus gave us a very clear answer in Matthew 24:30. He said, 'Then the sign of the Son of Man will appear in heaven, and then all the tribes of the earth will mourn, and they will see the Son of man coming on the clouds of heaven with power and great glory' (Matthew 24:30).

"Jesus' glory and power is the sign of His majestic power and authority. His glory shall fill the very heavens and banish the great darkness that is going to envelope the whole earth."

Andrew posed another question. "What will happen next?"

Again, John supplied the answer, "And He will send His angels with a great sound of a trumpet, and they will gather together His elect from the four winds, from one end of heaven to the other' (Matthew 24:31).

"Paul described it in this unique way, 'For the Lord Himself will descend from heaven with a shout, with the voice of an archangel, and with the trumpet of God. And the dead in Christ will rise first. Then we who are alive *and* remain [Greek: meaning, to survive] shall be caught up together with them in the clouds, to meet the Lord in the air. And thus we shall always be with the Lord' (1 Thessalonians 4:16–17)."

Andrew concluded the service with a few final comments. "Two more horsemen will still make their appearance. The results are going to be even more catastrophic, than the first two. Seven angels are still to sound their individual trumpets before Jesus comes to *rapture* us from planet earth. Jesus, is the world's only hope and security."

Andrew turned the service over to John, who in turn gave an invitation to the people who were ready to commit their lives to

Jesus. With the exception of a few, nearly the whole crowd committed their lives to Jesus.

. . . .

The pastors who attended a meeting with John passed on this message to their congregations.

John said, "Since the appearance of the black horse, the rain has stayed away, and the little rain that has fallen was too late to save the crops. There is going to be a great scarcity of food. Do not be anxious my brothers and sisters. Jehovah God is going to take care of us. Jesus said, 'But seek first the kingdom of God and His righteousness, and all these things shall be added to you' (Matthew 6:33). Share the little that you have with your fellow man whether they know Jesus or not. Jehovah shall replenish your food supplies. A little in the hands of God is much.

"Jesus said in Luke 6:38, when we give to others it will be given back to us. We will get more back that what we have given away. We must make sure that our measuring cup is not too small because, you will get the same amount back. Tell the believers to have a sharing heart as we see the Day approaching." One of the brothers dismissed the service in prayer.

. . . .

The United Nations appealed to the rich nations of the world for food donations, but it had fallen on deaf ears. In Africa, Asia, and the former Russian Republics, people were dying by the millions. Things were so bad that fathers would shoot their families and then turn the gun on themselves, just to save their families from starvation—or worse.

Terrible news was surfacing of fathers who had to catch rodents in order for their wives to prepare meals for their starving children. The once fertile farmlands had turned into deserts within a short space of a few months. Lakes, rivers, and dams had all but dried up. Those who were caught stealing food or water were shot on sight.

In Europe, marauding gangs were seen on television breaking

into the homes of politicians and the rich and the famous who were guilty of hoarding food.

The police were afraid to arrest the heavily armed gangs. The military had to be called in to protect presidents, prime ministers, royalty, and the rich and famous, but at a price. People were eating grass, roots, mice, rats, snakes, dogs, and cats, just to stay alive.

• • • •

As if the previous catastrophes were not enough, the time had come for the pale horse to appear. Pastor Andrew had prepared the believers for the coming of the pale horse. He began his e-mail with a passage from the book of Revelation.

> When He opened the fourth seal, I heard the voice of the fourth living creature saying, "Come and see." So I looked, and behold, a pale horse. And the name of him who sat on it was Death, and Hades followed with him. And power was given to them over a fourth of the earth, to kill with sword, with hunger, with death, and by the beasts of the earth. Revelation 6:7–8

> Beloved do not be afraid because of the pale horse. David the Psalmist said, "I have been young, and now I am old; Yet I have not seen the righteous forsaken, Nor his descendants begging bread" (Psalm 37:25).

> Our heavenly Father is responsible for us. Share what little you may have with your fellow brothers and sisters and with the stranger. Just as God multiplied the widow's flour and oil, so God will also perform miracles for us. You will experience how Jesus is going to multiply your food.

Soon after Andrew had sent the e-mail, testimonies came in how the Lord had replenished the food supply of the believers.

Hannah testified that night at the service, "We were down to our last few slices of bread when our neighbor knocked on our door. I asked her if there was anything I could do for her.

"She replied, 'My children have not eaten for three days, and they are very weak. Please give us something to feed them.'

"I was amazed that she would even come to us for food as she and her husband would not talk to us since we accepted Jesus as our Savior. I told her to wait, and I walked back into the kitchen. I was hungry myself, as I have not eaten since the night before. In the kitchen, I made the discovery—we only had four slices of bread left.

"There was only one slice of bread for each one of us. My dad had lost his job because he had accepted Jesus as his Savior. Both my dad and my brother were out looking for work. Mother went to visit my grandma who had taken ill.

"I asked myself, *If I give our neighbor the bread, what am I going to tell my parents when they ask me to prepare the bread for the evening meal?* I took the four slices of bread, smeared the last of the leftover lard on it, wrapped it in paper, and gave it to her.

"With tears in her eyes, looking down at her shoes, she said, 'May God, bless you.'

"I replied, 'Jesus loves you very much and so do we. If you need more bread, do not hesitate to come to us.' I could not believe what I had just said to her. I wondered *What am I going to tell her should she return again the following day for more bread? I would have to admit to her that I gave the last four slices of bread.*

"Then I remembered Brother John's admonition to us. I walked back to the kitchen. I could vouch that I heard the sound of angel's wings. I could not believe my eyes when I looked at the table. *I knew it was not my imagination playing tricks on me.*

"Staring me in the face were two loaves of freshly baked bread, butter, cheese, dates, and grape juice. When I touched the bread, it was still warm to the touch. My mouth was watering." The believers started laughing. "I thought, *My mom and dad won't mind if I just eat one slice of bread with butter and cheese.* I started praising God for His provision and started dancing around the table. *Yes, it worked. I had better get out of this house. The temptation was just too great.* I took half of the blessings we had received and took it to our neighbor.

"I told her and her husband what had happened and she replied, 'I have no problem believing you. We had asked all our neighbors for food, and they all said, 'We are sorry; we cannot help you, as we have only enough food for ourselves and our families.' I told my husband that you gave me your last few slices of bread.'

"I asked, 'How did you know that it was the last four slices of bread?' I had enquiring look on my face when I asked her the question.

"She replied, 'I tiptoed behind you, and I only saw four slices of bread on the plate. While you were wrapping the bread, I quickly hurried back to the front door.'

"I said to them, 'Jesus multiplied the two fish and five loaves of bread, and He fed five-thousand people. He is the same as He was two thousand years ago. He is the Bread of Life who died on the cross for our sins and rose again after three days and three nights.

"While I was talking to them, I asked for a jug and asked her to fill it with water. I then asked her for five glasses; she put them on the table and prayed, 'Lord! You turned water into wine. Please turn this water into milk for this family.' I poured the contents of the jug into the glasses, and to their amazement, I filled the glasses with fresh milk.

"Her husband said, 'Please pray for my wife, my children, and I. We want to accept Jesus as our Messiah and Savior.'

"I told them not to accept Jesus, just because of the food, I gave them, but because of who Jesus is, the Son of Jehovah God, the Savior of the world. The husband replied, 'We want to accept Him for *who* He is.'"

The believers were ever so quiet as they listened to Hannah's testimony. "I prayed the sinner's prayer with them, and they made peace with Jehovah God through Jesus His Son. They are present here in this service with us."

Hannah pointed them out to the fellowship and asked them to stand to their feet. The believers stood up and the believers started praising the Lord for His miracle of salvation and provision.

Hannah went on to say afterward, "Since I shared our last four slices of bread with them, the angels have been delivering four loaves of bread to us every day, with the extras. They deliver two loaves of bread for us and two for this dear family."

At the conclusion of the service, the whole fellowship welcomed the family into Jehovah God's family.

eighteen
CHAPTER

From the fellowship in Cana of Galilee Peter shared this testimony at his local church.

"At our wedding the caterers did not prepare enough food for all the people who showed up. Because of the famine, we have been experiencing in Israel, many uninvited guests showed up at our reception with the hope of getting something to eat.

"We got the shock of our lives when we entered the hall and saw about four-hundred people instead of the fifty close relatives and friends we had invited."

Someone commented, "Wow! What a predicament."

"I looked at my mother who is a firm believer in the miracle-working power of Jesus. She said, 'Peter! Today, you are going to prove to yourself whether you are a man or a boy. Call Pastor Andrew, your father, and Miriam. We are going to the kitchen, and we are going to ask our Savior to cook us up a delicious dinner for the extra 350 guests.'"

Peter continued, "I looked in amazement at her, and I could see that she was very serious. I knew that it was not the time to argue with her. I did as she ordered me, and we went to the kitchen. Mother did something amazing. She took two extra large saucepans the caterers use for large wedding receptions and placed it on the stove.

"She took a huge ladle and transferred some of the rice into the empty saucepan and some of the meat stew, in the other saucepan. "Then she said, 'Please tell the men to set up more tables and come back right away. We are going to feed all these hungry people.'

"I immediately returned to find my parents, my beautiful wife, Miriam, and pastor, Andrew, standing around the stove, and I joined them.

"Mother prayed, 'Father, let Your manifold blessings fall upon these near empty saucepans. Please multiply the food in the name of Jesus. Amen!'

"We only opened the saucepans when it was time to serve the guests who were now seated at the extra tables.

"Mother said to the kitchen staff, 'Dish a blessed plate of food for each person. There is more than enough for everyone.'" Peter took a moment to let what he was about to say sink in to those around him. He then continued and said, "When mother prayed the Lord's blessing on the contents of the saucepans, the staff was not present. I heard Amina, the Muslim caterer, saying to Fadilah, her Muslim friend, 'We are in a very great predicament. We did not cook enough food for all these people.' Peter said, "I overheard them and thought, *You are soon going to discover the power of our God and the eternal love of Jesus, His Son.* "I asked Pastor Andrew to pray the Lord's blessing on the festivities.

"He prayed, 'Jehovah, God of all creation. We know that there is no end to Your power and greatness. You created the universe out of nothing tangible. You only used Your creative word. Nothing is too hard for You. Thank You for all our guests. Thank You for having provided a delicious meal for all of us. We believe that this is only the beginning of many creative miracles that we are going to experience in Jesus' name. Amen!'

"Andrew had no sooner said, 'Amen,' when a commotion broke out in the kitchen. Amina and Fadilah were shouting with pure joy, and excitement.

"A guest who was sitting next to Andrew said, 'A mouse must have scared them.'

"Andrew replied, 'A mere mouse is not able to bring out so much joy and excitement.' "The ladies ran to the head table, and Amina said, 'I would not have believed it if I did not see it with my very own eyes. We only cooked food for about fifty-five people, and there is enough food for the whole Israeli army!' She exaggerated to make her point. 'The two saucepans are full to the brim with the beef-stew, and the other two saucepans with rice, likewise. Where did the extra food come from? It looks exactly like the food we had made.'

"I told her, 'I will tell you later.' "The servers entered carrying large plates, dished with delicious, aromatic food. The aroma set the taste buds of those present in motion, especially those who had not eaten a decent plate of food for a very long time. After everyone was served, the men and women servers were called to take their place at the tables.

"When Amina put the fork of food in her mouth, she exclaimed, '*Mmmmm! Mmmmm!* I did not cook this food. It tastes just heavenly! I have never tasted such deliciously marinated meat, and sauce in my whole life. I sure did not add the spices, which gives it such a uniquely delicious flavor.'

"Andrew and the rest who had prayed for the miracle knew exactly where the flavor had come from. After the main meal, while refreshments were being served, Andrew brought a short word. Again, they were about to witness a miracle. The angels must have worked overtime in heaven's kitchen because the cakes the servers were serving were not made at any Jewish or Muslim delicatessen we knew of.

"Andrew said, 'I want to tell you in real honesty that we did not have enough food for all the guests. While we were in the kitchen, we prayed that Jehovah-Jireh would multiply the food in Jesus' name. We have eaten miracle food. We know that many of you and your families have been experiencing starvation.

"'We who are born again of Jehovah's Holy Spirit have discovered that we serve Jehovah-Yireh. He, who is more than enough, will provide for His children. We do not need to steal to survive. I am not afraid to confess that we are followers of and believers in Jesus, our Savior and Messiah.

"'During these hard times He is taking care of our daily needs. None of us needs to starve. All we have to do is to forsake our sins and put our trust for salvation in Him. He is the good

Shepherd, and we are His responsibility. The Apostle Paul said, "And my God shall supply all your need according to His riches in glory by Christ Jesus" (Philippians 4:19).

"'He supplied salvation for our souls, deliverance from sin, healing for our bodies, divine protection, and He supplies our daily needs. We do not want you to accept Jesus just for the food but for who He is. He is the Son of the living Jehovah God.

"'He died for the sins of the world, and He rose again from the dead after three days and three nights. If you are convinced of who Jesus, really is, please stand to your feet.'

"To the joy of the believers, all the guests, including the Muslim servers, stood to their feet signifying that they wanted to accept Jesus as their personal Savior. Only after the converts were prayed for did the servers clear the tables. They then went back to the kitchen to clean up. Amina who was an Arab Muslim, came running back and talking excitedly.

"She said, 'Brother Andrew, you spoke the truth. Jehovah is the true and only God who supplies all of our needs.'

"'What has happened?' Andrew inquired.

"She replied, 'We have fed over four hundred people, and the saucepans were completely empty. But now, they are as full as when we started dishing up.'" Her face was beaming from ear to ear.

"Those present started praising Father God for His mercy and love. Because the kitchen area was not very big, about twenty guests went in at a time to witness God's miracle of provision.

"Mother approached Pastor Andrew and said, 'Please make an announcement that after the guests have returned home they must return with containers. I believe that our heavenly father wants us to share the miracle food with as many people as possible.'

"Andrew made the announcement, 'Brothers and sisters it gives me great pleasure to make this announcement. We are going to share the blessing of the extra food with you. Thank you for making it such a wonderful day for Peter and Miriam. Please return home now and fetch some containers. Bring as many as you can. Tell your neighbors to bring containers for themselves as well. We have enough food for everyone. One warning, however, if you want the food to last until the rain comes, you must share your food with those who are less fortunate than you are.

"'The day you stop sharing your food with others, your blessings will dry up. It reminds me of the widow woman in 2 Kings 4:1–7. As long as she kept on pouring the oil into the empty vessels, it kept on flowing. When she ran out of vessels, the oil stopped flowing.

"'As long as you share your food with others, you will have food until there is a harvest. Go and find someone to share your meal with. But at the same time, share Jesus, the Living Water and the Living Bread, with them as well. It does not matter whether you feed one or a hundred. The food shall never be used up,'" said Andrew under the inspiration of the Spirit. "It is when we become selfish and stingy that God's blessings, dry up. For the benefit of the new converts, we are gathering in this hall at six o'clock tonight for a great celebration and thanksgiving service. Go with the Lord's blessing. Amen!"

Peter took a sip of orange juice before continuing with his testimony.

"Amina, the converted Muslim reminded them by saying," 'Remember! The miracle of Jesus, is now in your hands. As long as you share the blessing of Jehovah our God the blessings will keep on flowing. If you hoard the food, it shall become rotten.'" It was a very happy group of people who went home that afternoon."

• • • •

The news spread like wild fire that the angels had supplied food for the guests at Peter and Miriam's wedding, reception. People turned up from everywhere with containers. It was only after the last container was filled, that the food in the saucepans dried up.

Before supper that evening, the believers went knocking on doors looking for needy and hungry persons to share their meal with! They gave them an open invitation to come for supper or bring their own containers with them in order that they may take the food home with them. The people of the neighborhood had not eaten this well in months.

That evening the new converts brought some relatives and friends with them. They wanted to hear more about this man called Jesus who has the power to multiply food. They were going to hear *far* more than that.

Because there were so many people, they were compelled to have an open-air service in spite of the fact that the false prophet had banned the followers of Jesus from having meetings. The service went on without any interference from the zealots that Wednesday evening.

The people heard that Jesus, the Son of God was able to forgive their sins and transgressions and give them a brand new life. They heard for the very first time that He is the only one who was able to give them eternal life. The majority of them accepted Jesus as their Savior.

The people who came to the open-air service also brought containers along. After the service, they asked the people to enter the hall fifty at a time to receive their miracle food. Many of the people were afraid that there would not be enough for everyone.

"Peter calmed their fears by announcing, 'We have enough food to feed four times the amount of people present here. Not one of you will leave this place with empty containers. Just be patient and wait your turn to enter the hall.'" Peter's announcement had the desired effect.

nineteen
CHAPTER

The afternoon after the Sabbath Bible-study, they announced that the baptism of new converts was going to take place at the Jordan River after the Sunday morning communion service. The new converts were very excited. The Sunday morning service started at eight o'clock and finished at ten thirty. That gave them enough time to enjoy their miracle lunch.

Many testified that since Peter and Miriam's wedding, the food tasted even more delicious every day. Every day Jehovah-Yireh replenished their food. Like the manna, it stayed fresh just for that certain day. Every evening the saucepans were to be empty and washed. The next day the Lord provided just enough food for them and for those they were sharing it with!

From all over the surrounding areas, the believers came to witness the baptism service. It was a good experience for the followers of Jesus to meet their brothers and sisters from other towns and villages. Some had come as far away as Tiberius to witness the baptism of the new believers.

Brother Luke, the leader of the fellowship in Tiberius, opened the gathering with prayer. The sound of anointed music and singing filled the air. The people who were picnicking at the river stood nearer to hear the sermon. The believers were handing out tracts and praying for the sick and needy.

Some of the people there were also present

when the plague fell on the soldiers and when the fire nearly consumed a man who wanted to fight with Jehovah's prophets.

John brought a brief message on baptism.

> Therefore we were buried with Him through baptism into death, that just as Christ was raised from the dead by the glory of the Father, even so we also should walk in newness of life.

Romans 6:4

"Beloved, baptism is only for those who have accepted Jesus as Savior. It sets us apart from the world to follow Jesus, and only Him. We cannot and must not follow the trend of the Mystery Babylonian Universal Church who sprinkle babies and calls it baptism. It makes a mockery of the death, burial, and resurrection of Jesus, our Savior.

"If you are not sure of your commitment to follow Him, it is not too late for you to postpone your baptism. We will not hold it against you. But when you are ready, we will baptize you. After today, there is going to be no turning back. Jesus said, 'No one, having put his hand to the plow, and looking back, is fit for the kingdom of God' (Luke 9:62)." Then he read another verse of scripture. "'Now as they went down the road, they came to some water. And the eunuch said, "See, here is water. What does hinder me from being baptized?"' (Acts 8:36).

"I want to ask you. What is hindering you who have accepted Jesus as your Savior from being baptized? Are the false doctrines you have been taught hindering you? Do the priests of the Mystery Babylonian Universal Church with her unscriptural doctrines still have a hold over your lives?

"Today, the curse of the false doctrines will be forever broken over your lives. Today, you will be signifying to the world that you have forever broken with the false religious system. Today, those from amongst Judaism are breaking free from the shackles of the man made laws of the Pharisees and the Sadducees.

"I want to say to you as Philip said to the eunuch, "'If you believe with all your heart [in Jesus], you may [be baptized]," And he answered and said, "I believe that Jesus Christ is the Son of God"' (Acts 8:37).

"You who have come from Judaism no longer have to put your faith in the commandments of men. A small number of you have come from the Babylonian religious background. You no longer have to put your faith in the Antichrist, or Elijah, the false prophet, the priests, the saints, or even Semiramis, the queen of heaven.

"You have now placed your faith in Jesus Christ. Antichrist and the false prophet may control the world's religious system from Jerusalem, but they cannot control you or me. We are under the control of the blessed Holy Spirit. We now belong to the Lord, because we have been bought with the blood of Jesus, His Son.

"We have been sealed with the Holy Spirit until the day of redemption. Do not be afraid, even if you have to die for Jesus. The eunuch was very eager to follow Jesus, all the way. He confessed that Jesus was the Son of God. Let's read on, 'So he commanded the chariot to stand still. And both Philip and the eunuch went down into the water, and he baptized him' (Acts 8:38).

"Even with the water is up to your chin still does not count for baptism. Only after they were in the water, did Philip immerse baptize (immerse) him. If the mode of baptism was infant sprinkling, Philip would have sprinkled the eunuch on the chariot because he had a safe supply of water with him for himself and for his attendants' use. Philip did not know about the man-made baptism because it did not exist during the time of the apostles.

"The true Church was born on the Feast of Pentecost or as we Jews call it—the Feast of Weeks. Not one of the converts was sprinkled with water on that High Holy Day. Jehovah put His seal of approval on the eunuch's baptism because the Holy Spirit was also present as we derive from the following verse. 'Now when they came up out of the water, the Spirit of the Lord caught Philip away, so the eunuch saw him no more; and he went on his way rejoicing' (Acts 8:39).

"The Holy Spirit is also present here today as you follow Jesus in baptism. From today onward, you shall be branded as heretics by Jesus' enemies, because you accepted Him as your Savior and have chosen the scriptural mode of baptism by total immersion. Today, you are going to be baptized into Christ Jesus, and into His death.

"Your baptism symbolizes a burial with Him. And even as Jesus was raised up from the dead, even so shall we also be resurrected on the day of the resurrection of the just. It shall coincide with the day of Jesus' coming on the Feast of Trumpets. He shall come to resurrect the saved dead and then He will *rapture* them together with the living saints.

"The believers only started to function as the Church after the outpouring of the Holy Spirit on that special feast of Pentecost. It was on that exact day that the Apostle Peter said to the converts, '… Repent, and let everyone of you be baptized in the name of Jesus Christ for the remission of sins; and you shall receive the gift of the Holy Spirit' (Acts 2:38).

"The majority of the baptism candidates here today are Jewish. We are going to do just as the Apostle Peter did on the day of the Feast of Pentecost. Remember that it was the first day that the believers were functioning as a local church.

"We are going to baptize converts from amongst the Jews, nominal Christians, and Muslim who have accepted Jesus as their personal Savior, the same way Peter and the apostles baptized the first disciples of Jesus Christ.

"We are not going to bow under the pressure of the false church or the false prophet in Jerusalem. They have declared it a criminal offense to baptize any convert by immersion, and it is even a greater crime if it is done in the name of Jesus Christ, who is the personification and representative of the triune Godhead.

"We who are born again Jews love the name of Jesus, and it is our heart's desire to see that those who claim that the Book of Acts is also part of the inspired word of God, to accept it in its totality. How can we possibly call ourselves followers of Jesus and refuse to submit to the highest name in the universe.

"I give our heavenly Father all the praise that we, as Messianic believers from out of Judaism, have been spared such confusion. We highly esteem the name of Jesus, the Son of Jehovah God. And we also highly appreciate the blessed Holy Spirit who worked the new birth in us.

"We just go to the origin of the Church as recorded in the Book of Acts, and we join our Jewish brethren as on the day of Pentecost, and we do as the scripture says. If you have broken any of Jehovah's commandments, you are a sinner. Confess your sins to God right where you are. He is a forgiving Father.

"After you have confessed your sins, you must repent and forsake your sins and the judgment over your lives shall be removed. You will experience our heavenly Father's grace through His Son Jesus, who paid the penalty for our sins on the cross."

The Holy Spirit convicted those who were spending the day at the river and heard the gospel. They confessed their sins before a holy God. The well-trained personal workers counseled each new convert. Everyone received a tract containing key verses concerning salvation, deliverance, and healing. John gave an invitation to the new converts who had accepted Jesus as Savior to be baptized.

"You must be aware that when we as Jews accept Jesus as our Savior and get baptized by immersion, we are declared dead by our parents, family members, and friends."

After giving them a moment to think about what he had just said, he then asked them, "Have you come to a decision to go all the way with Jesus? Have you made up your minds to be, immersed? If so, please raise your hand." All over the area, the new converts raised their hands. "If you did not bring a towel or a garment for baptism then please ask the gentleman at the kiosk for the articles. We shall pay for the articles afterward. Please get ready for baptism immediately."

Joel, the born again policeman said, "The kiosk owner, who rents out the garments is going to do very good business today. I am grateful to the Ministry of Tourism for having allowed the construction of these kiosks." *I wonder how long before they are going to ban the rental of baptismal robes?*

Amos, his friend, commented, "Isn't it beautiful to see about a thousand converts all dressed in white robes or in white trousers and white shirts? There are so many candidates. The elders and some of the brothers will have to help the pastors to administer the baptism. I wish I could help. It would be a wonderful experience for me." *Please Lord, let Pastor John call on Amos and me to help with the baptism.*

Joel encouraged him, "'…delight yourself also in the LORD, And He shall give you the desires of your heart (Psalm 37:4).'"

"I say *Amen* to that. Jehovah God could not have given us a more beautiful and warm summer's day. Even the birds are singing in the trees. It is as if they understand the sacredness of the moment of what is taking place."

At that same time, Pastor John's voice came over the P.A. system, "Joel and Amos please come and assist us with the baptism."

Amos looked at Joel and said, "The Lord sure moves fast," and they both burst out laughing with sheer joy.

I did not bring a change of clothing for nothing, crossed Joel's mind.

Amos went over to the kiosk and was fortunate to get the right size robe for himself.

The pastors, elders, and brothers who were going to help administer the baptism were already standing in the river. The brothers and sisters, who were going to assist the candidates in and out of the water, were standing at the water's edge. The new converts were already wading into the water. The voices of the redeemed could be heard on the riverbank as it was being carried by the light breeze. They were singing a very old song titled, "Where He Leads Me I Will Follow."

Brother John lifted up his hands and quietness descended over the congregation. He prayed, "Heavenly Father, we thank you for this beautiful day. We thank you for the followers of Your Son, Lord Jesus, who are willing to forsake all. They are willing to follow Him, even in the face of tribulation or even death. I pray that Thy blessed Holy Spirit would strengthen and anoint every believer here today. Help everyone to be faithful unto death or unto the *rapture* of the, redeemed.

"Bless especially the new converts who are going to follow the example of our brothers and sisters from the first century church, who were baptized two thousand years ago, on the day of the Feast of Pentecost. Fill them with Thy Holy Spirit and protect all of us under the redeeming blood of Jesus. This I ask in Jesus' name. Amen!"

Forty converts were able to be baptized at a time because of the number of brothers administering the baptisms. The faces of the baptismal candidates were radiating with Jehovah's glory as they came out of the water speaking in a heavenly language.

Some went in sick and afflicted and came out healed by Jesus' power. One young man, who had to be carried into the water because he was paralyzed, came out walking, completely healed. The spirit of celebration was in the air. The spirit of belonging to someone bigger than the universe took possession of the hearts' of the saints.

It took a few hours to baptize all the converts, and the bodies of the brethren were cold and tired, but to them, it was worth it all. After the baptism, they spread out blankets under trees and enjoyed sandwiches and juice and shared their food with those who did not bring any.

An hour and a half later about thirty huge trucks without canopies on, each carrying about twenty passengers, pulled to a stop in the parking area. Mean-looking men jumped off the trucks and ran toward the believers. They believers immediately knew that it meant trouble. The men were armed with broomsticks, batons, whips, and chains.

Because the P.A. system was not disconnected yet, John immediately switched it on. He told the believers, "Do not be afraid. Remain seated and remain calm. Jehovah God said, 'You will not *need* to fight in this *battle*. Position yourselves, stand still, and see the salvation of the LORD, who is with you, O Judah and Jerusalem!' Do not fear or be dismayed; ... for the LORD is with you' (2 Chronicles 20:17)."

John quoted another scripture, "'Then all this assembly shall know that the LORD does not save with sword and spear; for the battle *is* the LORD's' (1 Samuel 17:47a)."

The scriptures had a calming affect on the believers. Then John addressed the last phrase to the mob that was fast approaching. "And He will give you into our hands' (1 Samuel 17:47b)."

At the sight of the approaching men, some of the little children started crying. Their mothers shielded them with their arms. The brethren who were sitting with their families stood up. John again addressed the believers and said, "Start calling on the Lord Jehovah and thank Him for His great deliverance."

He then beckoned the leaders, both men and women who were present, to stand between the fast approaching men. All of a sudden, the birds stopped their singing and flew overhead, by the hundreds. John commented, "Jehovah is already intervening on our behalf."

The menacing men were about thirty yards away when a black cloud came toward them, and the sound of tens of thousands of angry bees filled the air. The bees flew over the believers and started attacking the mob.

They dropped their weapons and started fending off the bees, while at the same time screaming. Some of them started rolling in the sand. Others again ran to the river and jumped in. It was a very pathetic sight, to behold.

The new leader of the zealots crawled to John and said, "Please call on the name of your God and ask him to call off the bees. My men are going to die of the bee stings. Jesus your Messiah is stronger than Satan, Messiah, and Prophet Elijah!

"The prophet sent us to do you harm, so as to persuade you to forsake your Lord Yahshua. He sent us to arrest you and to commandeer your buses in order for us to drive you to a prison at a secret destination."

John asked him, "What is your name?

He replied, "My name is Jambres."

John said, "Jambres, Jesus loves you and your men very much. He is willing to forgive your sins, and we forgive you as God in Christ has forgiven us."

The majority of the men's faces were swollen beyond recognition, and they were groaning because of the pain and discomfort. John prayed in his heart, *Jesus, don't let any of Jambres' men, die.*

Jambres addressed his men. "I am going to dedicate my life to Jesus. You have to make the decision for yourselves. You used to obey me to the letter, but I can no longer decide for you." Tears were rolling down this once hardened criminal's face.

Dudley Fairbairn

The believers felt very sorry for Jambres and his men. John lifted up his hands and prayed, "Dear Father, these men have learned a sore lesson not to touch Your anointed. Please forgive them, in Jesus' name, and please call off Your little soldiers. Amen!"

Immediately, the bees regrouped behind John. They did not leave the area immediately, but hovered over the men. John gave the microphone to Jambres, and he called his men. "Men, we have fought against the Holy One of Israel, and we have lost. We have committed a grievous sin. These people have done us no harm. All they desire to do is to serve Jesus. The bees have only called a temporary truce. As you can see, they are still hovering just above us.

What happened here today is a miracle. Not one of Jesus' followers were stung, only us. Only those of you who are willing to accept Jesus as your Savior step toward me."

About fifty came out of the river where they were hiding. Others were hiding amongst the bushes, and the rest were just lying on the ground. Jambres prostrated himself on the ground, and the majority of his men came and did likewise.

John spoke to them and said, "By your actions you transgressed God's law. You wanted to do us harm. You had murder in your hearts, and you would have harmed our wives and daughters."

Jambres replied, "What you have just said is all true. We would have done that and much more," and his men nodded in agreement.

John led them into the prayer of commitment to Jesus and they repeated the prayer after John. Tears were running down their faces. The bees encircled them one more time then flew away, only after Jambres and his men had said, "Amen."

Jambres and those of his men who accepted Jesus requested to be baptized. John and the brothers were more than willing to baptize them. Jesus, the baptizer, baptized and filled them with the Holy Spirit as recorded in Acts 2:1–4. John informed him where their regular services were being held. "If you are really serious in your commitment to serve Jesus, and if you want to grow in your faith, it is very important that you regularly attend the services."

· · · ·

Every one of them returned home with great peace and joy. As they were driving home, the buses rang with the singing and the laughter of Jehovah's children. Their faith had increased because of His divine intervention and protection. The new converts were established in their newfound faith in Jesus, Israel's Messiah.

The anointing of the Lord came down on the praises of the established believers and new converts, and they started worshipping Him and singing under the inspiration of the Holy Spirit. The anointing was so heavy that the bus drivers had to pull off the road so they *too* could join in on the blessing of the heavenly visitation.

Dudley Fairbairn

twenty

CHAPTER

At Jerusalem, Prophet Elijah was furious when he heard the news about the conversions at the river. Jambres had gone into hiding after Prophet Elijah had lambasted him over the phone over the failed operation and because he and some of his men had accepted Jesus as their Savior.

Prophet Elijah said to him, "You know what happened to Judas when he betrayed me? One of the zealots slit his throat when he was on his way to the prayer meeting. He deserved to die because he accepted that imposter Esau, whom you prefer to call Jesus. There is not room enough for two Messiahs in Israel, or the world.

"There is only one true Messiah, and I can assure you that it is not Esau. The true Messiah is living amongst us, right here in Jerusalem. He is the one who made peace between Jew and Arab. The Messiah you believe in is a fraud. If you do not turn your back on Esau, I am going to have you all annihilated."

"You cannot scare me. You and Antichrist are going to hell. I am a man of my word. My men and I have made a promise to Jesus that we were going to forsake our sins and serve, only Him!" said Jambres, and he put the phone down on the receiver.

Prophet Elijah went red in the face, and his heart started racing very fast. He could have suffered a heart attack had his personal physician not come to his aid. His physician sent him to bed for the rest of the day.

When Jambres testified at the fellowship what had happened between him and Prophet Elijah, an elderly couple in the local fellowship, who had no children had compassion on him and offered Jambres, who was a single man, a place to stay. He was able to get a message to his men to inform them of the situation with Prophet Elijah. He told them where the services were going to be held.

The wives, mothers, and children of the men were amazed when their husbands, sons, and fathers came home with badly swollen faces. However, they were even more amazed by the drastic changes that took place in the men's lives. Wives received back new husbands, children received back new fathers, mothers received back new sons, and girlfriends received back new boyfriends.

A peace, which they had never experienced before, entered their lives and homes. Jesus, the Prince of Peace, came to dwell with them. Because of what Jesus had done for them, their families also desired to attend the services of the Messianic believers. The men shaved off their shaggy beards and had their wives and mothers cut their long, unruly mops of hair. They were unrecognizable when they attended the fellowship.

• • • •

Prophet Elijah was planning another attack against the followers of Jesus. He informed Messiah about his plan. "This time it must not fail. These low-life Christians are undermining our authority," he said to Messiah. He was so upset that he began to stammer. "Over … aaaaaah … thousand of them were … were baptized in that despicable name."

He could not bring himself to say Jesus. "aaand … my … my men were unable to stop them." With pitiful eyes, he looked at Messiah, and with a pleading voice he said, "Messiah, you must help me or I will go crazy." *You have been crazy for a very long time now. You look like a puppy whose bone had been taken away by a big dog*, thought Messiah.

Messiah looked at him with a smile and said, "Leave it all to me. We are going to strike at the heart of this rebellious Christian sect who refuse to join our Mystery Babylonian Universal Church."

Elijah continued with his griping. "The main problem is we are not dealing with people who belonged to the various Christian sects before our One World Church came into being. They are a minority. We are dealing with a rebellion against and a defection from organized Judaism. They are *challenging* your headship as king over Israel, your claim to the throne of David, and your claim to be the Jewish Messiah.

"If we do not act soon, your plan to declare yourself God in the middle of the seven years of false peace shall be in great jeopardy."

Messiah responded, "Over my dead body." Elijah felt much better after confiding in Messiah.

• • • •

In spite of the ban against open-air meetings, the believers still went ahead and held open-air meetings at strategic places. Their fellowship meetings were still held at secret venues. They were warned by scouts about the approaching danger.

The people showed great interest in God's word. The believers were not afraid to pray for the sick and the needy. They prayed right on the sidewalks and in the city squares. People were being healed from various diseases. The precious name of the Lord Jesus was mentioned thousands of times during that specific day.

• • • •

The public was beginning to associate the name of Jesus the Messiah with the many miracles that were taking place. A blind beggar named Jacob experienced an outstanding miracle. He had been begging at the same spot every day for the past three years. He would arrive early in the morning when people were on their way to work. He discovered it was the best time to beg for alms.

Simon, an eighteen-year-old follower of Jesus, witnessed to Jacob. He said, "Jesus the Messiah is able to heal you of your blindness." Jacob was very amazed, as no one had ever told him that before. He immediately showed interest. Simon asked him, "What are you going to do when Jesus heals you?"

He replied, "I will go back to practicing medicine."

Simon asked surprised, "Are you *really* a doctor?

"I was a doctor. Now I am a thirty-three-year-old beggar. I practiced medicine in the United States of America before I immigrated to Israel. The day after my arrival, I was attacked by a member of the *Intifada*, while I was on my way to the hospital for an interview.

"A terrorist threw a hand grenade at my car. It shattered the windscreen, and I was blinded in both my eyes. My face was also terribly scarred."

He removed his sunglasses, and Simon stared into his empty eye-sockets. The scars on his face were now more visible. He turned his face to Simon and asked, "Can your Jesus still heal me?"

A big crowd had gathered around Simon and Jacob, and with great interest, they followed the conversation.

One young man said, "I wonder how he is going to extricate himself out of this one?"

A woman interjected, "It is a crying shame that these deceived Christians would give people false hope. I know Jacob for three years now. I always bring him something nice to eat on Fridays." *Now they'll know that I am better than the followers of Esau.*

Simon heard the comments some of people were making, but he ignored them. Instead, he answered Jacob's question. "Yes, I still believe that Jesus can and will heal you."

Jacob did not put his sunglasses back on. He turned his face toward the people, and they recoiled in horror when they saw the empty red eye-sockets. They had never seen him without his sunglasses before.

Simon placed his hands lightly on either side of Jacob's temples and placed his thumbs over the eyeless sockets without touching them. He prayed, "Jehovah God, in the name of Jesus the Messiah, Your Son, please create new eyes for Jacob and remove the scars on his face."

Simon had not even finished praying when a man shouted,

"Blasphemy! Blasphemy! Esau is not the Messiah of Israel and you are a false prophet."

The interruption and accusation did not discourage Simon in the least. He just kept on praying. "Father, heal Jacob by the power of Thy Holy Spirit. This I ask in Jesus' name. Amen!"

Simon, removed his hands and Jacob shouted as he never shouted in his life before. "I can see! Thank you Jesus! I can see! Praise be unto Jehovah! I can see!"

Jesus had created two beautiful dark-brown eyes and new eyelids for Jacob. Simon lifted up his hands and started exalting Jehovah in a heavenly language.

The Jewish man with side curls hanging from either side of his skullcap, who had taken offense at Simon, shouted much to the amazement of the crowd who had gathered. "He is speaking Russian! He is speaking in my mother tongue all about the great things of our God. is saying through him, 'My beloved Son, Jesus, is Israel's Messiah.' "God is saying 'My Son was slain on the accursed cross for the sins of the world and that He rose again after three days and three nights, over two-thousand years ago. He is Israel's, and the world's salvation.'"

The Russian Jew stopped for a moment, lost in Simon's words, and then he continued speaking. "I was angry at first when this young man made the assumption that Jesus was the Messiah. I now also believe that Jesus was the promised Messiah. Only Messiah can make the blind to see." His positive confession made a great impact on the bystanders.

The people were amazed at what had happened. They also wanted Simon to pray for them.

With great excitement in his voice, a man shouted, "Jacob! The scars on your face are d*Isa*ppearing."

Jacob touched his face and was amazed at the smoothness of his face. He exclaimed, "My face feels like the face of a new born baby." Tears streamed down his face. The Russian Jew and many others responded to the call for salvation. Some of the brothers and sisters came to Simon's rescue and helped him minister to the needs of the many people who requested prayer. The blessed Holy Spirit multiplied the miracles and healings. The sidewalks and the grassy parks became altars where many were saved and healed!

A young man named Benjamin Hershel saw Jacob's miracle. He asked Simon to pray for him, as he was suffering from excruciating pain caused by an inoperable cancer of the stomach. Simon cursed the cancer and commanded the cancer to die and to be expelled from Benjamin's body. Nothing visible happened at that moment when Simon prayed for him. He walked away saddened by the fact that he did not receive his miracle.

Many people were late for work that morning, but they were not worried because Jesus had filled the great void in their lives. Many of their bosses showed great interest when they related the miracles they had witnessed.

Some of them even went with their staff during the lunch hour to listen to the preaching of the word and with the hope of seeing a miracle. Jesus did not d*Is*appoint them. What they heard and saw forever changed their lives.

. . . .

All the believers from Tel Aviv and the surrounding areas, who had come to do personal evangelism and to participate in the open-air services, were all heading toward the City Auditorium. Brother Jonah, the overseer of the Tel Aviv and surrounding home churches, was to be the main speaker at the three o'clock service.

The public was invited to attend the seven o'clock service. Many of them promised to come that evening. Jacob, who had received back his sight, and many others had asked if they could testify in the evening service how Jesus had healed them of their sicknesses and diseases.

Even with the fifteen-hundred believers in attendance, the auditorium looked empty. The worship team was already leading the praise and worship. The anointing was hanging like a glory cloud over the believers. After the opening prayer, a number of them came forward to share the great things the lord, had done.

Many testimonies of salvation, healings, and miracles were related. Everyone who testified gave God the glory. While testimonies were being shared, a few men dressed in the identical uniform the staff who worked at of the auditorium wore entered the auditorium. They did not disturb anyone but quietly continued with their duties. Unbeknownst to the believers, they were shutting all the windows that were about ten feet off the floor. They also secured all the inside doors of the auditorium, except the doors, which opened up into the foyer.

When the last song was sung after the last testimony, Brother Jonah waited for the music team to take their seats. As he was walking to the stage, all the lights in the auditorium went out. The switches at the power box which serviced the foyer and the auditorium had been was switched off. Soon after, the four main doors to the auditorium were flung wide open, and the bright sunlight, which shone through the large foyer windows lit up the entrance to the auditorium. It revealed men dressed in black with gas masks on, entering the large doorways to the auditorium.

Pastor Jonah immediately knew that something was terribly wrong when he saw them throwing objects, which looked like canisters, amongst the crowd.

He immediately raised his voice above the noise, and with a firm voice, he commanded, "Beloved, remain calm and start praying," then he shouted, "Brothers, grab those men."

A number of brothers immediately responded. It all happened so quickly. The men with the gas masks fired a few shots overhead to scare off the brothers. In the confusion that ensued, the men slipped out, locking the doors from the outside.

Brother Jonah said, "Beloved, our lives are in Jehovah's hands." Then he addressed the men, "Brothers, see if you can force open those doors. Do not be afraid of those who can kill the body. Jesus is our resurrection and our life. He is our eternal security."

The poison gas was very potent. Those present were already gasping for air. The children were screaming. Some of the adults were crying. But whatever they were doing, they were calling on the name of Jesus. The gas was already doing its horrible work of destruction. All over the auditorium the believers were dying.

Brother Jonah addressed his wife, children, and the believers. "Joanna, my love, Matthew and Abigail, daddy's sweet children. I love you very much! Brothers and sisters we shall see one another very soon in the presence of Jesus, our Savior."

The brothers who tried to open the doors were soon overcome by the poison gas and died.

With the last bit of life and strength Pastor Jonah prayed, "Jesus, into Your hands we commit our spirit. Thank you for dying for us on the cross. Jesus, we love you," Then he slumped to the floor and died.

Only here and there, a faint voice could still be heard praying. Within fifteen minutes of the attack, fifteen hundred of Jesus' faithful followers died and woke up in His presence. People were already showing up for the evening service, an hour before the time. They were amazed to find the doors to the auditorium were still locked.

Jacob shouted to the people standing around him, "Something is very wrong! I do not believe for a moment that the believers would invite us to the service and not show up themselves. If someone has a cell phone, please phone the police headquarters. Tell them it is a life and death situation. The lives of over fourteen-hundred people are in jeopardy."

The chief officer immediately informed the ministry of defense. Within minutes of receiving the call, the sharpshooters and soldiers showed up.

A police officer told the people, "For your own safety and protection please move to a safe distance from the building. We are not sure what to expect."

The soldiers forced open the main doors to the auditorium and entered the spacious foyer, which was lit up by the light shining through the large windows and the open doors. A soldier went to switch on the lights, but there was no power. He immediately ran to the power room. He used his flashlight, and switched on the main power switch.

One of the officers heard muffled sounds were coming from the men's restroom area. Then they heard someone shouting for help. They rushed to the restroom area and found an "Out of order" sign hanging on the doorknob.

The key was still in the lock, and when they unlocked the

door, they found the staff, both men and woman, tied back to back. Some of them were bleeding from facial wounds. While the soldiers were busy untying the staff, an officer took down a statement from the man who raised the alarm.

He said, "We had just finished cleaning the auditorium, foyer, and the various washroom areas when twelve masked men burst in on us. They threatened to kill us should we refuse to cooperate. When we resisted, they hit us over the head with the butts of their rifles."

The officer asked him, "Can you give us a description of the men?"

He replied, "It was difficult to identify them as they had ski masks on. They wore the same uniform that the staff wears. They must have raided our warehouse."

The officer then asked another question, "With what accent did they speak?"

"They spoke with a Jewish accent. One man had a skull and bones tattooed on the back of his right hand. The colors were red, blue, and yellow." The officer had a smile on his face. He knew who the owner of that tattoo was. He thanked the man and told him that he had been very helpful. The soldiers then unlocked the main doors to the auditorium because the keys were still in the locks.

When they unlocked the doors to the main hall, they made a very gruesome discovery. At that same time, a shout rang out, "How sad!"

More than twenty bodies were found in the area of the doors.

There was a strange odor in the hall. The soldiers who had opened the doors to the auditorium immediately stood back a few paces and told the soldiers to don their gas masks. Those who did not have gas masks were asked to immediately vacate the premises. When the soldiers entered the hall, the full extent of the horror that had taken place stared them in the face. It looked like a war zone. Not even one believer was alive.

Bodies were sprawled out all over the auditorium. Mothers were seen holding their babies or clutching their children. Husbands were embracing their wives and children. Young men were embracing their girlfriends. A young girl was clutching her doll. It looked as if they were frozen in time.

A few of the soldiers told the crowd that had gathered that all the Messianic believers had been martyred. All over the crowd, men and woman were crying and embracing one another. Others were kneeling and praying. Even the soldiers were visibly moved.

Within minutes after being notified, the medical staff and ambulances from the hospital in Tel Aviv were on the scene.

They unlocked all the inside exit doors and opened all the windows to allow fresh air to drive out the poisonous gasses. The real impact of what had really happened hit the crowd when the soldiers carried out the corpses by the hundreds. Some of the soldiers were very emotional and cried openly.

• • • •

The massacre sent shock waves through the communities of the followers of Jesus in Israel and abroad. Stories were filtering in through the grapevine that believers were being burnt at the stake in South America, and in the European Union, crucifixion was once gain becoming the mode of execution.

Also in France, the guillotine had again been reintroduced to deal with the nonconformists, as the followers of Jesus Christ, were called. They had to be eradicated by force because they were a scourge on the New Age Society.

The day after the massacre, John and Andrew came together with all the pastors from across Israel for an emergency meeting in Tel Aviv. They had to make arrangements for the funeral of their martyred brothers and sisters.

Andrew opened the meeting in prayer. "Heavenly Father, I pray for those who have been bereft of mothers, fathers, husbands, wives, sons, daughters, and friends.

"Blessed Holy Spirit, please bring healing where there is brokenness of spirit. Bring understanding where there is confusion. Where there is fear of the unknown, please give them peace of mind. Dear Father, strengthen them in the hour of their sorrow. This we ask in Jesus' name. Amen."

All the pastors pledged to help the poor families with the funeral expenses. They also reached a decision that the joint funeral service was going to be held in Tel Aviv and that buses would be hired to convey the mourners.

John addressed the leaders and said, "You know who are responsible for the massacre. It is none other than Antichrist and his sidekick, the false prophet. They are behind this monstrous and barbarous act. They are hiding behind their privileged position. Their demise is not far off. I do not feel sorry for them because they are already condemned by Jehovah our God.

"Many of our brothers and sisters have been killed, worldwide. We know that they are with Jesus at this moment, awaiting the resurrection of the just. We have the hope of seeing them again soon. Hold fast to the profession of your faith, beloved, Maranatha!"

After the discussions, One of the pastors dismissed them with the benediction. Some of members of the local churches, who had escaped the massacre because they were unable to attend the evangelistic outreaches, prepared a lunch for the pastors. It was a miracle meal. The food was supplied by a young man who received a miracle from Jesus the morning of the massacre.

twenty_one

CHAPTER

The day before the funeral service just as Andrew and John arrived at the community hall a young man drove up in a car. He approached them and asked if they could give him a hand carrying the food he brought to the kitchen. John and Andrew introduced themselves and gave him a helping, hand. The young man introduced himself as Benjamin Hershel.

When they were finished, they sat down to enjoy a glass of freshly squeezed pomegranate juice. While they were seated in the shade of a tree, Benjamin shared his testimony with them. "I was on my way to the hospital because I woke up with excruciating pain the morning of the massacre. I wanted the doctor to give me a morphine injection. I was diagnosed with an inoperable cancer of the stomach two months ago. I only had two more months to live, as the cancer was spreading at an alarming rate." Both John and Andrew were amazed at the healthy looking young man sitting opposite them.

He then told them about the miracle that he had witnessed when Jesus healed the blind man by creating two eyes in the eyeless sockets.

"I asked Simon, one of the martyrs, to also pray for me. He cursed the cancer in Jesus' name and commanded it to die and to be expelled from my body. I was saddened by the fact that I did not get my miracle immediately when Simon prayed for me. When I arrived at the hospital, the pain was very excruciating. I told Doctor Kissinger about my condition, and as I could hardly walk, I asked him to assist me to the washroom.

"We were both shocked at the sight of my shirt and trousers, which were stained with blood. When I pulled up my shirt, the huge cancerous growth fell to the floor.

"The thing that amazed us was that within seconds after Jesus healed me, the wound closed up right in front of our eyes, leaving no scar." The doctor was just amazed as I was. He took me to his office and gave me a thorough examination.

"I told him that a young man named Simon who believed Jesus to be Israel's Messiah, prayed for me. He commanded the cancer to be expelled from my body in Jesus' name."

John suddenly spoke up and asked, "What was his reaction?"

"For a few seconds he had a blank look on his face. Then he said, 'I also want to accept Jesus as my Savior.'"

Andrew asked, "What was your response?"

"I told him to ask Jesus to forgive his sins and to take possession of his life, which he did. The evening of the martyrdom the two of us went to a prayer meeting at a brother's house and were both filled with the Holy Spirit. We are going to be baptized after the funeral service." We both are very happy for you," said John.

They laid hands on him and prayed for the Lord's divine protection and unction upon Benjamin's life. Before he left, he said, "I would love to have a brief talk with you after the funeral service."

"You are most welcome," came Andrew's reply.

Many Orthodox and Reformed Jews, Messianic Jews and converts from amongst the Gentiles, which included the Muslims, had opened their hearts to the bereaved families by giving liberally toward the funeral costs. From the business sector in Tel Aviv and other surrounding towns, donations of food and money were pouring in.

As they were preparing for the service, Andrew said, "Never in the history of Israel has such an outpouring of love been experienced, except when Jesus died on the cross for the sins of the whole world. It was on the cross that Jehovah God poured out His love on humanity."

John replied, "Every time Antichrist and the false prophet issue a command for believers to be killed, it backfires in their faces. Jehovah's love causes thousands to accept Jesus as their personal Savior."

"You can say that again," said Andrew.

"We must encourage the believers to bring plenty of New Testaments to the funeral. Jesus did not make us fisher's of men for nothing. See you at the funeral service, Andrew," and they parted. They both still had much to do before the funeral.

• • • •

From all over the world the news media converged on Tel Aviv. Central News Makers, from America, beamed the breaking news to the world. All over Israel and from the neighboring Islamic countries, followers of Jesus were streaming in to attend the funeral and to show their solidarity with their fellow brothers and sisters.

They also brought with them tens of thousands of Euros and dollars to help the bereaved families to starts a trust fund for those who had lost their breadwinners.

Prime Minister Mordecai and Chief Rabbi David Cohen of Jerusalem came to the service against the direct order of Prophet Elijah. The prime minister was very adamant when he told Elijah, "I am not going to allow you or anyone else to intimidate me any longer. If you want to kill me, just as you are killing the followers of Jesus, then go ahead.

"I know where I am going when I die, but where will you be going? It is not you who put me in office but my Lord! I hear that your office is receiving tens of thousands of post cards from all over the world wishing you and Antichrist a very happy future in hell."

Red faced, Elijah glared at him and said, "Get out of my sight … you … you … imbecile." His voice took on a very high pitch when he screamed, "I will get you for this. I will make you pay. You will see! Your Jesus will not be able to deliver you in the day of my wrath," and he turned around and left the prime minister's office in a huff.

The prime minister thought, *"I have made an enemy for life,"* and bowed his head and had a quiet time with God.

• • • •

Thousands of people from various religious persuasions gathered at a new section of the cemetery. Fifteen hundred and twenty graves had been dug. A huge marquee had been erected for the bereaved families and dignitaries. Some military generals, government officials, and Jewish religious leaders were also present.

Many of them were openly sympathizing with the followers of Jesus. The military band requested to play the national anthem and a mass choir sang the song entitled, "Jerusalem." Ten brothers sang a cappella of "Amazing Grace."

As they were singing, the blessed Holy Spirit was busy ministering to the hearts of thousands of people who came to say their farewell to another group of tribulation martyrs. The mayor of Tel Aviv greeted the people and expressed his condolence on behalf of the citizens of Israel. He also read a few e-mails from other parts of the world.

Andrew took his place at the lectern. He looked visibly moved at the loss of his brothers and sisters. He bowed his head and prayed, "Heavenly Father! Just the thought of knowing that the spirits of our dearly departed are in heaven with You, brings comfort to our aching hearts.

"There are thousands here this morning, and we know according to Your word where they are going to spend eternity should they die without faith in Jesus, Your Son. Have mercy on them and save them from eternal destruction. This I pray in Jesus' name. Amen!"

John quoted the words of Jesus from the gospel of John 11:25–26. "Jesus said unto Martha, 'I am the resurrection and the life. He who believes in Me, though he may die, he shall live. And whoever lives and believes in Me shall never die. Do you believe this?' *I hope everyone present here believes the Gospel.*

"Jesus' body did not see corruption because He was the Unleavened Bread who came down from heaven. The empty tomb in Jerusalem bares witness to that fact and without Jesus there is no hope after death. Paul the Jewish Rabbi declared, 'For if *the* dead do not rise, then Christ is not risen. And if Christ is not risen, your faith *is* futile; you are still in your sins! Then also those who have fallen asleep in Christ have perished. If in this life only we have hope in Christ, we are of all men the most pitiable. But now Christ is risen from the dead, *and* has become the firstfruits of those who have fallen asleep' (1 Corinthians 15:16–20).

"Through the centuries the blame of our Savior's death was laid squarely on the shoulders on us who are Jews. Such a burden is *too* heavy for any nation to bear. But I have good news for you today. Jesus said, 'Therefore My Father loves Me, because I lay down My life that I may take it again. No one takes it from Me, but I lay it down of Myself. I have power to lay it down, and I have power to take it again. This command I have received from My Father' (John 10:17).

With great boldness, Andrew came to the defense of the Jewish People. "For too long our Jewish nation had to bear the blame off Jesus Christ's death. If we have to lay the blame on any nation then Imperial Rome stands guilty before God. It was the Roman soldiers who nailed Jesus to the cross, not the Jews. It is a historic fact that is purposely overlooked. But thanks be unto Jehovah, the tomb is empty. Jesus has risen from the dead. He is our Passover Lamb who made atonement for us."

"It was because of the sin of the nations of the world, including the nation of Israel that Jesus had to lay down His life on the cross of Calvary. It was Jehovah's plan for salvation for all humanity. Jesus had to die! If you want the life that Jesus has to offer you, you must repent of your sins. Raise your hand if you have never sinned." Not one person raised a hand.

Andrew picked up where John had left off and said, "We all stand guilty before God. We transgressed God's laws. We all deserve to be cast into hell. The wages of sin is eternal separation from God. Jesus, who is Jehovah's salvation, paid for our sins by dying on the cross for us. He is the only Savior.

"If you are sincere in your desire to serve the Lord, then I want you to go a step further. Confess your sins to Him."

The convicting power of the Holy Spirit descended on those present, and the majority of them started confessing their sins and crying out for forgiveness.

John took over from Andrew and said, "Those of you who have confessed yours sins, please pray this prayer after me, "Heavenly Father, I thank You for having forgiven my sins. Thank you for Jesus, who paid the penalty for my sins, and whose blood has washed away all of my sins. I now accept Him as my Savior. Amen!"

The people who heard the word and saw the miracles the morning of the massacre were amongst the thousands who accepted Jesus as their personal Savior. The choir sang softly in the background while the coffins were being lowered into the graves. The Chief Rabbi, who was also a believer, announced the benediction. Andrew thanked the people of Israel and those from abroad who had offered their condolences and who had sent financial gifts toward the trust fund for the families. He also thanked all the businessmen who donated food and beverages.

He said, "I bless you all in Jesus' name."

He then announced the addresses of the venues in Tel Aviv where the visitors and the local people could get something to eat and drink. The believers brought enough New Testaments and other spiritual literature with them, which they distributed to all the new converts and others who were interested.

• • • •

One morning, across time zones, 144,000 Israeli men around the world discovered an imprint of a seal on their foreheads. Twelve thousand out of each of tribes of Israel were sealed. In Jerusalem, the office of the local church was inundated with phone calls, concerning the strange phenomenon.

Many of them were worried that it was a sign of something evil. The staff had to work overtime, answering the calls and sending e-mails and faxes to explain to the relatives of the recipients of the mark what it signified.

At the same auditorium where the massacre took place, Andrew addressed hundreds of pastors from across Israel. "Beloved, please inform your congregants not to be afraid. Brother John and I have also received Jehovah's seal on our forehead. You will discover that all the men who have been sealed are from one of the twelve tribes of Israel. We all have one thing in common; we have all accepted Jesus as our Savior and Messiah.

"We, who have the seal on our forehead, have been set aside by Jehovah God to be His ministers on special assignment. We are going to take Jesus' message to the far outreaches of the world. Just as Philip was physically *raptured* by the Holy Spirit and taken to Azotus, so we *too* shall experience the joy of being transported to distant places, and countries by the Holy Spirit. Holy Spirit transportation will eliminate the need for passports and v*Isa*s.

"All the governments and countries who are under the control of Antichrist and the false prophet will not allow us to enter their countries to preach the gospel of Jesus. Through the intervention of the blessed Holy Spirit, the problem has now been circumvented. 'The gospel of the kingdom will be preached in all the world to all nations, and then the end will' (Matthew 24:14).

"We the followers of Jesus shall preach the gospel until the end of the (*Church*) age. The Church-age shall come to an end when Jesus comes to *rapture* His Church. Therefore, it is the responsibility of every follower of Jesus to share Him with their fellow man. What we have experienced is recorded in the Bible. I want to bring three verses from Revelation 7:2–4 to your attention.

> Then I saw another angel descending from the east, having the seal of the living God. And he cried with a loud voice to the four angels to whom it was granted to harm the earth and the sea, saying, "Do not harm the earth, the sea, or the trees till we have sealed the servants of our God on their foreheads." And I heard the number of those who were sealed. One hundred *and* forty-four thousand of all the tribes of the children of Israel *were* sealed.

"Every believer is already sealed by Jehovah's Holy Spirit, irrespective of whether they have the seal on your forehead or not. Every believer is in the full-time ministry because we are all full-time believers," said Andrew, much to the encouragement of those present.

"Paul declared in Ephesians 1:13, 'In whom you also *trusted*, after you heard the word of truth, the gospel of your salvation; in whom also, having believed, you were sealed with the Holy Spirit of promise, who is the guarantee of our inheritance until the redemption of the purchased possession, to the praise of His glory.'"

"The tribulation against Jehovah's redeemed is going to become more severe because the devil knows that he has but a short time. However, be of good cheer. Jesus overcame the world, and through Him, we are more than conquerors. Greater is He who is in us than the devil, Antichrist, and the false prophet who are in the world.

"Pray and fast as never before. Witness, win souls, cast out demons, pray for the sick, and raise the dead. The Holy Spirit has empowered both men and woman to do the works of the ministry Jesus. Remain faithful and full of Jesus' love. Brothers and sisters may the grace of our God, and the love of Jesus, and the fellowship of the Holy Spirit, be with your spirit. Amen!"

twenty_two
CHAPTER

Samuel, one of the newscasters of Central News Makers, informed his worldwide audience that soon after the sealing of the hundred and forty-four thousand Israelis, a strange worldwide phenomenon took place. The scientists were completely baffled. They had never seen anything so bizarre. People started phoning the local TV and newspaper offices reporting that they had seen an angel flying through the sky, sounding a trumpet.

Soon after the sighting of the angel, the people had to run for cover, as an electrical storm was unleashed across Planet Earth. The hail had the appearance of being on fire, and where it fell, it scorched the earth.

The forensic scientists, who were called in to inspect and analyze this mind-boggling phenomenon, were amazed that the consistency of the fiery-hail was like blood. News reports began pouring in at the offices of The Ministry of Environmental Affaires at the United Nations.

After the meteorologists studied a picture sent back by NASA's satellite, a very grim picture unfolded. A third of earth's forests and grasslands had been totally, destroyed. The once lush forests turned into deserts within hours of the electrical storm.

The scientists said that it was the severest electrical storm ever recorded in the last couple of hundred years. People claimed to have seen men with a strange seal on their foreheads. They were seen in various parts of the world preaching the gospel of the kingdom and praying for the sick.

Undeniable miracles were happening when prayer was made in the name of Jesus. One of the men with the seal on his forehead, who spoke in English said, "Leaders of the governments of the world, be forewarned, even more catastrophic judgments are on the way. Be warned, people of Planet Earth, your only hope is in Jesus Christ. Only through Him can you be assured of a place in heaven. He died on the cross of Calvary for your sins. Only through repentance and completely turning away from sin will you be spared from the judgment of hell.

"Your eternal security is only in Jesus, the Son of the living God, and not in Antichrist or the false prophet or the apostate church. Planet Earth is on a collision course with dIsaster, and there is no way of escape outside of Jesus, who is both Lord and Savior."

· · · ·

Everywhere in the midst of the destruction and decay that was left after the first angel blew his trumpet, the followers of Jesus Christ experienced a mighty Holy Spirit driven revival. The results were of such magnitude that the spillover resulted in the salvation of multiplied millions of men, women, and children.

Unprecedented since the birth of the Church, every country was experiencing the outpouring of the Holy Spirit. The believers were revived by the visitation of the Holy Spirit.

· · · ·

Prophet Elijah was pacing the floor of his large dining room, awaiting the arrival of Messiah. There was a knock on the door, and Ishmael, the valet thought, *It must be Antichrist.* He walked to the door, taking his time. Messiah knocked again. When he opened the door to let in Prophet Elijah's distinguished guest, there was a scowl on Messiah's face. Ishmael made a deep bow as was expected of him. "Welcome Your Holiness. Prophet Elijah is in the lounge awaiting your arrival." Messiah ignored his greeting. "May I have your coat, please?" Messiah nodded and allowed Ishmael to remove his coat.

While he was walking to the lounge, he said without looking at Ishmael, "Bring me a double Scotch."

Prophet Elijah's face lit up when Messiah entered the lounge.

While Ishmael was walking to the kitchen, he thought to himself, *The two drunkards are together again. I wonder what they are scheming against the followers of Jesus this time? Whenever they get together, believers are killed, soon after. I have to keep my eyes and ears open this time, so I can warn Brother Andrew and Brother John what the evil twosome are up to.*

The last time they came together, they sent me on an errand, and soon after, fifteen hundred believers were gassed to death in Tel Aviv. If I had known of their evil plan to martyr the followers of Jesus Christ, I could have warned them. They won't fool me this time.

•   •   •   •

Up to a month ago, Ishmael was a devout Muslim. His mother, Gadidja, was dying of a serious strain of diabetes. She had gone into a coma many times. A month ago, it happened again. He was at home at the time. Prophet Elijah reluctantly gave him a few days off to attend to his mother. Ishmael's mother was taken to hospital by ambulance and was immediately connected to a life-support system. Her heart was extremely weak. Very early that Thursday morning Doctor Levin phoned Ishmael. "Ishmael, your mother has taken a turn for the worse. It is only a matter of time now. Please come to the hospital immediately. You can phone your family members once you get here. Time is of the essence."

As he did not want to upset Ishmael, he withheld the information that his mother had died the night before. Doctor Levin decided, *I will tell him once he arrives here at the hospital.* Instead of going straight to the hospital as the doctor requested, Ishmael first phoned his Uncle Cassiem, his mother's eldest brother.

"Uncle Cassiem, Mother's health has taken a turn for the worst. If you want to see her alive then you must come to the hospital immediately. Ask one of the family members to contact the rest of the family," said Ishmael.

While Andrew the overseer of the Jerusalem churches was busy praying early that Thursday morning, the Holy Spirit specifically told him to go to the hospital. In an audible voice, he heard the Holy Spirit say, "Go to the hospital. You shall meet a young man named Ishmael. He is on the third floor at the phone booth around the corner from the intensive care unit. You must raise his deceased mother, Gadidja, from the dead."

Because Andrew had experienced the supernatural workings of the Holy Spirit before, he had no reason to doubt Him. He immediately took a shower, got dressed, said good-bye to his mother and was on his way to the hospital. He was on his last day, of a twenty-one day fast, so he no need of breakfast.

When Ishmael arrived at the hospital, he was just about to phone his *Imam* to inform him of the seriousness of his mother's condition when Andrew approached him. Andrew greeted him with the customary Muslim greeting. "*Salaam,* Ishmael."

Ishmael was amazed that the stranger knew his name. He returned Andrew's greeting with the customary Jewish greeting. "*Shalom!* Stranger!"

Andrew introduced himself to Ishmael and said, "This morning, while I was in prayer, Jehovah God told me to come to the hospital. He told me that I would find you at the phone booth and that I was to pray for your mother, Gadidja."

Ishmael was amazed at Andrew's revelation and that Andrew's God knew his mother's name. Their conversation was abruptly ended when thirty of Ishmael's relatives arrived. Doctor Levin, who Ishmael was to contact on his arrival at the hospital, appeared around the corner, and walked straight to Ishmael. He put his arm around Ishmael's shoulders.

He looked at him and said while addressing the whole family, "I bring you very sad news. Your mother passed away peacefully in her sleep. We did everything that was medically possible, but she was just *too* weak and could not fight the sickness any longer. We have moved your mother's body to a private ward for viewing. Please accept my sincere condolence."

The family was so shocked at the doctor's news that the mournful sound of wailing immediately filled the air. After the doctor had shaken hands with everyone, he excused himself and went back to his office.

Ishmael looked at Andrew, and with a very forlorn expression on his face, he asked, "Can you still pray for mother, or is it too late now?"

Andrew shook his head and replied, "Jesus also arrived *too late* in Bethany, and His friend Lazarus was already dead for four days. That did not stop Him Jesus from raising Lazarus from the dead."

Ishmael, who was a tour guide before he started working for Prophet Elijah, was acquainted with the story of Lazarus, as he had related the story to thousands of tourists many times before.

Then Andrew informed Ishmael, "Jesus told me to raise your mother from the dead."

Ishmael's jaw just fell open when he heard what Andrew said. Confused, Ishmael replied, "But it is senseless to pray for Mother, now that she is *dead*," came, Ishmael's argument.

"Have you forgotten how Jesus raised Lazarus from the dead?"

"But that was over two-thousand years ago, and He's not here, now. How can He raise Mother from the dead?" *What have I gotten myself into?*

"Ishmael, just trust Jesus Christ, with me, and you will see His power."

However, I have one request to make of you. I want only you, your late mother's eldest brother, his wife, your sister, and her husband, and the doctor to go in with me when I pray for your mother."

"Jesus lives in me, and I am filled with His blessed Holy Spirit. I am just following Jehovah's orders. I am one of His ministers on special assignment. Come let us go and tell your family that I am going to pray for your deceased mother."

Ishmael conveyed Andrew's request to his family. His brother Carriem became very outraged and began shouting, "How can you allow this ... this ..." He nearly choked on his own words.

" ... Jewish infidel with the strange mark on his forehead to pray for our deceased mother!?"

His uncle intervened and said, "Please control your temper Carriem! You should know better," his uncle scolded him. "A prayer won't harm anyone, especially someone who is dead."

"Uncle, I'm sorry. Please forgive me."

"Okay, son. It is all behind us now."

They called the doctor, and together they went to the private ward. Doctor Levin and the other family members, except Ishmael, were not ready for what they were about to experience. None of them knew that Andrew was going to raise Gadidja from the dead.

Andrew took his place at the right side at the bead of the bed, and Ishmael and his sister, Miriam, stood next to him. Ishmael's uncle, Cassiem and Hagar, his wife, and Hassan, his brother-in-law stood on the opposite side of the bed. The doctor stood at the foot end of the bed.

Andrew requested that they bow their heads, and he started praying, "Jehovah God, I come to you in the name of your Son, Jesus. I confess before these witnesses that Jesus is the resurrection and the life."

With a more commanding tone in his voice, he said, "Satan! You spirit of death! I command you in Jesus' name. Come out! Let go of Gadidja, right now!"

The doctor opened his eyes. He wanted to rebuke Andrew for making a circus out of the family's sorrow. Just as he was about to open his mouth, Gadidja gasped for breath and opened her eyes. Gadijah's sister-in-law fainted, and Doctor Levin had to summon another doctor to come and take care of her, as he had to give his full attention to Gadidja.

The doctor asked Andrew and those with him to leave the ward, as he wanted to examine Gadidja. When they left the private ward, they were immediately swamped by the rest of the family members, who were still lamenting!. They could not understand why Ishmael, Andrew, and the rest of the family who had come from the bed of the deceased, were in such a joyous mood.

Carriem, asked, "Is this a time for laughter or for mourning?"

Anger was written all over his face. He had completely forgotten the reprimand his uncle had given him.

Ishmael replied, "If you knew what we know, you would also be laughing." Then he said, "Mother is not dead anymore. Jesus has raised her from the dead. Doctor Levin is examining her at this very moment."

Carriem, could not believe what he had just heard. "Stop your tomfoolery at once!" came arriem's outburst of anger. "The doctor said that she was dead." *If Uncle Cassiem wasn't here, I would punch you in the face.* "Mother is dead, and no one can bring her back to life again. Do you hear me?" He burst out crying, and one of his sisters went to console him. "Ask Uncle Cassiem if you do not want to believe me. Here he comes right now."

Through his tears Carriem asked, "Uncle, is mother dead or is she alive?"

His uncle replied, "Carriem! Your mother is very much alive. A miracle took place when Andrew prayed for her."

Right at that moment the doctor made his appearance. Carriem's uncle said, "Here comes the doctor right now. Ask him. He will tell you." *The doctor will calm him down when he hears out of his mouth, that his mother is alive. The poor boy does not know how to handle his mother's death.*

Before Carriem could ask, Doctor Levin said to them, "Your mother is well and alive and is asking for you. Please do not ask her *too* many questions right now. She is tired but well."

Carriem and the rest of the family could not believe their ears as they made their way into the once deceased woman's room.

Doctor Levin said, "Andrew will you please follow me to my office." After he closed the door to his office and after they were seated he said, "Young man, I have experienced many strange happenings in my life as a doctor, but this tops them all. The computer that monitored Gadidja's brain showed on the printout that she had no brain function one hour before it was discovered by the sister on duty that she had died.

"My colleague, who was on night duty, was immediately notified. On his orders, the life-support system was switched off and disconnected. Her body was immediately taken to the hospital mortuary." Doctor Levin went on to say, "I have never heard of a person who was brain dead and frozen solid for over eight hours being resuscitated. What happened here today was indeed a miracle!

"Her family would have buried her today as is the Muslim custom. She was still frozen solid when you prayed for her. It all seemed so easy."

Andrew replied, "I did the easy part and left the difficult part to Jesus." The doctor just smiled. "Early this morning when I prayed, the Holy Spirit told me that I was to come to the hospital and raise Gadidja from the dead.

"I did not tell Ishmael that the Lord told me that his mother was dead. I did not want to upset him, as I already knew then that Jesus would come through for me. He only heard that she had passed away after you mentioned it to the family."

The doctor asked, "What is the meaning of that strange mark on your forehead?"

Andrew smiled and said, "Jehovah's angel sealed 144,000 Israeli followers of Jesus all over the world, and I am one of them. We are Jehovah's servants on special assignment. He is going to send us all over the world."

"Like this morning's assignment when you raised Ishmael's mother from the dead in Jesus' name?" came the doctor's inquiring question.

"Yes, like this morning," came Andrew's humble but assured reply. Then looking intently at the doctor, he said, "Doctor Levin. I know that Jesus has conquered your heart. All you have to do is to surrender to him."

In the privacy of his office, they both knelt on the carpet, and Andrew led him in the prayer of commitment. Another precious soul had come home to the Father. Andrew quietly slipped out, while the doctor was still talking to his heavenly Father and joined the Muslim family in the private ward. Carriem walked straight to Andrew, stuck out his hand in greeting, and then broke down crying.

He embraced Andrew and said, "Please forgive me for my rudeness. I am truly sorry that I called you an infidel. You are not an infidel. You are the servant of the Most High, Jehovah God. Can you find it in your heart to forgive me? You are a true follower of Jesus the Messiah," came, *Carriem's* honest confession.

Andrew replied, "The Lord has already forgiven you over two thousand years ago; accept His forgiveness. I hold nothing against you."

Andrew walked toward the bed and saw Gadidja eating soup and bread. When she saw him coming toward her, she put her spoon on the tray and stretched out her hand to greet him.

Andrew said, "Mother Gadidja! I know that you have a wonderful story to tell us."

She replied in the affirmative. She then started telling them of her experience with death. "I was falling down a very dark tunnel. As I was falling, all my sins flashed before my eyes and I was surrounded by ugly creatures, and I was very much afraid. I knew then that I was on my way to a place of torment.

"Then I saw a man clothed in a pure-white robe approaching me. He was enveloped in a brilliant white light. The demons immediately screamed and fled at the sight of him."

"He said to me, 'Gadidja! I am Jesus the Messiah, the crucified Savior of the world. I conquered death and rose again after three days and three nights. Go back to your family and friends and tell them that I, Jesus, am the only Savior. Tell them my coming is at the door and that it won't be long now.' "Then Jesus vanished, and when I opened my eyes, I saw you and my family standing around my bed."

Doctor Levin, who had quietly entered the room, heard the whole testimony. Ishmael walked around the bed to where Andrew was standing and said to him, "While you were with Doctor Levin we all accepted Jesus as our Savior. We all want to be baptized in the Jordan River, if possible."

To Ishmael's request, Doctor Levin said, "Please count me in. I also want to follow my Lord and Savior all the way."

"We can arrange a baptismal service after our Sunday morning celebration communion service," came Andrew's reply. "You are most welcome to attend our Sabbath Bible study on Saturday morning at ten o'clock."

Andrew told them where the service was going to be held and also what clothing they had to bring along for the baptism. They all promised to bring a friend along.

Andrew was very exhausted when he arrived home that afternoon. He greeted his mother and quickly told her about the miracles Jesus had performed that day. She was overjoyed at the testimonies that he shared with her. Andrew took a hot bath and just relaxed for the rest of the afternoon in the Lord's presence.

That evening at the prayer meeting, The Lord's presence hung like a glory cloud over them. He again anointed them with His Holy Spirit for the tasks and challenges that were still ahead. Afterward, Andrew told them about his experiences of the day, and they all rejoiced in the greatness of Almighty Jehovah and Jesus, His Son, and the blessed Holy Spirit.

After the prayer meeting, they all went to Andrew's home to break their twenty-one day fast with delicious vegetable soup and freshly baked bread. After the believers had left, Andrew went straight to bed. He was very tired and wanted to be rested for the Sabbath Bible study hour the following morning.

The news of the miracle, that Gadidja was raised from the dead, spread like wild fire through the hospital and the Jewish and Muslim communities. Gadidja was released early the following Friday morning. It enabled her to attend the Sabbath Bible study and the celebration and thanksgiving communion service the Sunday morning. The service was followed by lunch and the baptismal service at the Jordan River.

twenty_three
CHAPTER

At Prophet Elijah's penthouse, Ishmael could hear the subdued voices coming from Messiah and Prophet Elijah as he came in with a double Scotch for Messiah and a brandy for Elijah. They immediately stopped their conversation when he entered the room.

After a few refills, Prophet Elijah called out, "Ishmael, come here!" When Ishmael showed up, Prophet Elijah blurted out, "You are free to go home now. Your services are no longer required for the rest of the evening." *I don't want you to be eavesdropping on our conversation.*

Ishmael greeted them very politely and left their presence. He switched off the rest of the lights and hid in the adjoining room where he was able to listen undetected to their conversation.

He heard Messiah clearly say, "The time has come for us to make an example of those stupid followers of Esau, not only in Israel, but in the whole world. I want you to send an encyclical to the Church Universal and inform the bishops and priests to eliminate as many of the followers of Esau as they can lay their hands on as recorded in Revelation 6:8.

When Ishmael heard what they said, he nearly blew his cover. He wanted to cry out, *Stop you devils. You are going to be cast into the lake of fire, burning with brimstone.*

Then he realized that he was not supposed to be listening to their private conversation. He would be jeopardizing his own safety. He would be arrested, and be put in jail and then his plan to warn Andrew and John about the impending danger would not be possible. What Ishmael heard was enough to make him sick. He calmed himself as Messiah continued to explain his master plan to Elijah. "I have decided to make a public display of them three days before Passover."

Confused, Elijah asked, "But why?"

"Passover is a very important high holy day in the lives of Esau's followers! They are under the impression that he died on the cross on that day as their Passover Lamb. That is the reason they celebrate the atonement they believe he had made available to them" *I wish I did not possess the knowledge of who Jesus really is.* He tried to erase the thought from his mind.

"We must persuade them that Esau is a fraud and that I am the true Messiah of Israel and the Savior of the world. We will have to convince them that Mohammed, the great prophet of Islam, had the correct teaching concerning Esau. He did not believe that Esau died on the cross and that He was God's, Son.

"Mohammed believed that he only appeared to be dead and that his disciples revived him in the garden tomb." *That's old news,* thought Elijah. "I have many bishops in the United Kingdom, who for many years now, have rejected the belief in the Virgin birth or the physical resurrection of Esau."

Elijah, who looked as if he was thinking very deeply, said, "Now, I see the logic of your plan, and I agree 100% with you. Your plan is excellent. Why didn't I think of it before?" *Whether you believe it or not does not matter to me in the least,* thought Messiah.

Ishmael said to himself, *Elijah, you are a brainless idiot. You never think for yourself. You allow yourself to be influenced by Antichrist. Your mind is brand new because you never use it. You have been completely taken over by Antichrist.*

Messiah confirmed, "I plan on having two thousand of them killed in Israel alone and many more around the world."

Again confused, Elijah asked, "But why only two-thousand?" *Seeing that there are millions who cannot stand the thought of you.*

Messiah explained the logic behind his decision. "One person is to be killed for every year since the birth of Esau."

To which Elijah exclaimed, "That is excellent! That is brilliant!"

Ishmael just shook his head in dismay. If the situation were not so serious, he would have burst out laughing.

Messiah went on to say, "We are going to take a few believers from every village, town, and city in Israel. I do not want whole families to be taken. I want the survivors to suffer the pain of losing a family member. I want it to be a constant reminder to them that I will not allow them to interfere with my plans.

"We must make sure that they arrest the overseers of the Messianic believers in Israel. I have heard that one lives somewhere in Jerusalem and the other one lives somewhere in Bethlehem. They are the formidable ringleaders. I heard their names are Andrew and John. If we can kill them, I believe the sheep will scatter."

• • • •

Ishmael, who had heard enough, quietly let himself out and went directly to Andrew's home. He felt sick to his stomach. Andrew immediately responded to Ishmael's knock. In the light of the doorway, he looked very pale.

Andrew greeted him. "*Shalom*, my brother. Please come in. You look like someone who is the bearer of bad news. Come take a seat. I am expecting Pastor John. He is on his way here, now. He should be arriving in the next few minutes or so."

They had just sat down when there was a knock on the door. John let himself in, as Andrew had showed him before where the spare key was hidden. He joined the two brothers. They greeted one another, and John sat down.

"Mother made a few flasks of tea and a lot of sandwiches. We are going to be very busy until late tonight. Mother has asked to be excused because she is very tired. She is not that young anymore you know. She does not want to miss a service or a prayer meeting," said John.

Andrew served them tea and sandwiches, and they ate and drank in silence for about fifteen minutes. Ishmael's heart felt very heavy. He just *had* to share the information about Antichrist and the false prophet's plan as soon as possible.

Andrew said to Ishmael, "Please tell us the reason for your coming and take your time. I can see that something has you terribly upset."

With tears streaming down his face, he poured out his heart before them. They felt very sorry for him. When Ishmael was finished telling them what Antichrist had planned, both Andrew and John laid their hands on him and asked Jesus to strengthen him with a fresh anointing of the Holy Spirit. They prayed for strength for the believers for the approaching danger that was awaiting them.

John said to him, "Ishmael, you did the right thing by coming to Brother Andrew."

"Ishmael, it is a miracle that Antichrist and the false prophet have not as yet discovered, that you are a follower of Jesus. Your information is very important to the believers worldwide. You can be likened to the early Christians who, during the time of Imperial Rome, worked in Emperor Caesar's palace, and he was unaware of it," said Andrew. "Thank you very much for responding so quickly with this very vital information."

"Just as Caesar's servants were the ears and the eyes of the underground church, so you are our ears and eyes in Prophet Elijah's penthouse. We shall e-mail and fax the news you brought us tonight to the believers here in Israel and to the churches in North and South America, Africa, Europe, and Asia. They in turn shall contact the leaders in other countries."

John said, "All we can do is to pray and warn our brothers ands sisters and tell them to be very careful and to fast and pray as never before. We are on the last lap of our spiritual journey. The coming of Jesus is at the door. There is no safe place in Israel for the followers of Jesus. Let me rephrase what I have just said, There's no safe place in the world. Only in Jesus Christ is there safety and security, whether, we be dead or alive."

After they had prayed for an hour, they sent e-mails and faxes to the brethren in Israel and around the world. They stayed up until the early hours of the morning. They did not think about

Dudley Fairbairn

sleep until their work was finished in warning the Church of Jesus of the impending danger.

Andrew invited both John and Ishmael to stay overnight, which they gladly accepted. They were too tired to go to their homes. They decided to leave early the next morning after few hours sleep and a nourishing breakfast.

· · · ·

Men and women went to work but never returned home in the evening. Children went to school but never showed up for class and were reported to the authorities. It had become a worldwide phenomenon. It seemed that people were just d*Is*appearing into thin air. Everyday, articles about the d*Is*appearances appeared in the newspapers and was broadcast on national television.

The headlines of one of the newspapers read, "Members of the Christian Sect Have Been Abducted by Unidentified Flying Objects." Another newspaper's headline read, "The So-Called Rapture Has Taken Place."

All over the world, the authorities were being bombarded by anxious family members reporting missing relatives. In Israel alone, 1,999 of Jesus' followers were reported missing.

· · · ·

In the forests of Israel, the zealots were busy making crosses. Their counterparts in other parts of the world were also busy making crosses, not in the forests but in the factories Prophet Elijah had send out the following encyclical to the Bishops in the various countries.

> You must deal very harshly with the followers of Esau. You must send a clear message to the heretics that disobedience is no longer going to be tolerated. If they do not join the Mystery Babylonian Universal Church, they will be killed!

In the city stadium in Jerusalem, zealots posing as municipality workers were busy constructing a very large enclosure, which took up three quarters of the field. The electrified fence was ten feet high. It also had an electrically operated gate.

Five hundred eight inch wide pipes were being planted six feet apart and two feet in the ground around the circumference of the field. The pipes stuck out six inches above the ground.

A curious onlooker asked one of the men, "What is this enclosure for, and why are you planting those pipes?"

A zealot replied, "It's none of your business. Get out of my sight before I lose my temper."

Bundles of wood and huge piles of brushwood were also being off-loaded from huge trucks. It was distributed around the field. Many containers of gasoline were to be seen under a marquee.

Prophet Elijah told the spokesman of the zealots, "I want five-hundred stakes to be dropped into the pipes in the ground. I will make an announcement when it is time for a thousand volunteers from the crowd to tie five hundred heretics to the stakes.

"They must make sure that their hands and feet are well tied. Secondly, they must arrange the brushwood and the wood around the heretics. They must make sure that the wood is well doused with gasoline. Then lastly, the same volunteers must light their torches and set the brushwood on fire."

• • • •

Every thirty minutes the newscasters announced the Roman Games on radio and on television. The newspapers also carried full-page advertisements about the upcoming Roman Games. They made no mention that believers were going to be martyred.

The same events that were being planned for Israel were to be duplicated worldwide, but on a much grander scale.

Four days before the Jewish Passover, the believers who were abducted were taken from their places of incarceration and loaded onto huge trucks like cattle. The two-thousand believers were divided into three groups. Five hundred were earmarked to be burned at the stake. Another five hundred were earmarked to be crucified, and a thousand were to be fed to the lions.

Some of the children were crying and screaming because they

were separated from the strangers with whom they had bonded with during the time of their incarceration. The mature brothers and sisters were comforting those who were overtaken by the fear of the unknown.

Their nightmare had just begun. Grown men were wiping away tears. Women who had children of their own were comforting the little ones and teenagers.

Trucks entered the stadium and drove toward the enclosure. The circumference of the fence was covered with tarpaulins. The trucks backed up toward the entrance of the enclosure and the believers were commanded to disembark.

The trucks drove off after they had unloaded its cargo of human flesh, and the gates closed behind them. It was a cold and clear night, and the believers huddled together to keep warm.

The church leaders and the brothers and sisters who were strong in the faith encouraged those who were in need of encouragement. All through the night, the prayers of the saints could be heard. Then someone would start a song of worship and others would join in on the singing.

They would break forth into spontaneous worship to Jesus, their Savior. The Holy Spirit fell on everyone, and those who were not filled received the Holy Spirit.

• • • •

It was CNM who first beamed the news worldwide that the followers of Jesus were to die as martyrs. The believers were even more adamant that they would rather die for Jesus than join the Mystery Babylonian Universal Church. They refused to bow their knees before the modern religious system of Baal.

In the enclosure, some of the believers were so exhausted that they just fell asleep on the cold and damp grass. Early the next morning the brothers and sisters were seen moving amongst the crowd to give them words of comfort. The believers were all huddled together at the side where the gate was.

The rowdy voices of many could be heard outside on the bleachers of the stadium. They seemed to be in a very joyous mood. They were laughing and cracking jokes, and some were displaying a real frivolous spirit. People came as early as six o'clock to secure a seat for themselves and for their family members and friends. By eight o'clock the stadium was packed to capacity.

Messiah and Prophet Elijah were sitting in the booth reserved only for dignitaries such as the Israeli prime minister and his wife and the ambassadors from the various countries and other VIP's. The Israeli prime minister, his wife, and others close to him, including the Chief Rabbi, chose to boycott the Roman Games.

Instead, they went to a prayer meeting in Bethlehem to pray for strength and courage for their brethren who were to be sacrificed for the wicked ideals of Antichrist and the false prophet.

The crowd did not understand what the enclosure, the piles of brushwood and wood, and the rows of poles encircling the enclosure were for. They would not have to guess for long as the Roman games were scheduled to begin at eight fifteen.

twentyfour

CHAPTER

Pastor Andrew was also arrested by Messiah's thugs. He got the attention of the believers and said, "Beloved! I want you to know that no matter what happens here today, Jesus loves us very much, and He is in full control. 'He who finds his life will lose it, and he who loses his life for My sake will find it' (Matthew 10:39). We are on the verge of losing our lives for Jesus' sake. It is when we lose our lives for His sake, that we will possess it forever." Andrew continued preparing the hearts of the believers for the coming ordeal. "Jesus said, 'Then they will deliver you up to tribulation and kill you, and you will be hated by all nations for My name's sake' (Matthew 24:9)."

Then he quoted another scripture, "'... yes, the time is coming that whoever kills you will think that he offers God service. And these things will they do to you because they have not known the Father nor Me' (John 16: 2–3).

"Beloved we are to prepare our hearts to join our Lord, Jesus Christ, very soon. We are going to be martyred because of our faith in Him. So be ready, my beloved, to lay down your lives for Jesus, He who laid down His life for us."

At this point, many of the believers knelt on the wet grass and through their tears prayed to their heavenly Father. Andrew asked the believers to raise their hands in surrender to Jesus and to personally rededicate their spirit, soul, and body, anew to His divine safekeeping.

Some of the brothers and sisters gathered

the young children and teenagers together and formed a circle around them. Others again gathered the elderly, and they started praying and recommitting their lives anew to Jesus. They asked for His strength in the midst of the approaching and devastating storm.

In the background, the faint roar of lions could be heard. The zealots ran to the fence and let down the tarpaulins. When the crowd saw what the tarpaulins were shielding they went wild with frenzy. When Messiah and Prophet Elijah stood to their feet, a deathly silence descended upon the crowd. When they started applauding the crowd also stood to their feet and started applauding.

Messiah lifted up his hands and made the thumbs down sign, the zealots were waiting for. They immediately ran to the opposite side from where the entrance gate was. They started pulling on a rope from the outside. The gate that was level with the ground opened up, exposing the entrance leading to the holding pen of the lions.

The gate was not visible to the believers inside the enclosure because it was covered with grass. The opening revealed a tunnel that led to where the lions were being held captive in an underground holding pen. The roaring of the lions became louder and louder as they got nearer to the opening.

Then one after another, the lions started jumping out of the tunnel. At first, they appeared to be disoriented. It took them a few minutes to get their bearings, and then the lions headed straight for the believers.

Andrew was the only one present who had Jehovah's seal on his forehead. He and the other leaders of both men and women formed a line of defense between the lions and the followers of Jesus.

Andrew shouted above the noise of the crowd, "Pray, beloved."

The anointing of the Holy Spirit fell on them, and they started praying under the unction of the Holy Spirit. Then a choir of voices broke loose, and they began to sing a beautiful song.

"We are more than conquerors through the blood of Jesus Christ. Through Jesus' name, we are more than conquerors. We are conquerors through His name."

The crowd became very agitated when they heard the believers singing under the anointing of the Holy Spirit. Many of them stuck their fingers in their ears and started slinging obscenities at the martyrs. It was as if an evil spirit from hell had been let loose upon the crowd and they started chanting.

"Kill the heretics. Kill the followers of Esau. Down with Esau and up with Messiah and Prophet Elijah."

They quieted down when the first batch of lions started running toward the believers who were singing. Then a second batch of lions followed them. The moment the first lion pounced on its prey, Messiah and Prophet Elijah stood to their feet and started applauding. Soon after, everyone was on their feet egging on the lions.

The majority of those who were present were secular Jews from the former Russian Republics. When the Reformed and Orthodox Jews saw what was taking place, they loudly raised their protests. They stomped their feet to shake the dust off their shoes and left the stadium in disgust.

The lions pounced on their prey inflicting great pain and mutilation and in the end death to their victims. The cries of men, women, and children, overcome by fear, filled the air. Many of them started running blindly in different directions.

Groans could be heard all over the enclosure from the wounded and the dying. Many were in a serious condition and death was imminent.

An elderly woman was lying across a corpse. She saw Jesus kneeling at her side, and for a moment, her eyes lit up, and she died with a smile on her face. Jesus revealed Himself to each and every one of them in their dying hour. Some of the believers saw heaven opening up to them, and angels appeared unto them.

In most cases, death came instantaneously. Prayers and songs of worship still filled the air. Dead bodies were sprawled all over the enclosure. Some of the lions were seen dragging their prey to a more secluded place where they could devour it without being disturbed by the other lions.

A lion slouched toward Andrew, and as it pounced, Andrew lifted up his finger and pointed toward the lion that was coming his way. The lion that was in mid-air dropped to the ground as if it were full of lead.

It made whimpering sounds as if in pain and slunk off to join the other lions. Andrew walked across the field filled with mutilated bodies and knelt beside a brother from the fellowship in Jerusalem. He was barely alive.

He looked up into his pastor's face and his lips formed the words, "Please take care of my wife and children."

"With Jehovah's help, we will do all that we can to take care of them." It was as if he was just waiting on Andrew's assurance. Then his lips formed the words, 'Thank you,' then he died in his pastor's arms.

Right through the terrible ordeal the believers were going through, the crowd applauded. Every time someone was brought down by a lion they shouted their approval. The maddening crowd enjoyed every minute of the spectator sport.

When Andrew looked at the carnage of human suffering and degradation, a verse came to his recollection.

I saw the woman, drunk with the blood of the saints and with the martyrs of Jesus.

Revelation 17:6

Andrew said, "Jesus! Am I better than these who have paid the ultimate price? No! I am not better than any of these, my brothers and sisters. You said, 'Do not fear any of those things which you are about to suffer ... Be faithful unto death, and I will give you the crown of life ... And they overcame him [Satan] by the blood of the Lamb and by the word of [God in] their testimony, and they did not love their lives to the death' (Revelation 2:10, 12:11).

"Heavenly Father, You have given them the crown of life. They are better off than we who are still alive. Jesus, let your perfect will be done in my life. And when my time comes, help me to be faithful unto death or faithful until You come to *rapture* us."

. . . .

Messiah pointed at the man in the lion's enclosure. He said to Prophet Elijah, "There is still one man standing on his feet." *How is it possible? They should all be dead by now.* Then, the man d*Is*appeared before their very eyes. The spectators who were concentrating on the enclosure also witnessed as the man d*Is*appeared before their eyes. Messiah just scratched his head and said, "What a let down."

Prophet Elijah, was just as d*Is*appointed, and thought, *I would give a generous reward just to know who that man was.*

Soon, trucks carrying another five hundred believers drove onto the field. Men, women, and children were commanded to get off the trucks. Some were able to jump off the trucks. The elderly and the young children were assisted by brothers and sisters. No sooner had they alighted when they were forcibly dragged to the poles that were planted in the ground.

Prophet Elijah took his place behind the lectern, took the microphone, and announced, "For now, I want two hundred volunteers to help tie these deluded Christians to the poles and arrange the firewood around them." Although the services of only two hundred were required, a few thousand volunteers stood to their feet. "For the last item on the program, the services of more of you will be needed. If I tell you now what it is going to be, I will spoil the fun for you."

A few of the zealots selected men and women who were not *too* drunk, to give a helping hand. The awful presence of Satan could be sensed in the atmosphere. Some of the believers were screaming for help while others again were rebuking their persecutors in the name of Jesus.

Those who apprehended the believers kicked and beat them into submission because they resisted.

The believers called on the name of Jesus with the last bit of strength they had left. Messiah announced over the public address system, "You can call on the name of Esau all you want.

He cannot save you now. He could not even save himself when he was hanging on the cross." *What a stupid thing for me to say. I am not supposed to believe that He died on the cross. I hope they did not did catch on.* "Your salvation does not lie with him but with me. I am your Messiah, and I am your savior." Pointing to Elijah, he shouted, "and Prophet Elijah is your Pontiff. If you renounce your faith in Esau, then I shall be willing to pardon you!"

One brother shouted, "You can wait until hell freezes over. None of us shall recant." A zealot near to him hit him over the head with a baton. The spectators who saw it shouted for joy.

The volunteers quickly tied the hands and feet of the believers to the stakes. Some of them were still putting up a resistance. Because of fear, cries of anguish were still rending the air, but still no one asked to be, pardoned.

Some were still praying and singing, much to the dismay of their persecutors. Those who were helping the zealots, placed brushwood and wood around those who were tied to the stakes. Others were busy dousing the wood with gasoline. Some even went overboard and doused the believers as well.

Prophet Elijah stood up again and the crowd stood up with him. A number of the volunteers had already lit their torches, which had been dipped in gasoline. The torches were made of broomsticks with hemp tied to one end of the broomsticks.

The crowd went mad with excitement when the prophet took the microphone and shouted to them to set the brushwood on fire. The volunteers jumped to the occasion and did as they were, commanded. The moment the flames touched the gasoline-soaked brushwood, the flames leapt high into the air.

The horrifying screams of the martyr's filled the air. The screaming and the groans were unbearable. To people who were inflicting such awful pain on others, it sounded like music to their ears. Although a half an hour had passed, some of the believers were still alive. Eager hands quickly placed fresh brushwood and wood around the martyrs.

Again, copious amounts of gasoline was poured onto the believers from a distance. A can containing some gasoline, which slipped out of a man's hand, fell onto the hot embers and exploded.

It scared some of the volunteers but not enough to make them want to stop. They were on a high, and they wanted to maintain it to the very last minute.

They wanted their Messiah and Prophet Elijah to be proud of them. To a great number of Jehovah's children, death came very quickly. Others were still suffering and praying until death came as a friend to deliver them.

One brother said through his pain and agony, "I know that very soon I shall be with Jesus, my Savior, but where are you going should you die right now?"

The people who watched him burn became angry at what he had said. One woman said to the man next to her, "Quick! Bring me two full cans of gasoline. I will teach this stupid Christian a lesson not to mess with me."

The man came, running back with the cans of gasoline. They stood a safe distance away, or so they thought. Some of those standing nearby started running away from them.

They flung the cans of gasoline onto the fire. A *tremendous* explosion shook the stadium. The spectators were in shock. People jumped up from their seats, wanting to run away. Prophet Elijah grabbed the microphone and shouted to the volunteers, "Be careful. Do you want to blow us all up?"

There was no sign of the brother and numerous others who were tied to the stakes on either side of him. Their bodies had been ripped to pieces by the explosion. The explosion blew the burning cans against the heads of the man and woman who threw the cans, and they died instantly on impact.

Although the devil's show had gone on for hours, the carnage was not yet over. Prophet Elijah called on volunteers to remove the partially burnt bodies and the burnt-out stakes to make room for the last item on the program.

No respect was shown to the remains of the martyrs. They simply scooped up the remains and threw it onto a huge pile of brushwood and thick logs. Copious amounts of gasoline were poured over what was left of the bodies and set alight.

The flames leapt thirty meters into the air, and at the sight of the bonfire, the crowd again went wild with frenzy. People started running onto the field and started dancing around the pyre. They were in a very ecstatic mood.

Others again were unfazed at what was going on and were enjoying their hamburgers, sandwiches, and fruit. The fires had been burning for hours now caused palls of black smoke to hang over the city of Jerusalem. The awful smell of burnt human flesh and hair hung in the air, causing those with weak stomachs to get sick.

• • • •

Another convoy of trucks pulled up, and immediately the zealots and the volunteers started dragging the unsuspecting victims to the crosses that had been laid out by the open-ended pipes sticking six inches out of the ground.

Zealots were standing ready with hammers and leather bags containing nails, which were fastened around their waists. The believers who were resisting were dragged kicking and screaming to the crosses.

With brute force, eager helpers helped to pin them down. Their hands and their feet were held into place while one zealot nailed the hands, and the other nailed the feet to the upright beam. Because of the tremendous pain, many of the believers went into shock.

Many fainted and remained comatose until the crucifixion was complete. Others again remained lucid throughout the whole ordeal. Others died without regaining consciousness, which to many a spectator was a let down. They wanted to hear the believers scream and plead for mercy.

One sister cried out, "Jesus! Into Your hands I commit my spirit."

A brother cried out, "Thank You, Jesus, for allowing me, a sinner saved by grace, to experience a death similar to Yours. You were sinless when You died for me. Amen!" He died soon after when a zealot stuck a dagger into his heart.

He said to his comrade, "He wanted to emulate Esau in his death. All he needed was a wound in his side, so I helped him to fulfill his dream. All he still need is a crown of thorns," and they both burst out laughing.

After the martyrs were nailed to the crosses, the volunteers lifted up the crosses and dropped them into the holes. With every cross that was planted the spectators started chanting.

"Crucify the infidels! Crucify the heretics! Crucify the infidels! Crucify the heretics!"

Prophet Elijah took the microphone and said, "They deserve to die because they insulted Messiah by calling him the Antichrist and by calling me the false prophet." *It deflated my ego and hurt me very much*, he thought.

The people stood to their feet and a thunderous applause reverberated around the stadium. It was not clear whether they were applauding because the Christians were dying or because the *heretics* called Messiah the Antichrist and Elijah the false prophet. They just applauded at the wrong moment. Because of the many zealots and the volunteers the proceedings went off "smoothly and without a hitch" to use Elijah's exact words.

A number of the martyrs were still alive when the undisciplined mob dispersed to go home.

The handlers, armed with whips and stun rods, coached the lions back into the underground holding pen. The lions were loaded onto special trucks and taken to the City Zoo where they would to be taken good care of until their services were needed again for the next Roman Games.

Under the glare of the floodlights, the enclosure was quickly dismantled by the well-paid zealots. The corpses and the limbs that were lying on the field were completely ignored.

twenty_five

CHAPTER

When Brother Andrew was *raptured*, the Holy Spirit transported him straight to the prayer meeting in Bethlehem. He told them what had happened in the enclosure. After the prayer meeting, they made plans to dig a communal grave at the cemetery the following day.

An Orthodox Jew who was sympathetic toward the cause of the Messianic believers volunteered to dig the grave for free with his tractor loader backhoe.

Very early the next morning, the believers came with trucks to remove the bodies off the crosses. The sounds of lamenting filled the air as brothers and sisters cried unashamedly when they saw the carnage at the stadium. It was heartrending to see the followers of Jesus cradling their deceased family members in their arms.

A mother was reunited with her baby boy who had escaped certain death because he was shielded by two bodies. Together the believers cleared the field of mutilated bodies and limbs. Some of the bodies only had bite wounds around the neck area.

The blood and the ashes were also scooped up, put into bags, and loaded with the corpses onto the trucks. That very same morning, just before dawn, the men were already at the cemetery. The Orthodox Jew who promised to dig the grave with his backhoe was nearly finished digging the long trench.

One thousand six hundred and ninety-eight

martyrs were to be buried in that trench. Three hundred of the martyrs were burned to ashes. Of the two thousand who were kidnapped, only Pastor Andrew and the baby boy named Daniel escaped martyrdom.

Andrew said, "We are now experiencing how the first century followers of Jesus felt when their families were burnt at the stake, crucified, and fed to the lions." All the believers could do was nod. They were *too* overcome with emotion.

Because there was not enough time to make coffins, the bodies were wrapped in white sheets and laid next to one another in the trench. They first laid the women and children to rest then the men. Because of the difficulty that it presented to know what limbs belonged to what body, the limbs were wrapped individually in smaller pieces of white cloth. The ashes of the believers were also buried.

Although the funeral was not advertised, thousands of believers and sympathizers from all over Israel showed up. The martyrdom of their brothers and sisters made the followers of Jesus even more determined to serve Him, no matter what hardships were still come their way.

Brother John prayed, "Dear heavenly Father, our hearts are heavy at the loss of those who were so dear to us. We, however, have the hope that we shall see our loved ones again in the very near future. Comfort everyone who mourns the loss of a family member or friend in Christ.

"Please strengthen us in our faith that when our time comes to be imprisoned or martyred, should You so choose, please give us the strength *not* to deny You. Dear Lord, please let death come quickly. I ask this in the name of Jesus, Your Son. Amen!" John took his handkerchief and wiped his brow. Looking over those present, he said, "Pastor Andrew will take over from here."

"Beloved, the coming of Jesus is at the door. We have already experienced over two and a half years of tribulation. Millions of our brothers and sisters worldwide have died as martyrs. They have remained faithful unto death, and they shall receive the martyr's crown.

"Please read Revelation 6:9–11 when you get home. John

recorded that when Jesus opened the fifth seal, he saw under the altar the souls of those who were slain for the word of God and for the testimony, which they held. The souls cried out with a loud voice. They wanted to know when the Lord, the holy and true was going to judge and avenge their blood on those who dwell on the earth. A white robe was given to each one of them and they were encouraged to be patient a little longer, until the number of their fellow servants and brethren, who would be killed as they were, was completed.

"We see that these souls were encouraged to be patient until the rest of their fellow servants had also been martyred. Only when their number was full would Jehovah pour out His vengeance upon the perpetrators who were responsible for killing the followers of Jesus Christ. Until then we must remain faithful to Him and win souls for Him with the time that is left." *With every passing day, we are getting closer to Jesus' coming,* he thought.

"Jesus said, 'And this gospel of the kingdom will be preached in all the world as a witness to all nations, and then the end [of the Church-age] will come' (Matthew 24:14).

"The *rapture* of the redeemed brings the Church-age and the Great Commission given by Jesus to His disciples, including us, to a conclusion on earth. We must not allow the death of our beloved brothers and sisters to stop us in our tracks from serving our Savior. Antichrist and the false prophet want to scare us into submission." As the air was very stifling, Andrew asked Hannah to fetch him a jug of lemon juice. "I want to make a bold declaration of faith on behalf of Jesus' worldwide Church. A billion Antichrists and a billion false prophets are not able to stop us from fulfilling the Great Commission Jesus had entrusted unto us. We are going to preach Jesus, until either death or the *rapture* overtakes us.

"Beloved! When Jesus died on the cross, the curse was destroyed. It became a reality for us when we accepted Him as our Savior. After confessing and forsaking our sins, we must make a public confession of our faith. We must identify ourselves with His death, burial, and resurrection through baptism by immersion according to the Apostle Paul's revelation in Romans 6:3.

"Paul said that as many of us who were baptized into Christ Jesus were baptized into His death. Through the act of baptism, we were baptized into Jesus' death. The same way as He was raised from the dead by the glory of the Father, we too shall be raised by the glory of the Father. We should then walk in the newness of life. We should walk in our Savior's footsteps.

Sarah placed a jug containing lemon juice with two glasses on a small table next to the lectern. She filled one glass and handed it to John, which he gladly accepted.

"The reason the religious world hates us is because the name of Jesus was spoken over us when we were baptized. We are legally called by His name. Their hatred is so strong that they are driven to murdering Jesus' followers.

"Why are they so vengeful against us, because we are associated with His name? They hate us because we have put on Christ—because we were baptized in the name of the *Triune* God. Paul said, 'But put on the Lord Jesus Christ, and make no provision for the flesh, to *fulfill* its lusts' (Romans 13:14). 'For as many of you as were baptized into Christ have put on Christ' (Galatians 3:27).

"We have been made righteous through the blood that Jesus shed for us, and we have been clothed with His righteousness. Our hearts go out to those who have lost loved ones. But we shall see them again when we are caught up to meet Jesus in the air. And that day is not in the distant future. The signs of the times that we have already experienced are evidence enough that Jesus' coming is in the very near future."

Brother John took over from Andrew. "Dearly beloved, I am not telling you that serving Jesus, is easy. On the contrary, it could cost you your life as you see here before you this very day. One thousand nine hundred and ninety-eight of our brothers and sisters were brutally murdered yesterday with the full sanction of Antichrist and the false prophet.

"With heavy hearts but with the full knowledge that Jesus died for us as our Passover Lamb, we can prepare for the Passover which is the day after tomorrow." John then addressed the unsaved and said, "If you want to accept Jesus as your Savior in spite of the risk to your life, your family, and property, please raise your hand."

Like all the previous funerals of the martyrs in Israel and around the world, thousands accepted Jesus as their Savior. This time John did not lead them into a prayer of commitment. He asked the bereaved family members to pray and counsel individually with the new converts. While they were busy ministering to the new converts, their minds were taken off their own sorrows, and it also brought healing to their own hearts.

Their hearts were filled with joy and gladness for being responsible for introducing lost souls to the Savior, who hates sin, but loves the sinner. They shared with the new converts that their salvation was only to be found in Jesus, and that He is the only one who was able to deliver them from the bondages of sin.

Afterward, thousands of New Testaments and tracts were distributed amongst the new converts. It contained scriptural information that a change in lifestyle must now follow their conversion. They were now a new creation in Christ Jesus, and therefore, they must abstain from every form of evil.

The writer of the tract admonished them to pray and to make Bible reading a daily part of their spiritual diet. They were also encouraged to become part of one of the thousands of fellowships across Israel and that they had to share their faith with others. The Chief Rabbi, also a follower of Jesus, announced the benediction.

Andrew, John, and a number of the brothers stayed behind at the cemetery after everyone had returned home. They stayed behind to assist the Orthodox Jew who was so kind and generous to dig the long trench with his backhoe. In no time, the long trench was filled with sand.

While they were on their way home, John said, "Yesterday the kingdom of Jehovah, our God, became richer and not poorer because His children had paid the ultimate price because they refused to deny their faith in Jesus."

Andrew responded with, "The blood of the martyrs is truly the seed of the Church of Jesus, our Lord," *It has really taken on new meaning for me.*

twenty_six
CHAPTER

John invited the pastors to Haifa to Bethlehem to discuss with them the sounding of the second trumpet. As time was of the essence, he greeted them and opened in prayer and he started ministering right away.

"Beloved, I want to bring two verses from the book of Revelation to your attention in order that you may warn the flock of Jesus before it happens. Here follows the two verses. "Then the second angel sounded: And *something* like a great mountain burning with fire was thrown into the sea, and a third of the sea became blood. And a third of the living creatures in the sea died, and a third of the ships were destroyed" (Revelation 8:8–9).

Beloved a great destruction is on the way according to God's word. It is nearly time for the second angel to sound his trumpet. However, do not be alarmed because God, our heavenly Father, will take care of us. The trumpet judgments are only aimed at the ungodly. So stay close to Jesus. He alone is our eternal salvation. The coming of Jesus, to *rapture* us, is nearer than we think!

He ministered for about an hour and opened up the service for discussion. Interesting questions were raised, and answers were given straight from the Bible. John said, "Please pass this teaching on to your congregations and contact the brethren abroad. May our heavenly Father, bless and keep you safe and secure until we meet again." He asked one of the mothers who prepared refreshments for them to close in prayer.

The Appearance

Soon after, John warned the believers that people from various parts of the world claimed to have seen the second angel blowing his trumpet. When they contacted the authorities, they were ridiculed. They were told that they were lunatics and that angels did not exist. They were accused of causing consternation amongst the populations of the world.

The very same people who accused the followers of Jesus of being lunatics were themselves Satan-worshippers. The same day Central News Makers, Americas most prestigious Television Broadcasting Network, brought this breaking news. The newscaster said, "NASA's telescope, in the Nevada Desert, picked up a meteor of astronomical proportions. It is heading straight for planet earth.

"There is no hope of it breaking up while traveling through the earth's atmosphere or changing its course. It is heading straight for the Atlantic Ocean. Scientists are predicting that it could cause a tsunami with waves of one a mile high. It was going to plunge between the continents of Africa and South America.

"At this very moment, governments on both continents are busy evacuating millions of their citizens to higher ground. Help has been called in from the United Nations. The thing that is baffling to the scientists is; why did it take so long for the Hubbell Telescope, which is in constant surveillance of our universe, to pick it up?

"It snuck past without being detected, which in itself is a great impossibility because of the vastness of the meteor, which appears to be as big as a mountain."

While the newscaster was busy talking, consternation broke out in the vast studio of CNM. People were running in and out and talking loudly, leaving the impression that something was terribly wrong. Someone handed the newscaster a note. It seemed as if all blood drained from his face when he read the note.

While looking pale and nervous the newscaster said, "We just received very, very upsetting news from the desk of NASA's headquarters. They just received satellite photos. The coasts of Africa and South America have sunk into the ocean. Cities and towns along the coastline have been completely obliterated. Hundreds of millions of people have drowned. There is devastation as far as the eye can see."

The camera zoomed in and focused on a very renowned British scientist. He said, "Fifteen minutes ago, I was an atheist. I used to make fun of the flood of Noah, and I used to argue that the Bible was a myth. Viewing the film has made a believer out of me. I want to make an open confession of faith. I have accepted Jesus Christ as my personal Savior." His face was beaming with peace.

He still wanted to say something more when the screen went blank for a few seconds as they cut him off. Live pictures were now in focus showing the sea had turned the color of blood.

Because there was something wrong with the newscaster's earphone, they handed him another note. "As you can see, a strange phenomenon has occurred. A third of the seas have turned into the color of blood. It is having a deathly effect on the marine life. Multiplied millions of sea creatures have died, even hundreds of miles from epicenter where the meteor had fallen into the ocean. Millions of carcasses are being washed inland.

"The incredible heat the burning meteor had generated when it traveled through earth's atmosphere caused devastating electrical and windstorms. What the monstrous waves caused by the tsunami did not destroy, was destroyed by windstorms from up to one-thousand miles an hour.

He received another brief, which he immediately read. "The fishing industries in many parts of the world have been completely decimated. They will have to declare bankruptcy because a third of their fishing fleet was destroyed. Some of the boats and ships were washed up more than a thousand miles inland, and the waves are still dangerously high. There is still no signs of it abating.

"OPEC's oil tankers have also taken a terrible beating. They alone have lost three quarters of their fleet. The boisterous waves have snapped the tankers like twigs spilling its precious cargo and adding even more devastation to the already battered and fragile ecology. We shall keep you posted." and he signed off with, "God bless you."

A greeting, that had been banned by the Mystery Babylonian Universal Church because it made people who did not believe in a personal God feel uncomfortable.

• • • •

Brother Andrew sent an e-mail message to leaders of the house-fellowships in Israel and around the world.

Brothers and sisters I want to inform you what to expect next on Jehovah God's agenda. The third angel is soon going to blow his trumpet.

It is written, "Then the third angel sounded: And a great star fell from heaven, burning like a torch, and it fell on a third of the rivers and on the springs of water. The name of the star is Wormwood. A third of the waters became wormwood, and many men died from the water, because it was made bitter" (Revelation 8:10).

However, we do not need to be alarmed. In Exodus 12:22–24, Jehovah made the bitter water sweet. The same way He shall sweeten the bitter and poisonous water for us. Jesus declared, " …and if they drink any deadly thing [not on purpose], it will by no means hurt them" (Mark 16:18b).

We must have faith in the Lord's divine protection, and we must believe in His unfailing promises. The same way our Heavenly Father is supplying us with food by performing miracles in our food cupboards and deep freezers, so is He able to supply us with water until the three and a half years of tribulation comes to an end. We must continue sharing our food with the less fortunate.

In the same way, our God expects us to share our water with the thirsty. But at the same time, we must see it as an opportunity to witness to them and win them for Jesus. The waters that shall be available to us shall also be poisonous, but we must pray over it in Jesus' name, and He shall make it fit for human and animal consumption.

We can take heart from the Psalmist David. He said, "I have been young, and *now* I am old; Yet I have not seen the righteous forsaken, Nor his descendants begging bread. *He* is ever merciful, and lends; And his descendants *are* blessed" (Psalm 37:25–26).

We must keep our part of the bargain. With the help of the Holy Spirit, we must live righteously before our God, then we can freely avail ourselves of His benefits and blessings. We shall never lack when we follow Jehovah's principals of giving. As we share our bread and water with the unsaved, we must also share the Living Bread and the Living Water with them. How can we claim to be born again and not have the desire to win the lost for God's kingdom?

"If your enemy is hungry, give him bread to eat; And if he is thirsty, give him water to drink; For *so* you will heap coals of fire on his head, And the LORD will reward you" (Proverbs 25:21–22).

The greatest reward is to see souls saved and delivered from sin, and in return, our Heavenly Father will reward us. We are not working for our salvation. We are working for our God, because we are already saved!

I remain,

Your Brother in tribulation,

Andrew

Not long after Andrew sent the e-mail to the pastors, the third angel blew his trumpet.

• • • •

People from across the Islands of Indonesia reported to seeing the third angel. They also claim to have heard the sound of the trumpet. NASA reported that their telescope had picked up a huge meteor, which exploded when it made contact with the earth's atmosphere.

Reports were pouring in at the head office of the Environmental Affairs of the United Nations that a third of the earth's rivers and fountains have been affected by a toxic substance making the waters unfit for human and animal consumption. Reports were coming in from all over the globe of hundreds of thousands of people who died when they drank the bitter-tasting water.

The governments instructed their citizens that they should drink bottled water or fruit juices. The countries who escaped the showers of toxic debris were exporting millions of bottles of bottled water.

Supermarkets and shops were making a roaring trade. Racketeers were selling the most precious commodity on the blackmarket. Demonstrations and riots broke out between police and citizens of the countries where the waters had been poisoned. Supermarkets and shops were being looted.

Things were so bad in many countries that the help of their armies had to be called in to restore law and order. The soldiers had received orders to shoot the looters on sight. Men, women, and children who were shot dead still clutching their stolen loot. The businesses had received governmental orders to ration their stocks of water and other beverages.

twenty_seven

CHAPTER

Early the Monday morning, soon after the third angel blew his trumpet, Brother Andrew received an e-mail from a representative of CNM.

> This is from the desk of CNM, United States of America. We would like to interview you and John on our International Network for a live broadcast on our Thursday, 10:00 a.m. program.
> From our intelligence agents, we have heard that you are the number one enemy of Messiah and Prophet Elijah. You are also on the "most wanted list" of the United Nations. That is if they can catch you. Please reply immediately. You can reach us at cnm.com.
> Andrew jumped up and started shouting and swirling around, "Hallelujah. Praise the Lord. Thank you, Jesus. Thank you. Thank you. Thank you." He acted like a little boy who received his first chocolate.

Andrew immediately contacted John and informed him of the invitation. They got together for prayer that evening to get direction from the Holy Spirit.

"I have the conviction of the Holy Spirit that we should go to America and state the case for all those who believe in Jesus. I know that the American Government, or any other government for that matter, cannot do anything for us because they are also under Antichrist's dominance and part of the New World Order," said John.

"It will afford us the opportunity to preach the gospel to the ends of the earth," came Andrew's response.

Andrew's mother, who knew nothing about the invitation, shared with them that while she was praying in her bedroom the Lord impressed upon her heart to tell them to confirm the invitation. She said that God's Spirit will be upon them and that He will transport them there and back.

They immediately sent an e-mail confirming that they had accepted CNM's invitation and that they planned on being at the CNM's studio for their 10:00 a.m. appointment on Thursday, God willing.

When the chief programmer of CNM read the e-mail, he was wondrously surprised. He did not expect John and Andrew to accept the invitation. He thought, *What a scoop it would be for CNM to have them come to America.*

John and Andrew immediately e-mailed the believers nationally, and internationally requesting them to fast and pray the whole of Thursday, and they should bear in mind the difference in time.

After CNM had received their response, they immediately e-mailed Andrew and John again informing them to be at the CNM headquarters a half an hour before the scheduled time. That Thursday morning, CNM's crew was ready for action.

Neville Sash, who was going to interview them, was sweating under his collar as the chauffeur had returned from the airport without the guests.

The lady at the information desk told him that all the flights from Israel had landed, but there were no persons registered under the names of John Weisman and Andrew Levinson.

At the studio, three chairs were in place on the platform. Neville took his seat with only 30 seconds left before the program was to be aired, and yet there was no sign of either Andrew or John. Should the two Israeli guests not show up, then they would have to air a prerecorded interview.

• • • •

Only thirty seconds were left before they had to go on the air.

Suddenly, two men materialized in the two chairs facing Neville. His eyes nearly popped out of his head from fright, and the countdown immediately began.

Neville who was so confused asked them, "Did you come by airplane?"

"No. We came by plain air," came John's witty reply.

Neville quickly regained his composure as the camera zoomed in on him. "We bring you this breaking news. Believe it or not, these two men just materialized in front of our very eyes." While Neville was in focus, one of the staff quickly pinned on Andrew's and John's lapel microphones. "One moment they were not here, and the next moment they were sitting opposite me." One cameraman caught the materialization of the two men on film. *It reminds me of the space movie I saw when I was a teenager, where people just dIsappeared and then reappeared,* he thought to himself.

Because Neville did not know who was who, he allowed them to introduce themselves. He pointed to Andrew and said, "Tell our worldwide audience who you are."

Pointing to John, he said, "This is my colleague John, and I am Andrew."

Neville looked at their foreheads and asked, "What does that mark on your forehead signify?"

Andrew replied, "We were sealed by Jehovah's angel, and we are His ministers on special assignment."

Neville, who is always in control of any situation, looked somewhat confused.

John came to his rescue and said, "The Lord God, picked us up in Jerusalem at my home at 0900 hours, 59 minutes, and 30 seconds, Eastern standard time, and put us in these chairs 59 minutes and 30 seconds past nine o'clock. When the Lord is in control, there is no delay in time. You may ask us anything that is of interest to your worldwide audience."

While talking, Andrew opened his Bible, and without asking permission, he started reading a few verses. "In the Book of Acts, Philip had a similar experience. He was physically transported to Azotus in Israel (Acts 8:39–40)."

"We are living in the end of days. We are living in the age of the blessed Holy Spirit who is preparing a Bride for Jesus Christ the Lord. All the signs that planet earth is experiencing is written in God's Holy Word. We are Jehovah God's ministers on special assignment.

"We bare witness to the resurrection of our Lord Jesus Christ. God is going to destroy the Mystery Babylonian Universal Church which who has robbed billions of people from ever discovering that Jesus is the Son of God and the only Savior.

Andrew continued, "He is the only hope for the world and the *only* Savior who has the power to deliver from sin. Only He can forgive those who have repented and broken with their sin. The Antichrist, whom the world claims to be the Messiah, and the false prophet are going to be thrown into the lake of fire with all those who worship Satan.

"Everyone connected to the Mystery Babylonian Universal Church shall have their part in the lake of fire. You must repent and turn away from your sins and idolatry and accept Jesus as your Savior. There is no substitute for the Lord Jesus Christ. He is the world's only hope.

"The priests of the Babylonian Church have deceived the masses by way of spiritual deception and spiritual witchcraft. The governments and the nations of the world stand condemned before the Sovereign and Holy Lord. They are responsible for sanctioning the martyrdom of Jesus Christ's followers.

"They stand guilty before the Lord God because the followers of Jesus are being burnt at the stake, crucified, fed to lions, drowned, and poisoned." Pain was etched out on Andrew's face as he addressed the worldwide audience. He took a sip of iced water.

"The possessions and church properties of the followers of Jesus are being confiscated and the money donated to the fund of the Mystery Babylonian Universal Church for the advancement of witchcraft, Satanism, and the paranormal."

John took over and said, "The rot and decay, which is happening in organized religion, is prophesied in the Bible. I just want to paraphrase what Paul wrote in 1Timothy 4:1–3, He said, "That the Holy Spirit made it very clear that in the last days some will depart from faith in the Lord Jesus Christ. They will embrace and surrender to seducing spirits and doctrines of demons. Propagating lies will be second nature to them. They will have no remorse and they will twist the scriptures to their own destruction. Their conscience is dead concerning spiritual things. They forbid marriage which God has ordained, and they forbid certain foods which God had created to be to eaten with thanksgiving for those who believe the truth."

John and Andrew then took time to extensively explain the false doctrines of the Mystery Babylonian universal Church.

When they were finished Neville said, "I found your explanations to be very interesting and I hope the worldwide audience have found it as interesting as I."

Andrew continued by making an appeal to the billions watching, "By your association with the false church, a great number of you have made yourself guilty of transgressing numerous of God's laws. Many of you are guilty of stealing that which belonged to the followers of Jesus.

Repent and forsake your evil lifestyles. Accept the Lord Jesus Christ as your personal Savior. DIsassociate yourselves from the false church.

"This appeal is also to you who are followers of religions that deny that Jesus is the divine Son of God and who deny that Jesus was crucified, that He shed His blood for the remission of sins, and that He rose again from the dead! Accept the Lord Jesus Christ, and you shall be saved from eternal damnation. God is going to destroy the false religious system.

Therefore her plagues will come in one day—death and mourning and famine. And she will be utterly burnt with fire, for strong *is* the Lord God who judges her," No matter how hard she may try to deny or resist the truths of the Bible, the truth shall always triumph.

Revelation 18:8

For we can do nothing against the truth, but for the truth.

2 Corinthians 13:8

"Since the signing of the false covenant of peace, innumerable numbers of our brothers and sisters worldwide, have been put to death because they refused to have any part or parcel of the Mystery Babylonian Universal Church.

"The slaughter and martyrdom has not stopped yet. Only the coming of Jesus to *rapture* the redeemed will bring an end to the three and a half years of tribulation. In spite of the horrendous acts being perpetuated against us, the blessed Holy Spirit is very active on planet earth. Multiplied millions are being born again into God's kingdom."

Andrew gave John a sign to take over from him, and he flowed with the same anointing. "If it were not for the blessed Holy Spirit and the promise Christ Jesus made to us, we His Church, would have been annihilated long ago. Jesus said, '... I will build My church, and the gates of Hades shall not prevail against it' (Matthew 16:18b).

"I prophesy that multiplied millions are still going to come to salvation before the seventh angel blows the trumpet which is connected with a mystery. Christ gave divine revelation to the apostles John and Paul. John recorded that the seventh angel is going to blow the seventh trumpet, which is connected with a mystery.

"The apostle said, 'Behold I tell you a mystery: We shall not all sleep, but we shall all be changed—in a moment, in a twinkling of an eye, at the last trumpet. For the trumpet will sound, and the dead will be raised incorruptible, and we shall be changed' (1 Corinthians 15:51–52).

"John wrote, '... but in the days of the sounding of the seventh angel, when he is about to sound, the mystery of God would be finished, as He declared to His servants the prophets' (Revelation 10:7).

Andrew who took over from John and said, "Children of the Lord God, if you are listening to this program, listen very carefully. What I am going to say to you now is of utmost importance. Rather choose death at the hands of the enemies of Jesus. Whatever you do, *please* do not deny the Lord Jesus Christ who bought you with His precious blood.

"Should we die before the *rapture* overtakes us, then Jesus will raise us up when the seventh angel blows the last trumpet. It happens when the ministry of the two prophets comes to an end three and a half years into the last seven years of this generation, according to Revelation 11:3–15."

Still slightly in shock from all he had just heard, Neville looked at Andrew and asked, "Do you have any further comments to make? You have seven minutes left to make your final statement."

Andrew knew just what he was going to do. With strong conviction in his voice, he said, "I know that billions of people of various religious persuasions are watching this program. Maybe you have never heard the truth about Jesus and about the false religious system as you heard it this morning.

"The Spirit of the Lord has convicted you while you were listening to both John and me. You have been convicted of your sins and wrongdoings. Now it is up to you to repent of your sins and to d*Isa*ssociate yourself from the works of darkness. If you want to escape the eternal judgments of God then you must accept the Lord Jesus Christ as your personal Savior."

As if suddenly touched by the Holy Spirit, Neville and the cameramen and others were seen wiping away tears. Andrew said to his worldwide audience, "If you are able to kneel, then kneel right where you are and please pray this prayer after me. 'Lord God, I come to you in the name of Your Son, the Lord Jesus Christ. I confess that I have sinned against You and Your children. I confess that Jesus died and shed His blood on the cross for my sins.

"'I believe that He rose again from the dead. Save me now from eternal damnation. Give me the determination to break all ties with Antichrist, the false prophet, and the false church, or any Christ denying religion. I now accept Jesus Christ as my personal Savior and Lord. This I ask in Jesus' name. Amen!'"

All over the world where they were receiving CNM, multiplied millions prayed the prayer to accept Jesus as their Savior and to break with their sinful lifestyles.

Neville thought to himself, *It is a miracle that no church or government officials have commanded CNM to terminate the broadcast.*

As he was busy entertaining that thought, agents of the Mystery Babylonian Universal Church forced their way into the large studio area. They pointed their automatic weapons at Neville, Andrew, and John.

Their spokesman said, "We have come to arrest you. We have received orders from Prophet Elijah to shoot you without hesitation, should you offer resistance."

He continued speaking and said, "Lift up your hands above your heads and do not try to do anything stupid."

I knew this was coming. Andrew was just waiting for him to say that they had to lift their hands. As they lifted their hands, Andrew's hand touched Neville's hand and immediately the three men d*Isa*ppeared right before the eyes of the agents of the false church and those in the studio.

The agents were dumbfounded, as well as the cameramen, including those who were watching the program on the various monitors. The agents started cursing and shouting obscenities at the three men who d*Isa*ppeared into thin air. They were in a very foul mood when they left CNM's headquarters. Before walking out, they threatened CNM's bosses that the ministry of religion would see to it that they lose their broadcasting license.

The cameramen intentionally did not switch off their cameras but kept on taping when the agents burst in uninvited. The billions of viewers saw how the men they had been listening to for hours d*Isa*ppeared into thin air, and they also witnessed the angry reaction of the agents of the religious system.

Dudley Fairbairn

twenty_eight

CHAPTER

Multi billionaire, John Edwards, and his family were in complete shock when the men he and his family had just seen on television a few seconds ago materialized right before their very eyes. But the precious Holy Spirit taught the entire family very quickly.

John Edwards' family, consisting of Melanie, his wife, his son, James, and his daughter, Emma, were still on their knees having just given their lives to Jesus when the three men suddenly appeared in their presence. They stood to their feet, and they introduced themselves.

Mr. Edwards said, "Wow! You sure gave us a scare. But it is *good* to see you in person. You were on the program for a number of hours. You must be famished!"

"Yes, we are," came their response.

Melanie summoned the overseer of the kitchen staff and told him that they must set three extra places at the table for the guests on the patio. Within thirty minutes, delicious steaks and salads were served. Andrew, John, and Neville thoroughly enjoyed the wonderfully prepared meal, as they were very hungry.

After they had finished eating, they went to the lounge to recline and discuss what to do next. John and Andrew also wanted to know what Neville's plans were.

Andrew spoke to Neville and said, "You have to let your wife, family, and parents know what has transpired. If they had watched the program of the interview this morning, they will be very worried about you." *They must have seen what happened on television!*

Neville, replied, "I am still single at twenty-five, and I lost both my parents in a car crash soon after the Babylonian Church was formed."

"I am truly sorry to hear about the loss of your parents," came Andrew's response.

"I was sad up until an hour ago, but not anymore." Those in the room could not understand what he meant. Then he continued, "Both my parents were born again Christians. They were deliberately killed because they refused to join the Mystery Babylonian Universal Church. I now know that they are in heaven with Jesus. When the churches were forced to amalgamate, their church went underground.

"I was too busy enjoying life to find time to go to church. I had no time for God or Jesus. However, I have to confess that I have never experienced such peace in all my life as I am experiencing right now. And it is all because I gave my life to Jesus more than an hour ago." *I should have done it when my parents were alive.*

"While you were sharing the word in the studio, I was overcome with great guilt and shame. I have done terrible things that only God knows about. Since asking for His forgiveness and accepting Jesus as my Savior, I have a wonderful peace in my heart."

With a relaxed smile on his face, Andrew said, "Jesus, John, the Edwards family, the angels, and I all rejoice with you.

"Neville, you *are* aware that you will not be able to return to CNM as you will be immediately arrested, and thrown into jail or executed. You could, however, go to Israel with us," said John.

Neville knew that his work as a talk-show host was forever over. But he also knew his life was there in America.

Mr. Edwards who was following the conversation with great interest said, "I realize now that all honor belongs to God that I am a multi-billionaire. Both my wife and I were under heavy conviction when you spoke about breaking God's laws.

"While we were listening to the interview we asked our children's forgiveness for not always having been there for them and leaving them to the care of the nannies. Melanie and I also asked one another's forgiveness, as we had not always been faithful to one another.

Melanie and I both feel as if a heavy weight has been lifted off our shoulders. Even our children asked us to forgive them for being so unappreciative, lazy, and difficult at times.

Mr. Edwards then addressed Neville and said, "You are free to stay with us. We have a very large cabin hidden away in the mountains, which is well stocked with food that could last us for a number of years.

"There are various kinds of edible berries and the mountain streams are well stocked with fish, and it is also deer country. We'll have lots of fresh meat to eat. As there are no roads leading to the cabin, it is only accessible by helicopter. It has always been our hideaway, and our children just love it there very much."

John said, "Over two years and ten months have passed now since the tribulation started. According to my understanding of prophecy, Antichrist is going to break his seven year covenant of peace when the three and a half years of tribulation had run its course, just before the start of the three and a half years of The Great and Awesome Day of the Lord.

"According to Paul's revelation, Antichrist is going to sit in the temple of God claiming to be God."

John spoke on 2 Thessalonians 2:3–4. "Paul warned us not to allow any one to deceive us. He said *that that Day* of the rapture *will not come* unless the falling away or rebellion against God comes first. The rebellion shall usher in the man of sin who is also called the son of perdition. He will oppose and exalt himself above all that is worshipped, so that he sits as God in the temple of God, pretending that he is God.

"The day of his coronation as God in the temple of God is going to turn into a fiasco, because a total worldwide eclipse of the sun is going to engulf the earth. Jesus gave us a clue as to what was going to happen when the three and a half years of tribulation comes to an end."

John opened his Bible and began to read:

Immediately after the tribulation of those days the sun will be darkened, and the moon will not give its light; and the stars will fall from heaven, and the powers of the heavens will be shaken.

Matthew 24:29

"The tribulation is only going to last for three and a half years. The last three and a half years of the seven years are termed, The Great and Awesome Day of the Lord. According to Matthew 24: 29–31, Jesus placed His coming after the tribulation and the total blackout, just before the above mentioned *Day,* begins.

"Jesus placed the catching away of the redeemed of both Jew and Gentile at this juncture. What place are we going to be gathered to? Here follows Paul's answer, 'Then we who are alive *and* remain [survive] shall be caught up together with them in the clouds to meet the Lord in the air. And thus we shall always be with the Lord. Therefore comfort one another with these words' (1 Thessalonians 4:17–18)

After joining Jesus in the atmospheric heaven, we shall proceed to the judgment seat of Christ Jesus. After our works have been judged, we shall accompany Jesus to the throne room in heaven.

"The true believers are not going to be here during the implementation of Antichrist's mark. The receiving of the mark leads to the outpouring of God's wrath by the seven angels, with the seven bowls. It takes place during the second period of three and a half years of Daniel's seventieth week."

After John had finished his teaching session, Mr. Edwards again addressed Neville. "You do not have to worry about money. I have plenty until Jesus comes to take us to heaven. We have just heard that the coming of Jesus is in the very near future. I also have spare parts for the helicopter and thousands of gallons of fuel in tanks, buried about five thousand yards away from our cabin, for the helicopter.

"It is shielded by trees, and the landing-pad is also close by. I want to do as much good with the money the Lord has blessed me with, as I can. I want to help my brothers and sisters in the faith.

"Because I am an entrepreneur, they will not be suspicious of me if I buy food-supplies in bulk. I also have warehouses in every state and in other countries. All we have to do is to inform the underground church where they can get food for free."

Andrew replied, "Leave that to us Mr. Edwards. We have a very good networking system in place. We'll inform the leaders of the underground church worldwide. The Lord shall abundantly bless you and your family."

Then he addressed Neville again, and said, "Neville, what is your decision? Are you going to be part of our family? The choice is yours."

Neville answered, "There is no other alternative for me. I feel I need to stay in America, so my answer is yes. I will gladly become part of your family and thank you very much."

"Mr. Edwards. May I present the gospel message to your staff. We can gather under the patio roof. They, *too*, need to hear about Jesus," came Andrew's request.

• • • •

It took about a half an hour for all of them to assemble. Andrew explained the gospel as simply as possible that everyone is a sinner in God's eyes. He then presented the message of salvation through Christ Jesus, the crucified and resurrected Lord.

"We are all guilty before Father God and deserve to be eternally lost. But the Lord has made salvation available to us through His Son, the Lord Jesus Christ. You must forsake your sinful lifestyles and accept Jesus with all of your heart."

None of Mr. Edwards' staff was a member of the false church. They were not religiously inclined at all. When they heard the pure gospel message for the very first time and heard that they were guilty of breaking God's commandments, they were immediately convicted of their transgressions.

When Andrew gave the altar call, every one of the staff accepted Jesus as their personal Savior. John then gave them

Christian literature with sound teaching of what the Lord Jesus expects of them.

He also gave them tracts concerning the end times. Andrew encouraged them to make contact with the underground church leadership. He gave them only one contact number of Brother X. Anonymity was of utmost importance to the safety of the believers of the underground church.

．．．．

"I see that you have an indoor swimming pool," said Andrew as Mr. Edwards gave them a tour of his home.

"It is heated," came, Mr. Edward's response.

Andrew exclaimed, "Excellent! Excellent!" When Andrew, John, Neville and the Edwards family, joined the staff, he asked them, "What does hinder you from being baptized?"

With one voice everyone shouted, "Nothing hinders us to be baptized!"

They quickly got ready for baptism, and the staff who were mothers brought their babies and toddlers, wanting Andrew and John to baptize them as well.

John told them that infant sprinkling was unbiblical. He took his Bible and showed them from God's word what Jesus did when they brought little children to Him. In his own words, he told them the contents of Mark 10:13–16.

"Parents just like you, brought their little children to Jesus, that He may bless them. When His disciples saw the parents bringing their children to Jesus, they rebuked them. The action of His disciples greatly displeased Jesus. He told them to allow the little children to come to Him and not to forbid them because the kingdom of God belongs to them. Jesus stressed it to His disciples that anyone who does not receive the kingdom of God as a little child will by no means enter in. Jesus then took the little children in His arms, laid His hands upon them, and blessed them.

John explained to the parents that neither Jesus nor His disciples baptized babies but that Jesus blessed the little children.

Then he asked the parents whether they understood what he had just read.

And they collectively said, "Yes!"

Both Andrew and John took each child in their arms, prayed God's blessing, health, and protection over them and their parents, and blessed them in the name of the Lord Jesus Christ. The parents were overjoyed.

Everyone of the baptismal candidates first made a public confession of their faith in the Lord Jesus Christ. Then John and Andrew baptized the new converts on the confession of *their faith* in the Lord Jesus Christ, in the name of the Father and of the Son and of the Holy Sprit. In all, there were forty-five who were baptized.

Mr. Edwards then informed his staff that he and his family were going to sell their mansion and that they were relocating to another state. "The Lord spoke to my heart while you were being baptized to bless you because you were such faithful workers and I appreciate every one of you and I also speak on behalf of my wife and children. I am giving each of you a check in the amount of two million dollars. Be wise as to how you spend it. Tough times are ahead of us. Take care of your family and extended families and be faithful to Jesus."

The staff was *so* overcome with gratitude that both men and women started to cry. They embraced one another and promised to be faithful to Jesus. Abraham, one of the senior staff members, promised that he would keep in contact with each one of them. He was the one who got the contact number of Brother X. He promised Mr. Edwards, "I will inform them where the underground believers are gathering. We have been spiritually bankrupt, and we need to be instructed in the teachings of Jesus, and how to live lives pleasing, to God.

John advised them by saying, "Go to the second-hand book stores and garage sales to see if you can find the King James' Version of the Bible containing both Old and New Testaments. People have been getting rid of their Bibles by the millions, which most of them never read in the first place. The *New Age Guide Book* has now replaced the Bible.

"The Holy Spirit will perfect a quick work in you as He knows that the coming of Jesus as at hand. He will guide you as to what Christian books you must read. But take note! The Bible is the best book to read."

After changing into dry clothes, they gathered again for a few minutes. Andrew prayed the Lord's blessing upon them and asked their Heavenly Father to protect and guide them every step of the way.

Mrs. Edwards, gave Andrew a check to the value of two hundred million dollars signed by both her and her husband. As she gave it to Andrew, she said, "Use it for the gospel, the believers in Israel and abroad, and for the greater good of the poor and needy."

Andrew called John and showed him the check. Their eyes welled up with tears as they thanked Mr. and Mrs. Edwards for their generosity, hospitality, and love. Before they were to make their leave, they shook hands with everyone. John said, "Should we not meet here on earth, again, we shall surely meet one another in heaven."

Everyone started to cry again. He then lifted up his hands to heaven and announced the benediction, "May the grace of Almighty Jehovah God, the love of the Lord Jesus Christ, and the fellowship of the blessed Holy Spirit, God three in one, abide with you always. Amen!"

Andrew and John shouted, "*Shalom!*" They immediately d*Is*-*a*ppeared before the eyes of the new converts and reappeared at John's home in Bethlehem, in Israel. An e-mail message from one of their contacts in America was awaiting them.

Soon after your appearance on CNM, multiplied millions of all nationalities and other religious persuasions have accepted the Lord Jesus Christ as their personal Savior. They were swept into the kingdom of God, our Heavenly Father, by the power of the blessed Holy Spirit.

Both John and Andrew flung their arms into the air and started praising, Jesus their Messiah, the Son of Jehovah their God.

Messiah, Prophet Elijah, the clergy, and the demonized members of the Mystery Babylonian Universal Church were filled with indignation against the followers of Jesus.

Messiah said to Prophet Elijah, "We need new plans on the drawing-board on how to deal with the pockets of resistance against our Super Church. Did you hear how much damage those two imbeciles, Andrew and John, did to our cause?

"They had the audacity to expose our great Church to billions of people around the world! And they heaped great scorn on both of us, as if we *were* monsters." A smile crept across his face, and he said to himself, *yes, we are monsters,* "I hope they stay in America and die with the rest of Esau's stupid followers.

"We must finish them off because my father has great plans for me when the three and a half years of tribulation comes to an end. You already know everything about it, remember!? When I was in Tibet, you told me that Father told you everything there was to know about me. That time is close at hand."

"Yes! I remember," came, Elijah's reply. *How can I forget? You spoke about it for the longest of time.*

"We are going to strike against the Jews and the followers of Esau on the day of the Feast of Trumpets. Jews shall be converging on Jerusalem from all over the world to attend the feast—"

"Oh! How I hate that feast," interrupted Elijah.

"That feast is a prediction of Esau's return. They are going to be in for the shock of their lives. Elijah, my dear friend, please send an encyclical to our priests worldwide and inform them of our plans."

Prophet Elijah left Messiah's presence for about ten minutes and returned with the draft of the e-mail he was going to send. He read it to Messiah, "On the day of the Feast of Trumpets, the Jews and the followers of Esau worldwide must be completely annihilated. Not a single one of them must be spared this time. I wish you strength for the task. I remain, Your Savior, Messiah and King."

"Quite impressive and to the point my friend. Have it sent

immediately,'" said Messiah. It made Prophet Elijah proud to be Messiah's confidant. *He would be lost without my expertise.*

Dudley Fairbairn

twenty_nine
CHAPTER

Ishmael found a printed copy of the e-mail message, which Elijah had sent out, in the desk drawer. He immediately contacted Andrew and John. They in turn immediately warned the leadership in Africa, Asia, South, Central and North America, and Europe by e-mail of the impending danger, that was planned for the Jews and for the followers of Jesus.

They warned them about Antichrist's plans to have God's chosen people, the Jews, and all the followers of Jesus Christ killed on the day of the Feast of Trumpets. They encouraged them to be in fasting and in prayer a few days leading up to the Feast of Trumpets, and to bear in mind the difference in time.

They also had to inform the Rabbis in their communities what Antichrist and the false prophet had planned against them. That if they put their trust in Jesus, they would have nothing to fear because He would fight on their behalf. Let them know Jesus' coming was getting closer and that with each passing day their deliverance was drawing nearer.

They had to admonish the believers to keep their hearts pure, and their eyes focused on Jesus. Tell them to keep their hearts and ears in tune to hear the sound of the trumpet. Please have this message translated into the various languages and send it to the church leaders of the respective countries. It is imperative that this message reach them as soon as possible.

The Appearance

. . . .

With the excellent networking, which they had established, all the brethren should know of the impending danger within the following twenty-four hours.

At one of the pastoral gatherings, Andrew informed the pastors what to expect when the fourth angel sounds his trumpet according to Revelation 8:12–13. The pastors found it very informative. They found it quite interesting that the daytime was going to be shorter and the night time longer. They were very eager to share the knowledge with their congregations.

One of the pastors spoke on Revelation 8:12–13. He said, "When the fourth angel sounds his trumpet a third of the sun, and third of the moon, and a third of the stars would be struck. It will cause a third of the stars to be, darkened! A third of the day will not shine, and the night likewise. An angel flying through the midst of heaven will make an announcement with a loud voice, "Woe, woe, woe to the inhabitants of the earth, because there were still three more trumpets that were to be sounded by the remaining three angels."

Andrew dismissed them with the benediction.

. . . .

The meteorologists were dumbfounded and confounded when the days became shorter by a third and the nights longer by a third. They had no explanation for it until it was brought to their attention that it was predicted in the Bible.

They outright rejected that which was written.

The followers of Jesus Christ were already preparing for the sounding of the fifth trumpet. They knew that the judgment of the fifth trumpet could not harm them either because the judgments were aimed at the people who rejected Jesus.

John, Andrew, and the pastors from across Israel secretly gathered in Haifa. Andrew addressed the gathering after the opening prayer and said, "Brothers and sisters, I want to take the opportunity to thank all of you for having been such good co-laborers in the faith. Your lives had been on the line many times for the sake of Jesus. You denied yourselves many things just to help someone in need.

"Our heavenly Father keeps the Book. Someday soon all of us shall receive our eternal reward and that is to see Jesus face to face and hear Him say, 'Well done, My son and daughter.'

"Our responsibility is to watch and care for the flock; the Lord has put in our care. It is even more crucial now than ever before. The false prophet is not going to stop his threats and harassment against the followers of Jesus worldwide. He wants every believer to accept the false Messiah as their Savior.

"Even in the midst of the severest tribulation since the birth of Jesus' Church, we can cling to the blessed hope of Jesus' return.

"Beloved, it does not matter what stumbling block the enemy throws in our pathway. With the help of the blessed Holy Spirit, we shall triumph over the enemy time and time again. We can expect the fifth angel to sound his trumpet in the very near future. The results of the sounding of the trumpet may be very scary to those who are young in the faith.

"Tell the believers not to be afraid. Just as our God came through for us with the sounding of the previous four trumpets, so He is going to show Himself strong on our behalf who believe in His Salvation."

Andrew asked John to read Revelation 9:3–6 to the assembly. John gave a lengthy explanation on the four verses, as he painted the scenario of what the believers were to expect. He explained to them in detail how it was going to affect the unbelievers and that their suffering was going to be very horrendous.

• • • •

Soon on the heels of the fourth angel, the fifth angel sounded his trumpet, and demons were released from the bottomless pit. They were charged not to destroy nature, but only to hurt those who did not have the seal of Jehovah God on their foreheads.

Great consternation and fear exploded across planet earth as millions of demonic spirits started attacking men, women, and children. Their sting was like the sting of scorpions. The medical scientists had no cure for the suffering masses to alleviate the pain. Those who were stung desired death because of the awful pain. Some tried to commit suicide but were unsuccessful. Death fled away, and their suffering was to endure for five months.

. . . .

Andrew again warned the believers worldwide and spelt out what the consequences were going to be when the sixth angel sounds his trumpet.

At the congregation in Jerusalem, Andrew ministered what the consequences were going to be at the sounding of the sixth angel.

"Brothers and sisters, John, who penned Revelation 9:13–16, heard a voice from the four horns of the golden altar which is before God, saying to the sixth angel who had the trumpet to release the four angels who were bound at the river Euphrates. The four angels had been prepared for the hour and day and month and year. They were going to be released to kill a third of mankind. The number of the army of the horseman *was* two hundred million.

There is a fixed length of time when the four angels of Revelation 9:15 are going to kill about 2.2 billion people. It entails a third of the earth's population. Their methods of destruction are by fire, smoke, and brimstone, which proceed out of their mouths. Not one single country out of the 194 countries in the world is going to be spared. Be watchful, pray, and stay close to Jesus. Our lives are in God's hands."

Soon after Andrew warned the believers, killer locusts descended on planet earth like a desert storm. Governments made appeals to exterminators to kill the plagues of locusts. No chemical, no matter how poisonous, was able to kill the killer locusts.

Corpses were seen everywhere. The corpses were taken to hospitals, schools, churches, colleges, factories, and a 101 other places. The people who were working at the crematoriums were working day and night cremating the corpses. The gravediggers could not stay ahead with the digging of individual graves.

The local governments gave permission to burn the corpses

in open fields away from the cities, towns, and villages. To counteract the stench of the decaying corpses and out of fear of an outbreak contagious diseases, the municipal workers poured chemicals and gasoline over the corpses before setting it on fire.

Many of the elderly and those who suffered from emphysema, asthma, and other breathing and health problems died soon after inhaling the toxic fumes. People were advised to stay indoors.

In spite of the mass slaughter, many people still did not fear the Lord God. They refused to repent of their idolatry, witchcraft, and sin. Messiah and Prophet Elijah were reeling over the losses the members of the Mystery Babylonian Universal Church had suffered. It made them even more determined to take full control of planet earth and its inhabitants on schedule.

Messiah was under the impression that it was going to happen when he declare himself God in the temple of God when the three and a half years of tribulation drew to a close. He was very confident that he was going to win the war against Christ Jesus.

• • • •

In Israel, there was a beehive of activity as the High Priest and the Levitical Priesthood were preparing for the celebration of The Feasts of Trumpets. Not only in Israel was excitement building up, but also amongst the world's Jewry. The excitement was not confined to the world's Jewry alone, but also the Messianic Jews in Israel and the followers of Jesus worldwide.

However, the excitement was for a very different reason. The followers of Jesus were expecting the return of their Savior, Jesus Christ, to evacuate the redeemed of all ages, before the start of The Great and Awesome Day of the Lord.

The Rabbis from all over the world received a personal invitation from Messiah to attend The Feast of Trumpets in Jerusalem.

• • • •

In Bethlehem, Andrew, John, and all the local pastors in Israel were gathered together in a very large public gathering place. Andrew and John were to instruct them from the word of God concerning the importance of the seven Jewish feasts.

John welcomed the pastors after the opening prayer. "Beloved, the coming of Jesus is upon us. We have to keep on winning souls. I want you to know that we are on the winning side. There is no turning back for us. The only way out for us who are Jehovah's redeemed is up.

"Brother Andrew and I want to show you how near we are to the coming of Christ Jesus. We want to share with you how the seven Jewish feasts can only find fulfillment in Jesus. We shall show you systematically from the scriptures proving that the Jewish feasts point to Jesus Christ according to the revelation the blessed Holy Spirit gave to the Apostle Paul.

"Paul said, 'So let no one judge you in food or in drink, or regarding a festival or a new moon or Sabbaths, which are a shadow of things to come, but the substance is of Christ' (Colossians 2:17). A chorus of amen and hallelujah filled the air.

"Jesus is our Passover lamb. We read in Exodus 12:21, 'Then Moses called the elders of Israel and said unto them, "Pick out and take lambs for yourselves according to your families, and kill the Passover *lamb.*' Paul wrote in 1 Corinthians 5:7, "Therefore purge out the old leaven, that you may be a new lump, since you truly are unleavened. For indeed Christ, our Passover [Lamb] was sacrificed for us.'

Jesus is our Unleavened Bread. Moses wrote in Exodus 12:15, 'Seven days you shall eat unleavened bread. On the first day you shall remove leaven from your houses. For whoever eats leavened bread from the first day until the seventh day, that person shall be cut off from Israel.'

"The connecting verses are found in John 6:35 and Psalm 16:10. Jesus said, 'I am the bread of life.'

"Leaven speaks of sin. The leaven of sin was not present in the Spirit, soul, and body of Jesus. It was for that reason that His body did not decay in the humid tomb. David declared, 'For You will not leave My soul in *Sheol,* Nor will You allow Your Holy One to see corruption.'

"The connecting verse is found in Acts 2:31, '... he, foreseeing this, spoke concerning the resurrection of Christ, that his soul was not left in Hades, nor did His flesh see corruption.'

"If you have a question just raise your hand."

Simon raised his hand and made a comment, "It makes sense why we use unleavened bread when we celebrate the Jesus' death during the communion service."

"Well said, my brother," said John and continued with the study.

"Jesus fulfilled the Firstfruits Feast. We read in Exodus 34:26a, 'The first of the firstfruits of your land you shall bring to the house of the LORD your God … '" The connecting verse is found in 1 Corinthians 15:20. 'But now is Christ risen from the dead, *and* has become the firstfruits of those who have fallen asleep.'

"Jesus was the first of the brethren who received a glorified body. He was clothed with the incorruptible body when He arose from the dead. I will discuss one more feast then Brother Andrew will take over.'

"The following feast under discussion is the Feast of Pentecost. It is recorded in Deuteronomy 16:9. 'You shall count seven weeks for yourself; begin to count the seven weeks from *the time* you begin *to put* the sickle to the grain.'

"The Feast of Weeks starts the day following Passover. Seven weeks are then counted. Seven times seven plus the day of Passover brings us to the fiftieth day. Pentecost is the Greek word for fifty. The Feast of Pentecost falls on the fiftieth day. Jesus fulfilled this feast on the exact day when He poured out the Holy Spirit on the disciples. The Church was born on that very same day. *Thanks be to our heavenly Father for that very special Feast of Pentecost.*

"It is recorded, 'When the day of Pentecost [the Feasts of Weeks] had fully come [when the fiftieth day arrived], they were all with one accord in one place. And suddenly there came a sound from heaven, as of a rushing mighty wind, and it filled the whole house where they were sitting.

"'Then there appeared to them divided tongues, as of fire, and *one* sat upon each of them. And they were all filled with the Holy Spirit and began to speak with other tongues, as the Spirit gave them utterance.' (Acts 2:1–4). Jesus' Church was born on the day of Pentecost."

Hannah walked over to John and gave him a glass of orange juice, which he highly appreciated.

Andrew took over the teaching session from John. "I will discuss the fifth feast which is, The Feast of Trumpets, last. Let's skip to the sixth feast.

"The feast that I want to discuss is the Feast of Atonement. Moses recorded in Leviticus 17:11, 'For the life of the flesh is in the blood, and I have given it to you on the altar to make atonement for your souls; for it *is* the blood *that* makes atonement for your soul.'

"Paul wrote in Romans 5: 10–11,'For if when we were enemies we were reconciled to God through the death of His Son, much more, having been reconciled, we shall be saved by His life. And not only *that*, but we also rejoice in God through our Lord Jesus Christ, through whom we have now received the [atonement] reconciliation.' "Beloved, let's stand to our feet and lift up our hands and praise Jesus for the atonement He has made available to us." For a few minutes the believers were lost in praise and adoration to their Savior."

thirty
CHAPTER

Andrew said, "Jesus fulfilled the Feast of Tabernacles when he was born. Please give me your undivided attention and follow the scriptures along with me in your Bible.

"It is recorded in Deuteronomy 16:13, 'You shall observe the Feast of Tabernacles seven days, when you have gathered from the threshing floor and from the winepress.'

"Our forefathers made them booths during the Feast of Tabernacles and lived in them for seven days. It was in remembrance of our forefathers [Israelites] who lived in booths when they left Egypt.

"In 1 Kings 6:13, our God declared, 'And I will dwell among the children of Israel, and I will not forsake My people Israel.'

"Our Heavenly Father tabernacled with our forefathers in the wilderness according to Moses.
"Moses recorded in Exodus 13:21, 'And the LORD went before them by day in a pillar of cloud to lead the way, and by night in a pillar of fire to give them light so as to go by day and night.'

"In the millennium, Jehovah our Heavenly Father is going to tabernacle with us again according to Jesus' Revelation given to John. In Revelation 21:3, we read, 'And I heard a loud voice from heaven saying, "Behold the tabernacle of God *is* with men, and He will dwell with them, and they shall be His people. God Himself will be with them *and be* their God."'

"When Christ was born, Jehovah God clothed

The Appearance

Himself in human flesh and came to tabernacle with man. It is written in Matthew 1:23, 'Behold, the virgin shall be with child, and bring forth a Son, and they shall call His name Emmanuel,' which is translated, 'God with us'"

"Paul said in 1 Timothy 3:16, 'And without controversy great is the mystery of godliness: God was manifest in the flesh [when Jesus was born], justified in the Spirit, Seen by angels, Preached among the Gentiles, Believed on in the world, Received up in glory.'

"Jehovah clothed Himself in human flesh and for thirty-three and a half years He dwelt with man in the person [or body] of Jesus Christ.

"In John 1:14, John recorded, 'And the Word became flesh and dwelt [tabernacled] among us, and we beheld His glory, the glory as of the only begotten Son of the Father, full of grace and truth.'"

The brothers and sisters, who had prepared refreshments, were also sitting in on the teachings. Hannah raised her hand. "Pastor Andrew! The word dwelt in the above context also means—to tabernacle."

"Hannah, you are so right."

"You are welcome, pastor." The believers just loved Hannah for her spontaneity.

Andrew continued and said, "In the previous six feasts we have made the discovery that Jesus Christ had already fulfilled six feasts on the exact day of the exact month. The only feast that He has not fulfilled yet, is the Feast of Trumpets

"Because of the set pattern of the previous feasts and its fulfillment, I believe that Jesus is also going to fulfill the fifth feast, which is the Feast of Trumpets.

"Jesus cannot be fulfillment and a fraud at the same time. We as Jewish believers believe with all of our hearts that Jesus is the fulfillment of all our Jewish feasts.

"The Apostle Paul said in 1 Corinthians 15: 51 - 52, 'Behold, I tell you a mystery: We shall not all sleep, but we shall all be changed—in a moment, in a twinkling of an eye, at the last trumpet. For the trumpet will sound, and the dead will be raised incorruptible, and we shall be changed.'

"The only place in the Bible where mystery and trumpet are connected is when the *rapture* takes place. At that same time, we shall be clothed with incorruption. According to the revelation that Paul had received, he placed the timing of the *rapture* when the seventh angel sounds the last trumpet in a series of seven trumpets.

"Six angels have already blown their individual trumpet. The seventh angel is going to blow the last trumpet in the series of trumpets only after the two prophets of Revelation 11, have completed their ministry of 1260 days, which is equal to three years and six months." Andrew coughed and looked at Hannah. "Please pour me a glass of pomegranate juice," he said with a tickle in his throat. He slowly took a few sips before continuing with the study.

"When I was busy studying the subject on the *rapture* the revelation was birthed in my spirit that the Feast of Trumpets was going to coincide on the first day of the seventh month. At that time, I was not acquainted with Leviticus 23:24.

"I had to make use of a concordance to look up the scripture concerning the Feast of Trumpets. I found the scripture, and I could not believe my eyes. It was *too* good to be true."

"Here follows the verse, 'Speak unto the children of Israel, saying: "In the seventh month, on the first *day* of the month, you shall have a Sabbath-*rest,* a memorial of blowing of trumpets, a holy convocation."'

Andrew asked the eager congregation, "When you count, what month follows the sixth month?"

Someone shouted, "The seventh month follows the sixth month."

Andrew again asked the congregation, "Every month starts with what day of the month?"

Again, another believer shouted, "Every month starts with the first day of the month." Excitement was building up in the air.

Andrew continued, "I was not acquainted with the fact that

the Feast of Trumpets fell on the first day of the seventh month. This knowledge was revealed to me by divine revelation. It was also revealed to me that Jesus was also going to fulfill the Feast of Trumpets at the exact timing, just as He had fulfilled the previous six feasts.

"Why would Jehovah our God make an exception when it comes to the most important feast which concerns the Church of Jesus, His Son? He is either the fulfillment of the Jewish feasts, or He is not the fulfillment of the Jewish feasts. He cannot be both!

"I believe with all of my heart that Jesus is the fulfillment of our Jewish feasts. The question that may arise is … if we say that Jesus is going to come on the Feast of Trumpets then we know the day of His coming. And it has been widely taught for many years that nobody knows the day and hour of His coming." Andrew then quoted Jesus' words in Matthew 24:36. 'But of that day and hour no one knows, not even the angels of heaven, but My Father only.'

"To what event was Jesus connecting the day and hour to? Was He referring to His word that was going to pass away? *No!* A million times, *no!* His word shall *never* pass away. Jesus already clarified His position on that matter.

"He said, 'Heaven and earth will pass away, but My words will by no means pass away' (Matthew 24:35).

"Then the day and the hour that no one knows about must then be referring to when heaven and earth are going to pass away. Jesus has already stated that heaven and earth are going to pass away and that His word will never pass away. Why is it impossible to know, the day nor the hour, when heaven and earth are going to pass away? The answer is in Jehovah's unfailing word.

"From what we learn from the word we know that heaven and earth are going to pass away after the one thousand years of peace, and after the white throne judgment. But just when it is going to pass away remains a mystery. We learn from the Bible that the devil is going to be bound for a one thousand years.

"Afterward he is going to be loosed for a *little while*. Here is the cause of the problem. We do not know the duration of the *little while* Satan is going to be released. And we do not know how long the white throne judgment is going to last. Where the Bible is silent concerning a matter, it is better to remain silent.

"If we are really honest then we have to acknowledge that no one knows the day or hour when heaven and earth will pass away. Jesus did not say that no one knows the day or the hour. He said, 'But *of that day and hour* no one knows [have knowledge of], Not even the angels of heaven, but My Father only' (Matthew 24:36, emphasis mine).

"We do not have knowledge about the contents of that day, apart from the sun coming up that morning and the ensuing eclipse of the sun. Can we honestly say we that we know what is going to happen all over the world apart from us being caught up to meet Jesus in the air? Let us be honest! We do not know the contents of the day of the *rapture*.

Andrew said, "I want to paraphrase Luke 21:25–27 for you. There will be signs in the sun, in the moon and in the stars. There will be distress amongst the nations. They will be perplexed by tsunamis that causes the sea and the waves to roar, and causing great damage and loss of life. It will cause men's hearts to fail from fear from those things Jesus and the prophets prophesied about that were coming to pass. It is going to be of such severity that the very powers of the heavens will be shaken. It will be during this time of cataclysmic upheaval that they will see the Son of Man coming in a cloud with power and great glory.

"In the above verse, Jesus placed His coming after the heavenly disturbances. It corresponds with Matthew 24:29–31. He placed His coming after the tribulation and the total worldwide eclipse of the sun. In Matthew 24:29–31, Jesus prophesied that immediately after the tribulation of those days the sun will be darkened, and the moon will not give its light; the stars will fall from heaven, and the powers of the heavens will be shaken."

"The shaking of the powers of the heavens refers to the coming war between Michael and his angels and Satan and his angels. Jehovah God's heaven cannot be shaken. Then it must be referring to Satan's place of power in the atmospheric heavens that is going to be shaken. Satan is called the prince of the powers of the air in Ephesians 2:2. The war in heaven between Michael and his angels and Satan and his angels will cause a severe shaking of the atmospheric heavens (Revelation 12:7–9).

According to Matthew 24: 29–31, Jesus will appear only after the tribulation and the eclipse of the sun and after the powers of the heavens, had been shaken. Then Jesus will send His angels with a great sound of a trumpet, and they will gather together His elect from the four winds, from one end of heaven to the other. Here we see a very clear picture of the *rapture,*" said, Andrew.

"Did Jesus say when He was going to come? *Yes,* He did! He placed His coming when the three and a half years of tribulation comes to an end and only after the total eclipse of the sun and not before those events (Matthew 24:29).

"In Matthew 24:30–31, we see a very clear picture of the *rapture.* The Apostle Paul agreed with Jesus in 2 Thessalonians 2:1–2. He said in 1 Thessalonians 4:16, that Lord Himself will descend from heaven with a shout, with the voice of an archangel. It will be during that time that the dead in Christ will rise first. Then we who have survived the tribulation, will be caught up together with them in the clouds to meet the Lord in the air. We shall be with Jesus forever." *What a glorious day to look forward to!*

Many of the believers had the same thought.

"Paul addressed the believers. He said concerning the coming of our Lord Jesus Christ and our gathering together (Matthew 24:31) unto Him not to be shaken in mind or to be troubled, either by spirit or by word or by letter pretending to be from the apostles, as though the day of Christ which is connected to the *rapture* had already taken place.

"The coming of the Lord which leads to the gathering together of the redeemed, and the day of Christ refers to the same event. The coming of Jesus leads to the *rapture* of the saints when the gathering together unto Him takes place. It is called the day of Christ.

"Paul admonished us in 2 Thessalonians 2:3a, that we must not allow anyone to deceive us by any means. Paul said that *that Day which* ushers in the *rapture will not come* unless the falling away from faith in the Lord Jesus and the rebellion against Jehovah God comes first.

"The falling away began when false teachers introduced heretical teachings denying that Jesus Christ is the Son of God and that He died on the cross and that He rose again from the dead. I call them false teachers because they were not born again of God's Holy Spirit.

"The falling away from Jehovah God reached its apex with the formation of the Mystery Babylonian Universal Church.

"According to 2 Thessalonians 2:3b, the second thing that will take place, after the falling away from the truth is the revelation of the man of sin, who is also called the son of perdition. His characteristics exposes him to be the Antichrist because he will exalt himself above all that is called God or that is worshipped. He will be so brazen that he will sit in the temple of God, pretending to be God.

"We know that nearly three and a half years ago Antichrist made a false peace covenant guaranteeing Israel's security. He did not declare himself God at that time. It was still futuristic at that time. It is no longer in the distant future. The future has caught up with us. He is going to declare that he is God on the Feast of Trumpets. The three and a half years of tribulation will then have run its course.

"Jesus gave us the sequence of events in Matthew 24: 29–31. He said that He was going to come after the tribulation and the worldwide eclipse of the sun. It is also recorded in Luke 21: 25–27.

"What did Jesus encourage us to do in Luke 21:28? He said, 'Now when these things [the signs in the sun, moon and stars] begin to happen, look up and lift up your heads, because your redemption draws near.'

Some of the believers stood to their feet and started clapping their hands with excitement.

"This redemption is not the redemption of our souls. We were redeemed when Jesus died on the cross for us. It became a reality for us when we accepted Him as our Savior. This redemption, which is drawing near, speaks of the redemption of our bodies. We are going to receive new bodies. The redemption of our bodies happens at the *rapture*.

"The signs of Luke 21: 25 shall inform the followers of Jesus that His coming is at the door. The middle of Daniel's seventieth week of seven years spells the end of the tribulation for us who are followers of Jesus. On that same day, Antichrist commits the abomination that Jesus referred to in Matthew 24: 15. It is then that he declares himself God in the rebuilt temple.

"The worldwide eclipse of the sun shall throw Antichrist's coronation into d*Isa*rray. It will be the sign to those who have put their trust in Jesus; that the day of His coming has arrived." Andrew took another sip of the juice and asked, "Are you enjoying the study?"

"Yes," came a chorus of voices.

"I'm glad to hear that!" Andrew continued, "Beloved! Please forgive me if I have taken too long."

"No! You have not taken too long," said a pastor who sat in the front row. "I do not know when we shall be afforded another opportunity to get together like this again. Please bear with me for another few more minutes. I still have one more nugget of truth that I want to share with you. Afterward, there shall be time for discussion and then we are going to enjoy a delicious lunch our brothers and sisters have prepared for us.

"We have been taught that Jesus is going to come as a thief in the night for us. Let's check what the Bible has to say on that matter.

"Paul said in 1 Thessalonians 5:1–4, 'But concerning the times and seasons, Brethren, you have no need that I should write unto you. For you yourselves know perfectly that the day of the Lord so comes as a thief in the night [For whom is the day coming as a thief?]. For when they [the ungodly] say, "Peace and safety!" then sudden destruction comes upon them [the ungodly], as labor pains upon a pregnant woman. And they [the ungodly] shall not escape. But you, brethren [Who? You brethren], are not in darkness, so that this Day should overtake you as a thief. You are all the sons of light and sons of the day. We are not of the night nor of darkness [that that Day overtake us as a thief].'

"Jesus is not coming as a thief for us. He does not need to steal us because we are His purchased possession. Amen!"

A chorus of amen went up, and all the believers stood to their feet and started praising and worshipping Jehovah God. The sweet presence of the Holy Spirit filled the place and those present were endued with power from on high for the last lap of the race.

Interesting questions were raised by the believers, and answers were given directly from the Bible. Before the believers sat down to a delicious lunch, Andrew had a last word of admonition for the pastors. "Brothers and sisters tell the believers under your care to be very vigilant, and prayerful. Call for three days of fasting that leads up to the Feast of Trumpets. Only the young and the elderly are exempted from fasting. If the elderly want to participate, then they are free to do so.

"As you already know, Antichrist has sent out an encyclical to the bishops of the Mystery Babylonian Universal Church that on the Feast of Trumpets they must kill Jews and followers of Jesus. They have declared it *the mother of all tragedies.*

"Tell them to stay indoors and to only come out when the worldwide eclipse of the sun occurs. As you have heard from this afternoon's Bible discussion Jesus said that he was going to come after the tribulation and the total eclipse of the sun. Tell them that they have nothing to fear. The gross darkness is the sign that our redemption is drawing near."

After they greeted one another, a spiritually refreshed group of ministers went home that afternoon. They did not know whether they were going to see one another again on earth. After the church leaders had, left Andrew invited John to his home for further discussion. Andrew's mother was very happy to see John. She hugged him and said, "Make yourself, at home, my son. I hope you are staying for supper."

John responded, "Thank you very much! I sure will, Mother Hannah."

After they sat down in the lounge, John said, "I have a very strong intuition that we do not need to fear any new retaliation leading up to the Feast of Trumpets.

"Antichrist and the false prophet have already decided to revenge the deaths of their 2.2 billion comrades. We can expect a lull before the devastating storm. We can have peace in our hearts because we have already warned the believers, and the world's Jewry, what Antichrist has planned.

"Thanks be to God that we had taken it upon ourselves to warn them of the coming annihilation planned against them and us. Whether they are going to believe it is another matter. We who have broken with sin have this blessed and glorious hope that the coming of Jesus our Savior is going to deliver us from the coming annihilation that Antichrist has planned for us on the day of the Feast of Trumpets."

The announcement that supper was ready interrupted their conversation. Andrew's mother joined them for supper. After she had cleared the table, she sat down with them in the lounge to hear what her son had to share. It was very interesting to hear what God had in store for His children on the day of the Feast of Trumpets.

thirtyone

CHAPTER

Three weeks had now passed since John, had visited Andrew at his home in Jerusalem. Their time was taken up with encouraging and admonishing the believers not to allow anything to distract them from serving Jesus, and to keep themselves unspotted from the world.

. . . .

The Ben Gurion National Airport had not been that busy in many years. A few million Jews from all over the world were expected to attend the celebration. All the hotels, motels, and private lodgings were filled to capacity. All the camping sites were filled with tents and caravans. Again, an appeal was made to the citizens to open their homes to the visitors.

Just three and a half days before the end of the day 1260 of tribulation, people were blaring their car horns and the peeling of church bells could be heard. Messiah's soldiers were seen everywhere.

Messiah, and Prophet Elijah the Sovereign Pontiff, were riding in a bulletproof Messiah-mobile. They were followed by a motorcade of religious and political leaders who had arrived for the Feast of Trumpets. People were lining the streets by the thousands. Right at the end of the motorcade was a flat-back truck. Two men were on the back of the truck. Their wrists were chained to two rings, which were welded to the cab of the truck. They looked disheveled and they were covered in blood.

People were shouting, "Kill those crazy prophets! They caused us much harm. And they are responsible for killing millions of our comrades."

The believers worldwide were shocked when they realized that the two men they were seeing on television were none other than the two prophets whom they believed to be Moses and Elijah who fought on behalf of the worldwide followers of Jesus.

The motorcade came to a stop at the Western Wall. The soldiers unchained the prophets and dragged them off the truck, and threw them to the ground. The prophets were being kicked by the bystanders. Messiah and Prophet Elijah were seated on a podium. They were enjoying every minute of it. Satan's vileness was oozing out of them.

In the depth of the bottomless pit, a vile demonic spirit started stirring. It was filled with murder and hatred toward Jesus. With blinding speed, it sped upwards toward Jerusalem. Its evil anointing came upon Messiah, and he stood up and walked toward the prophets.

He looked like Satan incarnate. His eyes turned a reddish color. The people present were unaware of what was transpiring. Suddenly, Satan's fury was unleashed against the two prophets.

The prophets were buffeted and trampled upon. They were flung into the air, time and time again by the unseen force to the great amusement of the tens of thousands who had gathered. The believers, who were watching the suffering of the two prophets on television were horrified. Many a time they had to turn their faces away.

All over the world, the believers who were witnessing the happenings in Jerusalem, via satellite communication, were praying for the prophets although they knew what the outcome was going to be.

John asked Andrew, "How long are they going to be able to bear it?"

He replied, "They are no longer in their bodies. Their spirits have already left their bodies."

The followers of Messiah were applauding the terrible punishment meted out to Elijah and Moses. When Messiah and Prophet Elijah realized that the prophets were already dead, they became very angry.

Messiah stood up and screamed, "The bodies of these two imbeciles shall not be buried. Their corpses shall rot and be food for the fowls of the air, because they caused us so much harm. Where is their God now?" said Messiah with great bravado.

Messiah continued addressing his worldwide audience. "I declare a worldwide public holiday for three and a half days."

At the hearing of his words, the people went wild with excitement and immediately started celebrating. Orgies of drunkenness and perversion akin to Ancient Babylon and Rome were re-enacted all over the world. People were giving gifts one to another as they celebrated the deaths of the prophets who had tormented them. The worldwide followers of Jesus were saddened at what had happened to the two prophets.

However, at the same time they were filled with joy and ecstasy knowing that the two prophets were going to be resurrected in three and a half days time on the day of the Feast of Trumpets. On that very same day, the tribulation will comes to an end against the followers of Jesus.

. . . .

The day that the entire Jewry and the Arab world were waiting for (but each for completely different reasons), had finally arrived. They did not know of each other's expectations. Gentile, dignitaries from all over the world, and even Mr. Pharaoh, the former president of the Palestinians, were present. They had a special place in the outer court of the temple area.

Mr. Pharaoh whispered to his associate, "The day the Palestinians have been looking forward to has finally arrived." He ignored the Arab-tag Messiah had placed upon them. "Today, all the land belonging to Israel, including the whole of Jerusalem, will become ours. The temple shall become a place of worship for Allah and him alone. All memory of Jehovah shall be erased. Today shall be the mother of all *tragedies*."

· · · ·

The High Priest and the Levitical Priesthood were out in full force. Millions of Jewish worshippers from all over the world were in Jerusalem for this High Holy Day. Tens of thousands gathered around the temple area. They were anxiously waiting to get a glimpse of their Messiah. Many would be seeing him in person for the very first time.

Temple guards were seen everywhere. To many, it was not strange at all to see the temple guards armed with machine guns and not with swords as in Old Testament times. Huge screens were erected at strategic places around the City of Jerusalem and other Israeli cities. It showed what was happening both around, and inside the temple. Many were watching the proceedings from home—or from hotel rooms, lobbies, or wherever they could find a television.

Then Messiah made a brief appearance, flanked by the High Priest. He waved to the people then he d*Isa*ppeared out of sight. The people were in ecstasy and thankful just for the crumbs which were thrown to them.

An International Jewish Orchestra played the National Anthem. Sadness came over the people and many men and women were crying unashamedly. A few screens were also erected around the temple area and also in the outer court where all the Gentile dignitaries and guests were seated. People who had never seen the inside of the temple were amazed at the splendor and the magnificence of the place. It was truly breathtaking. The cameraman, a zealot dressed up as a Levite, gave the people on the outside a tour of the inside of the temple.

Then they saw the high priest giving instructions to two Levites to draw the curtains which separated the Holy from the, Most Holy Place. They were not Levites at all but zealots dressed up as Levitical priests, and the high priest was also an imposter.

Then they saw something they never dreamed they would ever see. The golden ark of the covenant, with the two golden angels mounted on the lid, was now in plain view. The gold glistened in the glare of the bright lights.

Dudley Fairbairn

The Orthodox Jews were appalled at what was transpiring in the temple and started tearing their clothes.

. . . .

At home and abroad, the followers of Jesus Christ were glued to their televisions, and those who did not possess one went to their neighbors to watch the proceedings that were taking place at the temple in Jerusalem.

They were neither shocked or appalled at the sacrilege that was taking place because they knew that Jehovah God had vacated the temple more than two thousand years ago.

The believers did not have to guess what was taking place in the temple. Jesus had referred to the abomination of desolation in Matthew 24:15. They also were aware that it signaled the last day of the three and a half years of tribulation.

They were now waiting for the total eclipse of the sun, the moon, and the stars that Jesus had prophesied about in Matthew 24:29. They knew that His power and glory would banish the gross darkness when He appears.

They were expecting the evacuation of the redeemed to take place at that moment in time. They refreshed their memories by quoting Jesus' own account in the book of Matthew 24, which they had memorized.

. . . .

All over the world, the followers of Jesus were in an ecstatic mood. The places of worship were filled to capacity. Crowds of believers gathered in open spaces, and on hillsides. They were not anticipating the end of the world, but the return of Jesus their Savior. In the Asian countries, the believers gathered in the forests.

Others, again, felt led to climb the hills and the mountains and wait for the coming of Jesus, their Savior. However, wherever they were, they were seeking the face of Jehovah their heavenly Father. The sounds of spontaneous praise and worship could be heard in millions of places. The believers gave Jesus praise and worship that was worthy of the King of kings and Lord of lords. They were truly worshipping Jehovah God in spirit and in truth.

• • • •

Back at the temple, abominable things were taking place. Two Levites carried in the golden throne and placed it next to the ark of the covenant. Then Prophet Elijah, followed by Messiah, entered the throne room.

When the high priest came back after discovering that he was deceived, he was shocked to see that the curtains were drawn open. The temple guards were instructed to grab him the moment he made his appearance. When he saw what was taking place, he screamed, "Abomination! Abomination! Antichrist! Antichrist!"

The cameraman received prior orders not to video him. They dragged the High Priest, Abraham *Isa*acs, to a small room where one of the zealots, slit his throat. Fortunately, for him, Brother Andrew had witnessed to him twice before that Jesus was Israel's long-awaited Messiah.

Andrew had painted the scenario to him of exactly what he had just witnessed a few minutes ago. He did not die immediately and still had time to pray in his heart while his life was ebbing away.

He prayed, Jesus*! I accept you as my Messiah and Savior. Please forgive my transgressions.* And with this prayer in his heart, he died with *great* peace.

thirty_two
CHAPTER

Messiah stepped onto the podium and sat down on the golden throne. Prophet Elijah took his place next to him. The camera zoomed in and he and Messiah was now in full view. Outside the temple, the Jews were mesmerized and at the same time in great shock.

Prophet Elijah held a golden crown in his hands that belonged to King David or so the people were made to believe. "Citizens of the New World Order," he began, "I now crown Messiah God of all creation and King above all kings." Prophet Elijah exuded pride and as he placed the crown on Messiah's head and declared, "Behold your God!"

Messiah stood up and said, "From this day on, I and only I, am to be worshipped. All the major religions, Judaism, Christianity, Buddhism, Hinduism, Islam, and all other religions must from today onward bow down and worship only me!"

Mr. Pharaoh, the former president of the Palestinians heard Messiah's announcement, he was shocked to the core of his being. He cried out, "That man is not the Jewish Messiah! He is the Antichrist. He has fooled the Palestinians, and the Muslim/Arab world. It is no wonder that the followers of *Isa* (Muslim name for Jesus) call him the Antichrist. Let's get away from here before we *too* get killed."

Outside the temple, the Jews started running away as confusion made way for great fear. Then the Antichrist gave the command, "Kill all the

Israeli Jews and the world's Jewry, and kill all the followers of Esau Jesus, wherever you may find them. No one must escape."

. . . .

Three and a half days had passed since the murder of the two prophets. It was now the day of the Feast of Trumpets. Thousands of revelers were still dancing around the corpses of the two prophets and kicking the corpses. Others were spitting and slinging obscenities at the slain prophets.

All of a sudden, the wind started blowing, but it was not the normal kind of wind. The wind was encircling the corpses of the prophets. It caught the eyes of the revelers. They immediately stopped what ever they were busy doing and looked at the strange phenomenon.

Then they heard a whistling sound. It was at that same time the breath of Jehovah God entered the corpses of the prophets, and their chests started heaving. They opened up their eyes and stood to their feet. A terrible choking fear fell on the people, and many of them were gasping for breath as the fear of God came upon them. Central News Makers, who was covering the story, caught the whole episode on camera.

Then a powerful sound came from heaven. It sounded like the roaring of a mighty waterfall, and a heavenly voice called the prophets.

And they [the people] heard a loud voice from heaven saying to them, "Come up here." And they ascended [they were not *raptured*] to heaven in a cloud, and their enemies saw them.

Revelation 11:12

The whole event was beamed live to the four corners of the earth by CNM. The revelers were horror-stricken when they heard the voice coming from the heavens calling the prophets to "come up here." They were filled with even greater fear when they witnessed the prophets ascending to heaven. Messiah's followers were in for even a greater shock.

Because in the same hour, there was a great earthquake and a tenth of the city fell; seven thousand people were killed, and the rest were afraid and gave glory to the God of heaven (Revelation 11:13).

Great damage was caused by the earthquake around the circumference of the greater temple area of the City of Jerusalem. However, the subsequent deaths of seven thousand people did not even put a damper on the celebrations of the Feast of Trumpets.

When the soldiers heard Antichrist's command, they advanced on the thronging confused crowd, killing men, women, and children.

Simultaneously, all over the world the satanic orchestration was unleashed against the Jewish people. Without warning, the skies grew dark, and a thick darkness descended on planet earth as the sun, moon, and stars withdrew its light in the middle of the day.

Demon spirits invaded every area of human society and brought forth their inherent depravity. The earthquake was soon forgotten, as the devil erased it from the minds of his worshippers. To Satan, the crowning of Antichrist as God was priority number one.

• • • •

The total eclipse of the sun caused complete chaos to Antichrist's coronation. It was now pitch dark in the temple. Prophet Elijah barked out orders to the zealots, some of whom took off as fast as lightning when the earthquake shook the temple.

All over the world, the believers were encouraging one another with the call, "Maranatha! Christ Jesus is coming!"

During this time, Andrew was surrounded by the believers from Jesus the local churches. He said to them, "The day we were praying, and waiting for as prophesied by the prophets, has come at last. Jesus said in Luke 21:28, when the signs in the heavens take place that we should look up and we should lift up our heads, because our redemption draws near."

• • • •

All over the world, the followers of Jesus came out of their houses, halls, and hiding places and moved into the streets and large open spaces. They wanted to experience that which was foretold by Jehovah God's prophets thousands of years ago.

In the atmospheric heavens, another scene was unfolding. The archangel Michael and his angels were busy waging a war against the devil and his angels. The odds were heavily weighed against Satan and his angels.

Michael and his angels cleansed the atmospheric heavens of Satan, the fallen angels, and the demonic forces. It now opened the way for Jesus the King to make His Royal descent, with power and great glory. The atmospheric heavens were now fit to receive the King of kings and Lord of lords.

• • • •

All across the world, the followers of Jesus were in a spirit of great expectation and rejoicing. The blessed Holy Spirit was witnessing to their hearts that Jesus was on His way. Wherever believers were finding themselves, whether in prisons in the former Soviet Union, China, Communist Korea, Europe, Africa, and in the Arab/Muslim countries they were anticipating the coming of Jesus, their Savior.

In every country, the pastors, elders, brothers, and sisters were encouraging multiplied millions of believers. They said, "It won't be long now. The darkness won't last forever. It is going to make way for the brightest and purest light the world has ever seen. Jesus who is the light of the world is going to banish the great darkness."

Wherever possible, families were grouped together. Mothers were holding their babies. Husbands had their arms around their wives and children. Young couples were embracing one another. Those who had lost family members during the three and a half years of tribulation had become members of other families.

The wife and children of the brother who was killed by the lions during the Roman Games were standing with Brother Andrew and his mother. She had moved in with them the day after the mass funeral of the martyrs. Fathers and mothers were encouraging their children not to be afraid of the darkness.

Even the great darkness did not stop the believers from witnessing to their unsaved family members and encouraging them to accept Jesus as their personal Savior. The Holy Spirit convicted them of their sins causing them to see their need of the Savior, Jesus Christ.

With no one prompting them, they confessed their sins and their transgressions aloud and gave their lives to Jesus. Millions upon millions who were in the valley of decision, whose loved ones had prayed for them, were crying out to God for forgiveness and mercy and God's grace did not let them down.

The cries of multitudes around the world reached the throne of their heavenly Father. They received forgiveness from the Father, who so loved them that He sent Jesus, His only begotten Son to die for them.

Not everyone was willing to receive the truth of God's word. The world's scientists with the brightest minds could not understand why the eclipse of the sun was lasting so long. When some of the followers of Jesus, told them that He had prophesied it two thousand years ago, they refused to accept the explanation for the eclipse of the sun.

Andrew told the stranger who stood next to him that Jesus had prophesied about the eclipse and quoted the verse from Matthew 24:29, to him. "Immediately after the tribulation of those days the sun will be darkened, and the moon will not give its light; and the stars will fall from heaven, and the powers of the heavens will be shaken."

The stranger said to Andrew, "I am a scientist and what you just quoted is nonsense." In the great darkness, he pushed his way through the crowd to get away from what he believed to be a religious fanatic.

While the unregenerate were afraid of the darkness that had now lasted for some time, the Lord's redeemed were singing praises unto Jesus. They broke out into spontaneous worship and it seemed that the angelic choirs also joined in with them. This scene was being repeated all over the world.

The redeemed sensed that Jesus' presence was getting closer and closer. To some it seemed as if the darkness was going to last forever when suddenly a chorus of voices shouted enthusiastically while at the same time pointing to the sky. "Look! Look at that brilliant light in the sky."

It was of such magnitude that it literally pushed the darkness away, and the light came closer and closer and closer.

Brother John shouted with many others, "Look! There is a silhouette in the form of a man, surrounded by that glorious and brilliant light."

Andrew recognized John's voice. John, his mother, and many of the believers from Bethlehem were standing just about eight meters away. As the darkness dissipated, John turned his head and their eyes met. John shouted, "Jehovah God bless you. See in heaven."

Andrew shouted, "Hallelujah!" Then his eyes were again focused on the approaching silhouette. Multitudes of believers, including Andrew, shouted as they had never shouted in their whole lives before. "We can see Jesus! We can see Jesus! We can see Jesus."

Their shouts were heard by hundreds of believers, who surrounded them. They knew that it was Jesus, who was coming to deliver them from the earth. A worldwide shout of victory broke loose when hundreds of millions of believers saw the light of Jesus' glory Jesus as it broke through the stark darkness. The victory shout of the redeemed reverberated around the world in many different languages and dialects.

The blessed Holy Spirit brought this encouraging scripture, to the memory of the worldwide redeemed.

For the Lord Himself will descend from heaven with a shout, with the voice of an archangel, and with the trumpet of God. And the dead in Christ will rise first.

1 *Thessalonians* 4:16

Dudley Fairbairn

As Jesus descended from heaven the shout, of the voice of the archangel could be heard. It was sweet music to the ears of the followers of Jesus. To the hardened sinners, it sounded like an announcement of the death penalty.

The sound of the archangel's voice rang out, and it too reverberated around the world at the speed of lightning. The sound of the archangels' voice put fear of Almighty Jehovah God in the hearts' of the ungodly, Christ rejecting nations of the world.

At that same instant, the seventh angel blew God's trumpet which was connected with a mystery. It shook the very earth. Innumerable crowds of people from amongst the nations who had put their faith in Jesus raised their voices in praise and adoration to their Savior. There was no more cause for fear. They were overjoyed at the sight of their Redeemer.

With an innumerable cloud of witnesses around the world, the followers of Jesus in Israel joined in with them in the victory shout. "Maranatha! Maranatha! Maranatha!"

"Look! Jesus is descending to the atmospheric heavens, we can see Him very clearly now," they shouted with great excitement.

An anointing of praise exploded over them, and it sounded like the rushing of mighty waters. This scene was being repeated wherever the redeemed were gathered together. Every believer was experiencing the glory of Jesus. Tears of joy were being shed for the very last time. Joy unspeakable and full of glory possessed Jehovah's children. The believers, who were imprisoned and chained in dungeons for their faith, sensed the holiness of the moment, and they too broke out in spontaneous praise and worship.

They knew that their deliverance was near. The brilliant light was getting closer and closer and as it touched the clouds, the physical form of Jesus was unmistakably recognizable. Jesus' power and glory reached down to the earth, and it also penetrated the very rocks and concrete and lit up the dark dungeons, prisons, and caves.

At the sight of Jesus, the unregenerate started screaming.

When the radiance of Jesus' power and great glory touched the earth, some suffered heart attacks and strokes. Others again suffered nervous breakdowns; while others simply went stark raving mad.

What looked like millions upon millions of white specks accompanied Jesus and spread out all over the earth's surface. As the specks got closer, it took on human form. It was then that believers realized that it was the disembodied spirits, of the redeemed Old and New Testament saints. It included the martyrs who had died during the three and a half years of tribulation. The spirits of the redeemed dead entered the graves.

The resurrection power the Apostle Paul spoke about was released, at that very same moment. Multiplied millions of elect came out of their graves, clothed with incorruptible bodies. For a fleeting moment, the living believers saw them all around them. Many of the resurrected saints were known to them as some of them were relatives and brothers and sisters in the faith. Then immediately after them, those who were alive and who had survived the tribulation, felt the resurrection power surging through them, and they too were clothed with incorruption.

The resurrection power of Jesus possessed them from the crowns of their heads to the soles of their feet. Immortality became a reality to them. Out of nowhere, myriads of angels joined them as escorts. Together with the resurrected saints the living translated saints, were caught up, with great force to meet Jesus their Savior, Jesus in the air. The joy of seeing Jesus in person for the very first time, just to look into his face, took their breath away. To them, it was truly an experience of joy unspeakable and full of glory.

Although there were an innumerable company of saints, it seemed that every one of them had a front row seat. Jesus was so near to them that they could touch Him. *The pain and suffering of the tribulation was worth it all. It was not even a memory anymore, so nothing had to be forgotten.*

The Bema Seat judgment was also now behind them, and they were on their way to heaven. In order, " … that He [Jesus] might present her to Himself a glorious church, not having spot or wrinkle or any such thing, but that she should be holy and without blemish" (Ephesians 5: 27).

thirty_three

CHAPTER

The saints were not prepared for what awaited them on their arrival in heaven. As it is written: "Eye has not seen, nor ear heard, Nor have entered into the heart of man the things which God has prepared for those who love Him" (1 Corinthians 2: 9).

The serenity, peace, and joy were indescribable. It left the saints breathless and speechless. The Holy City, Jerusalem, radiated with the glory of Jehovah their God.

Her (Jerusalem's) light *was* like a most precious stone, just like a jasper stone, clear as crystal. Also she had a great and high wall with twelve gates, and twelve angels at the gates, and names written on them, which are *the* names of the twelve tribes of the children of Israel: three gates on the east, three gates on the north, three gates on the south, and three gates on the west.

Now the wall of the city had twelve foundations, and on them were the names of the twelve apostles of the Lamb ... The construction of its wall was of Jasper; and the city *was* pure gold, like clear glass. The foundations of the wall of the city *were* adorned with all kinds of precious stones: the first foundation *was* jasper, the second sapphire, the third chalcedony, the fourth emerald, the fifth sardonyx, the sixth sardius, the seventh chrysolite, the eighth beryl, the ninth topaz, the tenth chrysoprase, the eleventh jacinch, and the twelfth amethyst. The twelve gates *were* twelve pearls: each individual gate was one pearl. And the street of the city *was* pure gold, like transparent glass (Revelation 21:11b-14, 18–21).

They were ushered into the throne room. The size was stupendous. There was a rainbow around the throne, in appearance like an emerald. Four angels stood about the throne accompanied by twenty-four elders clothed in white robes. They had golden crowns on their heads, and were sitting on thrones.

The demonstration of God's power was breathtaking. From the throne proceeded lightnings, thunderings, and voices. Before the throne was a sea of glass, like crystal. Surrounding the throne were four living creatures who were saying day and night:

> Holy, holy, holy, Lord God Almighty, Who was and is and is to come!

Revelation 4:8b

> Whenever the living creatures give glory and honor and thanks to Him who sits on the throne, who lives forever and ever, the twenty-four elders fall down before Him who sits on the throne and worship Him who lives forever, and ever, and cast their crowns before the throne saying: You are worthy, O Lord, To receive glory and honor and power; For You created all things, And by Your will they exist and were created.

Revelation 4:9–11

• • • •

After these things I looked, and behold, a great multitude which no man could number, of all nations, tribes, peoples, and tongues, standing before the throne and before the Lamb, clothed with white robes, with palm branches in their hands, and crying out with a loud voice, saying, "Salvation *belongs* to our God who sits upon the throne, and to the Lamb!" All the angels stood around the throne and the elders and the four living creatures, and fell on their faces before the throne and worshipped God, saying: "Amen! Blessing and glory and wisdom, Thanksgiving and honor and power and might, *Be* to our God forever and ever. Amen."

Rev. 7: 9–12

Now when He had taken the scroll, the four living creatures and the twenty-four elders fell down before the Lamb, each having a harp, and golden bowls full of the incense, which are the prayers of the saints. And they sang a new song, saying: "You are worthy to take the scroll, And to open the seals; For You were slain, And have redeemed us to God by Your blood Out of every tribe and tongue and people and nation, And have made us kings and priests to our God; And we shall reign on the earth.

(Revelation 5: 8–9)

[The saints heard the voice of]...many angels around the throne, the living creatures, and the elders; and the number of them was ten thousand times ten thousand, and thousands of thousands, saying with a loud voice: "Worthy is the Lamb who was slain To receive power and riches and wisdom, And strength and honor and glory and blessing!"

(Revelation 5:11–12)

[All of creation joined them saying,]
Blessing and honor and glory and power
Be to Him who sits on the throne,
And to the Lamb, forever and ever.

Revelation 5:13b

• • • •

The saints breathed in the very presence of Jehovah God and the Lamb. They bathed in His the love, which flowed from the throne. To them, it was beyond description. Outside the throne room, the scenery was breathtaking! The sky was the bluest of blue, they had ever seen. Mountains of enormous heights touched the fleecy white clouds.

Trees of various heights dotted the landscapes. They saw flowers of various colors they had never seen before, covering the heavenly landscapes. The only way they could describe the scent was that it smelled heavenly. It looked like multi-colored tapestries that could only have been woven in heaven. Brightly colored birds flew in the clear unpolluted skies. Birds were singing beautiful songs in the trees in honor of their Creator.

In the distance, the cascading of waterfalls could be heard as it plunged 2000 feet to crystal clear pools. The sounds that were generated by the babbling sound of the rivers as it flowed over the stones and rocks, and the sounds of the waterfalls sounded like the music of the song:

t

Lord, nothing can be compared with you.
Your fragrance is sweeter than roses.
Your beauty surpasses all human comprehension.
Your presence fills our hearts with love.

The rivers and lakes were teeming with fish, and they would swim up to the saints so as to inspect who the faces were of people they had never seen before. The animals would also walk up to you as if to say, "We welcome you to heaven." Multicolored butterflies were to be seen everywhere.

The saints were in awe to see the beauty of heaven, but to see their beautiful Lord and Savior Jesus Christ, was the *very* best of all. Just thinking about Him immediately ushered them into His presence where the great multitude was worshipping Him.

They would find themselves crying out, "Jesus, You are Lord! Jesus, You are Lord! Jesus, We love You! Jesus We love You! We love You!

|LIVE

listen|imagine|view|experience

AUDIO BOOK DOWNLOAD INCLUDED WITH THIS BOOK!

In your hands you hold a complete digital entertainment package. Besides purchasing the paper version of this book, this book includes a free download of the audio version of this book. Simply use the code listed below when visiting our website. Once down-loaded to your computer, you can listen to the book through your computer's speakers, burn it to an audio CD or save the file to your portable music device (such as Apple's popular iPod) and listen on the go!

How to get your free audio book digital download:

1. Visit www.tatepublishing.com and click on the e|LIVE logo on the home page.
2. Enter the following coupon code:
   bfaf-8da6-f63e-1a5b-7bdf-6f30-b3f5-b1073.

Download the audio book from your e|LIVE digital locker and begin enjoying your new digital entertainment package today!